FOR THEM THE EARTH WAS FILLED WITH SPIRITS . . . PERILS . . . AND PROMISES BRIGHT AS DAWN

ASHAN: Chosen by the spirits when Mahto the great bear killed her mother, she alone has the right dream, but her dreams trap her between desire and destiny . . .

TOR: A handsome hunter, he has a secret—a daring plan to make the forbidden Ashan his mate . . .

RAGA: Ancient, wise, and fiercely possessive, this shaman feels her magic slipping away. If she has to, she'll kill to keep the new Moonkeeper pure . . .

TSILKA: Sensuous as a she-cat, she has a mission—to seduce Tor and to convince him to betray Ashan . . .

EHR: Cast out by his tribe, he had grown old alone until his traps caught an unexpected prey—a beautiful woman and her extraordinary child . . .

D0954019

PATRICIA ROWE

KEEPERS OF THE MISTY TIME

WARNER BOOKS

A Time Warner Company

Enjoy lively book discussions online with CompuServe. To become a member of CompuServe call 1-800-848-8199 and ask for the Time Warner Trade Publishing forum. (Current members GO: TWEP.)

WARNER BOOKS EDITION

Copyright © 1994 by Patricia Rowe
All rights reserved.

Cover design by Diane Luger
Cover illustration by Mel Grant

Warner Books, Inc.
1271 Avenue of the Americas
New York, NY 10020

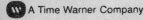 A Time Warner Company

Printed in the United States of America

First Printing: April, 1994

10 9 8 7 6 5 4 3 2 1

Dedicated to Don, my hero:
It's all because of you.

In memory of Steven:
spirit of smoke; wind song; flower scent;
proof that earthly life is but
a paragraph in God's novel.

Special thanks to:

My parents, Pat and Virginia Doherty, who with limitless love taught achievement.

The late Con Sellers, who gave me one end of a golden string.

Barbara Bickmore, soul sister disguised as mentor.

Barbara Charles, for special research assistance and support.

David Cutsforth, M.D., for medical advice.

Marcia Amsterdam, agent/fairy godmother.

Jeanmarie LeMense of Warner Books, sculptress of ideas.

AUTHOR'S NOTE

In the distant past, courageous human beings crossed a temporary land bridge from Asia to America. The place welcomed the people, and they flourished. Small bands split from larger ones, moving south and east, leaving behind artifacts we find and ponder today. By the time of this story, these scattered peoples had forgotten that their ancestors once had belonged to a single tribe.

The first Americans found new creatures, among them the horse. The archeological record shows that horses originated in America, evolving here with unbroken continuity for sixty million years. About nine thousand years ago, the horse died out in its homeland. Only because of earlier migrations to Asia and Europe does the genus *Equus* (horses, asses and zebras) exist today. The horse was reintroduced by the Spanish in 1519, bringing the indigenous peoples of America a prosperity never before known . . . a flowering lovely but brief, for the return of the horse also brought home the destruction of ancient, balanced cultures.

FOREWORD

Nine thousand years ago, ancestors of the Plateau Indians flourished in the forests and grasslands of southern Washington. Migratory hunter-gatherers who were led by women, the People of the Misty Time left a legacy of artifacts, legends, and petroglyphs carved in black basalt.

From high on a windswept cliff, a woman's haunting stone face looks out over the mighty Columbia River. Her large solemn eyes are gracefully ringed. Owlish horns perch above curved eyebrows. She Who Watches, known as the Moon-keeper, Ashan (Ah-Shan), is the heroine of an ancient legend:

> *A woman was chief of all who lived in this re-gion. That was a long time before Coyote came up the river and changed things, and people were not yet real people . . .*

CHAPTER
1

The canyon rim swallowed the sun, spreading a welcome shadow over ninety people snaking down the trail. With Ashan's every step, the river's thunder grew. She sighed in gratitude as they neared Loudwater, the last camping place of the autumn trek.

A hummingbird buzzed the red flower stuck in her headband. She shook her straight black hair to chase it.

"Fly, little warrior. Your friends left with the vultures days ago."

With a startled chirp, the bright creature flashed away from the talking flower. She smiled. Ashan, Whispering Wind—mistaken for a faded flower with the smell of a skunk lily! She looked at her torn moccasins, made only last moon, just before the tribe left Ancestor Cave. She had been so proud of her handiwork, but now a naked savage wouldn't bother stealing them. The long trek had chewed holes in the elkhide bottoms; loose laces trailed in the dust. Ashan laughed at herself: She knew little more of women's ways than she knew about the weapons of men. Well, no matter. Moccasin sewing was not an important skill for the next Shahala chief.

The trail widened, curving away from the river into thick forest. Ashan dropped her bundle of skins beside the path and sat on an old friend—a flat, moss-cushioned rock overlooking the camp. Some warriors had run ahead, and a fire billowed white smoke. She inhaled deeply. Her mouth watered. *Soon*, she told her grumbling belly—*the spirits sent us Yamish the deer today*.

Tingling warmth rippled through Ashan as Tor came into the clearing below, dragging a great oak branch to the fire. The sight of the young warrior stole her breath. Had he changed so much, or did the eyes of an almost-woman see differently? Taller than most men, Tor moved with a cougar's lean grace, deep-brown muscles standing out as he pulled against the unwilling branch. Ashan had dreamed of those strong arms holding her, his black hair brushing her face, his sweet breath in her nostrils. She knew what men and women did, though Raga would be shocked to learn the Chosen One even thought of such things.

"Is your rock big enough for two?"

Ashan jumped from her forbidden thoughts as her spirit sister sat beside her.

"Thanks to Shala, this trek is almost done," Mani said. "I can't wait to sleep in the huts of the ancestors. I hate sleeping under the stars." Mani looked to see if anyone was listening, then whispered, "Last night I saw spirits shoot across the sky."

Ashan couldn't help laughing at Mani's fear. Though she understood Mani's feelings, Ashan liked the darktime world and the spirits who wandered there.

"You're a mouse, Mani!"

"I may be, but soon this mouse will fear nothing. *He* will do all my worrying for me."

Mani pointed to Lar in the camp below as she stroked the braided band tied around her upper arm—strands of black hair laced with horsetail hair of several colors.

"Six horses for my pledge band! Lar is the bravest warrior Amotkan ever created!"

Mani squeezed Ashan's arm, spreading prickling resentment under her skin, and chattered on.

"Kamiulka, the Autumn Feast! Do you believe it's finally here? All my life I've waited for him. Only four days left!" The almost-bride drew a loud, deep breath, and shook out her straight black hair. "Seeing Lar renews my strength."

Mani shouldered her skins and started down the trail. "See you in camp."

Ashan frowned and pitched a rock down the cliffside, thinking of the coming three-day celebration that would bring so many changes. Little ones would take their spirit names. The pledged ones, Mani and Keeta, would take their mates. And at sunrise on the third day, Ashan would take the Shahala pledge band, becoming the tribe's Young Moonkeeper.

By ancient, spirit-given law, for Ashan, there would be no mate—not at this feast, not ever. No matter that her woman's body of fifteen summers yearned for a man's touch; that her mind longed to know the workings of Tor's. Her destiny was greater than that of any woman: to lead the tribe after Raga's last death.

As her people passed with words of greeting, Ashan looked beyond their faces, deep into their eyes, seeing them in a different, sharper way. Soon she would be responsible for all their lives. She loved each of them, from tiny Lia, born that summer, strapped in a cradleboard on Tira's back, to Ahnkor, the oldest man, carried on travel poles by two warriors. Ashan knew her people loved her: their looks and words said it. So did the gifts they were always bringing—special food, flowers, feathers and rocks found along a trail.

In many ways, the Moonkeeper's life was easiest of all. Ashan would not have to concern herself with gathering and cooking. Or mending, she thought, pulling her moccasin over her toes.

But how could she be happy without a mate, without her own little ones to love in the special way of mothers? Why must she be denied what every other woman had? If she was not to have a man, why had the spirits created Tor for her to want and never touch? Why had they cursed her with desire?

"What troubles you, Ashan?" growled a deep, bearish voice behind her. She stood at once and turned to face Raga; no one sat in the presence of the Moonkeeper. Shaking away the feeling of smallness, she tried to smile.

"Nothing."

The deep, leathery folds of Raga's face gathered into a smile that showed yellow, worn-down teeth. But her black eyes did not waver.

"A puff of wind cannot fool me. Your greatest moment flies on swift wings, yet you are troubled. I will know why."

Raga's eyes fastened to Ashan's. She could not look away, or stop the words that crawled up her throat.

"Can I change a law when I become Moonkeeper?"

Raga snorted and spat. "Spirits make laws; we cannot change them." She looked deeper into Ashan's eyes. "Tell me, Windpuff, what law would you change?"

"I would be the first Moonkeeper to take a mate!"

Raga's fists clenched. She roared, "Then you take him with you to death! The spirits will turn you to stone in their fury! And what mate will you feed to Coyote?" The roar became a snake's hiss. "Hear me, Ashan, and never forget! The Moonkeeper belongs to the spirits! They will not share her with any man!"

The firepoints in the old woman's eyes flared brighter with each heartbeat. Ashan had seen people fall dead from Raga's rage, their insides boiled to mush. But never had the force struck her! Her legs weakened and wobbled. The heat entered and the melting began.

Suddenly, Raga jerked her head skyward. "Aiyiii!" Coyote within her howled to the heavens. The inhuman sound echoed on and on. As if she had been leaning into the Moonkeeper's deadly stare, Ashan almost stumbled into the space between them. She willed her legs to be as oak stumps. She would not go on her knees before the old woman!

Raga's massive shoulders slumped. She looked down on Ashan, the burning coals of her eyes now misty clouds. Knobby, twisted fingers stroked the ragged brown feathers that hung from the pledge band, dark with age, tied to her stout upper arm. The voice that could kill was soft as a new mother's.

"My spirit daughter," Raga said. "At the Autumn Feast, you will become Young Moonkeeper. When I was a young one, I climbed Owl Rock to get feathers for my pledge band. It's time for you to do the same. You must show the spirits you have courage."

The old woman pointed up Yuna River's deep gorge to a small black cave in the overhanging cliffs. Long white streaks stained the smooth rock below. The strongest hunter—Tor himself—could not climb it!

Raga said, "Tucum the Owl Spirit lives there. The people hear his song as death, but for a Moonkeeper, it is life. Tell Death Singer you are the Chosen One, and no harm will come to you. Now go, before dark comes."

Ashan shuddered, but she would never let Raga see her fear. She grabbed a ragged lynx skin—her mother's only legacy—and started up the trail, with only riversound for company. Cooking aromas reached her. Everyone must be in camp by now, waiting for the fire to work its magic. The Old Moonkeeper's words echoed in her mind, churning with her own boiling anger, as her feet followed the narrow trail with an animal wisdom of their own.

She stopped. Some sense other than sight had found the Owl Spirit's home. Ashan had walked the Yuna River trail every autumn and spring of her life without ever once looking upon Tucum's face. The people passed under him silently, heads down, and never at night. No one wanted to wake Death Singer, or be nearby when he did his darktime work.

Taking a deep breath, Ashan squared her shoulders and forced herself to stare at the high cliff. No wonder the Owl Spirit chose this place to live—it was made in his own fierce image. Jagged stone feathers edged the sky, dark against the orange glow of the just-set sun. Below, where eyes would be, two flame trees clung to the rock, their powerful medicine leaves blazing red. A small black cave yawned between the guardian trees—Tucum's open beak, the door between worlds where every soul must someday pass.

Ashan shivered, pulling her lynx skin tighter. A squirming fearsnake coiled around her stomach. Trying to expel it, she shouted at the rocks.

"Tucum! The people hear your song as death, but for a Moonkeeper, it is life!"

The river's thunder swallowed the sounds as if she had not made them.

She thought of Tor, for a moment desperately wishing to be anyone but the Chosen One . . . to be like Mani, safe in camp, waiting for food, for her marriage, her babies.

For Ashan, it was much too late for hopeless wishing. It had been so since her seventh summer, when Mahto the bear had ripped out her mother's life, forever changing her own. The nightmare that could still strike terror night or day clawed her mind with its memory of shredded flesh, unseeing eyes, death-stained earth. Tears rose in her throat.

Ashan pictured Tor's soft, dark eyes to calm herself.

On hands and knees, she climbed a steep tumble of loose, broken rocks, reaching Tucum's great slabbed cliff out of breath. Stretching her arms high, she leaned against the solid rock, still warm from the sun's last rays. She flattened her face to it, touching it with her tongue, tasting its dusty roughness. Her body molded to the stone, every pore seeking to know its spirit.

Her searching fingers found a high crack where two slabs came together. She dug into it and pulled herself up, her feet toeing into unseen crevices. Less steep than she'd expected, the cliff slanted forward, away from her. Leaning into the solid mass, matching its slope, hand over hand, she slowly rose higher.

Near the top, the rock bulged out with a backward slant. It pushed Ashan away, forcing her to fight with all her strength for each bit of height she gained. She thought of nothing but the rock, talking to it, tearing at it, forcing her hands into tiny grooves. She clung to the cliff like a spider with half her legs missing. The remaining ones knew what to do but there were just not enough of them for the task.

She pulled herself onto a narrow ledge littered with bones and balls of fur, and crouched there. The cave was in reach above, but her pounding heart filled her throat and she could not breathe. The river's voice swelled her head with its low-throated, rolling thunder. Rumbling beneath the different sounds, tying them all together, Yuna's heartbeat rose and fell in a rhythm that entered Ashan's body and took over the flow of her blood.

For the first time, she looked down. Far below, the river ran smooth and glossy, then broke into ridges and gullies as it crashed through a path of massive boulders. Farther down the narrowing canyon, the ridges curled, exploding into clouds of spray as waves smashed against rocky cliffs. The whitewater slithered along, then collapsed into a whirling pit . . . a huge open mouth with teeth of spray, devouring an endless snake.

A tree hurtled through the boulders, its branches snapping like twigs. As it reached the whirlpool, its broken top filled the gaping mouth. Gnarled roots lifted slowly in the air, and the tree was swallowed.

Now she understood the vast pulsing sound, and knew why it was said that no creature went into Yuna's mouth and lived. The twisting sight below suddenly filled her with panic. Her leg muscles began to twitch; soon her whole body shook. The quivering seemed to come from the stone itself. Hostile, it shuddered, trying to rid itself of her, as a bison might shake off a fly. Bitter sickness rose from her belly to her throat. Her fingers curled into balls.

"Get out of me, fear!" she shouted, closing her eyes, leaning hard into the rock. Her hand touched soft moss which had clung there forever—never tiring, never giving up its hold, even now under clutching fingers. Its calm patience entered her. The heat subsided. Blood flowed smoothly again. The mad shaking stopped.

Slowly she stood, face flat against the rock, every muscle gripping the smooth surface. Ignoring the thick crust of owl droppings, she searched out a crack and pulled herself up.

Only darkness greeted her as she peered into the deep hole. An overpowering stench told her owls must have lived here since the Misty Time. Then she saw them: three perfect feathers, golden brown with darker stripes, stuck in a crack at the side of the cave. Tucum had left them for her!

Ashan reached for the feathers.

A piercing screech from the depths of the cave froze her. Two huge eyes opened in the blackness, glowing with evil yellow light. Time slowed as Death Singer dove for her head. Staring into the hideous eyes growing larger and larger, Ashan saw death.

She screamed as talons ripped her scalp, tearing her from the cliff. Sight-stealing blood poured into her eyes. Cold wind rushed up. She heard its whistling, and a screaming that seemed to come from everywhere. She begged Shala to stop the falling! The river's roaring voice rushed up in angry answer.

Ashan sucked in a last deep breath. Icy water engulfed her. Pain exploded in her back. She scraped the pebbled bottom and kicked into it, surfacing quickly. Through choking spray, she saw the boulders gleaming darkly ahead. She dug in against the fierce current, but the stones under her feet, hurle along by the powerful River Spirit, moved toward the rapids with her. The stones smashed against each other with angry, sobbing sounds, joining their quarreling voices with the crash of water turning over on itself. The whole world became one monstrous, drowning noise, squeezing through her ears into her brain. The sound filled her, became a solid rock that weighed her down. As the rivernoise held her in place, everything else slipped away. The clouds over the treetops became white tips on blue-gray waves; the trees on the riverbank, clouds of dark green spray. Even the cliff lost its shape and came blowing at her.

In a few heartbeats, the growing cloud ahead would break over her, and life would end in Yuna's swirling pit. As Ashan faced death, a terrible sense of failure eclipsed fear. Spirits demanded much of the Moonkeeper who would speak for them. She had questioned their laws. Angered, they had decreed her death.

As the warmth drained from her body and the strength in her muscles died, Ashan gave herself up to the will of the River Spirit, praying for safe journey to the otherworld. The sound in her head faded, then stopped.

CHAPTER
2

The young warrior Tor stood by a wide, bubbling pool, sharing water with Yuna as the river passed Loudwater Camp. He stared at the awesome scene upriver, wondering what terrible fury of spirits had caused the tumbled upheaval. Huge stone slabs blocked the canyon, higher than many trees. Near the bottom, Yuna's entire flow shot through a great gash in solid rock—a last violent gesture before the river went to nourish the valley beyond.

A high shriek cut through the pulsing thunder. Tor turned to the orange sky upriver, picturing an eagle defending its territory. The sight of the majestic black bird with white head and tail never failed to stir him. He searched the sky over the clifftops, hoping for a glimpse of his spirit guardian.

Another scream pierced the air, louder and higher, echoing on and on. Ashan! He knew it, though he had never heard her scream before. His heart stopped sending blood to his body as he saw the impossible horror far up the canyon: Ashan, tumbling through the air, falling to her death!

"Takeena, give her wings!" he cried to the Eagle Spirit.

You save her! the spirit screamed inside his head. *Now is the time you have known would come!*

Before Ashan's cry was cut off by Yuna's embrace, Tor bounded for the tumbled boulders that led to the deadly whirl-

pool above. Moss and green slime covered the rocks, kept
wet by escaping spray. His feet and hands were more cunning
than he thought they could be, ignoring the slickness, finding
hidden places to dig into. He became Suda, the ram with
curving horns who could climb anything, and in moments he
stood at the rocky edge of the great spinning hole.

The sight of it numbed his brain. The power inside overtook
him as Yuna's commanding voice tried to draw him in. Over
and over she rumbled his name in rhythm with his pounding
heart. The rocks beneath him obeyed the raging River Spirit,
pushing at his feet as she tried to suck him down. He dropped
to his knees and gripped the rock, shaking off the river's
trance.

In his mind he pictured Ashan, struggling, sucked toward
the jaws of the killing monster. He looked upriver and saw,
not the untouchable woman of his forbidden dreams, but the
spotted catskin she wore. It shot through the boulders across
from where he knelt, hanging for a moment at the lip of the
whirlpool. The spinning water snatched it and sent it spiraling
to the bottom, where it disappeared before his unbelieving
eyes.

Tor's cry of horror shook the canyon. The hideous power
inside the pit must not have Ashan! He would get to her first,
even if he died in the doing, even if she was already dead
from the fall. If he could cross the whitewater and reach the
boulders, he might grab her before she plunged into the pit.

He crept along the slippery rocks. Yuna grew fiercer and
wilder the further he penetrated her domain. She beat on him
furiously as he crawled on his belly, trying with icy fingers
to pry him loose. He breathed water now as often as air, but
he kept on, driven by terrible pictures of Ashan's ruined
beauty.

A cloud moved down from the sky and hung over Ashan.
Her mother's eyes, long closed by death, looked down with
unbearable sadness, saying, "I loved you before you were
born. For you only did I live until bear came for me. My
daughter . . . why do you hurt me by dying?"

Blackness closed around the eyes, then they became clear
again. Deep, dark pools of liquid, Tor's eyes looked into her

soul. Great tears welled up in them. They splashed into her face, and she coughed, choking.

Ashan saw the grieving faces of her people, and heard the voice of her guardian, Shala the Wind Spirit.

"Hear me, Chosen One who gives up life. The hope of the people dies with you. They will be lost."

The people! They might die of fear if the Chosen One died!

Life fire suddenly burned, dissolving the stone in her head. Blood flowed again, sweeping away the ice inside. Triumph bubbled out of her throat as laughter.

The rushing water split into waves. Ashan rode a small one that became a huge, slowly-moving fish, created to carry her to safety. Powerful, in control, she rode the river's neck, taking it where she wished it to go.

The fish wave hunched its back, swelling upward. For a moment, she clung to a high silver fin. When it broke away, she dropped into a world of pale-green foam—a tumbling, airless world with nothing familiar in it.

Crushed against a rock, she desperately tried to pry herself free, but the maddened water held her under. Her lungs cried. She begged to see the sky again. Kicking with all her strength, tearing the skin on her ribs, she lunged back into the current and broke through to life-giving air.

Ashan hung on the edge of the huge, churning hole, looking down into the belly of the devouring spirit. She clawed against the whitewater cave as she slipped slowly down its sides. Yuna threw sparks in her eyes, changing the world from bright to black. A new roar sounded in her ears—a roar more pain than sound, but louder than anything she had ever heard.

"AHH-SHAHN!" it thundered.

As the whirlpool swallowed her, black became all.

Tor saw the bright flash of Ashan's body at the edge of Yuna's screaming mouth. He threw himself across the impossible gap of pounding water in the moment she clung to the whirlpool's rim, then saw the foaming hole swallow her as he was smashed into a rock at its very edge.

Ashan was dead! Tor's death cry cut the air like a stone blade, echoed back and forth by the canyon walls—a sound of grief and rage unending.

Somehow, he hung on as the icy water rushed over him. His body took control from his tormented mind, bringing him slowly back along the rocks until he lay in quiet water. Gasping and heaving, he dragged himself onto the sandy bank.

Low animal moans rose up from deep inside, spaced with fits of breathless choking. Tor barely felt the pain of shredded skin, so great was the agony that threatened to crush his chest from within. Gripped with wrenching sorrow, he felt an awful kinship with Samar, the goose who flies with his mate for life, who mourns forever her loss. Like Samar, he would be forever alone. He cried out his rage to Takeena. What good was a guardian spirit who failed at the moment of greatest need!

Shouting voices reached him. Had Yuna decided to spit out the broken pieces? He sickened to think of it, but he couldn't stay away. Shaking, he walked along the rocks and looked over the edge. Far below, in the middle of the bubbling pool, Lar and Deyon paddled a tree limb toward the river's spewing mouth. Ashan floated there, then was pushed under by the mighty flood raining down on her.

Tor threw out his arms and dove. Takeena gave wings to his flight. He cut through the air clean as an eagle. Plunging deep into the foamy brightness, he reached for the black drift of Ashan's hair and tangled both hands in it. Pulling her up, he swam for the floating limb. As strong arms reached out to him, Tor closed his eyes and breathed deeply.

Lar and Deyon kicked, and the limb began moving toward the bank. Tor locked one arm around it, holding Ashan's limp body close with the other. He brushed away the tangle of hair that covered her face. His breath stopped at the sight of deep gashes over each eye, slashing her forehead from eyebrows to hairline. No blood hid the thin white lines of her exposed skull. Below the clean cuts, which looked like they had been made by a blade, her eyes were closed. No other marks spoiled her lovely face, which had the peaceful look of sleep.

Deyon said, "Is she dead?"

"No!" Tor cried. "Yuna has stolen her breath!"

He put his mouth over hers, willing his body to give her life. She shuddered and coughed up foamy water. Over and over, he breathed into her, unaware of the water, or the limb, or his friends paddling it to shore.

Tor struck out at grasping hands, but they knocked him away and took her. Shahala death cries rose and filled the canyon. He stumbled out of the water after the men who had Ashan, the men who believed her dead. *I can give her breath!* he tried to shout, but no words came.

Raga's bellow froze them all. "Put her down! The Chosen One is not a piece of meat for the fire!"

The men lowered Ashan to the ground. Tor stared at her small, fragile body. It seemed untouched except for the forehead gashes and a bit of torn skin on her belly. But her color was unnatural—pale, pale gray, as human skin should never be. Her breast did not rise and fall. Still she could not breathe for herself!

Tor fell to his knees and breathed into her again.

"Get away from her!" Raga shrieked, swinging her wooden staff at his head. It caught his ear with a heavy thud. He yelped, rolling away from her blows.

"You ignorant people—Ashan is not dead," Raga said. "She travels with spirits in their places of wisdom, as every Moonkeeper must. Now bring her near the fire. We must care for her needs."

Tear-streaked Mani took off her deerskin robe and covered Ashan. Deyon and Lar carried her to camp. They laid her beside the fire on a bearskin sleeping rug with her head toward Pahto, the sacred mountain.

The people gathered in quiet groups, their fear so strong Tor could smell its sharp, sweaty ugliness in the air. There was reason to be afraid. The tribe, indeed the world, would not survive without a Moonkeeper who knew the ways. If Ashan died, would the spirits give Raga time to teach another?

The Old Moonkeeper took a handful of red dust from her medicine bag. It flared in showers of sparks as she threw pinches into the flames—each bright flash a message only she understood. As the last sparks drifted into the pale gray sky, Raga spoke.

"The Chosen One is in the spirit world, as I told you. She fought the River Spirit without fear. Seeing her courage, Yuna spared her, as she has been spared before. But the struggle weakened her. She needs the life-force of her people. Each of you must go and find a stone—a special stone in the shape of your love for Ashan. Hurry now!"

With new hope, the people walked into the fading dusk, each man, woman and little one searching for signals given off by stones with healing power. One by one, they returned. Touching the rocks to their foreheads, combining their own life-force with the spirits in the stone, they laid the power-filled stones in a circle around the Chosen One. Tor rolled his large, shiny green globe just above her head, giving all he had of himself. When the last little one set her small pink stone, the circle of Shahala love was in place. Ashan was safe inside.

The people gazed at their hope for the future, so pale and still. For a long time, no one spoke.

Raga stepped inside the medicine circle and squatted beside Ashan.

"Yamish the stag gave his life to us. Go now and eat with joy that the Chosen One journeys with spirits and learns."

"You need food, Moonkeeper," a young woman said.

"For me there will be no food or sleep until the Chosen One returns to us."

Darkness covered the camp. Tor backed away from the broad ring of firelight, out of Raga's sight, and sat against a tree trunk. He vowed he too would not eat or sleep until Ashan awoke. He would sit and guard her from whatever harm might come while she lay helpless with only an old woman to protect her.

CHAPTER
3

Inside the stone circle of Shahala love, the Old Moonkeeper sat cross-legged beside dreaming Ashan, trying to ignore the complaints of her stiff body. When she was young, Raga could sit like this for days, but now . . . A groan slipped out. She wished for something to lean against, but the only thing large enough was the green rock brought by the First Warrior, Tor. And she was so angry with him for tempting the Chosen One! She spat, banishing every distraction, and focused all of herself on Ashan. Raga must be strong for her spirit daughter on this dangerous night. For not only was Ashan less in size and strength than she; Raga feared the girl was also less in courage.

In a distant part of her mind, the Moonkeeper was aware of people going quietly about their darktime work. Raga had tried to give them hope, to pass on her certainty that Ashan would return, but the sharp smell of fear still stained the air.

A little of the fear pierced the bubble of protection around the stone circle, invading Raga's heart. . . . If Ashan were found unworthy, she would have to die.

"I love you," the old woman whispered, squeezing Ashan's cool, limp hand. "Of all, I love you best."

Ashan's slack face drew into worried lines. Her mouth silently worked. Raga sensed that part of the fear she felt came from Ashan. A memory flashed in the old woman's mind . . . the night of her own testing, so long ago.

Raga, Raven Tongue, was a girl of ten summers when she died for the first time. No one knew what had covered the smokehole at the top of the hut, or why the Old Moonkeeper, Tsagag, had picked that night to go sit on the hillside. The sleeping little girl smelled too much smoke, but thought it was part of her dream. Then the choking started. In hot, suffocating terror, she felt her way across the floor, but when she reached the doorskin and pushed, something pushed back from the other side. *Spirits, of course, the same who had covered the smokehole.* And that was her last thought. While her body lay in a stone circle like this one, Raga's soul traveled in the spirit world to learn what a Moonkeeper needs to know. The trip was ecstasy and terror, but when she awoke, Raga was full of healthy life.

"You can do it, Windpuff. I know you can," she whispered, and hoped Ashan didn't sense her doubt.

The silence of the camp became complete but for rivernoise. All were asleep—except Tor. A finger of Raga's mind reached out into the dark and touched him. He was awake and watching. Trouble, that one would be. Raga had thought about wrapping his spirit in winter ice, making him miserable enough to leave the tribe. She'd also thought of simply killing him, with blade or spear or spell. Or perhaps another warrior . . . that would be easy to arrange.

But . . .

Raga sighed deeply. Wouldn't she be tampering with the spirits' plan for their next Moonkeeper? Raga believed Tor was Ashan's temptation to overcome . . . one of the tests of her worthiness to speak for the spirit world, no less important than the conquering of fear.

Well, it didn't mean Raga couldn't hate Tor for the pain he was causing Ashan. She thought of giving him great warts, but making him ugly would also ruin the test.

Nightmist hid the moon. The campfire had burned to coals. Since spirits are drawn to smoke, Raga got up to tend the fire. As she stepped over the stones and out into the air of the camp, something invisible snapped shut behind her.

Ahhh . . . she thought. *Spirit power is magnificent.*

A good stack of wood had been left, and it only took

moments to get the fire going again. The Old Moonkeeper was glad to get back inside the spirit bubble.

As the night deepened, Raga had little awareness of time, or even of her aches. The warm honey of the spirit bubble coated her soul, causing her thoughts to flit like a summerfly over a sunny lake.

The shaman-chief of the Shahala tribe, now thirty-seven summers, had never known her old ones. She was raised in the Moonkeeper's hut by Tsagag—a fierce woman who had little love for anyone, and no tolerance for mistakes. Tsagag punished the mind. Terror was her best weapon. She could make people see horrible things behind their eyes, and feel the feelings that went with them—like burning flesh, or dying breath. Young Raga had tried so hard never to make mistakes, but of course she did. She had learned fierceness from Tsagag—and it still worked quite well.

On most people . . . She thought of Tor, playing Tempter of the Chosen One, an ancient part.

Things are as they have always been, said one of Raga's inner voices, and in a way, the thought comforted the old woman.

For every Moonkeeper, there was once a man to tempt her. It would have helped to know this, but Raga hadn't known it as a girl, and Ashan did not know it now. Ignorance was necessary to the test.

Raga sighed as a faded picture entered her mind . . . a gentle, sweet warrior who would rather pick flowers than hunt. Lok . . . so wrong for Raga, even if she'd been only a woman. He was handsome in the way of a fawn, and shy as one, but when he raised his eyes, they saw into the young girl's soul and captured it, wrapping her in strands of desire, soft as spiderwebs, strong as sinew, that lasted to this day.

Of course, she had had to defeat her feelings. Tsagag somehow had known, and Raga had believed the old snake would kill Lok if she suspected that anything more than thinking was happening.

Lok . . .

Raga sighed as that still-empty place inside yawned wide.

Lok had finally taken a mate, a fragile thing named Keenya who was always sick with something. Alhaia the moon, in her wisdom, never sent little ones—Keenya probably would have died birthing. Raga still loved the man. Yes, she loved everyone, but what she felt for Lok was different.

They had spoken of their feelings only once: On the night before Raga became Young Moonkeeper. They ran off in the dark and sat on the hillside overlooking Anutash. They kissed, then their hands took control, and they touched in undiscovered places, breathing like men who have pursued an antelope herd too long. Explosions of hot pleasure seared Raga's loins.

Somehow, with more strength than she knew she possessed, Raga shoved him away, and when he came at her, slapped him hard.

"I will not kill you, Lok," she had said.

"I know that. You love me."

"I mean, I will not cause Tsagag to kill you."

"Raga, we can leave these people—go away and make a new life. I've seen how you look at little ones. You should be a mother."

"Any woman can be a mother. I will be Moonkeeper, a far more important thing. And one day, I will have a spirit daughter to raise."

Raga broke away from the memory.

A smile played on Ashan's dreaming face, and it made the old woman smile.

"No daughter of flesh could have been sweeter," she whispered.

Raga pulled all her powers tight, cloaking Ashan in their strength. She must, above all, protect this Chosen One. Raga had seen the future, terrible visions of babies and old ones dying. She had to stay here long enough to give the people their next Moonkeeper. For the spirits told her sweet Ashan would save them. Raga knew not how, but Ashan would give them a better life.

Love clotted Raga's face as she whispered to the one who did not hear.

"You are different, Ashan. I've always known it. You must be prepared for some tremendous task the spirits will ask of you. In this I must not fail."

CHAPTER
4

With no weight of flesh or bone to hold her back, Ashan drifted like a flower puff on a warm breeze, awash in sensations more pleasurable than anything she had ever imagined. Vivid flows of rainbow-colored light danced in pulsing rhythms, merging and mingling, then parting again. Bright flashes rushed by, trailing delicate ringing sounds. Intense aromas delighted her, sweeter than the blooms of spring.

The rivers of color carried her along as they flowed slowly back to their source—a distant white light so brilliant that the sun would cry his envy. Its warmth touched her, stroking her with feathers of softness. She longed to reach the radiance, to enter and become one with it.

A familiar presence enclosed her, lifting her in wavering, shell-colored strands. She drank in a fresh, washed fragrance and knew . . . Shala had come!

Her guardian spirit breathed: "This is not your time, Ashan. Turn from the light. Follow Shala, that you may lead. Learn, that you may teach."

In a heartbeat, Ashan became one with the flesh of her body. She looked down and saw with amazement her tiny feet, wrapped in the rabbit-fur boots of a little one. Small hands, stained bright purple, held a rough willow basket filled with berries.

In confusion, she looked at her surroundings. The sun beat on a brush-covered slope dotted with long-needled trees—tall, red-barked, sharply fragrant. Gentle hills in shades of misty blue climbed up and away. In the distance rose the blue and white splendor of Pahto, the sacred mountain who brought the waters of life. Clouds circled Pahto's high peaks, the only touch of white in a sky the color of a blue jay's wing.

A sweet-smelling breeze cooled her sweaty skin. All around, low branches offered ripe fruit. As recognition came, Ashan relaxed in the safe familiarity of the huckleberry field where her people always came in the last of the hot suns.

At a rustling behind her, she turned, flushed with warmth to see her mother rising from the brush. Kira was beautiful, but so tall! Ashan's head would not reach her waist! She knew suddenly that Shala had brought her to a long-ago time, when she was a little one and Kira still lived. She gave in to love long denied, forgetting all that had happened since that happy, carefree time.

"Come, Pella, we have enough. We will rest awhile before we look for the others."

The forgotten pleasure of her mother's voice so delighted Ashan that she couldn't speak. *Pella! She called me Pella!* Ashan took Kira's outstretched hand. They walked a short distance and sat in the shade of a tall grandfather tree on the thick mat of his fallen needles. A brook chattered beside them, bouncing and bubbling over small bright stones.

Ashan gazed into Kira's face, shadowed by a sunshade of woven reeds. Shining black braids wrapped with white leather thongs fell over her shoulders, ending in a free sweep of strands that brushed the golden skin of her breasts. She wore a short deerskin skirt in the summer heat, crossing dusty legs in front of her. Dark eyes smiled, crinkling around the edges as she spoke.

"I forgot," the lovely woman said softly. "You are Ashan now, Whispering Wind. No longer Pella, Kira's Pink Flower. Such an important name, my daughter." Kira smoothed Ashan's hair. "Already you are wiser than many fully grown. Shala loves the People of the Wind, and guides our journeys.

She must love you greatest of all to give you her name. You will be her special song.''

Her mother's words filled her with pride.

Ashan remembered the Naming Ceremony of the last moon. Standing before the tribe with her small friends, each in their seventh summer, she had never felt so important, so like a real person. Kira had made her a beautiful white leather cape, worked and chewed to downy softness. Long fringe fell from its edge, just touching the dusty earth of the ceremonial ground. The sacred colors of red, yellow and white adorned her face and arms in mysterious symbols painted by the old Moonkeeper. On each hand, three curving white lines ran to her wrist—the mark of Shala, the Wind Spirit.

Ashan waited while Raga chanted and shook deer-hoof rattles. When the songs were finished, the Moonkeeper commanded the little ones to step forward, from tallest to smallest.

''I am Tor, Eagle from the Light!'' shouted the boy she had known as Kendar. ''Takeena is my guardian spirit!''

Ashan smiled a secret smile. Once, making her swear to tell no one, her special friend had told her he flew with eagles in the darktime.

Next came Lar, Red Hawk; Mani, Earth Sister; and Keeta, Bluebird. Finally, Pella's moment came. Standing tall and proud, she spoke her true name, the name given by her guardian spirit on her power quest, the name only she and the Moonkeeper had known before.

''I am Ashan, Whispering Wind! Shala is my guardian spirit!''

Tor came awake at the sound of her voice, and cursed silently. He had slept, in spite of his vow. Had he been dreaming, or had Ashan really spoken? The dark of the night gave up no sound but rivernoise and the chirr of crickets. He shook his head, rubbing the sand of sleep from his eyes.

Ashan seemed to float before him in a pool of wavering light. Fireglow brushed her high cheekbones, and the tip of her nose and chin. Like stars in the darktime sky, it sparkled on long waving hair, and he remembered softness filling his hands. Full, ripe-berry lips held the hint of a smile. Her eyes were closed, thick black lashes quiet on golden skin. He longed to look once again into the flashing pathways of her soul.

Did he see sleep before him, or death? Everything about her said life. Still, he sensed an emptiness, as if the important part of her had gone; as if the butterfly had left her cocoon in pursuit of new life. He sniffed the air, searching for the odor of death. Only the smells of smoke and camp and people reached him. Among these, he found Ashan's sweet woman-scent, rich with healthy life. All Tor's senses said she lived. But this was more than sleeping, if less than death. Where was her soul?

Ashan's empty stillness drew him. He crept closer, his whole body aching from the war with the River Spirit. Stronger than any man, Yuna had won. He wondered why she had not killed him for his defiance.

Pushing away pain, he crawled toward the fire. He needed to touch her, to know that she lived. Suddenly, the lump behind her moved. Tor hadn't noticed Raga sitting there. Now he saw her, glaring at him. She looked away, mumbling, and he did not move again.

Ashan stirred, her eyelids fluttering. Her voice drifted to him, strong for a moment before trailing away into the night.

"Takeena Tor, Shala Ashan . . ."

She lives! The words almost escaped his lips. He held back an urge to run to her and throw off the old woman stroking her cheek. He rocked on his heels, regaining control, telling himself he could only wait and watch. He finished the song in his mind.

Takeena ku Shala kahni. Shala ku saika tahno. Suyano akaita; teahra, kahni ki.

Tor is the Eagle, Ashan is the Wind. The Eagle needs Wind to fly. The Wind needs reason to blow. Everywhere we see them; together, flying free.

Did Ashan dream of that long-ago day when two little ones played in a forest glade, and the boy sang for the girl the song of his heart?

The Old Moonkeeper dipped her fingers in a stone bowl of steaming liquid. She lifted Ashan's head and dripped the sharp-smelling medicine onto her lips. When Ashan moved no more, Raga laid her back. Tor wondered if the bowl held dark magic to make her sleep forever. His thoughts focused on the old woman who kept them apart, on her power over Ashan, over him, over everything. Ashan belonged to him. Even the spirits agreed—hadn't both their lives been spared?

He thought of taking her away, to live by themselves with all the little ones the Moon Spirit would bring. People said no one could live alone, but they only believed that because no one ever had. He and Ashan were different. Tor, the best young hunter of the tribe, would easily keep a family fat. And Ashan knew everything else. They would be happy—away from the others, the laws, the old woman.

His fingers curled around the pledge band he'd made and hidden in his medicine pouch. How could he convince Ashan?

The tribe's future Moonkeeper journeyed on through the night, living memory after memory—each complete in its joy or sorrow, fear, triumph or love. Some were sweet spices on her tongue; others burned with the bitter power of medicine roots.

Once again—small, alone and afraid—she climbed to the flat top of Kalish Ridge, a power place visited only by spirits and seekers. She would wait there without food or water, perhaps for many days and nights, until a spirit brought a vision, giving her its name and power of protection. Shala the Wind Spirit did not make her wait, coming in a blinding rush as the moon rose fat and orange. At first, little Pella could not believe the tribe's guardian would be her own. But the spirit left no question, naming her Ashan, Whispering Wind, Song of the People.

She lived again that day in her seventh summer when her mother took her to a honey tree after a morning of digging sweetroot. "Bees defend their food, but the happy laughter of Shahala little ones is worth many stings," Kira said. They didn't notice cubs hiding in the brush until it was too late. Ashan heard again the she-bear's roar as the massive paw slammed her mother to the ground, heard again the strangled screams. Unable to move or make a sound, she watched the bear claw Kira. Life poured out, staining the earth.

The beast looked up. Ashan stared into small black eyes. For long moments, they were locked together. Then the bear snuffled for her cubs, and the three lumbered off, leaving Ashan in numb horror by the mangled body of her mother.

The others came running. Raga knelt over Kira, then looked up, shaking her head.

"Mahto the bear has taken the life of our sister."

The voices of the women rose in wailing.

"But," Raga said, "she spared the little one. Ashan stood bravely, and Mahto knew her power. The message of the spirits is clear!"

Raga grabbed Ashan under the arms and lifted her high.

"Long have I waited for the sign of the Chosen One. I will take her and teach her the ways, and she will one day lead you as Moonkeeper." As Raga carried her back to camp, Ashan's tears refused to fall and melt the stone lying on her chest. Many suns slept before she spoke.

She walked again with Raga, listening for the signs of wind and sun and moon and star that told the time to move; searching for the healing plants; learning of the spirit in everything. Now she became sun, moon, wind and star—briefly, but long enough to know their purpose. Spirits of plants told her their strengths. Spirits of animals took her into their lives.

She flew as hawk, diving through the air at squirrel, her prey. With perfect vision, she saw the hunted one running for his hole, and knew he would not make the distance. She thrilled in victory. Just as her powerful talons reached out for the strike, she was thrust into the victim's body. Fear engulfed her, then killing pain. Then a moment of triumphant realization that life, given up to sustain life, had not been wasted.

As bear, she knew a mother's love, and her special fear and courage, killing cougar in a terrible battle of slashing teeth and claws as her little ones watched nearby. And she understood that Mahto was not to be hated for her mother's death.

More than once, Ashan drifted into some sweet memory of Tor. These would not stay, though she tried to hold them. Soon a spirit would whisk her away, to see and feel and know life through other eyes.

For the first time, Tor looked away from the circle of firelight. In the brightening mist of early morning, he saw the dim outlines of trees taking shape, and restless movements in the furry bundles of sleeping people. Soon Raga would see him, squatting in the open where dark had hidden him all night.

As he stood stretching cramped muscles, the Old Moonkeeper turned toward him, a firelit scowl twisting her face. Unmasked hatred crossed the distance between them, piercing Tor like a hurled spear. Suddenly hot and breathless, he feared Raga might strike him dead!

Then Ashan lifted her head and rose to her elbows, wide eyes looking all around. Tor could not follow the torrent of words spilling from her lips, but he understood the life in them.

"You live!" he cried, forgetting everything else.

She turned. For a long moment, he stared into eyes shining with wonder and love.

Ashan did not look away until the space between them filled with excited people. Then, leaning on Raga for support, she stood to face the tribe. They swarmed around her as bees to the mother—some kneeling, some reaching out to touch or hug her. Their rejoicing filled the dawn.

As he watched them, the young warrior Tor realized he might well lose the battle for Ashan. They would be a terrible enemy, these people who had always been his friends. They and their Moonkeeper, Raga, who held the power of life and death.

CHAPTER
5

In the hut of his ancestors, Tor lay on a bed of fragrant new boughs, listening to his father's rattling growl and his mother's soft snuffle. He gazed through a gap in the skin roof. The Five Wise Sisters sparkled in the black sky. These moon-guardians seemed no farther away than Ashan, nor more impossible to touch.

The Chosen One had risen from her spirit journey full of life, more radiant than ever—the only sign of injury a band of medicine leaves around her forehead. The tribe had set off the next morning, reaching their winter home, Anutash, Valley of Grandmothers, at sundown. All the way, people had surrounded Ashan; everyone wanted her attention. Tor had stayed clear of the noisy ones, his mind filled with thoughts of taking her away.

Now, as he lay in the darkness, he feared he would not get to talk to her before the ceremony that would take her forever.

As the newest of the tribe's seven First Warriors, Tor would be out before daybreak, hunting stallions for the Autumn Feast—two young rogues with no mares of their own. Tor's father and grandfather had been First Warriors in their time. Arth was proud of his son—at sixteen summers, the youngest so named that anyone remembered.

When the warriors returned from the hunt, the Autumn

Feast, Kamiulka, would begin. On the third morning, Ashan would become Young Moonkeeper, married to the tribe and spirits.

The air inside the hut was thick and hot. Tor could not sleep for the troubled thoughts chasing themselves through his mind. The wedge of sky brightened. Alhaia the moon had risen, spreading light on the ground outside like honey on a graincake.

He quietly crawled through the low door.

Stretching, breathing deeply of the sweet night air, he walked away from the village up a rise on ground washed white with moonlight. Unseen animals scurried in clumps of leatherleaf bushes as he passed. Three times a nighthawk called, flying high where the wind sighed softly through long needles. The moontime walking brought peace, emptying Tor's mind of questions that could never be answered.

A huge, shaggy-barked tree loomed up before him—Pusha, the old one. Surprised to have found the ancient tree in the dark, Tor stroked the soft bark, then sat in the familiar curve of massive roots. He laid his hand in the hollow where his grandfather had sat, remembering the talks of an old man and a young boy. An unseen fragment of the wise one—gone to the ancestors long ago—sat with him now, welcoming him back.

The village below shone in pale light, crossed by the shadows of scattered trees, which seemed even taller than when he had last seen them six moons ago. The rough circle of huts looked like a gathering of sleeping turtles. In the center, several girls slept by the glowing coals of the night fire.

His eyes settled on Ashan's tumbled hair. Watching her sleep, he curled his fingers around the pledge band hidden in his loinskin, made in secret and carried for so long. He pictured her holding it, tying it to her arm, breathing his name. Heat spread inside, swelling him to delightful, aching hardness.

"Ashan . . ." He whispered her name to the passing breeze. "I need you more than the love of Takeena."

Far away, a big cat screamed.

Ashan sat straight up, wide awake. Had someone called her? Nothing moved in the bright moonlight. She heard no sound but wind and the breathing of her friends.

Shreds of the forbidden dream clung to her mind. Tor and
Ashan, lovers and mates, the passion of hungry bodies set
free. Transformed by the dream into sleek cougars—circling—leaping—meeting in the air—writhing in the dust.
Trembling earth and shattered stars. A cry of fulfillment, his
and hers together rising in one perfect tone.

She shivered, the dying flames of the dream drenched by
her frustrated tears. What hidden part of her knew these
unknown things? How could *she* be the Chosen One, the Pure
One?

How could she go through with it?

She looked to the hut where Tor slept with his old ones.
Who would he choose to share it? Tashi? Loka? Ashan stared
at the unpledged ones sleeping beside her. The ripe expanse
of Tashi's hips and the heaviness of her breasts would invite
the Moon Spirit to send many little ones. Loka's pouting lips
and tiny pointed chin were delicately pretty, even in sleep.
Tor shared no blood with either. He could have his choice.
Or would he bring an Outsider?

What difference did it make? Soon, Ashan would lead and
love everyone equally—Tor and his mate included. Now, in
these last few days, she must make herself ready to receive
the ultimate power, coming to the spirits pure, cleansed of
human weakness.

Help me, Shala, she prayed.

The soft wind called her to walk in the moonlight. She tied
on her skirt and catskin and headed up the hill toward a giant
fallen tree. Many seasons ago, she had hollowed out a small
cave under it. She could sit there and look over the village
below, even in the raintime.

As she walked, Ashan tried to keep her mind on the right
things, thinking of her spirit journey and the knowledge no
one else had. She pictured the coming sunrise ceremony, the
sacred robe, the moment of spirit possession.

The excitement of all of it did not come close to a single
moment of her dream of cougars.

"Ashan?"

She stopped at the loud whisper.

"It's Tor. I could not sleep. Will you sit?"

A warning sounded in her mind. The Chosen One did not
belong in the moonlight with a young warrior. Of course,

as Moonkeeper, she would talk to anyone she liked. What difference did a few days make?

Following his voice, she went and sat beside him in the hollow of an ancient tree, cushioned by soft needles, a thick root curving behind her.

"I could not sleep either," she said. "It's the feast—all the changes coming. I can feel the excitement in the village, even now when everyone sleeps. Can you?"

Ashan stole a glance at Tor. He smiled, nodding, but did not look at her.

She said, "I thought my friends would talk all night. Mani has waited for Lar since we were little ones. Keeta is sure Takluit the Outsider will be everything she ever wanted. They were still whispering under their rugs when I found sleep." She sighed. "I should not complain of their chatter. After this night, we will never sleep together again. I will miss that."

A cloud shadowed them from Alhaia's watching eye. In the darkness, Tor's broad hand covered hers, and she did not pull away. As little ones, they had often held hands, but that was long ago. When had they become more like Outsiders than closest friends? Ashan sighed. Closest friends became lifelong mates, and mates they could never be. Was that why they had stopped touching?

For this moment, she didn't care. All her attention focused on her hand. The light stroke of Tor's fingers flowed up her arm in waves of shivering warmth. She wondered if the same sparks penetrated his hand, finding their way to his heart. He moved closer. The heat of his thigh spread along the length of her own. She knew she should pull away, but her body refused to obey, wanting his touch with its own will.

"Ashan . . ." His voice was soft as the new velvet of a stag's horn. "Do you not think of what else you will miss? A warrior's love . . . his little ones . . ."

"Oh, Tor, if you only knew! I do, and I . . ."

She slumped against his shoulder, sobbing, the flood of doubts and fears released by the question no one ever asked. His arms enfolded her. She buried her face in his chest, wetting the hard smoothness with her tears. He held her close, stroking her hair, making his body a cave to hide in. Lost in the dark wonder of his warrior's power, wrapped in strength and protection, she gave herself to his gentle rocking—a whimpering, frightened little one, safe for a moment from everything.

Impossible words penetrated her haven.

"I can change it, Ashan. Let me make it different for you."

She pulled away, wiping the tears from her face.

"You can't change my life. Rabbit drew our paths when we were born, and we must walk as the spirits say—side by side, not hand in hand."

"Who decrees this?" Tor whispered loudly, spitting out his words. "Bear could have killed anyone's mother. Are we to hear spirit words in the roaring of every beast? No, Ashan. Raga built this wall around you, and I can set you free. Free to live as you were meant to. I know a place of such plenty that we would never want. We can go there—"

The word slapped her. She pushed his hands from her shoulders. "Go? What are you talking about?"

"Wait! Please listen to me!"

A shaft of moonlight touched his face, and she could not look away from the naked yearning she saw there. Through her eyes, he entered her, found hidden pathways to the deepest places in her being, caressed her there and held her. Slowly, she sank back to her knees, eyes still locked on his glowing face.

He took her hands. "I have seen a wonderful place, and I have seen us there. You and me and a flock of little ones. Lar and Mani are with us, and many Outsiders. You are the one who keeps our ways. We live beside a great river, sheltered by high cliffs with many caves. The river is so wide . . ." Having no words, he dropped her hands and held up all his fingers. ". . . more than this many rivers flowing together. And the fish! They are huge and fat, so many that a man could walk across on their backs!"

Ashan laughed at a picture of Tor trying to balance himself on a river of moving silver. He went on, quieter now, as if sharing a precious secret.

"This river is the mother of all the fish in the world, and they swim in her waters in all seasons. Great herds come to drink. Everything we need is there. Hunger never visits."

His words drew pictures in her mind so clear she could

almost smell the fish drying in the sun. She shook the images from her head, amazed at his power to create them.

"You tell a fine story," she said. "But pretending is for little ones."

"It's no story. I have . . . been there."

"I've been every place you have. There is no place like that in our world."

"It's not in our world, but it is real, and someday you will go there with me!"

Ashan stared at him with growing frustration. It was one thing to dream of being someone else. But he was talking like a madman of taking the tribe's Moonkeeper to a place that did not exist. If he didn't find a mate soon, he would drag her into his madness. Her frustration exploded in ugly words.

"Can we talk about what is real? You are a warrior now. You must take a mate, bring little ones to our tribe. Or are you one like Obo?"

His dark eyes flashed. He pulled a short thick rope from his loinskin and thrust it before her.

"Does this look like something Obo would make? I am a warrior in *all* ways! I will take my mate when the time is right!"

Ashan's throat tightened. Tor held a pledge band more beautiful than any she had ever seen. Each twisted strand, each tiny object, a loving thought of someone. Who had filled his mind as he worked? Loka? Tashi? One of the younger girls?

This was the answer—for him to mate with someone else and leave her alone. Why were tears welling up?

She reached out to touch a polished blue stone.

"Who will wear this?"

With one quick movement, he looped it around her arm and tied it.

"You will, Ashan! Before Amotkan, I name you my mate!"

He spun away and ran into the night.

The band came alive on her arm, melting into her skin, as though Tor's power and soul were braided with the strands of his hair.

CHAPTER
6

First light painted the clouds above distant hills. Soft pink brightened to orange as sun pushed against dark sky. Tor put away his troubled thoughts as he quietly approached a spring hidden beneath the overhanging hump of a ridge. Here, in a time before his remembering, Shahala warriors had fought invading Snake Men, driving them back to Warmer in a battle of many deaths. Men avoided this place of tragedy. Tor would never have come here, but for his dream.

A steady breeze blew into his face, dragging thin fingers of early-morning fog. Sniffing the damp air, he found the warm, sweaty aroma he sought. Horse scent! He knelt in the almost-darkness, fingers tracing fresh-cut tracks with no wetness standing in them.

"Kusi," he whispered to the Horse Spirit, "I have found your sons."

On hands and knees, he crawled toward the spring, keeping close to the rocks edging the trail. Neck hairs bristling, he remembered the story of the Shahala hunter who, while stalking game, was bitten by a death snake that dropped from above.

Tor's thoughts of danger suddenly flew from his mind when he saw them, just as his dream had shown: nine mares and two leggy colts drinking from the spring, guarded by a watch-

34

ful black stallion. Apart from the band, on a low rise of yellow grass, two stallions with the short beards of youth waited to drink—one the color of dried leaves, the other of new-fallen snow. Heart thumping, Tor cupped his hands around his mouth and called out his signal.

"Whoot. Whoot-whoo."

The black's head went up, ears twitching, flared nostrils searching for peril. The two young stallions took no notice, and soon the black went back to grazing. Tor thanked Shala for sending the wind in his favor.

The air moved behind him as they approached, though the six warriors made no sound. In the speech of hands, they made a plan to take the rogue stallions. Kowkish would climb the rocks around the top of the ridge, coming as close as he could to the black's backside before he bolted, and then would shout and wave his skins to drive the band. Hidden on the trail, Tor, Lar and Tonda would bring down the snow horse; Lyo, Deyon and Totus, the golden brown.

The First Warriors placed their hands together, combining their powers into one so great they could not fail. In a whispered prayer to Kusi the Horse Spirit, they asked for help with their sacred task.

As Kowkish disappeared into the rocks, Tor, Lar and Tonda crawled farther up the trail, taking cover in a yellowing whipstick bush. Tor crouched, keeping his eyes on the young white stallion, his three-stone sling ready.

The black's high whistle broke the silence. As raving Kowkish ran toward him, the stallion charged into his panicked mares. Biting, striking out with front hooves, he turned them down the trail.

The earth thundered as the terrified animals neared. Stretching close to the ground, the white stallion passed the mares. The warriors leapt to their feet, slings whirling. On the third swing, Tor let go. Alive with its own power, his weapon whistled away, straight into the legs of the snow horse. The horse pitched forward, stumbling to the ground. Tor hoped its legs weren't broken.

The herd stampeded past as the three men fell on the downed stallion. He screamed in fury, struggling frantically to throw the attackers off, slashing out with his one free hoof. Lar threw himself on the kicking leg, holding it long enough for Tor to rope it. Even with four legs tied, the fierce swift-footer kept thrashing, swinging his head like a war club. Tor winced as strong, flat teeth ripped his leg, but he managed to tie the power mask over its blazing eyes. Blinded by the leather hood painted with the signs of men, the animal quieted.

They worked quickly with horsehair ropes, tying front legs to back with a length between for walking. A rope was made of the stallion's silvery tail-hair and braided into his mane. With the ropes in place, they cut the tangled slings. Snorting, the muddy snow horse scrambled to his feet, and could only follow as the warriors pulled him to the nearest tree. They tied him, nose tight against the trunk, then ran to help the others. Soon the brown was tied near the white.

Mud-streaked, smiling, the men squatted on their heels.

Kowkish slapped his leg. "Too easy! We'll have them back by high sun!"

Lar cocked his head and stared at Tor with narrowed eyes. "How is it you knew where to find them?"

Tor hesitated. Did he dare say he had seen it in a dream? The question scratched at his mind again. Was he the only one? How could he be? Why would dream spirits come to him, alone of all the men?

"Do you have the dark sight?" he asked.

"We are men!" Lar said.

Lyo snorted. "No spirits in this man's bed! Kill me while I sleep! Wake up dead!"

Tonda punched Lyo's arm. "Dead men don't wake up!"

They all laughed, a little too loudly, and Tor sensed their uneasiness. He should stop now, and talk about the horses. Or anything. But how else would he know? And, someday, he had to know.

"Well, do you or not?"

Lar's black eyes flashed a warning. He picked up a rock and hurled it into the canyon wall. "What's wrong with you! Men should not even speak of it!"

Tor knew what his friend was thinking; they were spirit brothers, closer than brothers of flesh. Lar lived in fear of the spirits. Some good, too many evil, they saw everything men did. Only the Moonkeeper heard their voices as she walked in the darktime world. Her dreams were messages to help the tribe survive. The Shahala learned as little ones to block the faintest memories of spirits in their sleeping heads. Sleep was a peaceful nothingness for everyone but Raga and Ashan.

And Tor? No . . . he still could not believe he was the only one. The secret took on its own power, crawled up his throat, and burst from his lips.

"I have the dark sight! I fly with eagle's wings!"

As soon as the words were out of his mouth, he knew he'd made a mistake. They hung in the damp air, a foggy cloud between Tor and his friends. He wished he could bring them back into his mouth and swallow them.

Lar jumped up, stamping off toward the horses, arms stiff, fists clenching and unclenching. The faces of the others were dark with alarm.

Tor knew in a flash what he had to do. Hands over his mouth as if trying to hold it back, he began to laugh. Snickers grew to howls, howls to roars, until he was completely convulsed and rolling on the ground. He stopped suddenly and looked up. Their expressions had changed from annoyance to outright fury as they realized he was laughing at them.

"You believed me!" he howled.

Without another word, the warriors walked off. Tor slumped. It had worked. By their looks, he knew they had believed him. Now they wouldn't know what to think. It was better to make fools of his friends than to have Raga find out the truth.

Deep loneliness filled him. He was alone, the only man who dreamed.

He thought of Ashan, out gathering turtle eggs for the feast. She dreamed . . . one more reason for them to be together. Would she believe him if he told her? Would she understand? Or would she tell Raga? Tor didn't know what to expect. The pledge band given in love could bring death to them both.

He shook his head and walked into the morning sun, following the men and horses already far down the trail.

Ashan sat with Mani on soft sand at the river's edge, trailing her feet in quiet water. Sun's warmth lay smooth against her shoulders, a soft fur garment brushing bare skin. *Like his touch*, she thought, remembering. She leaned back, tipping her face up. Against the deep blue sky, sunset-colored leaves rustled in the breeze. She closed her eyes, watching for a while the red and black spiderwebs on her lids, inhaling the ripe aromas of late summer. They mingled sweetly in her mind with the memory of Tor's musky scent.

Ashan had been stepping on the wind since first light, living each dreamlike moment again and again. She touched the medicine pouch tied at her waist, tracing the coiled treasure inside. She smiled. Yes . . . it had really happened.

Through half-closed eyes, she saw the digging sticks and flat horseskin sack—only a few turtle's eggs to show for the whole morning's work. This day everyone gathered first fruits for the Autumn Feast. The cooking women would accuse them of laziness, but she didn't care. It felt good to be with Mani on a last warm day.

Ashan sat up, listening. A faraway rumble told of the First Warriors' return. For three suns, the ancient wood drums would live, their stretched skin covers the voice, the very heartbeat of each ritual. She thought of the Mating Dance, its slow throb rising to a mad frenzy.

"It has begun," Mani said. "Tomorrow the tribe will know me as woman. Lar will know me as woman." A broad smile lit her face with a beauty Ashan had never noticed.

"Oh Mani, I am happy for you." She hugged her friend close, smoothing her straight black hair.

The breeze shifted, suddenly crisp, a reminder of the changing season. Ashan shivered. How soon she must trade her short skirt for the heavy skins of winter; trade even sooner her freedom for the Moonkeeper's sacred robe. She shook her head, suddenly sad for all that would never be.

"What's wrong?" Mani asked.

Ashan sighed. "Oh, nothing . . ."

"Your spirit sister knows you better than you think. What is it?"

Ashan felt a powerful need to share her forbidden excitement. Mani was her only real friend. But even she would not understand this.

Or would she? With everything else stripped away, were they not simply women?

Ashan opened her pouch and took out the treasure.

Mani gasped. "A pledge band!"

Made from the tail of a white horse, twisted with strands

of a man's black hair, the braided rope was similar to Mani's, but also very different. Compared to its impossible beauty, Lar's gift seemed clumsy and plain.

Mani took it, turning it over in her hands. Woven among the strands of hair—standing out, but somehow held tightly within—were bits of treasure that made the eye smile. A bright blue stone with threads of silver running through it. A tiny piece of stag horn, rubbed and polished as smooth as water. Several shells of different shape and color. At each end, a thin strip of leather ran through a loop for fastening. Two downy feathers hung from the tie.

Mani looked up, frowning. "Where did you get this?"

"I found it by my sleeping place, almost touching my fingers," Ashan lied. "Look! Have you ever seen such a thing?"

"You must give it back! You are Moonkeeper!"

"I am not—not yet. And how can I give it back? I don't know who put it there." She tried to keep the whine out of her voice. "It's too beautiful to throw away. I will keep it to remember when someone wanted Ashan as mate." She took the band and slipped it into her pouch.

Mani shook her head. "Someone? You mean Tor! Anyone could see that. Eagle feathers! It speaks his name with its own voice!"

"Tor?" Ashan pretended surprise, plucking a faded flower from the grass, breathing its faint sweetness.

"Who else would be so bold? First he attacked the River Spirit—now this! He should die for his rashness!" Mani took Ashan's hands. "The tribe will be your mate—all the men and women, all the little ones, yours to love. You will wear the pledge band of the people. I beg you to destroy this evil thing. You should not have shown even your spirit sister."

The increasing frenzy of the distant drums echoed the turmoil of Ashan's racing thoughts. If she had known how Mani would react, she would have kept the secret. Raga spent enough time telling her the laws of the tribe. She fought back tears.

"The law is wrong. I could be Moonkeeper and Tor's mate."

"Men would never allow it, even if the spirits did. Accept it, Ashan. You must be who you are."

Mani spoke the truth. In spite of her desires, Ashan could not deny it. Tor had put them all at terrible risk, inviting the spirits' deadly wrath, and her own forbidden thoughts could only increase the danger. Her spirit power would be destroyed if she took a man. The laws were old; the punishment unthinkable.

Mani's stern voice startled her. "So, not-yet Moonkeeper . . . what will you do?"

Ashan answered without thinking. "I will climb Eagle Rock and throw it to the River Spirit. She will know what to do with it."

"The spirits know too much already, my sister. Pray they are not angry."

CHAPTER
7

Mani tried to arrange the puny offering of blue-green eggs into two heaps that would seem larger than they really were.

"Hurry!" Ashan said. "The old one comes! She will never believe we dug all morning for this!"

"I can do no better. Ten eggs will cover only so much ground, no matter how I try to stretch them."

Laughing, brushing the dust from their white leather dresses, they stood as Raga walked up.

"Girls! This is the best you could do? The people will not even taste bites so small." The deep creases of Raga's frown refolded into a smile, and her dark eyes sparkled. "I only tease you. It's the giving that matters, not the gift." She patted their heads and walked away, stopping to admire Karna's dusty blue sourberries.

Ashan smiled, amazed at the change in the Moonkeeper. Some mornings, the stooped old woman was so stiff she had to be helped from her sleeping place. Yet she became a creature of beauty and strength when she wore the ceremonial garments. Her stretched-out flesh clung tighter to her bones. Tall and straight, she strutted like a long-legged water bird among her people, with the light step of one much younger than thirty-seven summers.

As Ashan watched Raga speak to Tia—a boisterous girl, now smiling with lowered eyes—she wondered how it would be to wear the Moonkeeper's robe and headpiece.

The sacred robe, made of fur and hide, tufted with feather clusters, strewn with teeth and claws, represented every animal and bird known to the tribe. Many times Raga had taken it from its painted leather pouch, unfolded it in Ashan's lap, and told her ancient stories of the Animal People. Ashan loved to stroke the soft furs, to bury her face in them, memorizing the unique fragrance of each.

But of all the Moonkeeper's trappings, Ashan thought the stallion headpiece the most wonderful. A stiff mane bristled out behind Raga's head, circling her face with every color worn by horses. An impossibly long tail sprang from the center and swept down her back, brushing the ground as she walked. The pure white plume was the gift of Kusi the Horse Spirit—his own tail given to the Shahala in the Misty Time, so they would be known by their brothers, the horses. Countless Moonkeepers had treasured the magic headpiece, wearing it only at Kamiulka, the Autumn Feast. Its power could not be doubted . . . the land dancers had come to the valley in great herds, at the same time as the tribe, as faithful as the rain and snow.

"The magic becomes the old woman," Mani said. "Think how it will be for you. Good will come running. Evil will hide."

"And all you will have is a warrior under your sleeping skins, and a tiny one on your back. Who is the lucky one?"

Mani sighed. "You will see, Ashan. When the spirits take you, everything else will pale."

Lar's gray-haired mother waved across the milling crowd.

"Well," Mani said, "today I sit with Lar's family." She hugged Ashan and left.

The laughter around her chased Ashan's gloom away. The dark blue sky and crisp breeze added their sparkle to the fruits of the day's gathering. The sight brought a wave of hunger. None but the little ones had eaten since yesterday, and they would not eat again until tomorrow.

But, oh, when they did eat! Belly grumbling, mouth watering, Ashan stared at the bounty. Heaps of berries—five different kinds. Wapato, the knobby round morsels from lake mud. Roots, both bitter and sweet. Acorns, seeds and grains to be ground up and baked into flat cakes. Honey for the cakes. *And small—no, tiny—bites of turtle egg*, she thought, smiling at the two puny mounds.

Observing ancient laws of Balance, the first foods lay divided in two parts, arranged side by side on new reed mats. Half was for tomorrow's feasting. The rest would be returned to the land, with words of the tribe's need for food, and thanks to Amotkan's creatures for providing it. Ashan tried to think exactly where they had dug the eggs. She could only remember blue sky, soft breeze, and thoughts of Tor. She hoped Mani could find the turtles' home again.

The cooking pits shimmered in readiness; oakwood fires had burned to coals and the rocks inside glowed. Nearby, fresh boughs and leaves were stacked. The boughs would go in first, to keep the food from burning. Then the layers of food, the leaves, and earth over everything.

When the sun rose tomorrow, the pits would be uncovered. Oh! The delicious smells! Her nostrils twitched, remembering other feasts. Hunger sank its teeth in her belly. Even tomorrow, she would have to wait. While tempting aromas curled under the noses of the famished people, Raga would thank Amotkan. Then they would sip water to remember its importance to every living thing. Not until everyone tasted each first food would the real feasting begin. Ashan planned to eat until she folded up in pain, then wait awhile and do it again. And maybe one more time before darkness fell.

"All is ready!" Raga commanded. "Bring the stallions!"

The First Warriors—all but Tor—headed to the brush pen behind the village where the horses were kept.

Tor had not left the brush pen since returning from the hunt. Something about the white horse drew and held him—something he had never felt before. Even as he wondered what Ashan was doing, he could not leave the stallion. It seemed the snowy beauty had something to say in a language of shared thoughts.

He loosened the power mask from its head. When the horse did not move, he took it off. They stared long into each other's eyes. The wild creature showed no fear, standing still as a rock. Tor stroked its soft nose and felt its warm breath. He gently blew his own into its nostrils.

You are mine . . . you are mine . . . The thought ran over and over as he gazed into the unblinking eyes.

He shook his head. It made no sense. Horses were food, the same as berries or roots. They belonged to no one, except perhaps the wind.

At the sound of approaching voices, Tor quickly retied the power mask. Still the stallion did not move.

Cougar-teeth wrist bands rattled as Raga raised her arms.

"Come," she called. "It is time to remember."

The people sat in family groups. Ashan sighed. At these times, she felt the most apart. She barely remembered sitting here with Kira. Her father, Kahn, had died before Ashan could know him. She would be glad when it was her turn to stand in Raga's place. Then she would finally belong somewhere.

She found a place near Arth and Luka, Tor's old ones. His small sister Tenka looked up.

"Ashan sit by Tenka?" the little one said, black eyes dancing as she patted the ground.

Ashan squeezed Tenka's bony shoulders, kissed her laughing mouth, and sat.

The drums raised their voices. The people cheered as the First Warriors brought the stallions. Legs hobbled, faces masked, they came quietly, not struggling against their fate. A good sign—it mattered that they understood.

"Do not fear," Tor whispered in the ear of the white stallion as they approached the ceremonial ground. "You wear Kusi's own color. You're the one who will be free to fly again across the wide spaces. Someday our trails will meet. I will know you, and you will know me."

The warrior crossed his wrists in the sign that meant "spirit brother." The stallion snorted. Tor believed he understood.

How brave, how handsome, Ashan thought, looking at Tor's red-painted face—the color of successful warriors. The polished claws of Mahto the bear gleamed at his throat, proclaiming his position as First Warrior. Painted on his chest was a black eagle over a yellow sun, the sign of Takeena, his guardian spirit.

She saw Tor whisper to the snow horse as he pulled the rope tight to a wood post, and wondered what he said.

"Unblind the land dancers!" Raga commanded.

The warriors pulled off the power masks. At the sight of light and freedom, the brown horse lunged, jerking his head free. The people gasped as the post trembled in the ground, but the rope braided into his mane held.

Raga extended her hands and looked into the eyes of the horses. The thrashing one quieted, and the warriors stepped away. The Moonkeeper placed a hand on the head of each animal.

"Sons of Kusi, forgive our need for food. We must have meat, as you must have the yellow grass."

To the brown stallion, she said, "You have no mares, no foals to protect. Will you give up your life for our need?"

Shaking off her hand, he lifted his white-starred head. His long, high whistle lingered on the air. Stamping his hooves, he lowered his head. Raga stroked his nose and nodded, thanking him.

Of the white horse she asked, "Will you take our words back to your brothers? Say the Shahala hunt as Kusi taught us, taking only young stallions, sparing the mares and foals. Yes?" she said, though the horse did not move.

"Then hear me. This is how it came to be so." Raga dropped her hands and shook out the white plume behind her. Ashan listened carefully, though she had heard the story of creation many times.

"First there was water, everywhere water with no living thing in it. Amotkan the Creator reached down and pulled up some land. Darkness covered it, so Amotkan called Kai the sun, Alhaia the moon, and Haslo the star, and sent them to light up the sky. Into the emptiness came the Animal People. First, Amotkan's favorite, Kusi the horse. Spun from the wind, he flies on the land without wings. Next came the hunter's friend, Spilyea the coyote . . ."

Raga's deep voice rolled on, naming the Animal People. Her hands spoke in the old way, moving rapidly as she talked. Every word and symbol was important. Nothing could be added or forgotten. Ashan thought she could easily speak the names. But would her hands remember all those graceful motions?

". . . because he was lonely, after some failures, Coyote made the first man. A man of pitch melted when Coyote left him too close to the fire. Rain washed away a man of clay. The man he carved of hot stone cracked. He wove a man of reeds, but this man caught fire and burned. Finally, Coyote mixed all these things together, and added wind, smoke, and fire. A handsome man took shape. Coyote named the man Shakala.

"Pleased with Coyote's creation, Amotkan gave Shakala breath, so he could live, and speech so he could talk. And the man said, 'Yes, I shall remember.'

"Shakana, the woman, was made of the same things . . ." Raga paused, and then went on.

"Amotkan saw a purpose for the people Coyote had made, for there were struggles in the world that sometimes threatened its very survival. Amotkan named the man and woman Keepers of the Balance—between Spirits of Dark and Light, between moon and sun, land and sky and water, predator and prey. Between people and the world—our mother—and all her creatures—our brothers and sisters."

CHAPTER
8

The wet-earth taste of sacred mushrooms lingered as Ashan watched flames leap above the feathered heads of the dancers—crackling, snapping, dancing against the black sky as if they too obeyed the commanding voice of the drums. Ashan's heart pulsed with the slow, throbbing rhythm.

The dancers chanted, the women's voices high, the men's low and warbling. Ashan saw the sounds rise over their heads, spiraling strands twisting together, joined by cloud puffs of drumvoice and thumping feet. Waves of fireheat caught the many-colored sounds, sucked them all up together, and threw them sparkling into the moonless night. She blinked. The sound pictures wavered and were gone.

Watching, swaying in time, Ashan stood in deep shadows near the four grayhairs who pounded life into four even older drums. Around her sat the old women, their laps filled with sleepy-eyed little ones.

All but the very young and very old danced the Mating Dance, forming two circles, one inside the other, moving in opposite directions around the fire. The dancers sidestepped, crow-hopping on their toes, their heels not touching the ground.

The women in the inside circle wore capes of white deer-skin. The soft leather barely covered their breasts, coming to a point in back just above their buttocks. Bare knees knifed up through long fringe swinging around their legs. The men facing them in the outside circle wore only loinskins, paint, and feathered rattles around wrists and ankles.

Dark against the firelight, the dancers nearest Ashan looked more like living shadows than real people. Those on the far side of the fire were brightly lit. Flickering yellow light played tricks with face paint of ochre and clay, turning the dancers into bright birds, fierce animals, pale ghosts.

The grayhairs pounded faster, harder. Ashan's heart raced to keep up the quickening beat.

In the dance circle, Tor emerged from shadows into brightness. His red-painted face spoke of manhood, stirring a warmth inside Ashan. As he danced, he stared in her direction, not meeting the eyes of the women dancers as he should. Could he see her in the deep shadows? Did he feel her body heat flow to him, as his reached her?

The ancient ones whipped the drums to a frenzy. Suddenly, the men jumped back, faces menacing, fists jabbing the air.

Mani and Keeta took refuge in the inner circle of women. Kneeling, holding each other close, they crouched near the fire. The women closed around them.

"Get away!" they shouted. "These girls are too young to be women!"

"Aiyiiiii!" the men yelled, charging into them to get at the huddled girls. The women fought fiercely, beating their fists against painted chests. Finally Lar and Takluit broke through. They picked up their almost-mates and carried them screaming into the night. The men stood aside as the shrieking women gave chase.

The drums stopped. The women froze. For a moment, the only sounds were the cries of the stolen girls. They grew fainter, then stopped.

In the penetrating silence, Ashan imagined Lar laying Mani on a bed of soft needles. He would pull off her cape, throw it aside, stretch his naked body next to hers. Touch her breasts and the secret place of her woman power.

What came next? Whatever it was, Ashan was sure it was glorious. Memories, or something like them, stirred her flesh—so real, so intense, she thought she must have lived them some other time, in some other life. Her body burned to know them again. This time. In this flesh.

The drums spoke again, calling the dancers back to the fire. They circled as before, their feet stepping to the Moon Dance, the ritual of fertility.

From nowhere, Raga appeared among the dancers, magnificent in a robe of condor feathers that shimmered purple in the fireglow. The Moonkeeper thrust the tip of her staff in the flames. Popping and sizzling, flashing with green-white light, it flared brightly for a moment, then went out, puffing acrid smoke. Chanting, dancing behind the women, Raga blew the fertile smoke over their heads.

Her voice rang out, calling to the unrisen moon.

"Alhaia, Keeper of the Future . . . it is the Time of Balance, when day and night are equal. The Moonkeeper commands you to shine on this night of greatest power!"

Alhaia heard Raga's plea. The first sliver of moonlight crested the mountains. The married ones left the dance circle for the dark of their huts. Watching and waiting, unborn spirits might ride down on moonrays, to grow beneath a mother's heart, creating bonds so strong even death could not sever them. In the warmth of summer, tiny ones would emerge, and the tribe would continue.

Raga's lilting song invited them. "Awake, little ones . . . bring us tomorrow. We give you a place to belong."

As Ashan listened to the words that had called her to life, she thought of the nights when *she* would sing to the Moon Spirit.

The dancers went twice around before she realized Tor was not among them. At the same moment, she smelled his scent, felt his presence behind her.

"Ashan."

She barely heard the whisper in a pause between drumbeats. What was he doing? He should be dancing with everyone else!

"Ashan!"

If she did not go to him, someone would hear. Raga and the dancers were deep in an unseeing trance. The old women watched; the little ones dozed. No one would miss her. She backed into the darkness. He touched her shoulder, took her hand.

"Tor—"

"Shhh," he whispered. "We must talk."

As he pulled her along, her eyes adjusted to the faint starlight. His back glistened with sweat, though the night was cool. Downy puffs of white eagle feathers hung over his shoulder, swaying as he walked. For a while, she followed, meek as a masked stallion, in a trance of Tor's making.

Distance muffled the drumsound, but its power followed them into the night. Low thumping came as waves of pressure in Ashan's ears, creeping into her mind, setting off flashes behind her eyes. Her blood pulsed hotly. Even this far away, she smelled the sharp fertility smoke. Suddenly, her head felt light, her legs weak. She pulled against Tor's grip and sat.

He was on his knees in an instant. "Are you all right?"

"I am now. Why did you bring me here?"

"Why did you follow?"

"You said . . . I . . . I do not know." She had no answer. Why had she?

"I will tell you why," he said. "We belong here at moonrise on this night."

"No, Tor. Not this again."

He held her shoulders as she tried to stand. "Why did you come? Say it, Ashan—you want this too."

His shining eyes reflected moonlight, filling her world. She could drown in them and not care. His lips brushed her cheek. A tiny mouse voice in her mind squeaked protest as a bear voice roared, *Yes!*

Standing, he untied his loinskin and dropped it.

"I would die for you, Ashan."

The rising moon washed his body with soft silver. The staff of his power jutted toward the brightening sky. Entranced, she reached out and touched his hot, pulsing hardness, wrapped in the softness of flower petals.

Ashan folded his loinskin and lay her head on it, drinking in the rich man-leather scent. She would never forget the sweet muskiness, would carry the memory deep inside until death took her senses.

Tomorrow the spirits would own her, but tonight there was only Tor. Ashan reached up to him, her eyes moist and welcoming.

Tor could not believe the wonder lying before him. Taking her outstretched hand, he knelt beside her on soft, needled ground. The long fringe of her cape curled across her slender body, parting around her breasts. With both hands, he pushed the white leather strands away. Moonsilver stroked her belly, lighting the darkness below, guiding his hand as he sought the warm mystery of her womanhood.

Sighing, then moaning as he touched her, she parted her legs and pulled him down. Slowly, gently, he pushed. Swaying hips rose to receive him, and in a delicious instant he was deep in her. His body knew the ways to move, leaving his mind startlingly clear, aware of each tiny detail. He buried his face in the web of her hair, the leaf-washed fragrance filling him as he ran his tongue along her neck, tasting her sweetness.

Every part of his skin tried to cover her, to bring her inside his flesh. The distant drums quickened their thunder. The earth beneath them shook with it. The thunder rose from the ground, swelled inside him. The drums were in his head. They exploded, and he fell into her.

He held her so tight that nothing could tear them apart as the earth turned over and they fell into the sky, adrift in a heaven of shattering stars.

CHAPTER
9

Raven Tongue . . . pull yourself along the silver strand . . . back toward the world . . . smell, hear, see . . .

Drumthunder . . . fertility smoke . . . breathy chanting . . .

All came back as Raga became one with her body, swaying in the dance circle, belying its great age. She had journeyed with the moon. Alhaia had shown her souls waiting for birth, flitting like summerflies in a canyon made of clouds . . . more souls than stars in the sky, fuzzy balls of light no bigger than her hand, each a different, soft color of its own.

The Old Moonkeeper had never been shown this sight. It told her that her time to become one of those souls was near. Ashan would become Young Moonkeeper tomorrow. Then *she* in her wonderful youth and strength could take over as much of the work as Raga wished.

"Thank you, Alhaia," the old woman breathed. "And you, Amotkan."

A terrible thought struck her: What if she was wrong, it was too soon, Ashan was not ready? What if Ashan was *never* going to be ready?

It was too late to worry. Raga reburied the thought under the stone in her mind where she kept fears, stamping hard on the stone so the thing wouldn't slither out again.

Her part in the Mating Dance finished, the gleaming black-purple condor backed out of the dance circle. She slowly danced to the grassy spot where the old people sat, watching her feet so she wouldn't stumble. Raga was tired. Her vigorous dance had taken great effort, at least until Alhaia had swept her mind away. She sat down and closed her eyes. No one would know if she dozed for a moment. She welcomed the peace.

A hideous picture struck her brain like lightning. *Ashan!* Raga leapt up, screaming, "No-o-o! Tell me I'm wrong!" The Shahala fell to the ground as one terrified creature.

Out in the darkness, the lovers didn't hear a thing.

Still the magic pulsed. From a volcano deep inside Ashan, lava streamed to every fiber. Still Tor covered her, but lightly now, his leg curled over her, arms holding her against his wet chest. Did she taste the salty sweat of their loving, or tears spilled in that moment of soaring oneness?

No sounds existed but those of their bodies. Breathing had slowed, but still her nostrils flared for air. Her pounding heart matched the heavy throb in Tor's chest. Swept by a lingering wave, Ashan thought no glory of spirit or human could match the joining of lovers.

Gradually sounds returned. A nighthawk called. Crickets sang. And still, the drums reached into the dark, as they would until sunrise, when they hushed in the presence of spirits gathering to consecrate the Young Moonkeeper.

Stroking her back and the rise of her hip, Tor said, "We cannot live with the tribe after this."

She touched his lips. "Shhh."

"I will speak! We must leave them tonight while they dance. There's no other way."

Ashan didn't answer, hoping her silence would bring his back. She wanted to stretch this moment, lock it in her memory forever. It was the best her life would ever have, and she wanted it to last.

"If you are to come with me, there is something you must know." Tor took a deep breath. "Spirits come to me, though I never invited them."

"No—I will not hear this!" She covered her ears as cold fear swept her.

"You will hear. This is part of me."

Ashan could not bear to leave him yet. Even though it frightened her, she knew he spoke from his heart. She glanced at the moon . . . the night held much more darkness.

Raga! The old woman's face flashed in her mind, as it did when the Moonkeeper called without words. Ashan threw up the shield she had made long ago. It blocked Raga's intrusion, and even her own unwanted thoughts.

Tor cradled her in his crossed legs. Everything else drifted away as she stilled her mind, relaxed her tensed muscles and settled into his warm cocoon.

"Takeena the Eagle Spirit—Sky Dancer—comes to my sleep. I leave my bed and fly with him. I fly! Sometimes on great feathered wings. Sometimes with only the smoketrail of my soul. It must be dark sight, the dreaming of Moonkeepers. I've looked for you, Ashan, tried to find your dream and join it."

Alhaia's silver light seemed warm on her skin, like the kiss of sunshine on a spring morning. Tor's rough fingers stroked her arm. A high breeze rustled the trees, but it did not chill the lovers, curled up together as if their bodies had always known one another. The distant drums were softer now, and friendly as he talked.

"My first dream came in the time of new grass as we trekked to the mountains of summer hunting. We camped in the canyon of Yahwah River. I saw an eagle and his mate soaring over the bluff, always flying back to the same high place, and decided to sleep near them. Luck, or a spirit, guided me to a rocky crag near a huge nest. I climbed no closer. I only wanted to see them, be near them—not disturb them.

"As I sat looking at the great tangle of branches, wondering how many lifetimes it had been there, I saw the most wonderful sight." His faraway eyes settled back on her. "Except for you." He touched her face, then looked back to the dark sky.

"Amotkan's ugliest creature poked up its naked head, opened its beak, and said . . . 'Skree-eek!' Oh, if you could have heard it! I laughed at the puny thing, wondering how it could ever become the soaring beauty of the sky.

" 'Skree-eek!' it cried again, and I saw the reason. White tail flared, black feathers scooping great wingfuls of air, an eagle flew over me with a fish in its talons. The great bird landed, dropping the fish in the nest. It shook out its feathers and turned to me. Its piercing gaze struck me as I ducked behind a rock.

"Another eagle screamed as it landed. I peered around the rock to see them tearing the fish for their little one. They did not look at me again. Darkness covered us, and I and the eagles slept. And that was the part that was real."

Tor's dark eyes clouded. He drew a long deep breath.

Ashan held hers, waiting.

"In the night I was suddenly awakened, by what sense or sound I do not know, shivering beneath dripping sweat, remembering what I now understand was a *dream*. I was . . . almost afraid. I remembered flying on man-sized wings, high over the valley, over trees, over the river. I was so light, I perched on the highest branch of a grandfather tree without shaking it. As I looked down at the river and away to the camp, the real eagles circled above, hunting. In a great splashing dive, one brought up a fighting salmon nearly as large as itself. Struggling to gain height, it flew toward the nest."

Tor paused. "I wondered if I could catch a fish. With the wondering, my wings spread and I soared over the river. With keenest sight, I saw through the water. Below the flashing surface of a deep green pool, a silver fish swam in lazy circles. Our eyes met. I folded my wings in a powerful dive, plunged into the water and caught it. I shot into the air with the great fish in my teeth, all my strength barely lifting me over the water. I understood then that an eagle's life is not all gliding on the wind.

"At the thought of wind, a current lifted me. I saw the Shahala camped downriver and thought . . . what if I flew over and dropped the fish among them? Would the people look up and see a winged man? Would they think it magic, or a spirit? The wind carried me closer. Just in time, I turned away, realizing it was Tor they would see—not a spirit, but a madman who should be destroyed!

"As I flew off, I thought of the meat in my jaws. To waste such a life is wrong. I would have taken it back to Luka for roasting, but . . . a fish with her son's teeth marks? I could not. So I flew back to the nest and dropped it for the little eagle.

"Suddenly the sky darkened, and I saw the gray beginning

of dawn. All my flying had been in the day. I did not understand how it had come to be night, but I knew I must return— to Tor, the man. Then I awoke.''

He sighed and spoke no more.

Ashan stared at the sky. The Three Hunters still chased the Four Elk. She looked for the Bear, then the Spear Thrower, trying to think of anything but Tor's dream. But such words, once spoken, will not be ignored. Scrambled thoughts buzzed in her head like angry bees. She could not sort them out or find her voice to speak them. She wanted to think Tor a liar, but his words had such power that she had seen and felt what he described. How could he have made it up?

For him to dream was a dangerous wrong—even deadly. Yet one question kept gnawing: Why had Takeena given him the dream and brought him back unharmed? It went against everything Ashan understood—about dreaming, about spirits and men. All the little ones stopped dreaming before their power quests. Their old ones made sure of it, watching their sleep. The Moonkeeper helped any who were troubled too long, by making a dream catcher to hang over the bed: A willow twig tied into a circle as big as a spread hand, woven across with sinew from the center out, as a spider spins a web.

Men never dreamed. Ashan thought they had forgotten how. They knew they might die from trying. She and Raga had the protection of spirits, a power no man knew.

Tor claimed to dream . . . but here he was, more alive than she had known a man could be. She shook her head. Out of the confusion, a picture took shape in her mind, a vision as clear as if her eyes were seeing it. In slowed-down time, a magnificent eagle-man rose from the water. Sparkling spray flashed in the sunlight. Head thrown back, jaws clamping a great salmon, tremendous black wings thrust skyward—the picture stopped and froze there. Ashan would never forget the vision of her winged lover lunging into the heavens.

To fly with him! she thought. *To glide on the wind in great sweeping circles, outstretched wings almost touching . . .*

''There have been other dreams, but we have lifetimes to share them.'' He looked deep in her eyes. ''Ashan, I have loved you since we were little ones, though I knew you would never be mine. Then, on the night before the River Spirit took you, I had a dream that changed everything.

"Takeena flew with me that night, and your guardian Shala. Though I had never known Shala, she whispered her name in the wind that carried us. We flew into sun, over plains and mountains. At last we saw water ten rivers wide. I thought it must be a lake, but no . . . it was one river flowing endlessly on. Long we followed it, landing finally in high black rocks.

"This is what I tried to tell you, but you didn't understand. My dreamself looked down on our new tribe, happy and fat, gathered around as you held a tiny one to the sky in a birth ritual. Our own little ones sat at your feet. I knew then what I cannot forget: Takeena and Shala, our own guardian spirits, showed me our future. You and I are to leave these people who live in fear. We are to gather a new tribe, and lead them to the river I saw. I must make it happen. I have been commanded."

"Oh Tor—"

"Do you understand why we must leave them tonight? Before you become their Moonkeeper?"

Ashan understood. But understanding did not stop the panic rising at the thought of leaving. It was impossible! No one could live alone.

"We have nothing," she said, "not even our warm skins. Winter is coming and there will be no food. A man cannot hunt alone. Our own brothers would track us like animals. They would not stop until we were dead."

The shaking fear quieted as Ashan realized the deeper truth.

"For you there may be another life, but I belong to them. Shala named me Song of the People, calling me to lead. I cannot turn from that."

"How can I go without you?" he cried. "What good will it be?" Dark liquid spilled from his eyes, falling on her heart like a knife.

"But I will," he said slowly. "Somehow, Shala will bring you to me. Just as I believe I loved you before this life, I know we will love again. Time cannot change what is."

With her hand, he pointed to the sky. "The Five Wise Sisters have guided us forever. We have danced on their rays in times between our lives." He took her face. "When we die, I will meet you there again. Will you remember? Will you promise never to forget?"

She nodded.

"Some morning when you wake, I will be gone. When you see our stars, I will be watching them too. Loving you."

There was nothing more to say.

Gray light smeared their shelter of darkness. How could the night have passed so quickly? They rose and walked silently back. Just outside the firelit circle he stopped and pulled her into his arms. They kissed, drinking deep of each other. On the honeyed sweetness of his lips, Ashan tasted the bitter salt of their mingled tears.

Too late, he stopped. His father waited by the hut, glaring. Tor took a deep breath and tried to smile.

"The mushrooms—I ate too many and had to walk them out."

"On this night? On this night you could not stay with your people?"

"Arth, I was ill—"

Disgust curled his father's lips. "I do not wonder. Why would one who shows no sign of manhood feel well at the fertility rite—no matter how important it is to his people?"

Arth jabbed his finger in Tor's face. "The spirits demand the presence of everyone! Because of you, they may send no little ones to the tribe! Did you think of that in your moment of illness?"

The fury suddenly gone, the old man squatted on his heels, rocking and shaking his head.

"What have I raised? What kind of man? You are sixteen—are there no thoughts of a woman's softness under your sleeping skins? Your mother cries for you. She prays you will look at someone, mention someone's name. She longs to welcome a daughter to our hut. Her fine First Warrior, the pride of the tribe—is he to give his mother no grandchildren?"

"You have Beo and Tenka. They will bring what you desire."

"The harvest of your loins is what I desire. You are my firstborn. No other can fill that place."

Tor looked down on his father. Arth's shoulders seemed thinner; they trembled in a soundless sob. Pity swept him. He felt like a father in the presence of an inconsolable son. How could he leave this man who had taught him a warrior's ways? Or the woman who had given him life, who loved him far more than reason allowed? Luka might die of a wounded heart if he disappeared without a trace, leaving Arth alone with Beo and Tenka. Tor could not shatter his family. He must try to explain. Now—while his father's eyes begged him to speak.

"My staff rises high as any man's. I love someone, but she can't be my mate. Not here, with this tribe."

"A cousin?"

"No. We share no blood. I loved her before I reached your waist. Even as a little one I knew. I've tried to protect her, and thought I would stay for that. But soon she won't need me. A Shahala warrior must have a mate, I know that. But I cannot have the one I love, and I will take no other."

Arth stared at him blankly, as though he made no sense.

"I'm thinking of leaving the tribe. You and Luka must understand, and believe your grandchildren will play in the sun. I will tell them of you, and someday you'll hear their laughter calling on a breeze."

Arth spoke slowly. "I do not understand. Your words have no meaning, yet your eyes say you speak the truth. There is no family who would not welcome the son of Arth—no woman who would not run to your arms!"

"I love Ashan."

Arth came alive in a fire of rage. He leapt up, clubbing Tor to the ground. Tor rolled away, but Arth was on him, punching and bashing, screaming over and over, "You will die!" Tor had no defense; no son would ever strike his father. He covered his face with his arms, but there was no escape from the wild beast. Fingers dug into his throat, squeezing the life out of him. His brain rattled inside his skull. A jerking picture of Ashan appeared, then began to fade.

"You're killing him!" Luka screamed, leaping on them— kicking, biting, scratching until Arth threw Tor back and jumped away.

She lifted his head, slapping him.

"Tor! Tor! Speak to me!"

"Get away from him, woman!" Arth screamed. "He is evil, and we who gave him life are doomed!"

"You're crazy! You nearly killed my son!"

"Luka, our son . . . the Chosen One . . ."

Choking, Arth could not go on. For the first time, Tor heard his father weep. Other than Ashan's scream, it was the most awful sound that he had ever heard.

It made him want to die.

In the Moonkeeper's hut, Ashan knelt in silent prayer. Smoky firefish oil glowed in a small stone bowl. Smouldering in another, dried kalla leaves sweetened the thick air.

Raga watched from her bed of skins as the gloom of night faded.

"Sun breathes gray on the sky," the old Moonkeeper said. "I will make you ready."

Ashan stood as Raga removed the porcupine quills that held Kusi's headpiece in her thin white hair. Poking and pulling, Raga stuck the quills in Ashan's thick mane. As the long strands drifted over her shoulders, a strange lightness almost lifted her off her feet. *No wonder Kusi's sons fly without wings!* she thought.

"You were not among the people tonight," Raga said as she mixed bear fat and pigment for Ashan's face.

The guilty one had her answer ready. "Shala called me to walk in the moonlight and pray."

"And Tor, the other I did not see—do you think Shala called him?"

A lump thickened Ashan's throat. She shrugged. She had no answer for this.

Raga's broad fingers traced the waving lines of Shala's mark across Ashan's forehead in oily white chalk. Stale breath filled her nostrils. Black eyes pierced her.

"You are pale, Windpuff. You must eat more of the green things. Soon the snow will cover them."

Raga's calm voice didn't betray the vomitous stew boiling inside her, but Ashan tasted it anyway.

CHAPTER
10

The drums hushed. The Shahala people gathered. Ashan waited with bowed head in the center of the ceremonial ground as dawn chased dark from the sky. Kusi's plume flowed down her back, and the robe of the Animal People caressed her, as if its furs and feathers had waited for this moment. The ancient odors were familiar and sweet.

Raga stood beside Ashan and raised her arms as the last sharp drumbeat echoed away. Into the silence, one by one, the old woman sang the spirits' names.

As the sun pushed the darkness higher, they came. They came in clouds gathering for sunrise; in the breeze that picked up and feathered the strands of Kusi's tail; in songs of awakening birds, and shrouding drifts of orange mist.

As the sun threw tongues of flame into the clouds, spirits thickened over the people. Ashan lifted her arms to embrace them. Warm, blissful recognition flooded her. Though she could not see them, she knew her fellow travelers of the long night. Their love fell down like gentle rain, washing away doubts and fears.

The sun's golden finger touched her cheek, and she looked to see him slowly rising above the black hills. She did not close her eyes as the thin crescent grew to a blazing ball. Spirits entered her as she stared into the dawn. Warm tingling under her skin spread from her forehead to her eyes, her ears, down her neck, until her flesh was alive with it.

As the sun burst free of the hilltop, she closed her eyes against unbearable brilliance. The spirits left her, rushing up and out her forehead between the talon scars. Her soul, suddenly empty and alone, leapt to fly out with them.

No! She must not! She clung tight to the part of her that sought escape, closing the hole, wrapping her body tight around her soul. The effort took her strength. Her muscles went limp. She collapsed.

She heard the people gasp, saw Raga raise her hand to silence them. Ashan gazed into the disappearing clouds. For a moment it seemed like an ordinary morning. She drank in its loveliness, tasting its warm kiss on her lips. As her pounding heart quieted, she welcomed the feeling of wholeness again—of body and soul united.

And then she knew—they were still within her. Lingering traces settled softly against her fibers, growing to them, becoming part of her.

And she knew they would never leave.

Ashan rose and faced her people. Lifting her chin, she shook out the long tail behind her. Tears filled her eyes as she looked at their faces, then over them into the far distance.

Deep with new resonance, her voice rolled into the silence.

"Amotkan said: 'Earth was born of the timeless struggle between Light and Dark. Light was given power, and the Balance was restored. But people must keep the Balance, for Dark never sleeps.'

"Shakana the woman heard Amotkan's words, but Shakala the man was already looking for something to put in his belly. The Creator said to her, 'Woman: You shall be keeper of the moon, and the sun and the stars, and give them your strength in their time of need. And the Spirit of Light will know your people as friends.'

"The woman said, 'I will keep the Balance, and my daughters after me.' "

Ashan raised her arms to the morning sky.

"I am Ashan," she cried, "Spirit daughter of Shakana. While I am Moonkeeper, Dark shall not control!"

* * *

Listening filled Raga with relief, for Ashan could not so speak without the blessing of spirits. The Young Moonkeeper was aflame with their power. A baby would know it, or a bug, or a mammoth.

I was wrong, Raga thought. *My mind, like any other old person's, is a worn-out pouch full of holes. Wisdom and memory fall out the holes, crazy ideas come in. It's a trick so we won't know what's going on . . . that we are old . . . that we are dying . . . that everything will be left to these young ones.*

We must trust them. They are all we have.

Tor saw nothing but the ground under his feet as he ran toward the refuge of mountains. Away from his weeping father and raving mother. Away from the marriage of Ashan. At high sun, he stumbled into the deserted Yuna River camp. He had not known his flight would bring him here, but now he understood: He should never have left here alive.

He climbed through blowing spray to the whirlpool's thundering rim.

"Take me, Yuna!" he roared. "I'm not fit to live!"

Tor threw out his arms and lunged, but his body refused to obey, rooting his feet to the rock. He fell on it, tearing at the moss, pounding until his hands bled. He could not even choose to die!

Spent, he lay on the rock, the cold spray swirling around him. Yuna had not even noticed the crazed insect clawing her flank! Where was the raging monster? The teeth, the jaws? Now he saw only rushing water struggling to be free. And a man too weak to join it.

He sensed them and looked up before he heard their faint cries. Wingtips touching, black against the sun, two eagles soared. Another dropped from the blue above and joined their circling flight.

Believe, Tor, believe, whispered a voice inside.

He climbed down from the rocks and sat in the stone circle where Ashan had slept, leaning against the largest—the dark green globe he had found in the dusk of that long-ago day. Long ago! Tor shook his head. Five suns seemed more like five moons, or five turnings of the seasons. He had thought himself a man then—how little he had known. The real man had awakened inside Ashan. With her at his side, he could have done anything. But without her? He tried to think. Should he keep on running, higher into the mountains? Or go back to face his father?

As shadows gathered in the canyon, he headed home. What else could he do? To go into the wildplace alone, he needed weapons, skins, food. Otherwise, winter snow would bury a starved fool.

Tor walked long in the dark before he saw the reddish glow of the burned-down fires of his village. He found Pusha, his grandfather's shaggy-barked friend, curled into his sheltering roots, and slept.

Birds greeted cheerfully the cold light of dawn. Tor kept his eyes closed against it. He had always loved mornings—the fresh beginning, the promise of all possibility. Now they brought endings and pain.

Pain. Everywhere. As it came alive, he remembered his father's beating.

"Oh Takeena," he groaned. "What have I done? Why didn't you let my father kill me?"

Shivering against the cold, Tor called for sleep to come back, but it would not. Instead, memories flooded him—gut-wrenching, all of them, but for the instant of joy with Ashan.

Ashan refused to come with him! How could it be? Had Takeena not promised, had Shala not offered her help? Their loving was to be the beautiful beginning of everything, not the tear-filled end. Must he wait until death brought her to him? Die to live again?

"To-or . . ."

"Beo?"

"Owww! Bat dung!"

What was his little brother doing, stumbling around in the thin gray light?

Beo pushed through the brush, rubbing a bleeding toe. He sat so close their bodies touched. Beo hadn't done that in a long time; his warmth was sweet and welcome.

"I thought you'd be here. Arth sent me to bring you back."

"Why? So he can finish killing me?"

"No, Tor. Our father is the wounded one. He and Luka talked long in the dark. I didn't understand everything, but our mother believes you will be different, now that the Chosen One has become Young Moonkeeper."

Tor sighed, tracing a waving line in the dust. *Gone . . .*

Beo went on. "Luka burned stinking leaves and prayed you would return. She told Arth he would never touch her again if you do not. Our mother said that—to Arth!" Beo rolled his agate-black eyes. "At first light, he sent me to find you. You will both forget what was said and no one else will know. Our father said he loves his firstborn. Will you come?"

Thanks to Takeena! He could stay with the tribe until he hid away the things he needed to leave. "I will. I'm hungry, and I hurt." Tor looked at the bruises left by Arth's fists. "If anyone asks, I fell down a hill of boulders. It feels like truth."

Beo mumbled thanks to his guardian, Kiark the Falcon Spirit. "Eat this, brother. I brought it in case I had to travel far."

Tor took a leathery roll of berrycake—mashed purple fruit sun-dried on flat rocks. The tart-sweet taste made his mouth juices flow. His hurts lessened, his thoughts lightened, as the cloudless sky filled with pink.

"There is more to tell!" Beo's voice rose with excitement. "When I left, Raga was telling the elders a dream-vision."

"What of that? She dreams every night." The word annoyed him. He never wanted to hear it again.

"This is different, Tor, the dream of her lifetime! She saw Manu, the Earth Shaker! A great mammoth, the last of his kind! The tired old warrior wants to join his brothers. The Shahala are to take him. His meat will feed us long into the snows. It's a spirit gift for the Young Moonkeeper."

Tor spat a berry seed. "The old vulture is crazy. Manu has not roamed the earth since the Misty Time, if he ever did. Does my little brother still believe the grandfather stories of heroes and giants?"

Beo looked hurt. "You do not? Have you forgotten the bones we found? The leg as tall as your body? Baku the bison is not half as large. I was a boy, but I will never forget."

Tor remembered the day. He was just a boy with a short practice spear, hoping for a fat ground squirrel. He loved to see the pride in Luka's eyes when he brought meat.

"My son," she would say, "so young to be so skilled!"

Food was shared by all, but the tribe had plenty, so he would ask her to fix it his favorite way—thin strips soaked with spicy leaves and seeds, slowly dried over a smoky fire. He liked to take leathermeat when he hunted. As he chewed, he pictured himself a First Warrior away on a trek of many suns.

Even as a boy, Tor liked to be alone, especially to hunt. His friends roamed in a pack like their fathers, but spent more time punching and laughing than they did stalking. They almost never caught anything larger than Kua the quail, who gave herself away defending her young.

Tor had not understood those boys. There was a time for testing each other's strength. His growing muscles thrived on it as much as anyone's. But hunting was serious—so much to be learned, so little time before manhood. Tor wanted to wear the claws of Mahto the bear—the proud sign of a First Warrior. He wanted to be the youngest First Warrior ever.

On that long-ago day, Beo had begged to go with him. Tor loved his lively, cheerful brother, and found it hard to refuse the pleading in his chubby face. Beo could make a tear rise in his black eyes just by thinking it; he usually got his way. Tor had given in, helping him smooth down a short stick, hardening its point in fire—Beo's first real spear.

The little one had quietly followed in his footsteps, listening to every whispered word, studying every sign. After that, they had often gone hunting. The brothers of blood by choice became brothers of spirit.

On that first hunt, they walked a good distance toward Warmer, finally making their way up a rocky canyon. As they crept in the sand on their bellies, they saw Rika the ground squirrel sunning himself on a smooth white rock, his reddish-brown coat gleaming with golden lights. Tor rose on one hand and hurled his spear, but Rika saw it coming and flew into his hole. They scrambled to it and tore away with their hands, but there was no following it—the ground was full of holes.

As they sat back, Tor noticed the rock. He had never seen one like it—smooth and white, shaped like the rounded top of a giant man's leg bone. They dug around it, uncovering a great length, before Tor realized it was the burial place of a mammoth, known to his people only through legend. In awed respect, they covered it and never returned. Many times they talked of the great beast, kin of the giant bison, who existed only in legends. No living Shahala had ever seen these creatures of the Misty Time. The brothers felt fortunate to have even touched the bones of one.

Beo's voice brought Tor back. "Raga may be an old vulture, but the spirits do not lie. I believe the mammoth waits."

Tor couldn't argue about Raga's visions. He knew they were always right.

It would be wondrous to see a mammoth, to hunt it home to its ancestors. Had it wandered a lifetime, searching for another, before finally whispering to Raga's sleeping mind? How long would Tor, spirit brother of Manu, wander alone? He wanted—needed—to be there, the first man to strike the beast, the last to see life in its eyes.

"They will go soon," Beo said. "You are First Warrior. You must join them."

"Where does the Earth Shaker wait?"

"Where Day Begins, at the foot of the Serpent Hills."

"Where Day Begins is tabu! The Shahala do not go there!"

"Raga says that story of old belongs to the past. The spirits lead us to a new beginning. It's part of Ashan's gift to the tribe. Two Moonkeepers protect us now. We need not fear."

Tor shivered to think a tabu so ancient could be broken because of an old woman's dream.

"Everyone is going." Beo said. "Only a few will stay with the women. I want to go, Tor! I want to see him too!"

"Arth will not allow it. You aren't yet twelve summers."

"But I'm a good hunter! You've seen me throw my spear into trees—I never miss. Rabbits and squirrels cannot hide from Beo, Falcon Wing. I run all day in the sun. I am ready, Tor! Help me tell our father!"

Tor would be lucky if Arth even spoke to him, but Beo bounced beside him in eagerness. And he did use weapons better than most boys his age.

"All right, little brother, I will try. But it is our mother who must be won."

When the brothers entered the hut, their old ones carried on as if nothing had happened. Luka packed food in two leather pouches, as though she had known Tor would come.

Arth sat on his heels, flaking a new edge on his chert stone knife.

Beo stood with hands behind his back, trying not to squirm, as Tor persuaded their father.

Arth nodded, not looking up from his work.

Luka's voice rose unnaturally high. "No! Beo is too young to hunt a beast taller than two trees!"

"Lu-ka," Beo said, "two men, not two trees!"

"Close your beak, falcon boy! I do not allow it!"

Throwing down his knife, Arth rose over her, fists clenched at his sides.

"Enough of what a woman will allow! Do you forget who is warrior here? Every man leaves his mother to hunt with his brothers. What better time than this? Beo's name—and Tor's—will be sung at campfires of men not yet born as takers of the last Earth Shaker. A woman's raving will not steal that from my sons!"

CHAPTER
11

On a clear blue morning, Raga stood with the tribe to watch the warriors begin the quest for Manu the Earth Shaker. Something special was needed to celebrate the consecration of the Young Moonkeeper, and what could be better than the huge beast thought to have died out long ago? There were doubts, but the Old Moonkeeper had already answered them, and now she ordered doubt to leave her.

Raga watched as Ashan moved along the line of men, drawing her red-daubed finger down each nose to complete the fearsome paint they had put on themselves. When Raga, as large as any man, prepared the warriors, they could look her straight in the eyes, and some even had to turn their faces up. Ashan was so short, they had to bend down so she could reach them. Raga smiled and shook her head. The wispy little thing reminded her of wind-blown grass.

The warriors seemed awed by this first ritual of their Young Moonkeeper. More than one gazed at her with improper eyes. Raga wondered why the spirits had cursed Ashan with beauty and fragility that begged to be cared for . . . as if it weren't hard enough just to be a Moonkeeper.

Raga watched carefully as Ashan approached Tor.

As she did for each man, the Young Moonkeeper spoke to

Tor's guardian spirit, in a voice surprisingly potent for her size.

"Takeena! Protect this man valued by family and tribe."

She moved on to the next man, stopping not one moment longer with Tor than with any other.

When the ritual of painting was finished, the warriors stood in a circle around Ashan. They flung their arms high and shouted triumphantly as though they had already brought down the mammoth.

With last glances to their families, the warriors ran from the village like a massive, noisy beast, their shouts lingering as they disappeared from sight.

What was left of the tribe stood silently gazing after them, until a loud thump broke the stillness.

An old one had fallen.

When Raga and Luka reached Shandar, they turned her over. A trickle of blood came from her ear. Luka knelt by the old woman, holding her shoulders, gazing into her closed-eyed, slack-mouthed face.

"Oh, my mother, do you have to leave us now?"

Raga knelt and placed her fingers on the loose skin of Shandar's neck. Nothing. Then she put her face close and smelled for life. Nothing.

Luka's breathing was ragged and loud. The Moonkeeper held out her arms.

"I'm sorry, daughter," Raga said, though Luka was almost as many summers as she. "It's your mother's time. At least she lived to see her grandsons off on their greatest adventure." Raga continued to whisper words meant to soothe, but her deeper spirit self spoke in a louder, fearful voice. *Journeys christened by death are marked by battles for life.*

After a long, stealthy run across a sagebrush plain—once passing a herd of horses who never sensed them—the Shahala warriors stopped at Andor, River of No Crossing. They did not talk as they filled their water pouches and rested in the shade of a few clinging yellow leaves.

Tor sensed fear in his silent brothers. It settled on him as he stared at the Serpent Hills, forbidden to the Shahala since time before remembering. Ragged stone fingers stabbed the washed-out sky; the high dark edge had a look of malice.

Everything, he thought—their lives and the future of the tribe—held in the wrinkled palm of an old woman's dream. Did everyone fear it, or was he the only one who doubted Raga's sight?

Tor counted on his fingers. The warriors were four hands and four. That left only eight, and the grayhairs, to guard the women. He looked toward the sheltering mountains of his homeland. A long gray cloud hung over the valley of Anutash. Small snakes shivered up his back as he wondered if that was where the evil would come.

"Guard her, Takeena," he whispered, cupping his hands for a last drink.

Evil stayed hidden from Tor's searching senses as he ran, though lonely desolation surrounded him. There was little to hide the warriors in the flat, dry land but scattered rock mounds and thin gray bushes that looked as if they had never lived. He didn't trust the empty nakedness, glad in his heart for the trees and rivers of Shahala land. No soft dirt cushioned the rocky ground, and soon his elkhide-padded feet were as sore as his leg muscles from the low, crouching run.

Gard, the Headman, led them toward a gap in the hills where Raga said she had dreamed the mammoth. As they ran, the warriors kept a good distance between themselves, following brother-scent and a bobbing head occasionally seen. Tor wondered if Beo was still thrilled with the aching reality of his first hunt. Compared to the homeward run, burdened with more meat than a man believed he could carry, this was easy.

Cool and dark were Pahto's welcome gifts as the sacred mountain swallowed the sun behind them. The rocky ground sloped upward, and they passed a few stunted trees. When coyotes began calling across the loneliness, and darkness concealed their way, Gard stopped among some low boulders, signaling no talk or fire.

Tor laid out his huntskin—paired antelope hides laced together down one side. The familiar scent took him for a moment back to Anutash, to his old ones' hut and his bed of boughs on the earth shelf. He was glad for the clean, dry skins to sleep on tonight. Tomorrow night, the skins would be stuffed with meat, and he would lie on stony ground.

Beo crawled over and untied his pack. He rolled his big

round eyes and shook his head. Tor laughed inside. They ate leathermeat and berrycake, washed it down with Andor's stale water, then chewed bitter senna leaves for tomorrow's strength.

Before Beo finished, his mouth went slack and he slept. Smiling, Tor took the half-eaten leaf from his lips and brushed the wing of black hair from his eyes. As he pulled the antelope skin over his brother's shoulders, pride swelled his chest. Beo had done well, never falling behind. And, though tired, he was happy on the hunt. And who had taught him what he knew? Tor looked at the smile on Beo's sleeping face, glad of his part in it.

He lay back, wide awake. In the dark, the tabu land seemed less threatening. Laughing howls of coyotes filled the crisp air, many more than sang in Shahala night. Coyote, hunter's friend . . . if so many chose to live here, could it be so bad?

The darktime sky was another thing Tor liked about the lonely place. He would tell Ashan how it spread wide above, the stars more brilliant than he had ever seen. No treetops blocked the path of his eyes as they traveled around deepest blue, hung with points of sparkling light.

He sought out all the stars he knew, then rested his gaze on *their* stars, the Five Wise Sisters.

Ashan's feet knew the way to the burial ground near Anutash, and it was a good thing, for her eyes could barely see.

The black around the stars is darker on nights of death, she thought.

She found the young woman Ursa asleep on the bearskin that the dead woman's family had placed there for the vigil.

Ashan stooped to touch her. "Ursa, I'm here. You may go."

Ursa jumped. "Moonkeeper! I wasn't really sleeping."

"It's all right. Shandar knows your love."

Ursa disappeared in the dark, and Ashan settled on the soft bearskin next to the body wrapped in white leather.

One at a time, each Shahala old enough to have a spirit name would sit with the dead woman during the three-day ritual called The Soul's Growing. Ashan was here not as Moonkeeper, but as a person of the tribe who had loved this woman—here to help Shandar understand, accept, and take her place with the spirits.

Because of the great importance of the ritual, Raga would see to the Moonkeeper's duties. Ashan wouldn't be good anyway . . . all deaths affected her, but some more than others . . . and this was one of the hurtful kind. Shandar was a good woman who never wanted anything for herself. She gave all her sweets to the grandchildren, and told funny stories of old times. Tor and Beo would be sad. Ashan was glad they could enjoy the mammoth quest without this loss in their minds.

She picked up the time ball lying on Shandar's chest, and began to unwind it. The slender string was longer than two legs of a deer, and showed Shandar's great age of forty-six summers.

Every woman started a time ball at her marriage to keep track of the changes in her life. Only she who made it knew the meaning of the stone beads spaced on grass-fiber string. The time ball would be burned with Shandar so she could take her memories—the only thing that could be carried from this world—with her to the otherworld.

Ashan gazed at the unwound string lying in her lap . . . a whole life in grass and stone. She caressed the beads with her fingers one by one. Which was for Tor? Probably more than one . . . Shandar had been proud to bursting about her first-born grandson's feats.

"Ah, Shandar," Ashan murmured. "So many loved you and will miss you."

She slowly rewound the time ball and placed it on the wrapped body.

Ashan looked at the sky for a while, then turned her gaze to the center of the burial ground, where a great fire would burn on the third day. It was too dark to see, but she saw it in her mind: a bed of large, flat stones fitted together as one, black with the fires of the ages.

Ashan sighed as tears stung her eyes. She knew this wasn't the right way to feel, but . . . it would be hard to see Shandar burned to ash. She knew a soul could only be freed by burning the body; she knew the dead feel no pain; still . . . burning always seemed so scary. Ashan hoped she'd get used to it.

The ritual of The Soul's Growing was one of the most important things a Moonkeeper did for her people.

Couldn't the spirits have found a kinder way? Ashan wondered. After the fire, Shandar would be happy beyond knowing. But now, her spirit was confused, maybe frightened. Ashan felt it flitting around her in the dark.

She gazed at the slender shape wrapped in doeskin and spoke to the hovering spirit.

"This flesh that was Shandar lived well, blessed by spirits, useful to her people. But now the flesh has died, and the spirit must leave."

Ashan took a deep breath, and her voice changed from a sad whine to a Moonkeeper's resonant rumble.

"If you see dark, do not fear . . . soon you will be in light beyond imagining. If you feel cold, ignore it . . . the waiting warmth is greater than the sun. If you are lonely, do not stop. Your loved ones gone before seek you. The fire that is coming frees you to join them.

"And every moment, remember: *you are alive*. Know this, spirit of Shandar, and you cannot die."

On the third morning, the tribe gathered with Shandar for the last time. Raga made fire and carried it to the pile of wood where the dead woman lay. Flames leapt high and hid the body. Smoke carried her spirit to the sky, where loved ones gone before would show her the way to the Light. When the fire had done its work, what was left was buried beneath a jagged gray basalt stone brought here by Shandar as a child. Life's circle was complete.

Deep in the tabu land, Tor dreamed . . .

Great feathered dreamwings carried him high over an unfamiliar world. No green brightened the dead land below—a forbidding place where a man could wander until he died for lack of water. Behind him, the setting sun was turning blue sky orange. Ahead lay the Serpent Hills, dark under gathering storm clouds. He saw the gap between pointed fingers—the place of Raga's dream.

Now he knew where he was, and why. *Tor . . . Mammoth Finder! What a song to leave on Shahala tongues!*

Scattered trees grew taller and thicker as the rocky ground climbed beneath the dreaming man. He flew over a cluster of animals gathered around a muddy waterhole, and was disappointed to see no mammoth. But every other creature must be here. Horses; elk; stags with antlers high, ears pricked, searching the wind for danger as does drank. Smaller animals darted among the forest of legs.

Tor had never seen such a bounty! He wondered what kept the animals from fighting, how they had learned to share the only water—the last effort of a small stream winding out of a rocky canyon. Not a drop escaped the thirsty ones to nurture the dry land below.

From Colder, a long line of bison shuffled along a dusty trail. Baku! Rarely did his kind wander into Shahala land, but Tor remembered the sweet, rich meat with a watering mouth. Bison skin made the warmest winter rug, and he had not yet taken one. He would take three—for Ashan, his mother, and himself! A joke, of course . . . a man never killed more than he could carry.

Even if they found no mammoth, the warriors could take enough from this one waterhole to make the trek worthwhile. The many different kinds of meat would be riches for the tribe in the long winter.

And Tor, *Tor* had found it!

The dreamer flew higher, studying the wind and cover. He saw that the warriors should approach from Colder, hiding among rocks upwind of the waterhole. Unseen, unsmelled, they would surprise many bison.

Tor was sure Gard would listen to him. Had he not found the First Stallions?

Dusk and thickening clouds darkened the sky. The breeze became a wind, ruffling the feathers on his back, making gliding difficult. The sky flashed with blinding light. A monstrous thunderclap shook the air. Pain roared in his ears. For a moment, he feared he would fall into the mass of animals. The terrifying thought and the pain passed as the thunder echoed away.

Fat raindrops fell around him, splashing onto the thirsty earth. A clean fragrance rose up—sharp and pleasant, but different from the sweet, earthy rainsmell of Shahala land.

Animals continued to come and leave, their heads higher, their steps livelier than before. The rain must be as welcome to them as it was to him.

He saw a thin dustcloud up the canyon and flew toward it. Oh, Takeena!

Manu the Earth Shaker lumbered slowly along a creekbed, heading to the waterhole. The shaggy beast was huge—Tor's head would not reach its shoulder! Long brown hair fell in graceful waves. Small eyes scanned the surroundings as it tossed its head from side to side. One great horn curved up and back around—the tip nearly touching its face. The other horn was broken.

Tor darted back and forth in the air like a giant summerfly, excited, trying to remember everything.

Men!

He saw men, crouched among boulders farther down the mammoth's path. He flew toward them. There were many, but he felt safe in the air. No earth-bound creature had ever noticed the eagle-man as he dreamed in the sky above.

When he saw them up close, Tor shuddered. They were naked but for a coating of chalk dust, showing dark patches where the chalk had rubbed off. Jagged stripes of red slashed across faces smeared with black ash. Matted hair sprouted bright feathers. Bones swung from their ears. Each held a hooked stick and several thin spears tipped with stone points. Tor wondered how they used the puny weapons. Stone knives at their waists, twice as long as Shahala blades, left no doubt about their usefulness.

They were like no men Tor had ever seen or imagined. As he hovered over them in air thick with fierceness and a smell of dried blood, the tremor of fear in his gut rose to shaking panic.

Still, they didn't notice him, their eyes fixed on one man lying on a high rock.

The lookout stood, gesturing wildly, silently. With a chill of horror, Tor saw an upside-down human skull hanging on his back. He gripped a staff with a skull on top, finger bones dangling from the jaw.

What kind of thing wore human bones?

No! It could not be! The story of man-eating men was a trick to keep little ones from wandering! Suddenly weak and dizzy, Tor felt his stomach tighten, forcing bitterness up his throat. For the second time, he feared he would fall—to be shredded by long knives and eaten.

The skull-bearer pointed furiously to the flats below.

Tor's heart stopped. Among the rocks at the foot of the hill, he saw Shahala warriors creeping toward the waterhole, unaware of the peril above them. The dreamer saw himself at the rear, as blind to danger as the rest.

The savages regrouped, the mammoth forgotten for new prey. Slowly, the Shahala entered the jaws of the trap, never hearing their dream-brother screaming in the sky above.

The man-eaters closed around them.

Horror froze Tor. Was he to watch them die and then be eaten, or would death take his sight? He prayed for death.

His wings disappeared and he plummeted head-first. Useless, featherless arms sliced the air. Lung-bursting pressure built in his chest and filled his throat. His faint whisper grew to crazed shrieking.

"Man-eaters!" he screamed over and over.

"Tor!"

The dream shattered. The pieces rattled in his skull. He opened his eyes.

Arth was slapping the skin off his face. Tor threw his arms up to stop the blows.

Arth was alive, and Beo, and all of them, standing there staring down at him! Relief swept him. But it was gone in a moment as Lar condemned him.

"I told you he dreams, Gard, but you would not hear it!"

My spirit brother! Tor thought. *How could you?*

"He dreamed the First Stallions," Kowkish said.

"Is it true?" Gard asked.

Tor's mind spun. Dreaming would be punished. A lie about eating strange mushrooms took shape, but he stopped it before it became words. What if it had been a dream of the future like Raga's or Ashan's? Could he allow all of them to die?

"I know dreaming is wrong. I tried to stop, but—"

"You should have asked Raga's help," Gard said. An ugly look twisted the Headman's face, disgust hardening to hatred, as Tor rambled on, unable to stop himself.

"But I did not. Now Takeena has sent me a dream of warning—a future dream. Man-eaters wait in the Serpent

Hills, hungry for Shahala hearts. We must go back, or we will die here.''

Gard shook with rage and flexed his arms, fists ready to split through skin as if they were straining to choke away Tor's life.

''We thought you a man Tor, but only a child challenges the Moonkeeper! Raga saw no man-eaters! Are the dreams of a boy more powerful? She will want to know this. It will add strength to the blow that severs your finger—the least her wrath will deliver! I would not want to be you when we return to Anutash.''

Tor already knew he could not return to Anutash.

Sun peered over the forbidding hills. Gard turned to the men and snapped, ''Get ready to run! The crazed one has left us no time to eat.''

CHAPTER
12

High sun beat on Tor and his tribesmen as they ran toward the Serpent Hills with backs bent, arms swinging, legs pumping in a smooth, ground-eating lope practiced from boyhood. So well did the Shahala warriors blend with the tabu land that only birds would see them.

In torment, Tor followed brother-scent, strong in the heat. Hideous pictures churned in his mind, blinding him to the surroundings. Some would say there were punishments worse than losing a finger—death, or banishment, which was the same thing. But Tor would not agree. To think of having his finger chopped off was gut-wrenching. To imagine Ashan's role—it was she who would wield the knife of spirits' will—was beyond pain.

A proud warrior would rather die!

As he ran, Tor couldn't shake the memory of the time he'd seen the ceremony as a child. Everyone, even the children, took part. This was how they learned the law.

Tor remembered himself as a boy holding his mother's hand, watching with his gathered tribe as a warrior who had done some terrible wrong knelt before the Moonkeeper. It was night, but the child Tor wasn't cold. He felt one with the energy of the tribe, like a single fiber woven into an invisible blanket of belonging. He reminded himself that this was not so much punishment of a man as healing for the good of the tribe.

"One of our parts has gone bad and must be fixed," the Moonkeeper had explained.

Part of young Tor's mind was fascinated; another part wished he weren't there. He couldn't look away or close his eyes. Even if he wanted to, it wasn't allowed.

The face of the kneeling man was pale. His eyes and skin glistened in the firelight. The Moonkeeper was speaking, but only garbled, growlish sounds reached the boy. A sour smell was in the air, like when he wet the silver lines in some kinds of rocks. The smell of fear. The boy wished he understood the sin.

The condemned man positioned his shaking hand on a flat stone—thumb and first three fingers clenched together, the small finger wide apart. He stared at it, then up at the hulking shaman.

Raga wore a bearskin—not cut like a robe, but sewn back together complete with feet, claws, and head—the dead eyes replaced with shiny black stones. The mouth gaped, human eyes sparking behind blood-daubed fangs.

The bear-woman held out a blade of gleaming red stone, hafted to a stumpy antler handle. The man—Tor couldn't remember his name—had made the weapon as part of his punishment. The time spent finding a mother-stone, chipping out a rough shape, flaking it to sharpness, was time to think about his sin.

The man took the blade from the bear-woman and held it over the finger he'd chosen. Raga raised a stone hammer in both paws and hewed down on the red stone blade with all the strength of her man-sized shoulders.

The finger flew, chased by red spray, and landed with a sizzle in the fire. Without a cry, the man fell over. The tribe sucked in a common breath. A scent of urine reached the boy.

The Moonkeeper bent and gripped the man's spurting hand at its wrist. The bleeding stopped. One by one, the people went to the limp man and touched him, ready to forgive and to help him heal.

He did heal. He lived and was almost, but not quite, the same as everyone else. Seasons later, he didn't return from a hunt, and only his family mourned.

Tor finally remembered: his name was Bhut, and his sin was dreaming.

Tor had dreamed last night, but as he ran in the morning sun of today, he only remembered the dream's terror. The details were gone from a mind full of grim reality. When and how to disappear? Where to go? Did it matter?

He barely noticed the ground rising under his feet as the cloud-hooded hills drew near, or the scattered, stunted trees becoming tall and thick, or afternoon shadows growing long.

The loping men emerged from pine woods to flat, barren ground. Rock cliffs loomed to one side. Thunder boomed in the darkening sky. Fat raindrops raised a smell so sharp it almost brought tears.

"Kii-yark!"

The bit of Tor's mind still in touch with his surroundings heard a falcon cry, but the cry did not reach the part that was busy with images of life and death and finger sacrifice.

It wasn't a falcon's cry, but a good imitation. It was the Headman's signal to drop and crawl. Everyone but Tor obeyed.

A few more blind strides, and Tor tripped over his brother. As he went down, he saw animals massed ahead. Bison and stag side by side! And—

Where have I seen this? No answer came.

Tor asked for protection of spirits and the skills of his ancestors. He became one with his tribesmen and one with the ground as he crawled behind Beo toward the kill. He picked out the bison whose skin and meat would help him survive, alone in the wildplace that would soon be his home.

The silence shattered. Mind-numbing shrieks spewed down on the warriors, echoed by rock to sound like the raging of uncountable spirits.

Tor's will deserted his muscles. The only thing that moved was his head, to turn toward the savage howling. Looking up, he saw cliffs—that was all. Cliffs that shrieked. Rocks enough to hide as many men as there are bison in an endless herd.

Ahead of him, Shahala warriors fell in screams, pierced by a rain of spears.

Tor scrabbled to a bush and tried to cover himself. Ear-rending cries of hate and death paralyzed thought. Dust choked him. Through gray leaves too sparse to hide a fox, Tor saw them, pouring out of the rocks—so many—

—Chalky, shrieking ghosts, swinging war hammers, slashing with long blades, hewing down fleeing men as women hew down grain. Standing higher, others hurled spears with a kind of throwing stick that gave more distance and accuracy than Tor had ever seen.

The cries of men were lost in deafening thunder as the animals, bellowing and braying, charged toward the doomed Shahala. The new sound was like the roar of a waterfall, or a thunderclap overhead. It blocked out all hope.

Tor's brain and body finally connected. Better to die speared like a man than squashed like a bug.

He took off running, faster than a cougar-chased antelope, for the cover of the vaguely-remembered trees.

A voice rose out of the clamor. "Tor!"

Imagination—

—*Just run, run with the heart of an animal, run to save your body, to save your soul!*

Tor remembered the details of his dream now, and it gave him even greater speed.

Bone-wearers . . . human, but not human . . . soul-killers . . . man-eaters . . .

"TOR!"

At Beo's scream, Tor's feet dug in. He turned to see his brother running toward him in white terror, arms flung out, legs pumping so wildly they had to stumble, face all mouth, screaming.

"T-O-O-R-R!"

A savage ran behind the boy. Without breaking stride, he raised his spear and hurled it.

"TO—"

Beo pitched forward. The savage stumbled into him, jerked his head up by the hair and put a blade to his throat.

Tor's spear flew into the soul-killer's gut.

He ran back and kicked the dying thing from his brother. It flopped and twisted, hands clutching the heavy Shahala spear buried in its gut. It screamed out alien words. Tor stopped them by cutting its throat with its own long blade.

Face down in the mud, Beo didn't move. A short, thin

spear stuck from a hole in his back, just below the shoulder on the side of the heart.

Tor knelt. He turned Beo's head, wiped at the mud, and pushed an eye open. It wandered, unfocused, glazed with tears. His breathing was ragged and shallow. Blood and spit drooled from his broken lips.

Tor put his foot against his brother's shoulder and pulled on the slender spear. As the barbed point tore out, Beo shrieked. The sound pierced Tor's soul, but he was glad for proof that his brother was alive. He needed some. To look at Beo was to see the silent approach of death.

Tor made a decision: Whether his brother was alive or dead, the man-eaters would *not* have a chance to destroy his soul.

He picked up the alien weapons—the long knife, the thin spear and the stick it was thrown with—and put them in his loinskin. He hoisted Beo over his shoulder, barely feeling the weight. He ran, Beo's legs to his chest, head and arms banging on his back. He ignored the blood running down his legs into his moccasins. His brother's blood.

Tor ran and ran, expecting pain to hit when a spear found him. But none did, and the noise of battle dimmed. Was it over? He listened, still running. No, it wasn't over. But it wasn't following them.

The trees! It was like running into night. He realized he was on the homeward trail, and set his nose to follow it without bothering his mind. No thoughts would be the best thing, and for a while he ran blank, putting distance between himself and the massacre.

The sun was gone before the cries behind Tor had faded. The only sound now was his own gasping, loud as a lake edged with bullfrogs, a ragged pain in chest and throat. His heart thudded. His lungs hurt as if he were breathing flame. Each stride brought cramping pain to his gut.

He had to rest—had run as long as he could—had done nothing *but* run since he had awakened screaming from a dream this morning. Beo, at first like so many feathers, had become the weight of an elk's rear haunch.

Tor saw a large, long-needled tree off to the side of the trail. Halfway up, ancient lightning had caused the tree to

split in two. It would be easy to climb, tall and thick enough
to hide them. Tor turned from the trail. At the sheltering tree,
he unloaded his burden and laid him on needle-cushioned
ground. He looked on Beo's face for a heartbeat, then had to
look away.

His mind screamed: *He's dead, Tor! Your brother's dead!*

The part of him bent on survival screamed back: *He's warm
and limp and any fool can see he lives!*

He shouldered Beo, this time wearing him like a robe—legs
over one shoulder, belly at the back of his neck, head and arms
over the other shoulder. He tied Beo's wrists and ankles together
with a thong, so he could use all his own limbs for the climb
to get his brother up to the crotch of the tree without killing
either of them. He barely noticed bark peeling the skin inside
his thighs and arms as he went up. The pokes and scratches of
unseen twigs were no more to him than bug bites, though they
bled and dug out pieces of flesh.

The tree crotch was wide enough to sleep in. Tor draped Beo
onto it. The tree would hold its burden safely—needing no help
from the unconscious boy—far enough from the ground that
men on the trail wouldn't see him.

Tor did all this without looking at Beo's face. He didn't want
to see it. It would tell him—

Soon it would be so dark he *couldn't* see his brother or
anything else, and that would be good. For now, he didn't want
to be with Beo.

If he climbed to the top of the tree, maybe he could see back.
It was a thing he didn't want to do, but had to do. If any Shahala
lived, he must help them. If all were dead, he must take care
of their bodies and souls.

One man to do this for how many? *Oh Takeena, how many?*
His guts pushed bitter liquid up his throat. He spat, but the taste
stayed.

He climbed as high as he could, and saw nothing but treetops.
Arms and legs wrapped around the slim trunk, he stayed there
for a while, imagining what he couldn't see, thinking first of
his father, and then each of his tribesmen by face and name.

Which were dead with spear or hatchet buried in their backs?

Who had died beneath the hooves of stampeding beasts?

Had any escaped, or were they being dragged away, dead in
body, but horribly alive in spirit, dragged away to be stored and—

He had to stop these thoughts or he would go crazy!

—Eaten, EATEN! The part of him going crazy wondered if man-eaters cook their meat, and if that's enough heat to free the soul.

Stop it, Tor!

No, don't! Think of your people facing winter with no hunters. Think of them starving. Think of Ashan.

Hot tears spilled from his eyes. Everything went dim. He lost his grip and ripped down through branches, leaving more skin and meat. He thought of Beo and caught himself.

Save your brother's life, or soul if life has already gone. It's a thing worth doing before you die. Isn't it?

Dark was complete at the crotch of the tree. Feeling his way, Tor wedged himself between Beo and the trunk and instantly slept.

He awoke in dim light, wrapped in fog, wet with drizzle. The boy across his lap was cold and stiff.

Tor thought he screamed as he pushed his brother away and blindly clambered up the tree. Beo hit the ground with a hollow thump, and Tor screamed again. The pain of Beo's death, heaped on his other griefs, could not be carried. He meant to climb as high as he could and throw himself out, to die on the ground beside Beo. He had failed at other chances to die. He wouldn't fail this time.

A sound of dragging. A voice; another. Someone coming on the trail—man-eaters—

The speech was familiar Shahala.

"What's that?"

"A brother!"

"Alive?"

"Who?"

The voices came closer to the tree, but Tor, near the top, couldn't see the men through the thick needles. His mind and lips formed words: *Brothers, look up! It's Tor!* But something stopped the sounds in his throat.

"My son!" cried his father's voice. "Dear Amotkan, not my Beo!"

"It's only right that Arth pay with one son for what the other did!" The voice was so thick with hate Tor didn't recognize it.

"Your son dreamed it on us!" Lar said.

"Told the man-eaters where to find us!" Brok said.

The desire to make himself known left Tor, though he wanted more than anything to join them and receive comfort.

Comfort? No. A very bad death was what they hoped for their brother, Tor.

"You are wrong." This voice belonged to Gard, the Headman. "Tor's sin is not Arth's, not Beo's. Tor's sin belonged to Tor, and he has paid. May the man-eaters choke on his flesh. If his spirit survived, it will know it is not welcome. No Shahala will speak his name, as if he never was. If he must be mentioned, say the Evil One."

"Yes."

"It is so."

"Get the boy ready," Gard said. "We must go."

Like a hunk of moss, Tor clung to the tree above them. He couldn't think, could only listen to sounds that told him they were making travel poles to carry Beo home.

That had been the dragging noise Tor heard. They must be taking three or four others, dead or injured, home with them.

Tor recognized voices as they worked. Gard, Lar, Takluit, Brok, Snomish, Garend. And Arth, who cried softly instead of talking.

Seven left, out of four hands and four!

Tor listened to their leaving, to voices fading, listened, finally, to nothing. When he could no longer hear them, he imagined them in his mind—shattered, broken, burdened with their dead—getting smaller and smaller until they were a black dot that would simply disappear.

No Shahala will speak his name, as if he never was.

Everything went with Tor's tribesmen: hope, love, future, and even who he *was*. The most hated of creatures—one who betrays his brothers—could never go home again. He'd be dead right now if they had discovered him.

There was no reason to go on living. As a man guilty of destroying his people, Tor hoped his soul would die with his body.

But you betrayed no one! cried a voice in his mind. He shook his head against it.

Slower this time, not in panic, Tor climbed the tree to the highest limb that would hold him.

"Ashan," he whispered.

CHAPTER
13

Ashan awoke from dreamless sleep—for a heartbeat, at peace born of ignorance. Then her mind attacked her with counting, as it did every day.

It's been three hands and two since the Time of Sorrows began. Since the world ended. Since Tor died.

A sharp ache slammed behind her eyes. Her nose let go a watery stream as she denied the need to cry. With effort, she threw the cruel thoughts away for now.

Raga's snoring made the Moonkeepers' hut sound like a den of winter bears. There was no reason to wake the old woman. Dressing carelessly, Ashan crawled through the doorskin.

Icy wind swirled snow in the gray dawn.

"Thank you!" she muttered. An early winter was the last thing the tribe needed. The last thing Ashan wanted to do was visit those who needed her: grieving mates, hungry little ones, the seven who remembered the massacre.

Ashan heard their pleading voices in her mind: "Why, Moonkeeper? Why?"

Who was she to answer them? A moon ago, just a girl with nothing on her mind but a man. Now she was supposed to know everything!

She stamped her elkhide boot, making a cloud of snow for

the wind to snatch. *Oh! That the proud Shahala had been brought so low! That their Moonkeeper could do so little! That her beloved Tor was to blame!*

Or was he?

Ashan shivered as the wind found gaps in her antelope robe. She'd forgotten her beaver hat, and hair lashed her cheeks. She raised her arms in the ritual to welcome a new day. Cold crept down her sleeves and under her breasts to make hard little cones of her nipples.

She meant to say: Spirits of all who love people, awake and bring us this day.

But this slipped out: "Spirits, we did not wrong you! Why have you left us?"

Raga lumbered by, a fur-covered mound heading toward the hillside where she sat on a rock, day after day, staring toward Where Day Begins. The Old Moonkeeper should have been angry to hear Ashan curse spirits, but she spoke to no one. She was like one who has died inside, but lives on by refusal to believe it. It hurt Ashan to see proud Raga like this, to know of no medicine to cure her, or what to say to heal her mind. Raga could not help with anything, though the Moonkeeper's work was now enough for three. Ashan was exhausted.

Raga plodded along, barely aware of the first snow that had fallen last night. She was thinking of Ashan, yelling at spirits. A tongue of fear licked her. The Old Moonkeeper hoped spirits understood, and didn't blame her for not teaching Ashan better.

Raga offered a prayer. "Whispering Wind is young and small, and carrying a great weight, and . . . she's never been as respectful as she should be . . . I should have been harder on her, but—"

Why don't you help her, old woman? whispered a weak voice in Raga's mind. She let the other, stronger voices answer.

I'm too old for this much pain . . . to watch my people suffer and die . . . not to know why this happened, or what ritual I should make to stop it. Or if I bear any of the guilt. So easy to blame Tor, but how can I be sure? Who first dreamed the mammoth and sent her people to death? Bitter tears rolled down her face. *I don't know what to do anymore. I am too tired to live.*

When Raga finally reached her sitting rock, she flopped on it, not bothering to sweep away the snow.

Amotkan, I long for the peace of death . . . I just can't do this anymore . . .

Raga's foggy mind heard Shakana the First Woman speak. *If not you, Spirit Daughter, who? That skinny blade of grass you call Young Moonkeeper?*

She shook her head from weariness.

I'm sorry, Shakana . . . I am only human . . . you don't understand that I'm helpless.

Hmmmph! answered one of her voices.

Raga let the dark fog of her mind close around her. Not thinking was so much easier.

Like the snow this frozen morning, thick grief blanketed the village. Each hut Ashan went to would be filled with it. She had to get control of her own pain—*never to see Tor again!*—so she would have room in her heart for everyone else. She prayed, but not to Shala as she once would have.

"Spirit Within, help me this day."

A flicker of courage straightened her back.

Ashan approached the dark, silent hut of Tor's old ones. Smoke should be coming from the smokehole; light should be showing through gaps in the skins. Why had no fire been made to chase out the cold? The village fire, covered for the night to keep the coals, was just outside their hut.

As Ashan stooped to enter, Arth pushed past her into the blowing snow. She felt heat as he glared at her, hatred beyond grief for his sons and tribesmen and guilt at fathering the Evil One. Why should Tor's father hate her? Did he blame her, as she thought some did, for not knowing tragedy was coming? Or did Arth know the last thing she and Tor had done?

One hostile man was the least of the Moonkeeper's worries. She shrugged and shut the doorskin behind her. The cold air smelled of unwashed bodies and sour despair. She'd brought dried leaves from the moth-wing bush to make tea for Luka. The mother of Tor and Beo was wasting away. In the di light—no one had bothered with the oil lamp—she saw I

lying on a raised earth bed, staring up at the branches covered
with skins.

"Hello!" Ashan said with unfelt cheer. "Snow Spirit came
to our world last night, and it's very pretty!"

"Thank you for coming, Moonkeeper, but Arth's family
has no need of you." Luka's voice was a single flat sound.

Ashan spoke to the little girl with watching eyes who sat
on the floor pushing an unsoaked piece of leathermeat around
a stone plate.

"Tenka, get startwood. I have tea for your mother."

"There is none, Moonkeeper, but it's not my fault. Beo
always kept a big stack, and now he's died!" The little girl
whined, then started to cry.

"There's no time for that! Find some!" Ashan shouted,
sounding more like Raga than herself.

Little Tenka wrapped her arms around herself and howled.

Ashan remembered her own pain when Mahto the bear had
taken her mother. This little one, only seven summers, had
lost two brothers, and in a way, her elders too. She went to
the sobbing child. The stiff little body softened in her arms.

"I'm so sorry," the practiced voice of the Moonkeeper
soothed. But the words of Beo and Tor flying on the wings
of Kiark and Takeena stuck in her throat. It wouldn't comfort
this hurting child any more than Raga's mouthings had comforted motherless Ashan.

She squeezed Tenka, then pushed her away. "Garend's
family has startwood. Go ask for some."

"Yes, M-M-Moonkeeper."

Tenka's sobs became little gulps. She put on a skin and
left in a draft of frozen air.

Shivering, Ashan pulled her own robe tighter. *No wonder
they're miserable*, she thought. *It's freezing in here!*

"I'll be right back, Mother," she said. Luka wasn't her
mother, but respect made many call her that.

Outside, the wind still howled in the gray light. Icy air
burned her nose as she breathed. Hers were the only footprints
leading to the snow-covered remains of the village fire. No
one else had been here. Did no one desire a morning fire?

How sad, she thought. *How far we've fallen*. Kneeling,
Ashan brushed away snow and dug beneath branches cut
~~~n last night. Heat and sweet smoke rewarded her—she

wouldn't have to use her firesticks this day. She took the clamshell fire carrier from her medicine pouch, scooped a coal into it, and replaced the branches to save the coals for any who might want them——though she doubted anyone would.

In Luka's gloomy hut, she found a hollowed stone lamp. She touched her coal to the firefish oil. Yellow glow pushed the shadows back. Ashan returned the coal to her fire carrier and sat on the unswept floor beside Luka, who stared up as if she weren't there.

"Oh, Luka," was all Ashan could say.

Luka turned. Her eyes had a hollow look. "I did not want Beo to go."

"I know, but Beo is gone. Tenka is the one I fear for."

"There's no need. I've been giving her my foodshare."

"That's not what I mean."

"But it's best. Tenka is a growing thing. I'm only an old woman waiting to be with my sons."

"Waiting for death?"

Luka's answer was the steady gaze of her flat eyes.

An icy draft followed Tenka as she brought in an armload of startwood. Ashan arranged it in the firepit over a handful of grandfather-tree needles. Opening her fire carrier, she blew ash from the coal to make it hot, then placed it under the wood. The orange coal was hungry for the dried needles. The Fire Spirit awoke, snapping and popping, reaching for the twigs. The light that danced shadows off the inside of the hut should have been cheerful, but wasn't.

She put a cooking rock in the fire, then took Tenka outside while it heated. Each made a ball of snow the size of a man's fist. Ashan could have done this herself, but it was good for Tenka to help.

When the cooking rock was hot, Ashan grabbed it with a piece of leather and put it in a stone bowl with the snow and moth-wing leaves. To make it taste better, she added bright red pods the size of her thumbnail, fruit of the sweet-smelling thornflower gathered at the best of flavor the day of first frost. She thought thornflower pods were good for smiles, but wasn't sure. She cursed her failure to learn enough, and cursed Raga for falling apart. A Moonkeeper should have strength beyond the ordinary. Raga might as well be dead, and all the knowledge Ashan had not yet learned, be dead with her.

Luka drank the finished tea. She refused the piece of crystal honey Ashan offered, the rare sweet she'd been saving for a little one who needed cheering.

"Then give it to Tenka," Ashan said. "She needs to know you care."

To her surprise, the honey made the little girl smile.

The tea seemed to revive Luka, though her eyes still looked empty. She insisted she would go with the gatherers to a grove of nut trees a half-day's walk away, though Ashan tried to talk her out of it.

The snow stopped, the wind calmed, and the day's work began. The men, too few to hunt herd animals, left the village hoping to kill a deer driven from the mountains by snow. The boys went to gather firewood, and the girls to search for seed caches hidden by animals in the ground. The very little ones stayed in the village with Tira, who was still nursing, to pick through baskets of grain, removing stones and bugs.

Women made the largest group to leave Anutash on the first snowy day. The gatherers: more important to the tribe's survival than hunters. Ashan was with them. There was a time when the Moonkeeper would not have gone, but now everyone was needed.

She stayed by Tor's mother on the way to the nut grove. Luka stared at her dragging feet as if thinking about how to walk. She wore a faint smile, and her eyes were far away.

Ashan tried to get her to talk. "Do you think the small animals had time to fill their burrows before the snow?"

Luka said not a word the whole walk.

The nut grove was a hard disappointment. The women were too late. Animals had already harvested, leaving the ground under the squatty, short-needled trees littered with cone petals.

Ashan should have said something to make her tribeswomen feel better. She should have said: The thieves were smarter or hungrier than we. But she didn't. It was becoming harder to speak as the Moonkeeper. Her heart no longer believed many of the honeyed mouthings.

It didn't take long for each woman to gather her handful of unravaged nuts. They started home. Floundering in an avalanche of grief, Ashan lost awareness of her silent sisters.

Her plodding feet left long slashes on the snowy trail instead of footprints. This time her pain was made of guilt. She tried to stop her mind from asking: *Who is to blame for this Time of Sorrow?* She wanted to scream—so loud it would cover the voice grinding her insides—that spirits were to blame.

A Moonkeeper's sin is the greatest of all.

She strangled the unbearable thought.

For now, she had to watch her footing or fall. They had come to a dangerous part of the trail—steep, narrow, winding among unstable rocks at the high edge of a ridge.

Ashan, the last one to pick her way through, was relieved when the ground leveled out. Ahead in a group, her tribeswomen sat resting.

A sound like distant thunder boomed behind her.

Ashan spun around. The thunder peaked, then died away.

No, not thunder—a rockslide!

Someone yelled, "Luka's not here!"

Ashan dashed back up the trail, clambering, slipping, tearing the skin on her hands and knees. Crying as if she already knew.

And praying: "No, Amotkan! Please, Amotkan!"

The others came behind her, shouting Luka's name.

At a flat spot near the top of the ridge, she stopped to catch her breath. Beside her, the trail's edge fell away to a rock-strewn ravine. Dust hung in the air.

At the bottom, Luka lay like a sleeping child, curled up with her arms around her head.

Ashan shook her fists. She took deep breaths, fighting for control. *Tor's mother isn't dead! Just hurt!* Dropping to her knees, she forced herself to the edge and crawled over. Feet first, belly clinging to the loose shale, she slid all the way down to the crumpled body.

Ashan raised Luka's head. None of the many cuts seemed deep enough to cause death. Blood trickled from her ear. Her open eyes were clouding. She wouldn't speak, though Ashan called her name over and over.

She knew Luka was dead, but could not accept it. Unthinking rage filled her. She became a madwoman, slapping and shaking the body.

"Give her back, Amotkan!" she screamed. "We need her!"

Blood flew from Luka's head, but Ashan couldn't stop.
"Give her back!"

Rocks clattered as three others slid down to the Moonkeeper ravaging the body of their tribeswoman. They pulled
Ashan off. Mani tried to calm her.

"Don't touch me!"

Breaking out of Mani's grasp, Ashan scrambled up the
rocks. She had to get away! She felt like killing someone,
and Luka, the only one to blame, had already killed herself!
Rage burned her like a grass fire pushed by wind as she
clawed her way up.

Hands grabbed her and pulled. She tried to stand and collapsed. She couldn't feel her bleeding arms and legs; her
bones had turned to water. The women sat her against a rock,
and stood around her with terrified faces.

Ursa held out a water pouch.

Ashan slapped it away. "Leave me," she said, slumping
over with her head on her knees. She closed her eyes and the
dark was good. The voices of the gatherers swirled around
her as they tried to understand yet another death. No one
wanted to believe Luka had jumped, but it didn't seem possible to fall from this place.

Keeta said, "I saw her looking over, wearing a strange
smile. I asked if she was all right. 'Go on by,' she said, 'I'm
fine.' "

Tahna said, "I was behind you and I didn't see her."

Nor had Ashan. As deep in sorrow as she'd been, she
couldn't have missed Luka standing at the edge of the cliff.

Luka must have hidden until everyone had passed.

Kahnya said, "I know the answer. One who falls cries out.
One who jumps doesn't."

No one had heard her cry out.

"How selfish! What about us? What about Tenka?" Young
Challa's rising voice told Ashan she was near panic.

From inside the numb lump of her flesh, the Moonkeeper
found her voice.

"We will never know how Luka died, but we know how
deep her pain was. If she did end it, I believe Amotkan
forgives her. So shall we."

CHAPTER
14

The Time of Sorrows became ever more sorrowful. Death was not finished with the Shahala. Horses trampled a hunter who'd have been safe in a larger group. Some lost too much flesh to hunger. A few like Luka just gave up. As Ashan's shadow stick told the coming of winter's darkest day, the tribe was in danger of losing two more—the youngest and the oldest. She saw it as Amotkan's bad joke that they were kin, grandfather and granddaughter.

In the old people's hut, Ashan was feeding the grandfather, Ahnkor, in his daughter's place. His daughter, Tira, had trouble of her own. Her baby, Lia, born that summer, was losing strength to a racking cough.

The small hut was musty with the odor of too many old people. Two men and a woman lived here with Ahnkor. This was where people spent their last days, when the larger huts were needed by growing families. They were cared for here by their kin.

Ashan was on her knees beside Ahnkor's raised bed. His head was propped on a bundle of skins. In the light of the oil lamp, his hair and beard were yellow-white moss. The yellow-gray skin on his canyoned face folded like the bark of an ancient cedar. The folds were pulled into a scowl.

Scooping her fingers into a stone bowl of warm mush,

Ashan held them to Ahnkor's thin lips. This time, instead of taking the food, he jerked his head away. Her fingers left a mush-smear on his scraggly beard.

"Take it away!"

"I'm sorry, Grandfather." Ashan used the name out of respect. Ahnkor was fifty summers, a very great age. He'd been weak long before the Time of Sorrows; it was a wonder he was still alive.

She wiped his beard with her sleeve. He slapped her arm.

"Stop it! You tire me, woman, when you should be giving me respect!"

Anger flared! *Talk of respect!* No one would call Raga *"woman!"* But—Ashan took a deep breath—age deserved patience. Sighing, she lowered her glance, as his own daughter would.

"Forgive me, Grandfather."

Ahnkor fixed her with glittery, deep-sunk eyes. He smiled to show toothless gums, a smile cold as the rain pattering on the roofskins, that didn't reach his sly eyes.

"Bring me the sleeping vine and I'll forgive you."

Ashan shook her head. "Too many have died who couldn't help it. You do not have pain."

"There are kinds of pain a barren Moonkeeper will never know! The daughter of my daughter is dying! It's wrong that a man live longer than his grandchild!"

"It's not up to you to decide when to die."

"Did you tell Arth's mate that before she jumped?"

"Luka fell. I've told you."

Anger on Ahnkor's face changed to pleading.

"Please, little Moonkeeper. I can't bear to see my grandchild die."

Ashan didn't know the good of an old man's life, not really. He was just another body to feed when there wasn't enough. All he did was complain. But it wasn't up to Ashan to decide the value of a life. Shahala law, old as the Misty Time, was clear. Every person was important to the whole. Each life must be kept as long as possible.

"I understand, Ahnkor, but I cannot help you."

"Then send Raga! My old friend won't deny me!"

"Raga cannot even help herself!" The bitterness in her

voice surprised Ashan. She softened it, as she would with a child.

"Lia will be here long after you're gone. Don't you remember last night? I cast the evil that choked her into the fire. It turned the smoke green as it fled. Remember, Grandfather?"

"You didn't get it all. The noise of coughing from Tira's hut kept me awake." His bushy brows lowered. "As I lay here, too weak to even go and hold her little hand, I heard Death Singer call her name."

"No one can hear the Owl Spirit call for another. I tell you, the little one—"

The doorskin whipped open. Tira stepped in holding a fur-wrapped bundle.

"The medicine worked! She's sleeping without a cough!"

"Of course it worked," Ashan said, hiding her relief.

"I'll wake her so you can see."

"No. She needs sleep now."

Ashan gently opened the fur blanket in Tira's arms. Lia's color was a good pink-brown, her breathing even, her smell sweet. The back of Ashan's hand on the baby's forehead gave the best tidings: cool and dry.

"Take Lia to your father. They need each other."

"Spirits bless you," Tira said, bowing as she backed away.

"It's why I was born, daughter."

"Forgive my disbelief, Young Moonkeeper," Ahnkor said.

She smiled. "I do. But please remember—every person is needed by his people, even the oldest."

Ashan pushed the crossed sticks that held the doorskin and stepped outside. The rain had stopped, the clouds opened. Sunrays made tiny colored flashes of clinging drops.

Two lives have been saved this day!

She flared her nostrils and the bright air swelled her. That and pride. She was able to take care of far more than any person of fifteen summers she'd ever known.

Two lives!

Ashan thought of her mother. Kira would be proud. As would Tor. Might the spirits also be proud? Might they forgive her sin?

The sun warmed her upturned face. She sensed a turning

place in the Time of Sorrows—a beginning of the tribe's strength returning.

On a bright, cold morning, Tahna brought her daughter of nine summers to Ashan in the Moonkeepers' hut.

"Akaila made blood in the night," Tahna said with pride. "She's ready to be a woman."

Raga's mind was still gone from her body. She remained useless to the people. The teachings of womanhood fell to Ashan, as did all the needs of the tribe. But she'd enjoy this. Time spent in the women's hut was the most pleasant time.

"So," Ashan said, taking the girl's hand, "spirits have spoken. You are no longer a child."

Nine summers was young for womanhood, but spirits had their reasons. Maybe girls would become women sooner, to have babies to replace the dead. Ashan smiled. Akaila still looked like a child—short and thin, no hint of breasts. With hair singed short in mourning for her father, it would be easy to think of her as a boy. Her deerskin dress was old and too small, but in these times there weren't enough skins to make new ones.

Tahna kissed her daughter and left.

"Your mother showed you how to use the inner bark of the waterside tree?" Ashan asked.

"Yes," Akaila said. "She gave me some of hers, and showed me how to wrap it in grass fiber and tie it on."

"And what to do with it after?"

"Bury it outside the women's hut."

"And if we are traveling?"

"I walk behind everyone, and bury it away from the trail."

"That's right. We give our woman-power back to our mother the earth."

Ashan laid out a grass-fiber mat for Akaila to sit on. She put bits of yew bark on a stone lamp and set it smoking with a twig from the firepit. Spirits like smoke.

She opened the leather pouch that held her paints, and laid out the smaller pouches inside. Red, brown and white came from rocks she'd found and ground up. Yellow from the prickly grape. Blue came from crushed berries. Green from dried beetles. Black was burnt bark. Ashan smeared bear fat on a flat stone and put it by the fire, to mix with the color when it melted.

"Now," she said, settling beside the girl. "How to present you?" Akaila's name meant Sweet Berry. Ashan thought of a picture. "I see red and blue berry clusters on your forehead, green leaves on your cheeks, yellow vines—"

"Could I be a butterfly?"

"A butterfly?"

"You could paint my nose black, like its body. And then use all the colors to make wings, one on each side, big wings covering my eyes and cheeks."

Still mindful of the need to name the new woman to her sisters and the spirits, Ashan said, "And we can have berry clusters on your arms and legs. You'll be Butterfly On Sweet Berry."

"Oooo . . ." the girl sighed.

Ashan stirred black ash into the melted fat, keeping it to one side of the stone so there'd be clean fat for the other colors. Dipping her finger in the greasy black, she drew on Akaila's face. She talked as she worked of things women need to know.

"Woman-power is the life of the tribe. We are daughters of Shakana, the First Woman, and as you know, Amotkan gave Shakana all the important tasks: gathering, mothering, healing, speaking with spirits, leading the people. Think of a man giving birth, or being Moonkeeper!"

They shared the laugh of sisters.

Ashan put a black dot between Akaila's eyebrows—the butterfly's head.

"Only a woman bleeds without being hurt. Only a woman brings new life to the tribe. So you see, you are special to be born a woman. Your work is greater than a man's, but so are your joys."

Pleased with the body shape on Akaila's nose, Ashan used black to outline a wing on one side of her face, thinking of the firewing butterfly who comes to the mountains in springtime. Orange wings. She mixed red into yellow, then added more red. Firewing butterflies are bright creatures.

"Every moon, spirits visit to renew our woman power. This is when we bleed, from the fullness of it. Do you feel the power, Akaila?"

"Where?"

"Sometimes I feel it outside my eyes, like a small tightness. And sometimes like a warm blush on my cheeks."

Akaila touched her high cheekbones. "I do! It's like . . . a little tingle!"

"Yes. It's a sign of woman power. Do you like it?"

"I do!"

"For men, it is not a good thing. Our power at the time of bleeding is too strong for men, dangerous to them and anything they do. They know they must stay away from us. We make it easy for them by going to the women's hut. They think we do this for them, but we do it as much for ourselves. You will love this time spent with sisters."

When the painting was finished, the Moonkeeper and the girl held hands and walked the curving path to the women's hut. It sat away by itself, hidden from the village behind thick leatherleaf bushes that kept their gray-green leaves in all seasons.

Like every woman, Ashan looked forward to the several days spent here each moon, resting or working with skins and beads—peaceful days away from men and little ones, except those still at breast.

Babies were born here, with a woman's sisters gathered around.

A Moonkeeper's power was woman-power, but stronger. Filled with it all the time, a Moonkeeper came here whenever she wanted. Others, only when they bled or attended a birth.

Akaila's first visit was important. It marked the end of one part of life, the beginning of another.

They came through bushes to a clean-swept clearing around a horseskin-covered hut. The round doorskin, painted with signs of women and warning, was closed. A bare arbor of thin fir poles stood against the back of the hut. In warmer times, leafy branches covered the pole frame, making a shady place for women to sit and do their work.

Ashan said, "This same hut has been used by Shahala women since the Misty Time."

"How has it lasted?" Akaila asked. "It looks like others."

"From outside, yes. You can only see the skin cover. Like any other hut, new skins are sometimes needed. Have you helped your family work on their hut when we come here in the autumn?"

Akaila nodded.

"Put on new skins, or patched the old ones? Sometimes

branches must be replaced because they're old and weak. Sometimes it must be torn down and built again. That never happens to the women's hut. It has antlers for a frame, not branches. Antlers too many to count, fitted tight by our ancestors like a turtle's shell. Antlers last forever.''

"Why did we build our power place from male animals?"

"Hmmm . . . I don't know, but Raga might. I'll ask."

Tashi's head poked through the doorskin.

"Akaila! Join us, little sister! We're happy to have you!"

When they were inside the hut, Tashi, Challa and Mani fluttered around Akaila, admiring her butterfly face and berry body. They were the first of many who would praise her during this day. The tribe's women would bring gifts—the proud mother made sure all knew—a needle, a small skin, some beads, whatever they could spare. It wouldn't be much in this hard time.

Ashan settled into her favorite place across from the door, leaning against a wide moose antler that touched the reed-matted floor. The smokehole let in soft light. The warmth of friendly bodies made it pleasant even without a fire.

Ashan took the time ball from her medicine pouch. She needed to work on it before she forgot what had happened to whom, and when.

The Moonkeeper's time ball was different from others. It was the tribe's. It named births, deaths, matings, great hunts, good seasons and bad. Ashan's couldn't yet be called a "ball." She'd started it the day she became Young Moonkeeper. There had been little time for it since. But in time, hers would be much larger than those made by other women. The time balls of others were burned with them at death, so they could take their memories to the otherworld. Not the Moonkeeper's. It would be kept by her follower in a bison skull that now held eleven.

Ashan had made the beads for each person, keeping them in a little sack inside her medicine pouch. Pretty stones, bits of shell and antler; shaped, rounded, polished, then carefully drilled with a stone awl. It took a long time—half of them broke in the making. This was time for thoughts of the person named by the bead.

Pouring them onto the reed mat, she arranged the beads as they should go on the string. She lingered with the one made of eagle talon, touching it to her lips. Tears rose. She pushed them back before they fell. This was the bead for Tor.

Tobi came in. The stout old woman had thin white hair and skin like bison hide, thick and crossed with lines. Women her age didn't bleed, but still might come here for the pleasures of sisterhood. After praising Akaila and giving her two rabbit-ear mitts, she sat beside Ashan.

"I worry about you," Tobi said in a whisper. "I have seen you in the early light, spilling your gut on the ground."

"Many people have this sickness," Ashan said. "I think it's from eating carrion."

It was a sad thing. In the Time of Sorrows, the tribe was forced to steal from condors and coyotes, even eat bugs.

"Do you still bleed?" the old woman whispered.

The words struck Ashan like lightning. "Why do you ask?" she snapped.

Tobi's uneasiness was in her quivering voice. "You were late coming to the women's hut last moon. The old do not have much to think about. We notice small things."

"What are you trying to say?"

"I was Raga's spirit sister when we were young. Raga is sick, so I must help by warning you as she would." Tobi hesitated, then took a deep breath and went on. "If you were not Moonkeeper, I'd say you bear all the signs of a little one in your belly."

Ashan whirled, scattering the beads in front of her.

"But I *am* Moonkeeper! I could sew your lips together for saying such a thing! A child must have a father, and you know the Moonkeeper has no mate! Spirits have never sent a child to a Moonkeeper!"

"Yes. That's true. Such a thing couldn't happen."

"No, it could not!"

Ashan knew why she had made no blood for two moons, and it had nothing to do with a little one in her belly. It was punishment of spirits for the sin of wrongful loving. Tor died for his part. For Ashan's part, spirits no longer came each moon to renew her woman-power. What would happen when it was all used up? Would she die? Fade away like smoke?

A scarier question filled her thoughts: What would happen to the tribe when its chief lost her spirit power?

CHAPTER
15

Storms in the tabu land were as strange as everything else—thunder like spirits warring, but only a spatter of rain yesterday on the battlefield, and none since. Now wind-chased, black-bottomed clouds hurried dusk.

Early dark to fit dark deeds, Tor thought, clinging like moss in the high treetop, remembering the sight of Shahala brothers disappearing through a stream of tears. His body felt heavier than a bear—so heavy his soul was being crushed; so heavy it would leave a pit when it hit the ground. One last time he searched his mind, trying to find some hope. There was none—nothing to live for—and never would be again.

Tor, a young man just beginning real life, couldn't stand hopelessness.

How foolish young men can be! There is always *hope where there is life!*

"Takeena!" he shouted at the voice in his mind. "You betraying trickster, you carrion-eating beetle! I hate you and every eagle you ever sent to the sky! I hate the day you lied and said you'd guide me! You guided me to this—the death of my body by its own will!"

Takeena's voice weakened: *The death of your* soul.

You will not be forgiven! thundered a different spirit.

Could Amotkan be speaking directly to him?

"I don't care," Tor said. "Love drives men, and I'll never have any again."

The mind-voices fell silent as Tor looked down through the branches shivering in the wind.

Everyone knew falling causes death. Tor remembered a Shahala little one who fell from a tree while gathering moss; she died. Driving animals over cliffs made a hunter's work easier; he didn't have to face slashing horns and hooves with only courage and a spear.

But how far did a man have to fall to die? How bad would it hurt? He couldn't know. He'd just have to do it, remembering all the way down not to protect himself with arms and legs. His last thought would be to keep his head straight down, to drive it into the ground like a post. He'd allow no other thought.

Tor eased himself up, his back to the trunk, one foot wedged behind a branch. He thought of tying his hands together so they couldn't help, even if fear took over.

No! I'm stronger than that!

Hands clasped behind him, Tor leaned out, testing the slant of no retreat. The tree shuddered, from wind or dread. His leg muscles tightened as moccasined toes dug into the branch.

Fuzzy light spread on the ground below, taking the shape of his beloved's face, stained by deepest grief.

"Ashan," Tor whispered.

Her name was almost enough to stop him . . . the sound of wind feathering long black hair . . . the world's most beautiful sound.

Her name alone made him want to live!

He threw out his arms, but it was too late. Falling had taken over on its own. Flapping arms were as useless as the wings of a stupid goose who ate enough grass for ten. On the way down, he had time to think: *This will hurt! This will hurt! THIS WILL HURT!* Small things got bigger as the ground rushed up. When the blur of brown needles became countless individuals, Tor made a knot of himself—knees to stomach, head to chest, arms wrapped tight to keep himself from bursting like a dropped egg.

The ground punched him in the back, punched out breath, crushed his lungs so they could never hold air again! The sun's light exploded behind his eyes . . . white to orange to red! Pain pounded, ground him up! He hadn't known there was such pain! He twisted on the ground like a mess of writhing snakes.

I told you this would hurt! screamed a voice inside—no spirit, but the voice of his own body and soul. He groaned, pushing down shrieks that wanted release. A Shahala warrior, even dying, might cry from sadness, but not from pain.

He begged Death Singer to be done with it.

Gray fog slithered through his mind to put the red pain out, and Tor thought death was near. Then his throat betrayed him, opening to suck in a breath as huge as a cloud. Icy air tore his chest like spears, new pain to add to the rest, giving voice to the heart of the boy who suddenly did not want to die.

"Takeena! No-o-o . . ."

Black wings wrapped around Tor's mind and took him away.

It's morning, Tor thought, opening his eyes to deep blue sky. *And summer*.

No, not summer . . . bright cold winter in the tabu land. Frost covered everything but his skin. He was colder than he had been the night he'd spent as a lost little one in a snow cave, colder than ever in his life.

Squinting sky and shriveling cold weren't enough to tell him he was alive, but the pain that came with awakening did. Everyone knows there's no pain in the afterlife. He was not dead, no matter how much he wanted to be.

This day's hurt was bad enough, but not as bad as before— just throbbing in every part, instead of shrieking agony.

And not nearly as bad as the pain of heart and mind.

Tor, son of Luka, was a creature more disgusting than vomit, lower than unburied dung, a creature so worthless even death wouldn't have him. And the saddest thing was this: His heart wasn't low and disgusting. His heart wanted only the best for the people he loved so much.

How could a man this good cause suffering so great?

And what would happen now, now that such a man was doomed to live?

Tor's death-leap brought only things that made life harder. His throwing arm had twisted under him, taking his whole weight. He didn't think bones were broken, but it burned fiercely from elbow to wrist, and his grip was gone. The rest of his body sang a mean song of bruised, torn flesh.

And then there was his wounded soul: another failure in his miserable failure of a life. He hated himself.

Tor lay at the foot of the tree for a time he wouldn't remember, his drifting mind a fog of confusion, his pain a numb kind of thing . . . he knew it was *here*, but it didn't seem to matter, since he didn't feel *here* himself.

His shrinking water pouch finally got a message through: *Death by thirst is an ugly thing.* The Rain Spirit seldom visited this needful land. Water would be hard to find. Tor forced the numb lump of himself to stand and began walking—more like dragging, not bothering to notice the direction. It didn't matter, as long as it wasn't back to the battlefield or toward his lost home.

Days ran together. The Winter Spirit wrung warmth from the sunny, desolate land. The broken young warrior wandered without aim, filled with loathing—for himself and his hateful destiny, but most of all for spirits who were supposed to love people.

Sorrow fought with loathing to rule Tor's breaking heart— no one had ever known greater sorrow. *So many Shahala dead!* The rest couldn't survive winter with so few hunters. First they would hunger, then—shrunken and weak—they'd die. His beloved Ashan, their Moonkeeper, would die with them. There'd be no one to see to the burning of bodies at the end. They would lie in their huts and rot, souls trapped forever. Sorrow brought tears that flowed for days. Cold wind that never stopped chapped his wet face; knowing he deserved it, he told himself the raw hurt felt good.

Tor believed he didn't care if some animal favored him with death in the night, but he found safe places to sleep—a rare tree, a narrow slot between rocks, inside a bush. Predators filled the dark with eerie song: long-eared dogs and coyotes who wouldn't attack a man; wolves, who might. And other sounds that made him wonder if man-eaters prowl at night.

He had no hunger, or desire to hunt, and it was just as well. His injured throwing arm was too weak to hold a spear. His aim was so bad with the other that a rabbit wouldn't flinch. So he ate bugs, snakes and the like—low food that will keep life for a while, if not strength.

Water was not to be found in the tabu land. When his pouch ran out, he sucked its smooth inside to wet his mouth. After that he sucked pebbles. His tongue swelled; lips cracked and bled; skin dried up like a winter-shriveled leaf.

Thirst or starvation—which death would release him?

Just when it seemed thirst would win the race, the alien-bright sky clouded, thundered and poured rain . . . poured until he felt like a sodden mountain cat and wondered why he'd ever prayed for it. He started counting the days of rain, but lost track at ten—the more hands a number took, the harder to keep count. He made snakeskins into two water pouches. With these and the well-seasoned deer bladder his mother had given him, he'd never, ever be thirsty again. The weight of full water pouches on top of his soaked antelope skin was almost too much to carry, as weak as he'd become. The heavy skin stank, tempting him to leave it.

Finally the Rain Spirit left to torture some other place. Tor was glad he'd kept the antelope skin, though it was drying hard and would have to be chewed all over again.

On a day thick with mist that isolated a man, Tor was trudging along when the fog cleared to show starred black sky. Night had snuck up on him. He dropped the antelope skin, flopping down on the flat, unprotected plain, too tired to care about safety. The stony ground dug into his fleshless bones, but he ignored the discomfort, staring astonished into the sky.

The rising moon was round as the morning sun! A *whole moon* had passed since the massacre—fattened, shrunk, died and fattened again—a thing that took nights of five hands and three.

Five hands and three! And he was still alive! How? *Why?*

The next day, a windy, frozen day of squinting blue, Tor wandered onto the field of massacre, and that day he knew why.

With weeping heart, Tor stood where Shahala warriors had fallen, imagining a lingering odor of decay. Traces of blood stained the stampede-scarred earth, even after all the rain.

But there were no bodies. Nothing was wasted in this home of predators and scavengers.

The place was smaller than Tor remembered—just a little valley edged by cliffs on one side and forest on the other, blocked at the far end by animals at a waterhole.

No wonder so few had escaped! It was the perfect trap! Tor's people knew a canyon near the winter village much like this where they drove horses for easier taking.

Anger flared. The Headman should not have led them into such a place! And what good were Moonkeepers, who should have had warning dreams!

Better than men who ignore *warning dreams!* accused his mind.

"Be silent!" Tor yelled at himself.

His words rang off the rocks and returned, startling him.

Flesh-bumps skittered up his arms. Was he really alone?

The silence was complete but for a whooing in the rocks— a high wind passing.

Or did he hear the voices of Shahala souls, crying for release?

His guardian spirit spoke. *Trapped in flesh, the dead cannot fly to the otherworld.*

Tor knew. Having to leave bodies behind made the massacre all the more tragic. Hunters feared a distant death. Women and old men usually died near home, but hunters might die far away. If a hunter wasn't brought home to be burned and buried, everything ended. No afterlife with his family. No coming back to this world for another life.

You owe your brothers, Tor. You are the only one who can free their souls.

As Tor understood, the heaviness inside lightened. To rescue the trapped souls of his dead brothers—even one—was a worthy thing. If he did, would the spirits stop his pain?

The sun dropped behind the forest where a moon ago his brother Beo had died. A cawing raven flew out of the trees. Tor smiled and nodded as it winged over him: Spirits show their approval of men's doings by sending ravens.

Filled with confident hope, he climbed into the cliffs to sleep. He saw several protected places among the jumbled slabs, but kept looking for something better.

What he found was perfect. Squeezing through a narrow cut, he stepped into a small clearing edged with steep rock. It was like a tall hut with solid sides and no roof. In one spot, the rock face didn't reach the ground, but hung over a low, shadowed opening. He crawled inside and back two man-lengths. Under him was sand, soft for a good bed; over him, rock so close that a careless man waking might crack his head. The dark smelled clean. He saw some rabbit-size bones, and cat dung growing hairy black moss that showed its age. It was the closest thing to a cave he'd found, and no other creature claimed it.

Tor slept feeling safe as a wintering squirrel tucked in its groundhole. He awakened with a thought running through his mind.

Fire frees souls . . .

This had been known to his people since the Misty Time. And this also: There is soul in every part of a person. Freeing a finger is as good as freeing the whole body.

Leaving everything behind but his antelope skin and his spear, Tor went down to the battlefield. At the upper end, animals crowded the waterhole as they had the day of the massacre—but they were calm now, not bellowing and stampeding.

Cold sun shone on Tor as he crawled over the battlefield on hands and knees, putting the remains of his fellow warriors into his antelope skin. Blood-dark dirt. A strand of hair caught in a bush. A tooth. Anything that might have been part of a Shahala warrior. When the sun went down, he took the sacred remnants to his place in the rocks.

Hunger growled in his belly, and after the growls came pain. He hadn't eaten for several days. And then what? A bitter green lizard. Ashan wouldn't admire his body now, with fleshless ribs and shrunken thighs. If he found her suddenly and tried to love her, his jutting hipbones would bruise her perfect skin. He begged Amotkan to forgive what he'd done to his mother's gift.

He went back down out of the rocks. A choice of food waited at the waterhole. As he approached in dimming light, the wind blew in his favor. A snow deer drinking with its mother never smelled death's approach. Tor jumped on it and—*snap!*—broke its neck. He ran with the fox-size deer under his good arm, full speed back to his place in the rocks, though it was foolish to think animals would follow him.

He would have liked a fire, but smoke was a sure sign of men. Tor might be alone now, but these rocks had sheltered man-eaters. This was part of their home, as Ancestor Cave and the Summer Hunting Grounds were part of Shahala home. The man-eaters knew much about their home that Tor could not.

So, ignoring the sharp taste, he ate the warm heart of the little deer raw, then the liver and tongue. These parts were full of an animal's spirit, and eating them raw was best. He felt a twinge inside as a bit of the snow deer's spirit joined with his. The rest of the meat would be better cooked, but Tor would be sure of his safety before he made fire.

Soon enough, he'd *have* to make fire—not for cooking or warmth, but to burn the things of the battlefield in the ritual of The Soul's Growing. The next day he gathered wood for the huge blaze he'd need. He thought of going into the forest, then realized the sagebrush of the battlefield would be best— hot and quick. Armloads of sage grew to a pile. When the pile was the size of a young black bear, he strapped it with fresh thongs from the snow deer's hide and slung it over his back. The weight stooped him; the height made tipping over a danger. Looking like a man stealing eagles' nests, he made several trips to the clearing in the rocks.

That night he risked a cooking fire. His fire sticks, old friends given to him by his father, were clumsy at first, but a man never forgets how to use them. The light and warmth cheered him even more than he expected. It had been a long time . . . low food doesn't need cooking, and sometimes lonely men don't want to be cheered.

He stripped the deer with his rock scraper, poked a green stick through the back and the hind legs—the best of it—and held it over the fire. The smell of fat dripping on flame made his mouth water. He began eating before it was done. Juice ran down his chin. He'd never forget the rich, sweet taste. When he'd eaten all he could—far less than he once would have—he strung the rest on grass twine. Tomorrow he'd find a place where animals couldn't reach to hang it for drying.

Tor's fire gave up its flame for smoke, then glowing coals. Drowsy, feeling fat as a bear before winter, he crawled into the shelter under the rock.

Watching the fireglow with half-open eyes, he made a decision. This was a good place. He would stay here, maybe forever. The best food was close by, and water. The little clearing was hidden from easy sight. Tucked back under the rock, he would sleep dry.

Man-eaters? He spat. He hadn't seen any.

The new home near the waterhole was good to him. He ate well and slept peacefully. A bison gave up its hide to make life warmer with new moccasins and a robe that hung to the ground. Flesh began to pad his bones; strength returned; his throwing arm was healing. Hunting at the waterhole was so easy he wondered why no tribe lived here.

Tor put off the ceremony of burning, telling himself he needed more and more wood. But that wasn't the real reason. Doubts bothered him. Everything must be just right. He'd taken part in death rituals and remembered the words to be spoken. But what if only a Moonkeeper could light the fire and speak to the dead? What if all this was wasted?

At least spirits would know he'd tried, and maybe they'd think it enough.

Yet days went by and he couldn't do it, though he had a stack of wood as large as a hut.

In a dream he realized why: All that he'd gathered belonged to just *a few* of his brothers. What about the rest, the ones who'd been carried off by man-eaters? He realized that burning the stuff of the battlefield wasn't enough. He would have to find whatever was left of the others. And so he made a decision to leave this good place.

Part of Tor was sorry. He would miss the easy food and water. But he'd been here almost a moon—he couldn't stay forever—someday the man-eaters would stumble on him. Healthy again, he could throw his heavy Shahala spear far and straight. He'd been practicing with the man-eater's light, sleek spear-thrower, and one day he'd be very good—better than Beo's killer.

His mind was healing, too. He was past endless wading in

a swamp of grief. Ideas sparked, plans for the task required of him—the most important of his life—to change his name in the minds of spirits from "Evil One" to "Soul Saver."

Tor wiped out every sign of himself from the place that had been home for a while. Campfire rocks were turned with blackened faces down; food bones buried; footprints swept with a bush; the huge pile of firewood scattered to be gathered again when he returned . . . *if* he did. This might not be the place the spirits wanted the ceremony to take place.

He thought about whether to take or leave the Shahala remains he'd already collected. The antelope skin wasn't heavy, but it would slow him down. In the end he decided to take it, to keep them all together.

After a last night of peaceful sleep, Tor set off in a bright, frosty morning, toward Where Day Begins . . . deeper into the tabu land to find the man-eaters' home.

CHAPTER
16

Tor followed careless signs through the tabu land's canyons and ridges. The man-eaters didn't hide their trails or even bury their waste. It must have been long since they had worried about becoming prey.

Stalking the evil creatures, Tor fed murderous thoughts to the fire blazing inside.

Man-eaters! Tor the Destroyer comes! If you ate my brothers and stole their souls, I will burn every man, woman and little one to free them!

Tor didn't worry about how one man would do this. It was the will of spirits, and up to them to make a way.

Late in the day he looked for a sleeping place. When tracking, a warrior knew it was good to sleep high. He could study the land, and there was less danger of being found in the night by the pursued ones.

Turning off the canyon trail, Tor started up the ridge that edged it. What he'd thought was the top was not. He kept climbing, realizing that when, and if, he did reach the summit, he'd have a view toward Where Day Ends and his lost homeland. If he gazed hard enough, pretending he was only away on a hunt, it would bring good feelings, and that might bring a good dream.

When he finally topped the ridge, there was a narrow strip

of flat ground, then a sheer plunge into a wide, scrub-brush valley. Tor saw the ridgetop as the backbone of a great beast. Lower ribs of rocky ground spread in both directions, forming several narrow canyons with only one mouth—good for trapping horses, or men.

The setting sun flamed the sky. Tor sat on his bison skin, smiling, breathing deeply of the high, clean air. He felt close to some great victory. Leaning back against the antelope skin with its Shahala remains, he sensed that the souls inside were hopeful too.

His eyes searched the horizon, looking for smoke to tell him where the man-eaters lived, but the sky was still too bright. He settled back to wait for that twilight moment when smoke lit by the setting sun can be seen from a great distance.

Tor sat straight up, startled by a sound from below, part bellow, part grunt . . . something like a bull elk before a mating battle, but different, louder . . . as if it came from something even larger . . . *but*, Tor told himself, *there aren't any creatures larger than elk*. The hairs in Tor's ears stood up listening, but he didn't hear the strange cry again.

Tor was the kind of warrior who had to know the meaning of sounds, and he'd never heard that one. Taking only his spear, he made his way down the sheer rocks toward the valley. Twilight faded as he walked along the top of a side ridge.

The ground fell sharply to a small canyon shaped like a medicine pouch—rounded at this end, almost closed at the other. Tor dropped to his hands and knees and peered into the canyon, but it was too dark to see—

Wait! Something moved! He narrowed his eyes to slits and stared into deep shadow. A shape was barely visible in the waning light—a *huge* shape—

Oh, Takeena! It's Manu the Earth Shaker! Lying on his side with his head on the ground, looking so old, so tired . . . so huge!

The sight shocked Tor. Then rage set him aflame. If it hadn't been for this mammoth, the Shahala never would have come to the tabu land! Never would have died! In fury's blindness, Tor wanted to rush the beast with his spear! Pierce it full of holes! Shriek triumph as it spurted blood!

The Earth Shaker's size stopped him. Tor didn't want to

die. A man could stamp on the beast and it might not even wake. A spear-thrust might be a mere bug bite. As well as being the largest creature Tor had ever seen, Manu must be cunning and wise if he really was the last of his kind, as Raga said.

Darkness soon hid the Earth Shaker. Tor thought he heard Manu's labored breathing, but it could have been the wind. A heavy, sick odor rose up and touched him with sadness. A deep sigh carried his rage away. Compassion entered him. Manu, the great creature whose legends filled his people with wonder, was not the one who had killed the warriors. Whoever was to blame for the tragedy, it was not the beast. Manu deserved pity, not hatred.

Pity? No . . . respect.

For the same reasons he'd once decided that he and Beo should leave a mammoth's grave and never speak of it except to each other, Tor decided to leave here as quietly as he'd come. In darkness lit only by early stars, he moved carefully up the tumbled rocks.

Tor! shouted a voice inside. *That thing could save your people!*

No First Warrior worthy of Mahto's claws would turn his back on such a feast. True, Manu was too large to be killed by one man, but if this were another time, Tor would run without stopping to reach his village and tell the others. A mighty Shahala band would find and take the beast. Manu would feed his people all winter. Manu would save them from starving.

What a waste to walk away! What tragedy to heap on tragedy!

Who says the Earth Shaker's too large to be killed by one man, if *the man is Tor, Shahala First Warrior, pride of his people in another time?*

Tor had known something about himself as long as he'd known he loved Ashan: Hunting was different for him. It meant more. His mind was better at working things out. And then there were the forbidden dreams that spirits sent to guide him. If the Shahala knew how much of their food had come from a man's dreaming . . .

He flared his nostrils and took a deep breath.

Pride of his people . . .

Tor felt spirit power swelling inside, filling him like a
breath blown into his mouth from Amotkan's. He knew how
to use spirit power to work himself up to the clear, pure place
in his mind where truth and the answers to questions were
found.

Over and over, he told himself: *Spirit power grows within.
I am smart. I am brave. I can kill the beast, I can save my
people. And Ashan.*

And if you kill the beast, squeaked the voice that always
tried to ruin his ideas, *how will you get it home?*

He didn't know and didn't want to think about it.

"Spirits will take care of that," he said.

The question didn't return to bother him.

Alhaia the moon rose, almost full again. Tor took her smile
as a sign of spirit approval. Finding his way back, he squatted
on the rocky edge of the medicine-pouch canyon. Moonlight
crept across the ground below, but the place where the mammoth slept was shadowed by the far canyon wall.

Was Manu still down there? Tor's nose said yes. Old scent
under fresh told him the mammoth had slept here before.

And it *was* the beast's breathing he heard. His pity deepened . . . even in sleep the Earth Shaker had to work to stay
alive. Tor listened and let the sad, uneven sound empty him.

A thought drifted up from the shadowed canyon.

*Young warrior, I am tired, and lonely in a way you would
not know.*

I do know, Tor's mind answered. *I will free you.*

He sensed no answering thought, but it seemed the great
beast breathed easier in his sleep.

The young warrior sat thinking as the moon crossed the
sky, making one plan after another, finding flaws in each that
would mean his death. The mammoth, in his monstrous heart,
might be yearning to die, but Tor was sure his instinct to
survive was strong. Otherwise, Manu would have died long
ago with the rest of his kind, as he should have.

Finally, Tor thought of a way that seemed, while not at all
certain or safe, the best it could be. He would trap the beast
in the medicine-pouch canyon and kill it from above with
rocks.

Dawn fingered the sky. Night was almost over, and the
mammoth would have to be taken at night. Tor started back

for the high ridgetop where he'd left his skins, hoping Manu would return to the sheltered canyon to sleep tonight. Tor would get the sleep he needed today, while the mammoth tired himself searching for the great amount of food he must eat. Tor wondered whether mammoths ate plants or animals—legends didn't say. But legends left no doubt about fierceness. Many people had been lost to Earth Shakers in the Misty Time, crushed beneath monstrous feet or gored by face-horns and tossed in the air as easily as a child tosses a pebble-filled sack in a game of kick.

Tor reached the high ridgetop and went to sleep under a scrub bush. He dreamed that his plan was working . . . the mammoth came back to the medicine-pouch canyon, and—

Sun poked through a hole in the bush, struck his eyelids, and woke him. He felt rested and confident.

It was only halfway to high sun.

Good, he thought, stretching. *There's much to do, and time enough to do it.*

He first checked the mouth of the medicine-pouch canyon, approaching from the valley side, careful to keep the wind blowing against his scent. The entrance was a gap between rock slabs so narrow that there were tufts of long brown hair where the beast had scraped itself coming through . . . narrow enough, as Tor had thought, to be blocked.

He worked harder than he ever had before, piling sticks and brush behind cover of rocks near the canyon mouth. Roaming far into the valley for wood, he decided Manu probably ate plants, and that's why there weren't many. But the woodpile grew until it was larger than the one he'd made to burn the remains of his tribesmen.

When he had all the wood to be found in his hidden pile, Tor decided it was enough to block the narrow entrance. A charging mammoth could break through, but he hoped it would be confused. It seemed that as creatures got older, they became easier to confuse.

Shadows growing long told him it was time to get back to the rocks and finish his work. Then wait. And hope. What a waste of effort if Manu didn't come!

Up on the ridge near the canyon's mouth, Tor began stacking the rocks that would kill the beast.

At twilight Tor sensed Manu. He asked for spirit power.

His senses came alive to chase away weakness from lack of food—a warrior close to a kill, Tor had eaten nothing.

He couldn't see the beast, but he heard great weight shuffling a weary approach.

Manu came into sight, lumbering up the narrow, zigzagging pathway to the canyon. Tor held his breath.

Manu stopped. Did he sense danger? He stood below Tor, his great head bobbing as if trying to figure something out. Heat rose, and scent . . . unhealthy scent, Tor realized again.

But what a creature, even in age and weariness!

The Earth Shaker looked nothing like any animal in the world. Hair covered him, longer than the hair of a wolf's tail, shorter than the tail of a horse, the dull brown of an autumn leaf. Manu's legs were like oak trunks, his body like a hill. His ears were folds of hairless skin. His eyes seemed small for his size. Below the eyes, a long piece of flesh grew out of his face, something like a man's arm, except that there were nostrils at the end of it where a hand should be. The long nose waved, sniffing the air. From each side of the nose grew a brown-yellow horn as thick as Tor's wrist. One was broken off. The other swept in a great curve away from, then back toward the mammoth's face. Once, when Manu was younger, those horns could have killed a man, but no longer. The threat was size and weight. Tor's head wouldn't reach Manu's shoulder. And the weight—he swallowed hard.

Manu must have decided it was safe. He entered the trap, headed for the far end of the medicine-pouch canyon, and collapsed with a huffing grunt. The earth thundered in protest.

The beast slept, though it was still light. Quickly and quietly, Tor filled the canyon mouth with wood, crossing the longest sticks and tying them with strips of bison skin, weaving thinner pieces in and out. Dark was full by the time he finished. The brush wall was high and thick. But not strong. Wishing there'd been more wood, he offered up a prayer that it would hold.

Full and bright, the moon came up. Tor climbed the ridge and crawled with moonlight in his face until he was above the prey of his dreams. The beast lay in deep shadow, but Tor could make out its shape.

He'd brought and stacked many rocks here, each the heaviest a man could move. He put his hands on one and whispered a prayer.

''Find your way true. Not for myself do I ask, but for the Earth Shaker, so he will not suffer.''

The warrior hefted the rock. It felt lighter. The Rock Spirit was on his side.

Tor hurled it with all his strength, then another and another. The deadly hail flew out and down and true.

Whump! shouted the Rock Spirit as flesh and bone gave way.

Whump! Whump!

Blaring in pain and terror, Manu struggled to his knees, then fell back. Tor kept on, glad he'd gathered so many rocks. He was hurting the Earth Shaker, hurting him badly! Manu might die right here, and he wouldn't even need the brush wall!

The wounded beast bellowed as though he was brother of the Spirit of Thunder.

A chilling question flashed in Tor's mind: *Am I the last on earth to hear this sound?*

Manu lumbered to his feet, crying loudly enough to scare the dead. Lit by the moon, he ran slowly and painfully for the canyon mouth. Tor flew along the ridge above, pelting him with fist-sized rocks. Manu stopped when he saw the brush wall. He lowered his head and charged, backed up and charged, again and again. Tor heard breaking wood. He reached his rockpile above the canyon mouth and started hurling. Bellowing each time he was struck, the beast kept charging the feeble wall, even though there were bloody wounds all over him, and a man above inflicting more and more. Pain only seemed to enrage the Earth Shaker.

His plan to trap Manu in the canyon and kill him with rocks was not going to work. He would run out of rocks before the mammoth ran out of life.

Listen! He's going to break through! He'll never come back!

''No!'' Tor shouted.

Without thinking, he scrambled down the rocks outside the canyon mouth.

The wall of wood bulged, snapping and cracking as the bellowing monster threw himself at the other side.

Get out of here! Tor's mind screamed. *It's going to go!*
An idea hit.

With his father's fire sticks and some wood shavings from his medicine pouch, working faster than lightning Tor kindled a glow. He picked up the burning kindling, shielded it, and ran for the brush wall. Terror shook him. Less than a man-length away, the monster bashed the puny barrier. Tor's trembling hands tried to start it burning before the glowing kindling burned a hole through his flesh. But the sticks were green. Then he found dry ones.

The wall flashed.

Tor heard a fear-sharpened blare on the other side.

The earth shook as the beast ran back from the entrance.

Thank the spirits! Manu feared fire!

Tor knew now that he'd never kill the beast by pitching rocks. When the burning brush was gone, Manu would flee. Tor would never have another chance at him.

He scrambled back up the rocks, then down into the medicine-pouch canyon.

Flame was devouring the brush wall. The brightness rubbed out sight. Somewhere in the dark, Manu cried.

"Be strong!" the warrior said to his Shahala spear.

Tor saw a piece of wood thick as an arm and long as a leg, fiercely burning at one end. He pulled it from the blaze. With his spear in his best hand and the torch in the other, he ran into the darkness, yelling with the noise of five men.

"Earth Shaker! Welcome me! I bring you death!"

Torchlight struck the monster where he cowered against the canyon wall. Tor kept coming, shouting and jabbing fire. Manu reared on oak-stump legs, blaring, pawing the air, blocking the moon. Tor was a numb-brained ant with death's feet looming over him, but he kept yelling.

"Die, Earth Shaker! Die!"

Manu threw back his head and screamed at the sky. His earskin flew up, and Tor saw a hole behind it—a hole into his brain. He drew back, took aim, and hurled his spear almost straight up.

Takeena the Eagle Spirit carried the spear to Manu's ear and plunged it home, cutting off his hideous scream. His huge body hung in the air, then crashed forward. The earth shook, knocking Tor off his feet. The warrior's muscles were quivering mush. Dust choked him.

Then there was silence, so deep that the sound of Tor's breathing was like a windstorm.

Crouching by the beast, Tor wept without knowing why, until sleep took him.

Dawn lit the canyon. The young warrior stared at the thing he had killed . . . a hill covered in blood-matted hair. But there was no rank smell of death, no horde of flies or circling vultures. Felt but not seen, a misty blanket of peace lay over the carcass, telling Tor he'd been right to free Manu from his desperately lonely life.

But he'd been wrong about saving his people. What had he been thinking? Guilty questions tumbled in his brain.

What are you going to do now? How are you going to make this right? You thought you could save your people—even thought of marking the meat so they'd know their savior's name.

Did you kill the last mammoth on earth out of pride?

Tor shook his head, and focused on the carcass. *Meat. Food. Nothing more.* He marked it with cutting lines in his mind. How many packs would be filled? How many men to carry them? Ten? Thirty?

Tor, Tor . . . you're one man, and it's two suns to Anutash. What have you done, Tor? What have you done?

An animal's life was precious, its meat a gift. Shahala warriors only killed in need or in defense—never in pride or anger. It was a sin against the spirit of the animal, our brother; against the earth, our mother; against Amotkan, who created Each as part of The One.

What was the punishment for this sin? Spirits could give another of the victim's kind a chance to kill the wrongful man.

What, though, if the animal was the last of its kind? What punishment for this surely greater sin?

There *was* no rule. How could a kind run out?

Tears poured from too many wounds inside—wounds named Manu, Shahala, Ashan, Tor, sorrow, guilt. He fell to the ground at the mammoth's head, face in the blood-dark earth, a hand on the beast's nose.

Over and over he cried, "Spirits hate me! I am not fit to live!" Tor felt himself slipping . . . down, down into the numbing darkness of mind that could last for moons, or perhaps forever . . . galloping on and on like bad sickness . . . until *spirits* thought he'd paid enough . . . until *spirits* decided to loose him. He'd been here before . . . different times and places, the same self-hate and overwhelming desire to die . . . for dying *must* be easier than suffering the spirits' agony of mind.

A man, he pleaded. *I'm only a man!*

It seemed terribly, cruelly unfair. What gave something as powerful as a spirit the right to torture something as powerless as a man?

I am a man! *Not some powerless beetle scrabbling on the ground!*

Another realization struck him: Self-caused death is a mean trick. And a desperate gamble. One man loses by dying. Another—by miracle or chance—lives through the attempt, and learns to overcome the demon.

Tor picked himself up from the dirt and shook his fists at the sky.

"No!" he screamed, and meant it with every shred of will. "Not again!"

Tor had overcome the demon of self-destruction before . . . if he could only remember how . . .

His inner voice whispered: *Purpose of supreme importance is reason to live . . .*

He had killed the last Earth Shaker with two clear purposes: The creature would be freed from misery, and the meat would save the Shahala from starvation. The first, he'd accomplished. But he'd failed in the other. As any fool would have long ago known, there was no way to get the meat to his people, no way to save them from starving.

Tor heard the voice of his inner self, saw the picture it drew in his mind, and began to understand another way Manu might save his people.

Prey is more than food for the body. It is an animal's spirit, will and strength.

Manu's spirit could give the Shahala hope, his will give them desire, his strength give them ways to survive, as *he* had, against the impossible.

Memories of the Moonkeeper's sacred teaching swirled in Tor's head . . .

. . . *Souls of people must be freed by burning, but animal souls fly away at death . . . except the part that they give to people . . .*

. . . *Eating flesh is eating the animal's spirit, especially the heart, liver and tongue . . .*

. . . *but spirit moves in other ways—on wind currents, in smoke . . .*

An idea took shape and became a plan.

Manu's spirit would save Tor's people. All he had to do was get it to them.

Tor climbed the mammoth's shoulder and pulled his spear from its ear, whispering, ''I'll be back.'' He went to the ridgetop, carefully emptied his antelope carrying skin of its Shahala remains, and returned to the medicine-pouch canyon.

Manu's hide was tough. Tor sharpened his stone blade several times before it found heart and liver under thick fat.

Oh, how his people could have used that fat.

The tongue was the last thing he took.

It was strange, but still no flies or vultures came.

He would have liked to burn the rich carcass; the thought of man-eaters finding it enraged him. But he had already burned most of the valley's wood. It would take days to get enough, if it was even possible. Who knew if the monstrous thing *could* be burned? There are things on earth that cannot.

Tor would have to leave the kill of a lifetime.

He prayed over the partly-butchered beast.

''Spirit of Manu, come with me. Don't look back at this poor body. Even scavengers have to eat. Let them have a good winter for a change.''

Tor climbed out of the medicine-pouch canyon for the last time, the mammoth's organs heavy on his back. When he reached the high ridgetop, he lay down and slept for a time, awakening as the sun left the sky.

Hunger chewed his insides, but he had decided to eat no part of the mammoth himself. Nor would he ever speak of his impossible accomplishment. Manu had died for a whole people, not for a single man.

Tor broke dead branches from the few scrubby trees and made a woodpile on the ridge's highest place . . . a place with a view to forever. He took the heart, liver and tongue from his antelope skin, laid them on the wood, and fired it. Flames crackled the dry sticks and sizzled the juices of the raw meat. Kneeling, Tor stared into the flames and prayed.

"Spirit of Manu, leave this flesh, and go in the smoke to my people, the Shahala, who need you."

He stood before the fire, stretched his arms wide, threw back his head and shouted.

"Spirit of Shala, this smoke has power your people need. Carry it to them on your wind."

With his arms raised, he turned to the four directions, and said to each: "Spirits of everything else, forgive me for what I have done. Shower my people with your blessings. If you are pleased with my efforts, smile upon the Shahala."

A breeze touched Tor. It carried thick, fragrant smoke into the darkening sky, toward Where Day Ends, his people, his beloved.

When the fire was finished, Tor let it cool and then put the ashes into his antelope skin.

CHAPTER
17

Tor continued his quest to save his tribesmen's souls, going farther into the man-eaters' barren land.

Darkness closed as he walked down a canyon with high rock sides. His searching nostrils found a faint smell of smoke. A bit of lighter sky puffed ahead. He moved toward it, hugging the canyon wall. A faint hum became voices, laughing and shouting in ugly alien speech.

Full moon now lit the darkness. The canyon narrowed ahead, its walls coming almost together. Fireglow flickered beyond a narrow slot. Voices told of people on the other side.

People? No, man-eaters! Rage flamed as Tor thought of what they'd done to his tribe. He wanted to run in and spear as many as possible before he died!

No, Tor! Get control!

He'd come to rescue the souls of his brothers, not to avenge them—no matter how tempting that might be. Blind rage smoothed to clear determination.

Moonlight showed a way up the rocks that edged the canyon. Though it was cold, Tor left his new bison robe behind, wanting nothing between man and rocks who'd be brothers for a while. He hid his spears and the antelope skin with its Shahala remains. With his stone knife in his teeth—in case there was a guard—Tor began his climb. At the top, the moon flung light on a strange, flat surface—part bare rock, part humpy dirt covered with dry grass. Though he saw no one, he kept low, crawling toward a firelit spot in the night sky.

The ground dropped away. Tor crept to the edge.

Past the narrow slot he'd seen, the canyon opened into a small valley. Many huts hugged the rim. Women tended cooking fires, wearing furs against the cold. Little ones played. Shouts, laughter and alien speech rose in a confusing din.

In the village's heart stood a circle of wood poles buried in the ground. Each was taller than a man, and topped with a human or animal skull. Dancing men ringed a bonfire inside the skull-circle, calling like night animals, naked bodies steaming. One man struggled to dance with the head of a bison over his own. The others led him to the only pole with no skull and lifted him. He tied the shaggy head to the top, then jumped off their backs, shrieking and shaking raised fists. All of them fell, as if to pray to the gory head.

The sight made Tor sick. As he scrambled away, stumbling over the humpy ground, he stepped in water—a sunken place that collected rain. He cupped his hands and took some. It tasted of rock, but that was better than his snake-tasting water. His gut quieted, he crept back.

Their sick dance finished, the savages were going into huts.

As Tor watched, familiar words startled him . . . from somewhere down there . . . in a voice so soft, he might have imagined it. But it came again. He traced it to the far side of the skull-circle.

Shahala words were rising from a hole in the ground! Brothers alive! Why? The only answer disgusted him: Live food doesn't rot.

The wavering voice in the ground strengthened in a Shahala prayer to Keeli the White Swan Spirit, who sometimes flew to men's rescue—at least in the Misty Time.

Two man-eater boys not old enough to hunt came from a hut dragging a bulging pouch larger than a bear bladder. They struggled with it to the edge of the pit and dumped it in, shrieking with laughter. A woman grabbed a switch and went after the boys.

A shocked cry rose from the pit—a woman's voice! Shahala hunters weren't the only captives! Desire to get to them stampeded inside him like a herd of horses, but Tor waited. Finally the last savage was in his hut. The moon climbed to the other side of the sky, and long silence blanketed the village before Tor the Rescuer made his way down.

As he came through the opening in the rock walls, he wrinkled his nose at a thick, dead-animal smell. Moonlight left nowhere to hide. Tor was tired of crawling like a lizard, but he still had good sense. Face in the dust, he scuttled through the village, past silent huts, past the skull-circle, past a heap of fresh-cut poles.

He smelled the pit coming, then was at its edge. Deeper than a man could climb, too deep for moonlight to touch, it wasn't wide enough to stretch out in. The jumble in the dark bottom could be three or four bodies, sleeping or dead. The stench was terrible, but Shahala.

The idea of freeing them was powerful enough to die for.

But they must not know who set them free. Like the others, they'd believe Tor's dreaming had caused the massacre. They would never forgive him, no matter what he did.

Tor froze at a sound behind him . . . scuffling, a cough and muttered alien words, a trickle of water hitting coals with a sizzle. Only an ignorant savage would make water in a firepit, or be blind enough to miss a flattened stranger not two man-lengths away! Tor's heart thudded in his ears so hard it seemed he'd shake the whole place awake.

Finished, the savage shook himself and went into his hut, proving that too much food and too little fear deadens senses.

Quiet as a shadow, Tor crept to the heap of poles, loosened one and carried it to the pit. The captives didn't wake as he lowered it thick end first.

Yearning swept him as he looked down. To be with his people, to die with them, or even at their hands—anything was better than being alone.

He rubbed wet eyes, and did what he had to do. Backing away, he threw a handful of dirt in the pit and whispered loudly enough to wake them.

"Shahala warriors! Escape!"

Tor fled without looking back and scrambled up the rocks. Over the sound of his thudding heart, he heard running below.

His tribesmen were free! *Oh, thank you, Takeena!* he whispered to his guardian spirit. *And Keeli, and Shala, and . . .*

Almost floating from happiness, Tor watched the village for the rest of the night.

When the escape was discovered at dawn, the enraged men slapped women and little ones, then went after their running winter food. After they left, the women cooked a haunch of meat for a morning meal, chattering as if used to abuse.

Tor noticed that all the women were young, and wondered if the old ones were killed when no longer useful. Could these people really be that evil?

More evil than a Shahala man can imagine, he understood as he stared at the circle of poles in the heart of the village, the mounted human skulls, older ones smooth and glinting in the morning sun, newer ones dark with bits of clinging flesh. Some of these belonged to his tribesmen.

Why is such evil allowed to exist? Why don't all people have to follow the same laws? he angrily asked the spirits.

They do. Why don't you remove their kind from the earth, as you did so well with the mammoth?

A shocking answer, but . . .

Tor was a man who needed purpose to live. What greater purpose could there be than ridding the world of men who would eat other men?

He thought about purpose, how quickly it could change, and how a man could sometimes see no farther than his fingertips.

First he had been determined to free Shahala souls trapped on the battlefield, but that wasn't enough once he realized others were trapped in man-eater bodies. He'd been *glad* to know he'd have to kill savages . . . revenge would be soothing medicine for his hatred of them.

But he'd been sidetracked, and had to kill a mammoth, for reasons he could barely remember now.

And then he'd found Shahala brothers alive, freed them.

What was it to be now?

The pursuit of purpose wasn't easy for anyone, but Tor felt sure that no had ever had a harder time than he.

Longing for his old life stabbed him . . . to be merely Tor again, son of Luka . . . longing as hopeless as that of a mother begging spirits to give back the life of her child. Tor's old life was as dead as any mother's child could be. Revenge upon the man-eaters would not bring it back. And any fool could see that ridding the world of men who eat men was nothing but fantasy. Tor would die trying, and that would ruin everything. The souls of his tribesmen would not be freed. The Shahala, not the man-eaters, would be wiped from the earth.

Purpose was clear to Tor once again: He must save the people of his tribe, in soul or body, each one that he could. Each one saved increased their chances to survive as a tribe. Tor understood that *this* was what really mattered. Manu had somehow taught him the importance of a kind.

Some of the skulls in the man-eater village belonged to Tor's people. He decided to take them from this evil place, then free their souls with the ones from the battlefield in a monstrous fire. After that, he'd take them back to the homeland, to be mingled with the ashes of Manu and scattered on the sacred burial ground.

Only then did Tor think he'd be free of pain and guilt for whatever laws he'd broken . . . though he still didn't think dreaming and loving a Moonkeeper were so wrong.

Free . . . he thought, sighing. *What good will freedom be to a man with no mate or tribe?*

All day Tor lay watching the man-eater village, vengeful ideas filling his head.

When the women left to go gathering, he might rush down and massacre the children. But the lazy women didn't go gathering. They sat around all day talking, not even bothered by the fights their children kept having. *Do they eat* only *meat?* Tor wondered. *Is that what makes them so savage?* Tor imagined himself invisible, running through them slashing with his blade. He heard their screams in his mind. But it was only something to do until darkness came and he could go down there and get the skulls.

The man-eater men didn't come back that day, and Tor tried not to think about where they were. The women and little ones were in the huts soon after dark. When the fat moon was higher than the early winter star, Tor stole into the village.

He stood inside the skull-circle looking up, senses swimming. Which to take? Which to leave? Where to begin?

He'd have to take them all to be sure he had his brothers.

He started to count, then stopped. He'd just have to trust his antelope skin to hold them.

The poles were smoother and harder to climb than he'd expected, but his legs were strong again, enough to keep thighs clamped around a pole while he cut each skull loose from its tangle of thongs. Careful as he was, he made noises. Several times he was seized with an urge to drop everything and flee. He couldn't stop thinking of being trapped up a pole by man-eater women—no doubt as savage as their mates.

Questions tortured him as he did his terrible work. *What friend did he hold in his hands? What might the bone look like fleshed, with nose, hair and eyes?* He'd have vomited if there'd been anything in his gut; instead he gagged on bitter slime.

The moon continued its trek across the sky. At last, all but the poles with animal heads were empty, and his antelope skin was so full he couldn't tie it closed. Bones clattered in the bulging skin as Tor ran through the night. Early morning found him in the clearing near the waterhole where he'd spent a moon.

A cawing flock of ravens told him spirits wanted the fire here, where the warriors had died.

Tor pulled the bone-filled skin under the rock shelter and slept most of the day. When he awoke, he laid out the skulls and stared at them. The gruesome sight took away his idea about raiding the waterhole for a victory feast. Time for food and celebration would come when the task was finished. Tor wrapped the bones in the antelope skin and lay back down, wishing he hadn't left his new bison robe behind.

He didn't sleep well . . . kept waking up thinking he was in a group of people . . . invisible people who seemed quite real. Strong feelings filled the unseen ones, but Tor didn't know *what* feelings. It might have been love, frustration, or malice. He was still tired when morning came, but he was glad to see it. He'd waste no more time. They needed peace; he needed peace most of all.

Working with the speed of bees before winter, he gathered the wood he'd scattered earlier. Ignoring his own growing doubts about the spirit world, he sang to all the spirits he knew. The sweetest song called to the loved ones of these whose souls were beginning their journey to the spirit world.

When long shadows lay on the day, the woodpile in the clearing reached his shoulder, with more stacked on a ledge above.

This time, the feel of it all was right. Tor placed his antelope sleeping skin, bulging with its sorrowful load, on the woodpile's flat top. He unlaced the paired skins for the last time, remembering hunts of the past, sleeping in some wildplace with brother-scent thick in his nostrils.

He picked up the remnants one by one and put them down again, calling the names of missing Shahala warriors, so the spirits would know who to look for.

Then he dusted Manu's ashes over them.

Satisfied, he knelt with his father's fire sticks.

Surging flames forced Tor out of the rock-walled clearing. He squeezed through the entrance and climbed to the ledge above, to the brushpile he'd left on a flat place as wide as a man's stride where rock had fallen away. He squatted on his heels and threw pieces of wood down to feed the blaze. It crackled like the laughter of old people. The smoke, white as owl down, was thick with spirit. The taste was oily; the smell bitter, but clean. His eyes and nose watered, draining the lake of poison inside him. Joy filled him almost to bursting. Only the sight of Ashan could have made him happier.

The fire ate all the wood Tor had to give it. He lay back on the ledge and slept.

Tor dreamed. A mist like puffs of cloud surrounded him, twisting and curling as the smoke of a great fire, but smelling of the sharp herbs Moonkeepers burn to call spirits. Light glowed behind the fog. An unfelt wind pulled out feathers of gray and twirled them away, opening a hole on a flower-strewn meadow. Ashan knelt in the grass, little ones before her. Singing fell out of the air. The little ones smiled at their mother.

They were his! Boys and girls, fat and brown, black hair shining in the sun! How many? As he started to count, the fog closed around them and they were gone.

Tor awakened to pink-and-gold-streaked sky. He was filled with love and hope, feeling better than he'd thought he ever would again. He closed his eyes and saw the dream. He could not have created a more perfect vision: Tor, father of the loveliest children Alhaia ever sent; Ashan, Tor's mate.

Why hadn't he run to them, as he surely would if he ever really saw such a thing?

It's enough, he thought, *to be given the picture . . . a memory never to be lost . . . a thing to sleep with in the lifetime of lonely nights ahead.*

Sun crested the clifftop. Tor squeezed his eyes tight, trying to hold the dream. But he couldn't hold out. He stood and smiled, giving in to the glorious day. Arms raised, head back, he cried in an eagle's voice to greet spirits, forgetting that not so long ago, he'd wondered about the very existence of spirits.

Takeena came—Tor could feel him in the air. It was good to have his guardian back; he missed the sureness of knowing what to do. Takeena wasn't angry anymore. Tor thanked him for that, and for the gift of the dream. There'd been few since the massacre, another thing he missed. Now that the outcast couldn't harm his people, he hoped he'd be allowed to dream.

Enough idle waking-up thoughts. Tor slid down the rock face to the clearing. His work wasn't finished; the dead must be taken home.

As hot as he'd made it, the blaze had not consumed everything. The ashpile contained unburned skulls—something he'd forgotten in his plan to scatter ashes in the burial ground at Anutash. Unburned bones should be buried along with ashes beneath the gravestone, but Tor wouldn't have time for digging holes—nor would he know which stone belonged to which man. He couldn't stand the thought of just leaving them there on the ground unburied.

He could only think of one thing to do. It seemed terrible, violent, but these bones were no longer his brothers. Their souls were gone with last night's smoke. Still . . .

Do it, Tor. There is no other way.

He poked through the ashpile with a stick, pulled the skulls out, and crushed them to powder between stones.

With careful hands, he scooped the ashes and powdered bones into his horseskin sack. He tried not to think of what it *was*, thinking instead of his sister who'd made the sack. Tenka's love shone in the painted shapes of hunted beasts. By folding in a certain way, he could change it from a large carrier to a small pouch. The design was so clever others had copied it. And Tenka was only seven summers.

Dear Amotkan! How could he *not* think about the grainy

stuff that clung to his fingers? So little left of the bones that had overflowed his antelope sleeping skin! And yet, Tor knew this was how it must be . . . no weight of body to hold the soaring spirits down.

He set out for home with the horseskin sack and the sun on his back, leaving the tabu land forever.

CHAPTER
18

A shan hated this dream! She couldn't look anywhere but down on a moonlit village with . . .

Please don't make me see this . . .

. . . A circle of skulls mounted on poles. Shahala voices rose from a hole in the ground. Her tribesmen were here! Someone—Tor!—was crawling toward the pit. She knew he'd try to get them out!

She cried his name, but he didn't look up.

Someone shook her, someone outside the dream.

"You're shouting! What are you dreaming?"

She sat up. "He's alive!"

"Who?"

"Tor! And Raga, you're wrong! He's *not* a betrayer!"

Raga slapped her, knocking her back down. "Speak not the Evil One's name! Haven't your people suffered enough?"

The pain brought Ashan awake. Her eyes widened. What had been spewing from her mouth?

Unexpectedly, Raga embraced her. "I scared you. I'm sorry, Windpuff. I know the pain you are feeling."

The old woman, naked from sleep, took Ashan in her arms, smoothed her wild hair, rocked her in the way of mothers. Raga once had been the softest pillow a little one could know, but now her large bones poked through empty skin. Still, her warm breast—such a comfort that Ashan sometimes crawled to it in dreams—smelled familiar and safe. A little girl inside Ashan wanted to cry herself back to sleep. But she couldn't cry anymore, not even to Raga. Anyone else in the tribe could cry, but not the Moonkeeper. It would terrify the people, and disgust the spirits.

Raga stroked Ashan's hair. "The Evil One has sickened us. It's a sickness of the mind that gets inside our sleep. The dream you had was not spirit-sent, but made of your own longing. The Evil One is dead. You must not think otherwise. In time, his poison will leave you."

"I hope you're right," Ashan lied as she pulled out of Raga's arms. She took a deep breath and straightened her shoulders. No one, not Raga, not even Amotkan, could take away the dream. Tor was alive, Ashan knew it now . . . if not in this world, alive in another. His soul still existed. They'd be together again. It seemed almost enough to make up for the endless sorrow life had become.

Rain began beating on the hut.

Raga backed into herself like a threatened turtle, went to her bed and pulled the skins over her head—the rare moment of reality gone.

"Raga, please! Stay with me!"

Still as a stone, Raga made no answer.

Ashan felt herself crumbling, overcome with yearning to be back in Raga's arms. She let anger loose to fight yearning.

"Get up, old woman!" she snapped, partly in disgust, partly to anger Raga—anything would be better than this living death!

"Get up, I said! Tobi's dying and she needs you! You were little ones together!"

Leave me alone! Raga wanted to shout. *Who do you think you are?* But she knew who Ashan thought she was—the shaman-chief Raga had raised her to be. A chief must do whatever she must do to make her people obey . . . not that Ashan was any match for her teacher.

But shouting took more strength than Raga had, so she made a snore-growl in her throat. It was easier to pretend sleep. Not that the Old Moonkeeper would sleep. No matter that she was the most tired person alive, she would only lie here and think. How could sleep get to a mind so full of bad thought?

Snores rose from the lump of skins—fake snores.

"Bison dung!" Ashan cursed, but even that got no response.

She sighed and shook her head. She jerked fingers through her hair to untangle it, laced long winter moccasins over her knees, and wrapped a stained old deerskin around her waist.

"Bison dung!" she said again, jerking at the edges. The skirt barely touched in front—the same skirt that had always lapped over itself to cover what needed covering.

Something was wrong with her body, *very wrong*, and had been for two moons, since the Time of Sorrows began. First it was vomiting in the morning. Then spirits stopped coming to renew her woman-power. And now, somehow, while everyone else shrank, Ashan was getting fatter.

When would her punishment end?

She threw on her antelope robe, opened the doorskin and looked out. What an ugly day! Rain would soak her before she got to the old people's hut! She thought of trying again to rouse Raga, but snores from the pile of skins said not to bother.

Someone had to visit Tobi, and it would have to be Ashan. She didn't want to see the crazy old woman, who had it in her head that the Moonkeeper was with child, but her duty to the dying was clear.

Though she ran, Ashan was soaked when she entered the old people's hut.

She wouldn't have to hear Tobi's accusations ever again. The old woman's spirit had gone in the night.

The Old Moonkeeper, pretending to sleep, was grateful for the silence Ashan left behind.

Raga already knew the woman called Oak Heart was gone. Tobi's spirit had visited her in the night, lighter than owl down, the soft purple of peace. Raga was glad to know her old friend was prepared for death; out of confusion or fear, many spirits were reluctant to leave their bodies.

Though her head was under sleeping skins and her eyes were closed, Raga could see Tobi now, in the gray light on the other side of the hut . . . a faint purple mist hovering over the bed Ashan had just left.

"Tobi?" Raga said.

The purple cloud glowed brighter for a heartbeat.

"I need someone to talk to."

I know.

"There are too many horrors in my mind," Raga blurted. "They eat me. I can only fight them by hiding . . . hiding . . . it's getting harder to hide . . . I am too tired to live . . . I want the peace you know . . ."

Your work is hardly begun.

"And do you know everything, now that you are dead?" Raga said with dangerous sarcasm.

I thought I would, but I was wrong. I do know this, my old friend: You must not give up. If you die, our people will vanish like the mammoth. Believe me, Raga, and find your strength.

"I raised Ashan to take my place. She is Moonkeeper now."

I fear a mistake was made. Ashan cannot *be Moonkeeper.*

"What do you mean?"

A Moonkeeper cannot bear a child.

If a living person said such a thing, Raga would make them wish they hadn't. But what can be done with voices in the mind? Sometimes they can be controlled, sometimes not.

Raga managed to still her mind long enough for the picture of her beautiful spirit daughter swelled with the unforgiveable to go away.

When thought came back, it was time for the other horrors in her mind to speak.

Where is your power, Raga? a mind voice asked. *Where has it gone?*

"It doesn't work anymore," the old woman mumbled.

When the massacre began the Time of Sorrows, for a while *Ashan* was the Moonkeeper who couldn't cope. Raga had used all the magic she knew . . . every spell, herb, prayer. Nothing helped. It got worse. The Shahala grieved, weakened, died . . . as if a sickness were loose among them . . . a sickness of the mind . . . a sickness with no medicine.

"I fought it as long as I could," she said.

Her mind answered: *But not as long as you will.*

Behind her eyelids, Raga saw a golden light where the purple mist had been before. Spilyea, the Coyote Spirit, was in it. The light shone from his golden eyes. Raga took a deep breath to steady herself before such awful power.

A voice came from the yellow light, though the creature didn't move its mouth.

Daughter of Shakana, the old ways are dying. Soon the world will change.

Raga had been told this many times before, by different spirits. She had no idea what it meant, so as always, she replied with a question.

"What do you mean? How can the world change?"

As always, her question was ignored.

Unprepared, your people will not survive.

"Then tell me what magic to use! I have tried everything!"

Magic is the old way.

"But magic is all I know!"

A few days after Tobi's death, the Winter Spirit turned kind. Welcome sun shone on the Shahala village of Anutash.

When clouds hid the sun's light, as they often did in this season, a shadow stick could not be used, and the shaman-chief had to keep the passing of time in her mind. Ashan was thinking of a better way—perhaps wooden beads on a string, one for each morning she awoke to clouds. Today, thanks to the sunshine, she was able to check with her shadow stick. She hadn't lost track: Winter's shortest day—the dark one of the Days of Balance—would soon be here. It was a dangerous time. The Moonkeeper would have to stay out with the moon all night, a cold, unpleasant part of her work. But with her help, the season would turn, days grow longer, and food get better. Ashan hoped her people's moods would also get better.

Today, for a change, the tribe's puny band of seven hunters had met with luck—a mountain goat had stumbled as they chased it.

Now, as darkness fell on the village, two women turned a pole mounted over a fire. Tied to the pole by its legs, the skinned goat sizzled and smoked. Most of the people sat around waiting, breathing the sweet smells of cooking. No one was talking, but still . . . there was something different, something *easier* in the air.

As she chopped yellow-green shoots with a stone knife, hope fluttered in Ashan. Might her people survive after all?

A noise startled her. She looked up, dropping her knife. It must be animals crashing in the brush outside the village. But at night?

"Man-eaters!" someone yelled.

A filthy, naked man staggered from the brush, arms thrust out, mouth agape in a silent cry.

Two more followed him.

Shahala women and little ones shrieked and ran. Warriors grabbed spears.

The intruders stumbled and fell. The warriors charged.

Ashan's dream flashed before her.

"No!" she screamed. "They're Shahala!"

Ketral, Deyon and Chok—terrible as they looked, there was no mistaking them.

Cheers erupted as the people surged toward them.

"Get back!" Ashan said. "They're hurt!" She elbowed through the mob, kneeling by the three ghosts.

"There's another," Deyon said, rising on his arms, weak voice trembling. "She's afraid to come in."

Ashan gasped. "She?"

"An Outsider, and she is mine!"

The startled people murmured. "Amotkan!" "A woman!"

"Call her," the Moonkeeper said. "She's welcome."

"Cheronyak!" Deyon yelled. "Kaia! Kaia!"

What kind of speech is that? Ashan wondered.

The people were quiet, waiting, but no answer came from the dark.

The Moonkeeper stood in the firelight. She spoke in a kind voice, though she knew the Outsider wouldn't understand the words.

"Kalatash, New Woman! The Shahala welcome you!"

The stranger must have understood the meaning. The tribe gasped as one as she stepped out of the brush. She was as filthy as the men. Her hands hid the place of woman-power as if ashamed of her nakedness. Her bones showed through skin grayish from sickness or filth. But her chin was up. Her eyes held Ashan's, not looking at the ground as many would. She seemed stronger than the men, in body and spirit.

Admiring her courage, Ashan opened her arms.

The woman glanced at Deyon. He nodded, and she went to Ashan for the comfort that comes from a Moonkeeper's embrace.

Women grouped around them. Stinking dirty as the stranger was, they hugged her, clucking in sympathy, then led her away to the women's hut to wash and dress her. The Outsider Cheronyak was their sister now: Kalatash, New Woman.

Ashan could feel the emotions of her people on her skin . . . joy, excitement, fear, confusion. They assaulted her with questions.

"Are they real? Are they ghosts?"

"How can this be? What does it mean?"

Raga, where are you? Ashan thought desperately. She needed time to sort this out for herself before she could interpret it for her people. But they weren't going to leave her alone until she gave them answers.

Ashan didn't know where the words came from, but as always they came when she needed them. She held out her arm toward the three filthy men lying on the ground.

"See before you a gift to ease Shahala pain. The spirit world wishes us to survive, and has given us the way, by returning these fathers and mates, these desperately missed hunters. It is a sign: Amotkan's favored people will not perish."

A great breath of relief came from the people. Joy unleashed, they slapped and hugged each other.

"Brothers," Ashan said. "Carry the Men Born Again to the old people's hut. The old will sleep with their families for a while."

Surrounded by joyous people, noisier than Ashan had heard them in moons, the Men Born Again were carried to the hut, where each took the bed of an old person. Laughing and crying, mothers and daughters and mates went to work, washing their men and picking things out of their hair. People packed the hut to get a look at the unbelievable—this was the first time anyone but a Moonkeeper had returned from death.

Ashan looked them over, exploring their flesh with her hands and her mind. The woman of medicine found healed wounds but no fresh ones. They weren't starving; in fact, they were flabby. Nothing seemed wrong with their bodies except exhaustion, but something was very wrong with them. They should be as thrilled to be home as the people were to have them, but they were barely responsive. Slack faces and glazed eyes told of deep pain of the mind.

Ashan dreaded questioning them. She'd been to their place of suffering in her dream and never wanted to think of it again. But listening was part of healing, part of Moonkeeper's work. Listening often made Ashan uncomfortable, or worse . . . sometimes she felt another's pain as her own. Raga said it got easier with age.

Raga should be handling this, she thought. *The reappearance of dead men is no small thing. Where* is *Raga? Could she have slept through all this?*

Ashan sighed. Like everything else, she'd have to do this herself. Tomorrow would be soon enough . . . right now, the men needed rest.

"Everyone out," Ashan said. "All but the mates of the Men Born Again."

"Bring me Cheronyak," Deyon said.

Ashan smiled. He looked better already.

"Get Kalatash," she said to his sister. "Now out of here, the rest of you."

Shoulders slumped, feet dragging, Ashan walked back to the Moonkeepers' hut. And there was Raga, snoring away. The old woman had missed the whole thing. Ashan lay down and slept without a dream.

She didn't try to wake Raga in the morning. For a while after the massacre, the Old Moonkeeper had trudged to a hillside to spend her days moping. Now she rarely left her bed.

Who cares? Ashan thought with morning grumpiness. *Why doesn't she die so someone else can have her foodshare?*

Guilt surged as soon as she thought it. Thank Amotkan she hadn't said it out loud. Raga wouldn't act like this if she could do otherwise.

Why am I turning into a crone without sympathy?

The sky had turned drizzly again, more like winter should be, enough to dampen Ashan's hair on the way to the old people's hut. She chased the women out, noticing the hut smelled cleaner than it had in a long time.

The Men Born Again were much better than she'd expected

after one night's sleep. They looked ready to begin living again. But first, as a poisoned tooth sometimes has to be pulled out, the poison in their minds must be relieved.

"Tell me what happened," the Moonkeeper said.

Words tumbled like a rockslide. Ashan's dream had shown her just the tip of a buried bone. The returned warriors uncovered the rest of the foul carrion.

At first there'd been eight Shahala warriors . . . wounded, bound, dragged by the hair over rocks, and shoved in a pit. Too much food was thrown down; most of it rotted, adding stink to the warriors' own filth. Every few days the maneaters tossed a tangle of ropes down and hauled someone out by his head or leg or whatever caught. The men told of long screams and sickening cooking odors, of mixed dread and yearning to be the next one to leave this hell.

When the woman came, they thought her a spirit sent to rescue them. They were wrong. Cheronyak was plaything to the man-eaters; she was taken out of the pit and abused in ways men couldn't speak of, even to the Moonkeeper. Enough to say they were glad to be men. Deyon took to comforting Cheronyak when she was thrown back down. He came to love her.

The returned warriors agreed on all but one very important thing: *how they had escaped*. About that, their stories were wildly different.

"Yes, the moon was full-bright!" Deyon's voice rose in annoyance. "But we were *all* asleep!"

This made a lie of Chok's story. He claimed he'd gotten out while the others slept, found the pole and put it down for them.

Ketral said, "I can't believe it, Chok. We'd been trying to get out of that stinkhole for two moons."

Ashan's dream had shown her the answer, but she foolishly asked, "If Chok didn't get the pole, who did?"

"My guardian spirit," Deyon said. "Keeli. I prayed to him all the time. That night, White Swan grew huge, plucked up the pole like a pond reed and brought it to me. I saw his wings, and the pole in his beak."

Chok snorted.

Deyon threw him a dark look. "My woman saw what I saw!"

"How would you know?" Chok said. "You can't talk to her!"

"Stop!" Ketral's voice was sharp. "I'm sick of this!" He turned to Ashan. "I love my brothers, but—" He laughed. "If you were thrown in a hole with these two, for three lifetimes, with no skins—"

They were all laughing now. Ashan realized Ketral had become their leader. This proved what Raga taught: People must have a leader to survive.

Ketral fixed the other two with his eyes. "I *know* what happened. Why won't you accept it? Do you hate him so much?"

"Who?" Ashan asked.

"Tor."

She had baited Ketral, knowing what he'd say. Now she must warn him.

"Don't speak his name. We call him the Evil One."

"Call him what you wish," Ketral said. "I will honor his name."

"You're a fool!" Chok snarled. "Tor gave us to the man-eaters!"

"I know. But his spirit came back for us. I *heard* him!"

"Well, I *saw* the great white wings of Keeli!"

Ashan left them. Arguing was a good sign: The Men Born Again would recover.

That night there was a feast of celebration. Even Raga came out to watch the dancing and singing. Of course, there was little *real* food in the starving village, but the women were clever at stretching it with black moss, shredded alder bark, and chopped grass. No celebration was ever grander.

"Thank the spirits!" people said to one another. "The Time of Sorrows is ended!"

They were wrong.

CHAPTER
19

Tor couldn't believe how good it felt to be leaving the tabu land forever, to be on his way to the Shahala burial ground to finish the task of freeing souls. The horseskin pouch of ashes was as light as his heart . . . he was free for the first time in moons of the hatred of spirits.

Tor knew he was doing the right thing.

The sun was a warm smile on his back. He turned the walking over to animal spirits, and gave his mind to the wonderful dream he'd had last night. Over and over he saw it from beginning to end, and little by little, the picture changed. First Tor was looking at the meadow; then he was *in* the meadow, smelling, touching, holding his mate and little ones.

Such a dream could not be without meaning. He tried to understand. Thoughts floated, then began to shape themselves into a plan.

To go on living, a man must have *more* than a purpose. He must have a future.

Ashan was Tor's future.

A Shahala warrior takes what he must have.

Wouldn't he doom his people by taking their Moonkeeper?

No. He told himself how silly it was for one man to think he could doom a whole tribe.

But what if he was wrong? Tor wondered what the spirits would do to a man who brought extinction to his own tribe, as he already had to the mammoth kind.

Fear tried to overtake him, but Tor had become too strong.

"What spirits?" he said out loud, though he wasn't sure if he believed it.

He listened to the voice in his heart, and the one in his loins: *You must have Ashan to live*.

"I must have Ashan to live," he said, and repeated it. It became a chant in time with his steps. Time and the tabu land passed without notice. The words of his chant changed as the mountains of his homeland neared.

"Soon I will have love and life. Soon I will have Ashan."

Darkness came and slowed him, but he didn't stop to sleep.

Late the next day, Tor waded through the knee-deep water of Andor, River of No Crossing. Words could not have told his joy as the mist of Shahala land wrapped him. Two moons had gone since he'd been here last, with Beo, and Arth, and Lar and . . . Two moons . . . dried out, drowned and frozen by the tabu land's excuse for winter. He'd been through more than a man could survive, but all bad would soon end. Soon he'd have Ashan.

As darkness deepened, he lay on ground so soft he didn't miss his burned-up antelope sleeping skin, or the bison robe he'd left behind. He snuggled into the bed of pine needles. With his head on the horseskin pouch of his brothers' ashes, he fell asleep thinking of ways to love Ashan.

The next day, under high clouds easy on the eyes, Tor loped along familiar Shahala trails, soaking up moist air, grinning big enough to catch bugs. Halfway past High Sun, he smelled bear, then saw a young black stretched against a yew tree, moaning with pleasure as it stripped a branch with its teeth.

It was early in the season for a bear to be out of its den. An omen? No, a gift! Spirits were with him! A bearskin was what he needed most!

Tor thought of using the man-eaters' sleek weapon. On small prey, it worked better than his heavy Shahala spear. But a bear?

Why not? What could go wrong on such a day?

He put a stone-tipped spear in the thrower and raised it

over his shoulder. A smooth, graceful stroke with a snap at the end, and the thin spear flew.

Red splashed black shoulders. The bear screamed.

Tor shouted, "Yes!"

The bear turned—roaring, twisting, rubbing its back against the tree. Tor heard the puny spear snap. The enraged beast fixed its eyes on him and charged.

No man could outrun a bear. Tor stood, legs spread, gripping his Shahala spear—tall as a man, thick as his wrist at the butt. He jammed it into the ground between his feet and held it with both hands, up and out in the path of death.

The killer bear didn't see its intended victim's weapon. So close that Tor could smell its stinking breath, the bear lunged into the heavy spear. The spear easily pierced fur and hide, then stopped at bone. Pushed back to his knees, Tor held on. Bear screams terrorized him; guts splattered him; claws raked his arms. Then the beast went limp and fell on him.

Tor gasped. "Thank Amotkan!"

There was no time to rest. Heart and head thumping, he shoved the bear off. He cut the hide away, and gave it a quick scraping. Later he'd take time to work the skin. He dug out the stone point and broken shaft of the man-eater spear. The wonderful new creation had failed, but he still wanted to keep it, without knowing why. Leaving meat behind sorrowed him, but at least it would feed some creature. He was back on the trail with the rank skin draped over his shoulders before he remembered to thank the bear and the spirit who had sent it.

Tor reached Anutash long after dark.

Nothing moved in the village where he'd grown to be a man. Lar, the hunter left to watch, slept by the burned-out fire. His once-best friend snored to call attention to the tribe's unguarded condition. Any predator, man or animal, could take what it wanted from his people this night.

Shaking his head in disgust, Tor circled the village.

The Shahala burial ground was a short walk up a mild slope, out of daily sight. Families kept brush cleared. Grass grew even in winter. While they were still alive, people picked the spot they liked, and a favorite stone. Placed here and there, some of the stones covered ashes of the dead; others waited for the living.

Less than full, the moon was bright enough to throw shadows on the grass. Tor would be killed if discovered, but thinking of Lar, sound asleep, he decided that didn't seem likely.

He put the broken man-eater spear and its thrower where they would be found. The new weapon could help his people . . . if they had better sense than to try it on bears.

Tor sighed. It was time to do what he had come for. He unfolded the horseskin sack on the grass. The ashes glowed white in the moonlight. He walked among Shahala graves scattering handfuls, until light powder dusted the burial ground like thin snow.

It was finished. His brothers were home, and with them, the power of a mammoth.

Now! he prayed, to Takeena and all other spirits who might have ever been. *Now let my new life begin!*

Tor hid in brush at the lower end of the burial ground.

Sooner or later, Ashan would come.

Ashan opened the doorskin of the Moonkeepers' hut and looked out at a high-cloud morning. She touched the grass and smiled . . . dew enough for plants to drink . . . it would not rain this day. The air was warm, so she changed her antelope robe for a catskin.

No one asked for the Moonkeeper this morning. Ashan sat and watched, hungry but accepting, as little ones ate hot grain mush. In the Time of Sorrows, the very young and old were the only ones given morning food.

In the Time Before, there would have been laughter and playing; today there were round eyes in shaking heads. Looks of disbelief flew through the village thick as a hatch of sticky-flies over a lake. The minds of the people were numb. They couldn't make words for their feelings. The Men Born Again and New Woman couldn't be explained, even by the shaman.

The women and girls went to the river to wash. After quick splashes with biting water, Ashan sent the others upriver for pond reed shoots, late winter's first green. The gatherers could do without their Moonkeeper, whose mind was full of spiders spinning questions instead of webs.

Her heart wanted to believe Tor lived. Why not Tor? Hadn't others survived?

Yet Ketral was sure they'd been rescued by Tor's *spirit*. If he was right, Tor was dead, and her sick grief must go on.

No! She was tired of pain. She wanted him *alive!*

She clung to her dream. If a spirit had done the rescuing, why had she seen a real man crawling on the ground?

Yes. She was certain: The hunters had been rescued by the *actual living Tor, not by some spirit*.

No, she wasn't certain of anything.

She shook her head. The Moonkeeper needed to speak with spirits. Why did she always think of it last?

The burial ground was the best place to hear them. Ashan decided to go there with her questions.

The clouds opened when she reached the sacred ground. Sun sparkled on the grass.

Tor's heart jumped to his throat! *And I thought I could live without her!*

Dew covered the ash he'd scattered in the night. Lost in thought, Ashan didn't notice it under her feet as she walked up the slope to the large green stone she'd dragged there when they were little ones. Tor remembered offering to help, but she'd refused—if it was too big to carry, she had said, it wasn't the right one for her. She'd surprised him by doing it.

Ashan settled on the stone that would someday mark her grave and looked out over the burial ground of their ancestors. The white catskin slipped from her shoulders as she stretched—like a waking cougar in the bright winter sun, it seemed to Tor. A breeze played with her hair. Eyelids fluttered in her tipped-up face, then closed. Slender hands drifted into her lap and crossed palms up at the wrists.

This was not the first time Tor had hidden breathless watching her slip into a trance. She cleared her throat, and he knew she'd soon know nothing outside her mind.

When this time came, when she was as still as her gravestone, Tor circled his prey with cougar's stealth.

Within a leap behind her, he unfolded the skin of the new-killed bear, thinking again it was a sure sign of spirit approval. Another sign: Ashan should have noticed its stink, but she didn't.

With the bearskin in both hands and a coiled horsetail rope in his teeth, Tor sprang.

He had her! He whipped the rope around the bearskin full of thrashing woman, slung it over his shoulder and ran. She was wrapped so tight that her struggles were a pitiful effort. Her muffled screams would not be heard.

Tor ran and ran, lungs bursting from demand, heart bursting with joy, ever further from their home, toward Warmer and another tabu land . . . the mountains of Snake Men.

The Shahala would not follow them there.

When it slammed her, Ashan was a butterfly floating on her trance, breath and heart slowed, waiting for spirits to come—

She was hit and swallowed, like the prey of a snake.

Like in a dream, her shrieks made only the smallest sound.

Like a dream, she thought.

No, like death.

But Ashan still *felt*: crushing pain; smothering stink; jouncing darkness. Her nostrils were smashed shut; her lungs barely worked from squeezing. It didn't matter; there wasn't enough air in here.

Not enough air . . .

Her mind fogged and blackened. Ashan knew no more.

Too soon, knowing came back. Death by swallowing wouldn't be quick. The dark was complete, the smell worse—her own vomit mixed with the stinking slime of the beast's belly. She couldn't move anything, except toes and fingers, and her neck just a bit. How long had it been this way? *A long time*, answered her crushed body. She thought of her time ball, mashed around her waist in its doeskin bag . . . stone beads on grass twine . . . more and more added over the seasons, until those trapped in the center must feel like this.

She wished for black to come forever.

Fight, you mouse of a Moonkeeper!

Shala was with her, angry as a she-bear. Ashan knew *one* of her ideas was wrong: She hadn't been snatched by a spirit, as in the blackness she'd dreamed.

No. Whatever had her was a living thing.

She struggled as Shala said, but it was hopeless.

Her mind sorted out the smell: uncured bearskin. A bear's stomach must smell like its skin.

No! She remembered the bear who'd killed her mother—big, but not big enough to swallow a whole woman.

Ashan knew there were creatures she'd never seen. Stories from the Misty Time told of huge animals who'd once lived. She'd been swallowed by one left over from the Misty Time—what else could it be?—something that smelled like bear, but was much larger; something that jounced as if running . . .

The joucing stopped. Her shoulder screamed as it hit the ground. She was dragged over stones, and it hurt!

Something had eaten the bear! Something even bigger!

Amotkan! Let me die!

Movement stopped. The creature must have sat down to digest its meal of bear and woman. Terrified, Ashan was still as her time ball, or a thing already dead. She heard chopping and dragging, then she was lifted and placed on something stretchy, like the hammock of moosehide straps she used in good weather.

The moving started again—different now. She swayed like a deer slung on a pole between the shoulders of hunters, but the swaying was full of bumpy shocks.

Suddenly Ashan knew: She was wrapped in bearskin, dangling between travel poles.

The man-eaters had come. The Shahala Moonkeeper, useless with grief for a lost lover, had been sacked up and carried away.

It didn't take sight to know where she was going.

The scream that started up her throat was smothered by retching. Vomit pooled around her cheek. She turned her neck to a hurtful position to get her nostrils out of it.

Man-eaters were taking her to their home, far from Shahala land. She'd be helpless like this for two days . . . if she lived that long . . . then . . .

She knew what they did with men. The Men Born Again were glad to share every detail of what it meant to be food.

What would man-eaters do with a woman?

For a moment, Ashan was glad strange-talking Kalatash hadn't said much she understood. But New Woman's eyes had spoken of horror beyond imagining.

Ashan's knowing slipped away and came back over and over. Moments or days passed. Each time her knowing returned, it was weaker and left sooner. She thought she might be allowed to die before they got where they were going.

They? Ashan wondered. She hadn't heard a word, not once.

Were man-eaters a people who did not speak? No. The Men Born Again told of their noisy village.

Am I captive of a single man?

The swaying stopped. So numb she barely felt it, Ashan touched the ground. It felt good to stop moving . . . she could go to sleep . . . maybe for the last time.

She felt the bearskin loosen. Breathing eased, and brought sharp knowing back. Hot pain stabbed as she struggled to unfold. With heart full of fear, she pushed the bearskin away.

The moon shone bright in unfamiliar sky. Freezing air swept her face.

She was alone! And free! But where?

The moon showed scattered bushes and ankle-deep snow, and the travel poles she'd been dragged with. Someone had cleared a spot, built a fire, and left leathermeat and a water pouch. She knew better than to take anything from a captor— it could be poisoned with something to rob her of her fight.

Ashan fell when she tried to stand, so she crawled away. The slashes of travel poles in the snow were easy to follow. Her legs strengthened as she scrabbled along, and soon she could run.

The moon went behind a cloud. She cursed Alhaia for quitting on her!

Ashan splashed through water she hadn't seen coming, then stopped and ran back to it. The stupidest savage could follow her disgusting scent. In the shallow trickle of a stream, she washed bear guts and vomit from herself and her clothes.

Smelling new again, she ran on. Somewhere in a place of trees, she lost the trail of the travel poles. Bare above her wet deerhide skirt, her skin burned with cold. Her feet were beyond feeling. She didn't know where she was. She would freeze to death whether she kept stumbling, or quit.

There came the chilling sounds again . . . sounds feared by people since time before remembering. She shut her ears.

She was so sleepy.

Ashan stumbled, and slumped against a tree.

Distant howls moved closer, no longer to be ignored. Wolves wouldn't attack someone with fight in them, but Ashan had almost none left. She told herself to welcome death by wolves. They'd be quick; they went for the throat. She waited with closed eyes. The predators talked as they came—sad moans, happy yips, hungry growls.

Then silence.

Ashan opened her eyes.

Eyes alive with their own yellow light circled her.

She wailed as resignation turned to terror.

Beyond the evil eyes, a screaming orange glow flew out of the night. The yellow eyes turned, winking out. The charging light took the shape of a man with a grass-fired torch. The wolves fled yelping like dogs.

As her rescuer came toward her, terror and fascination paralyzed Ashan. He glowed large in the shimmering torchlight, his face hidden in its center so she couldn't make out his features.

She'd never seen a spirit, but what else could it be!

She fainted.

Tor dropped the torch and gathered limp Ashan in his arms.

Dear Amotkan! She's too cold!

There was no time to make fire, but Tor was hot from running. Ashan must have his heat or die!

Kicking snow away, Tor used their clothes to make a bed on the ground. He lay Ashan on her back and spread himself over her, softly at first, his hot skin covering every bit of her icy skin. His hair fell over her as he kissed her frozen face. Biting wind raked his naked back, but he didn't care.

Warmth grew between them. Tor thought that she would live.

Ashan's breathing evened, then became ragged in a different way. Small sounds came from her throat. She began to move beneath him as a lover. His body moved with her, not asking his mind. He grew hard. Even though he understood he was taking advantage of her, he couldn't help it.

Tor was just a man, and men are greedy, needing more food, more danger, more mating.

Ashan's flesh burned. To be warm was the most delicious feeling a human could know, and if the source was another body, so much the sweeter. She dared not open her eyes. She'd die if he left her.

The being of light and warmth lying on her was not human, no, but a spirit come for his bride, Ashan, Whispering Wind, Shahala Moonkeeper. The Spirit of Tor—behind closed eyes, she knew his scent and taste, and the feel of his muscles molding around her. Their bodies stirred. The spirit's power grew hard between them. He wanted to make love. Ashan wanted the power inside, where once Tor had been, but the spirit loved more slowly than the man, making her wait, driving her beyond frenzy with want. She thought she might die from pleasure, and what would it matter? Ashan and Tor, soulmates, were together.

Afraid to end the ecstasy, afraid to look on the face of a spirit, she kept her eyes closed. When she could stand no more, his heat flooded her and they flew as eagles into the sun. Her body pulsed with scorching waves. She would never be cold again.

He lay over her for a long time afterward, a light weight breathing heavily. Then he picked her up in his arms and began walking.

Ashan never did open her eyes. She pretended to be sleeping as the spirit carried her, and soon it was true.

CHAPTER
20

Ashan shivered with pleasure as waking began.

Dear Amotkan! She hadn't known a spirit could make love to a human! She must have died and gone to the otherworld!

But . . . why would there be bearstink in the otherworld? Or the all-too-human scent of Tor?

Full awakening struck. Ashan was under a bearskin with her lover—warm and naked, arms and legs entangled. He breathed slowly and deeply, a satisfied smirk on his face.

She'd been kidnapped by Tor, not a man-eater! Then tricked into lovemaking!

"You're no spirit!" she screamed, shoving him away.

Tor's eyes flew open.

Ashan burned with humiliation, shook in an earthquake of rage. She pounced on him, fingernails slashing, teeth tearing his hateful *human* face.

"Animal!" she shrieked. "You're dead!"

He grabbed her wrists in one hand and jerked her up.

"Stop!" he shouted in her face.

She drove her knee between his legs, into the ugly thing dangling there. He'd never use that again!

Tor howled, but he didn't let go. He slapped Ashan to her

knees, tied her wrists with a leather strap and shoved her down on the bearskin.

He clutched his groin, barely able to stand.

"What's wrong with you?" he whined, his face ugly with bleeding scratches. "Last night you couldn't get enough of me!"

"You pretended to be a spirit!"

"Bat dung! I saved your life! Do you remember wolves?"

"Better the Moonkeeper be eaten by wolves than be entered by a filthy dung-beetle of a *man*!"

He snorted. "You want to be wolf-food, Ashan? I'll take you back and tie you to the tree where I found you! As soon as you cook!"

"I'd rather eat dirt than cook for you!"

"All right! Tor and the woman he loves will starve together!"

Ashan used her coldest voice: "You can starve me or beat me senseless, but it won't change this: I hate your spirit, Tor! I will hate it forever!"

He heaved a deep sigh. "Bigger things have changed."

Ashan controlled her rage. Tor must have been as crazy as one who ate speckled red mushrooms to kidnap the Moonkeeper. Next to an angry spirit, a crazy man was hardest to deal with—she couldn't think like him to figure out what he'd do. Even fear, her best weapon, might not work. But it was the only weapon she had.

"Don't you know you're going to die for this?"

"You're wrong. Our brothers will not come here."

"Not your brothers, dung-face! You've stolen the Bride of Spirits! Do you think they will let you live?"

"I don't fear what I don't believe in."

How could anyone *not* believe in spirits? She pretended she hadn't heard it.

"Take me back and I'll ask them to show you mercy."

He laughed. "You're never going back. That life is done. Your new life is Tor. Your new home will be Chiawana, Mother River, the place of my dreams. And in time, you will be Moonkeeper of a great new people."

His certainty, and finality, struck her like a blow. She couldn't think. When she spoke, there was no power in it.

"Our people will die with no Moonkeeper."

"Don't be so fat with your own importance. Our people will manage."

"I will kill you while you sleep."

Tor laughed like a man gone mad as he tied Ashan's bound wrists to the long horsetail rope, and tied that around his waist.

"Get up. We're going."

She would not move. He began dragging her, then stopped. *Good*, she thought, *I'll wear him out.*

Red with anger, Tor strode back and slapped her until her cheeks burned and her brains rattled.

When he started walking again, she plodded after him. He looked like an evil spirit with the bearskin over his back—a beast with a man's head. The snow deepened as they headed into mountains. Clouds hid the sun. Ashan couldn't tell what direction they were going. With only her skirt and moccasins, she was freezing, but she'd rather be food for a man-eater than say one word to Tor. Whenever he looked back, she made her face ugly with hate.

The sky turned darker gray as night neared. Ashan's numb skin was the blue-white of fish belly. Breathing was like sucking in porcupine quills. She was exhausted when Tor finally stopped under a rock overhang.

He put the bearskin down and pointed. She glared at him and plopped on bare ground.

"So freeze," he said, tying the rope that held her hands to a bush rooted in rock. "I'm going for wood."

The moment he was out of sight, Ashan brought her bound hands to her teeth and began working at the knots. But he'd only gone far enough to hide and watch.

She cringed as he strode toward her. He retied her hands—behind her, very tight—and left again.

Too worn out to fight, Ashan gave in to tears. At first, she wept in hatred for Tor and pity for herself. Then she wept for her people. Each sob had a wretched Shahala face and was made of a ripped-out piece of the Young Moonkeeper's heart.

Of this, there was no doubt: The Shahala would perish without a shaman-chief who knew the ways, and Raga had long since given up.

About the rest of the world, Ashan wasn't sure. Raga believed the death of the last Moonkeeper—who kept the

Balance between Light and Dark—meant the end of everything, but that didn't make sense to Ashan. Amotkan must be smarter than to create all this, then entrust it to a single woman. The Shahala were the favored people, but not the only people in the world. There were probably other shamans of other tribes who could speak with spirits. Then again, she might be wrong.

But this, I know: The Shahala will perish without a Moon-keeper.

Racking sobs tore her apart.

It was near full darkness when Tor came back. She turned her face, but too late. He saw her shameful weeping, dropped his armload of wood and started toward her.

"I never wanted to hurt you!"

She let him untie her. Then she snarled, baring her teeth. He backed away.

Kneading her hands, Ashan glared at him . . . nostrils flared, lips pulled back over clenched teeth in the most fearsome look she knew . . . a look that would melt any Shahala man, woman or child to a puddle of mud. Her eyes hurled icicles of murderous intent.

Tor should have quaked and gone white with terror, but he just stood there staring at her. Did he question her power as he questioned the existence of spirits?

Or did he simply lack the sense to be afraid?

Keeping his eyes on her, shaking his head, looking completely confused, Tor picked up the scattered wood, squatted on his heels and made fire.

He sighed. "I don't understand you, woman. How could you love me last night and hate me today?"

Having seen that he could be stupid as dirt, Ashan could almost believe he *didn't* understand.

The fire sparkled on shiny specks in the rock around and over them. Its warmth felt good, but she didn't show it.

Tor opened a painted horseskin sack, the only thing he had besides the bearskin and his spear. He held up brown-red flesh, smiling nervously.

"Meat from the back of the bear. There wasn't time to take more. I only brought this so I'd have something special for you. Will you cook it for us?"

Ashan spat on the meat, then turned her head so his slap

wouldn't hurt so much. But he didn't hit her. He ate some raw, and offered her a piece.

"Stinking savage!" she said, flinging another gob of spit.

He laughed. "You call *me* a savage, you daughter of a spitting snake?"

In fine spirits, he finished eating. He tied each of Ashan's wrists to a bush at her side. With slack in the rope, she could lie down, but couldn't bring her hands together to work at the knots.

Now, she thought, *he'll force himself on me.*

He tossed the bearskin at her and crawled to the other side of the fire.

"Sleep in peace, snake-daughter."

Ashan seethed with rage and wounded pride. Tor could *not* make her cook, could *not* make her eat. He could take her in her sleep if he wanted to, but he couldn't make her get under the stinking bearskin. She kicked it away. Sometime in the night, she pulled it close.

It snowed with fury for two days. The rock overhang kept them from being buried. Tor kept a small fire burning, and talked without stopping.

Ashan huddled under the bearskin and acted as if he weren't there.

How could she have thought she loved him? Or thought him the smartest man in the tribe? Never had she been so wrong! She hated him more than the Ice Spirit who took the lives of sleeping babies! The fool had stolen her without the simplest plan. No food but two hunks of bearmeat. Almost no clothes. He said he was taking her to some river he dreamed of, but they couldn't travel like this, not in strange mountains in winter.

Even Tor realized it. He told her many times how sorry he was it had to be this way.

On the third snowy day, he left Ashan with her wrists tied to the bushes. He brought back a bighorn ram, skinned it, cut it and hung pieces over the fire. It was five days since she had eaten. The smell of cooking overcame pride. When he held some out, dripping fat and juice, Ashan knew she wasn't brave enough to die of hunger with food in front of her. She tore into it like a savage. Tor watched with delighted eyes as she gobbled piece after piece, until she fell asleep with fullness.

In the morning, Tor untied Ashan's hands and offered her cold cooked meat.

She took it, realizing that starving herself was no answer—a dead Moonkeeper couldn't help her tribe.

What *could* she do?

She remembered Raga's words about men: "The weakest man is stronger than the strongest woman, but the stupidest woman is smarter than the smartest man. Use your strength against their weakness."

Tor's greatest weakness? Blind, sick love.

He brought her the ramhide and a pouch with the animal's brainflesh.

"Work this. I'll beat you if you refuse."

Ashan put on a look of meekness, and held the ramhide up to find the place to start chewing.

"Cut a cape for each of us," he said, tossing his knife at her feet.

His knife! Yesterday, she'd have grabbed it and gone for his belly! But now she could wait for a better time. With Tor's weakness, she'd be free soon enough—and not dead in the effort.

Ashan peeled the ramhide and cleaned it with Tor's black-stone scraper, which was too big and hurt her hands. She chewed and stretched, rubbed in brainflesh and fat, then pegged it to the rock wall to heat by coals. The Shahala Moonkeeper did not work skins, but she had watched other women, never knowing how disgusting it is to chew fresh hide. Pride made her do a perfect job: The warm capes were soft on the inside, with long, pale-gray fur outside. They fit the shoulder's curve, and closed with thongs at the chest.

Ashan tried to be friendlier. Tor seemed thrilled when she talked to him, but still he kept her tied. He took her outside to tend to her body needs, looking the other way. He slept alone by the fire, making no attempt to touch her.

Though Ashan wore the look of a caught rabbit, her fire of hatred raged. When it waned, she remembered all that Tor had caused.

She thought again about his man-weakness. Neither fear

nor friendliness worked against him, but Ashan knew one other thing that would.

That night as he settled by the fire, she spoke softly.

"Make love to me."

He scrambled to her.

She took him under the bearskin, clenched her teeth and endured until he finished and collapsed.

When he breathed like a wintering bear, she wormed out from under him, crept to his sleeping place, and found his knife in the horseskin sack. Firelight sparkled on the blue chert blade. The leather haft felt good in her hand.

Ashan's heart flamed with hatred as she stood over Tor, staring at his fire-shadowed back. *Do it!* said Shahala voices in her clear, cold mind. *Kill him!*

Focusing on his heart side just below the shoulder, she gripped the knife in both hands and raised it high.

Something fluttered deep inside her . . . something she'd never felt. Not rage, not hate, not any kind of passion, but . . .

. . . Life?

Again . . . a caress of butterfly wings . . .

Life!

Ashan dropped the knife. Eyes round as moons, she stared at her belly, touching it with her fingertips. It was quiet now, but she could not deny the feeling.

Dear Amotkan! Why didn't you tell me it was a baby?

It cannot be a baby! It takes a mate to have a baby! The Moonkeeper doesn't have a mate!

Then what was it?

A wail tore out of her. She wrapped her arms around herself, swaying, seeing nothing through a flood of tears.

Tor reached out. "What is it?"

"Leave me alone!" She shoved him away, pulled the bearskin over her head, and cried herself to sleep.

Ashan's dreams that night were a jumbled mess, seething with love, hate, and everything between.

In a dream she held her own perfect baby . . . boy or girl, she didn't know, it didn't matter. Petal-soft skin smelled like sun-warmed dew. Tiny lips found her nipple. Love flowed from and to her, sweeter than she'd ever dared hope, as she fulfilled the desire all women are born with.

Then she dreamed of Tor, her lover; adoring father of her

child. He changed into Tor, the trickster who stole her; evil spirit in human flesh who destroyed his people.

In a dream of the tribe, Raga was as useless as fleas. Ashan saw the light of life go out in each doomed Shahala face. There was no survival without a Moonkeeper, but she knew her people would rather die than follow a chief who was also a mother.

In the morning, the butterfly fluttered again.

Ashan had to face it: The impossible had happened; the Shahala Moonkeeper was carrying a child. If this could happen, what else might?

CHAPTER
21

Birth was joyful for the Shahala, proof of Amotkan's promise that the life of the tribe would continue. The Moonkeeper was the first to touch new life. Raga loved that part. Each perfect birth confirmed the shaman's worth, and the love of spirits, and the value of every Shahala soul.

But not all births were perfect.

This day in the Shahala winter village of Anutash, Tisu's fourth child had much against it as it struggled to be born. No Moonkeeper waited to welcome it. In deep mourning since Ashan's disappearance, Raga had refused to come . . . even though winter was the worst time to be born: The Ice Spirit was hungry for tender little souls and often stole winter babies.

On its way into the world, Tisu's child became stuck in her womb. The women didn't know what to do, but they knew mother and baby might die without help. Finally, Tisu's sister Inra ran to the Moonkeepers' hut. Raga, who hadn't left her bed in almost half a moon, did not want to go. Inra fell on her knees, weeping, begging, pounding the dirt. She jerked out a handful of her short hair and held it out to Raga.

"All right!" Raga said. "Go so I may dress!"

Babbling, sobbing, Inra backed out.

As Raga approached the women's hut, she smelled a cloud

162

of sour fear hanging over it. From the cloud came unhearable sound, like future keening. The tired old woman stopped for a moment and took deep breaths.

Inra opened the doorskin. "Please hurry!"

Raga steadied herself and stepped inside. Women parted to let the Moonkeeper pass, their panic striking her like invisible lightning.

Tisu hung over the birth log—limp, pale, wet with sweat.

"How long?" Raga asked.

"Since she awoke this day," Inra said.

Tisu looked up. She looked near death. Her eyes were pain, her voice a grunt. "Hurts . . . too . . . bad . . ."

Raga said, "I know. The baby needs a piece of your soul for life. It hurts, but the sharing binds you forever. This must be a special child to want so much of you."

A birth pain gripped the exhausted mother. Raga knelt and embraced her hot, convulsing body.

"Hold back, Tisu," the Moonkeeper said. "Don't push."

The pain released Tisu. Raga reached inside her womb. The baby's backside was where its head should be. Reaching up, Raga pulled the legs into the birth tunnel in front of the buttocks. The next pain brought a pushing that finally moved the legs and body out. The Moonkeeper again reached inside, shifting the arms along the outsides of the chest. Now only the head remained, and if it too was not delivered, the baby would die.

"Get a sling to hold the child's weight," Raga said, and one of the women did.

Raga slipped two fingers in the baby's mouth and pulled. Tisu gave a last giant push. The head of a tiny girl slipped out. She scrunched up her face and howled without being slapped.

A sigh of relief escaped the women.

Raga cut the birth cord with the red agate blade she used for chopping herbs, and wondered about the mother-child bond. The special white blade that should have been used— a gift in the Misty Time from Alhaia the moon to Shakana the First Woman—had been lost with Ashan.

As Raga looked at the baby, she saw the third bad omen attending this birth: On her neck, below her ear, the baby bore a dark red mark shaped·like a leaf, or a fish, or a blade.

The Moonkeeper didn't know the meaning of the shape. It was just one more question unasked and unanswerable in the Time of Sorrows that grew ever more sorrowful.

The sacred burial ground near Anutash was the best place for speaking with spirits, and Raga knew that it was long past time. Alone there on the gray-sky morning of the marked child's birth, she hunkered down beside her gravestone—a large, shiny-black chunk that brought to mind a raven's wing. Wind stung her face. Though it hadn't rained for several days, the ground was winter-wet. The Old Moonkeeper barely noticed.

Sometimes I think I'm the tiredest creature alive, Raga thought, sighing deep and sad.

She felt more than bad enough to weep, but she didn't do that anymore. She had no tears left. They'd all been cried when the Time of Sorrows had begun and her people had died off like spiders at first frost. She finally found a way to turn her tears back, but it had turned her cold and dead inside.

If only I had my girl! Raga's throat closed. *Her that I loved best!*

"Spirits!" she cried, finally breaking through her shell to ask for help. "Why couldn't I have died before you took my Ashan?"

Spirits were quick to answer in her mind.

The world is changing. The Shahala are not prepared.

"Then we are doomed without our Moonkeeper?"

You are the Moonkeeper. That is why you still live.

"But Ashan . . . does she live? Will she come back?"

Raga's mind was silent, empty. She shook her fists at the sky. "Please! You must tell me what became of her!"

But the spirits had gone.

Raga crumpled—a lump of boneless flesh. She thought that the pain of not knowing was worse than if she'd seen the dead body of her spirit daughter. Death could eventually be accepted. But no one knew what had happened to Ashan. They only knew she hadn't been killed by animals, for that would have marked the earth with blood or bone. Had she run away? Been kidnapped? Whisked away by spirits?

Raga picked up the only clue—three pieces of wood that had been found after Ashan disappeared. Two of the pieces were thin as a finger, perfectly straight, the end of one sharply pointed and blackened with fire. These two had once been one. Most people thought it was a broken spear—though it seemed useless as a weapon, too small and weak to kill anything; too light to be thrown straight—unless the third piece had something to do with that. It was grooved at one end, and notched, and sized to fit nicely in the hand. Ketral had said it could be a man-eater weapon, and he wanted to try it. Just the word *man-eater* brought such fear to the people that the Old Moonkeeper had said no . . . it was bad medicine and should be left by her burial stone where it had been found.

Raga absently stroked the alien wood, but there were no answers in it. She was afraid that she would never know what had become of Ashan.

The Young Moonkeeper had last been seen at the river— Raga had a hard time remembering how long it had been. Ashan had sent the women to gather pond reed shoots, then vanished as if into the air. At first the people thought she'd gone walking alone, as Moonkeepers do. When she didn't come home by dark, they thought she had journeyed to the spirit world to plead for her desperate people. They began searching—it was dangerous for the Young Moonkeeper to be alone at such a time—but found only some scuffle marks by her gravestone. And the strange pieces of wood. On the fourth day, hopelessness set in: A shaman never died for more than three days, unless it was her *last* death.

The people thought Raga knew what had become of Ashan, and what would happen to them. They couldn't understand why their Moonkeeper refused to tell them.

Raga knew nothing but this: She loved the girl far more than she ever had dreamed. *Ashan* . . .

The Old Moonkeeper hadn't cried all her tears after all. They spilled in a torrent to her robe, blending with the stains of new life brought into the world this day. Gulping sobs ripped her like swallowed knives. Hot tears felt like the bleeding of her soul. The flood went on and on until her body had no more water. But that didn't stop the racking; the dry sobs hurt worse than the wet. Raga wept until she ached like one run over by bison, until her guts were raw.

When it was over, the Old Moonkeeper was a rag lying on the ground, with no more thought than a rag has. At dark, she allowed herself to be led back to the village, supported on the shoulders of unnoticed men.

Still Raga had no real answers to her questions, but at least she had asked them. And she had stayed awake all day.

The healing of tears had begun.

CHAPTER
22

Warriors live by knowledge of unspoken messages all around. The messages in the tabu mountains of Snake Men told Tor it was time to move on—he wouldn't find Mother River while hiding under a rock. Pale blue sky said the next storm was far away. Deep snow covered everything outside their shelter, but Tor smelled spring waking beneath it.

There were messages from Ashan, too, but they couldn't be trusted: She had invited lovemaking while planning to kill him—he knew because he found the knife she had dropped. How could anyone, especially a Moonkeeper, be so stupid? Tor's death would mean her own—frozen, starved, or caught by Snake Men.

Stupid, stupid woman! But he saw no purpose in punishing her, not even reason to keep her tied. Something had happened to her. She was silent now, the dangerous spark gone from her eyes, dull heaviness where fight had been.

Much was not meant for men to understand. Women, as Arth taught his sons, were the Creator's greatest mystery; might as well ask why sky is blue and leaves are green, instead of the other way around.

Tor had better things to do than try to make sense of a woman. *Get on with it!* he told himself. *Find the great river*

*and new tribe! Too bad about mountains, winter, and the
cougar-snake-woman who could love you or kill you, de-
pending on her mood.*

Tor packed what little they had and led silent, stumbling
Ashan from the rock overhang that had sheltered them for
half a moon. They headed higher into the mountains, ever
farther from Shahala land, toward Warmer, where Tor knew
Mother River waited for her children.

The wanderers had blue sky, but the sun didn't melt the
shin-deep snow. The going was slow. Tor was right about
one thing: He didn't need to tie his captive. She followed in
the trench he stamped out, meek as a baby quail.

He would *never* understand her! People stayed who you
thought they were, but not Ashan! He couldn't count all
the creatures she was! Passionate lover. Murderous cougar.
Medicine woman. Mother of little ones and chief of a new
tribe . . . in his dreams.

Of all the Ashans Tor had known in his sixteen summers,
this unseeing, unfeeling lump was the worst. She seemed
gone from the world of living people. It scared him. What if
she never came back?

When night came, Tor was almost sorry he'd left the rock
overhang. There was nowhere safe to sleep. He settled for a
juniper tree whose branches hung to the ground, except on
one side where deer had bedded. Ashan lay on the skins he
put down with her back to him, and Tor stretched out beside
her. Careful not to touch her, he pulled the bearskin over
them. Her warmth caused thoughts of lovemaking that he
chased away with thoughts of wormy meat.

They walked for days up the slopes of the juniper-covered
mountain range, making slow time in ever-deeper snow. Tor
didn't know how large the world was, but they'd walked a
lot of it. He was sure they must be nearing Mother River.
Still, he had to fight thoughts of mountains going on forever.

Nights were cold and uncomfortable. Though Tor saw no
sign of Snake Men, or anyone, he hated sleeping in unprotected places.

Worse, he had no idea what to say to his silent mate.

One day they came upon a noisy river, swollen with snow-
melt and angry about it, strewn with water-beaten boulders
too far apart for crossing. Tor was bewildered. His dreams

had shown nothing like this in the way. They followed the angry torrent all day, going far out of the way.

Finally he saw the answer.

"This will have to do," Tor said, pointing to a tangle of wood that stretched across the rushing water.

He must be crazy!

Ashan stared at the beaver dam—brave or stupid, barely holding its own against the mean-spirited river, nothing but a jumble of sticks and tree trunks with pointed ends, stripped of branches by the toothy animals who lived inside. In kinder moons, there'd be a calm, wide pool behind the home of the beaver tribe, but now white water swept over everything.

Ashan shook her head so hard that her whipping hair stung her cheeks. She found her voice for the first time in days.

"No!"

"Please . . . we must!"

"No, I said!" She hoped he wouldn't try to force her.

"I'll go first, then you take my hand."

"I will not!"

Tor shrugged. On hands and knees, he crawled out onto the beaver dam—slow, careful and light. He tested each handhold by trying to wiggle it apart. A piece that seemed safe broke loose when he put weight on it. Caught by the angry torrent, the limb shot downstream.

Ashan shrieked.

Dropping to his belly, Tor shouted, "Don't worry! I promise it will hold!"

How like a man to promise what isn't his!

He crept toward her and reached out.

"Come." It was a command.

"I'm not going out on that thing!"

"Don't make me drag you."

His hard voice and tight face said that he would. Ashan had to believe it. Choking down terror, trying to be numb again, she gave him one hand, praying silently to Shala to protect the baby inside. Tor's grip was strong, his pull steady, but every slippery thing Ashan touched shifted. The wood groaned. Freezing water beat on her skin. The river's mind-numbing roar awakened awful memory—battling Yuna, choking, dying!

"No," she whimpered, "the baby . . ."

She twisted out of Tor's grip and scuttled backward.

He lunged for her.

"Asha—"

Cra-a-a-ck!

A monstrous noise swallowed his voice. The dam that had taken too much broke apart like a bird's nest smashed against a rock. The water tore it to pieces and swept it, and Tor, away. Noise deafened Ashan, terror pounded her brain to flour, as she scrambled for the bank, her only thought the baby . . . *the baby could have been killed!* She reached solid earth and lay there gasping, "Please please please be alive!"

By the time she could breathe again, and think, the sun and its warmth had gone. The beaver dam was gone. Tor was gone. Ashan was a nearly-drowned thing spit out at the last moment.

She was finally free of her kidnapper. But free meant alone . . . wet . . . sure to freeze tonight. No one would ever know that a woman and her unborn baby had died beside this unnamed torrent.

What could be sadder? she wondered, and it came to her.

Tor . . . He'd done terrible deeds, but all because of love. Any other woman would give everything for such love. Ashan loved him still, of course she did, no matter what he had done.

And now he was dead. Or should she say, dead again?

The spirits were especially cruel to some people. Ashan had grieved for him once already, suffered enough to kill anyone else. But it was all a trick. The spirits had given him back, just to take him again. By the pain welling up, she knew she'd have to grieve all over.

Just as well she die, here and now!

But the new Ashan—Ashan the almost-mother—could not just lie here and die. She got up, and found the man who was in many ways her mate, not far downstream, caught in a tangle of wood jammed against a water-beaten boulder in the middle of the river. His head and one arm floated. He looked dead. The woman in love wanted to shut her eyes and shriek, but her twin the chief found a hooked branch and pulled her hope for survival from the water.

Tor was barely alive—icy pale, breathing slow pink froth,

aware of nothing. Blood flowed from a deep hole in his chest. Ashan stopped it with a handful of moss. The horseskin sack—its painted designs washed to memory—was still around his waist. She untied it, found his knife, and cut fresh cedar branches. She took off her cape and skirt and laid them out for a bed. Rolling limp, unknowing Tor onto it, Ashan covered him with her naked body, and brought cedar branches over them like the earth on a grave.

In spite of her exhaustion, Ashan stayed awake through the night, watchful as a warrior protecting his tribe.

Morning found the soulmates alive, and warm. Tor breathed more of heavy sleep than dying. Ashan had to think—no, talk with spirits—and she couldn't do that lying next to her lover. She shivered as she crawled out into the clear, cold air. She couldn't talk with spirits naked and freezing, either. With Tor's fire sticks from the horseskin sack, she started a glow in shredded bark, and soon had dry twigs crackling.

Moss hung from the trees like bundles of long gray hair. She pulled some down, wrapped herself, and sat staring into the fire. Shaking fear chased away thought. Then her baby fluttered, bringing calm. Ashan smiled and rubbed the small rise of her stomach.

"Thank you, little soulmate. More than once you've saved me from myself, and you aren't even born yet!"

Powerful beings were on their side, Ashan could not doubt it. The three of them had survived the impossible . . . so far. Continued survival was up to her now. She asked the powerful beings to stay.

They told her to think: What was lost and what was saved?

Lost—the bearskin that kept them warm at night; Tor's cape, loinskin, and one moccasin; dried meat; water pouches; the new grinding stone and bowl; the long horsetail rope; the heavy Shahala spear.

Lost—Tor's usefulness as hunter and protector.

Saved—the horseskin sack with its knives, scrapers and fire sticks; Ashan's clothes and medicine pouch, with its needle, herbs, time ball, pledge bands.

Saved—a family bound beyond understanding, blessed with protection of powerful spirits.

After Tor stole her, Ashan stopped wearing the pledge

bond of the tribe, choosing to wear nothing at all, for she belonged to no one. Now she took Tor's pledge band from her pouch and tied it to her upper arm.

"We can survive," she said.

Ashan removed the cedar branches and blanketed Tor with dry moss. That should have awakened him, but it didn't. She took a pinch of sharp sage from her medicine pouch and crushed it under his nose. Gummy slits opened in his battered face. Cloudy eyes wandered. Love and pain choked her.

"Oh Tor . . ."

He blinked. His eyes cleared.

"Ashan?"

"Yes!"

He drifted away, and she gave him another whiff of sage. His eyes opened. His voice quavered with hope. "Baby?"

So he *had* heard it! And wanted to believe it.

There was no reason to lie, no reason to fight him anymore. Though there'd been no mating ritual for them, Tor was her mate, and she loved him! She'd never doubt it again.

Ashan took his hand and put it on her belly.

"Our baby," she said.

His smile was full of wonder. He closed his eyes in sleep— the medicine his beaten body needed most.

Ashan sat by her moss-covered mate, listening to his even breathing, smelling his scent. Calm filled her. The strange sense of not really being here was gone. Her thoughts were clear and stood in a line so she could look at them, take them apart and put them back together as a plan.

With his terrible injuries, Tor wouldn't be able to move for a long time. Staying by the angry river was the only thing to do. Rivers bring food. That might bring other people— evil people—but why waste strength thinking about what she couldn't change?

The first thing they needed was shelter. Ashan worked while Tor slept. The ground under a massive, nearby cedar was soft and free of snow. With pieces of the shattered dam, she made a small hut against the trunk. She covered the frame with fresh boughs, layering the fan-shaped needles to shed water and snow.

Tor screamed as she dragged him on her ramskin cape. It hurt Ashan to hurt him, but she had to get him inside.

The small space warmed with his gasping breath. He lost knowing, and she was glad that his torture would stop for a while. Dim light came through the opening. Ashan probed Tor's wounds. He had cuts and bruises everywhere, but they were like bug bites compared to the ragged hole in his chest. One of the beaver-sharpened trees must have tried to go through him. Through shredded muscle, she saw bone and torn pink stuff—very bad. She pulled the edges together, covered the wound with river-washed moss, and wrapped and tied leather strips cut from her skirt all around his chest to hold it in place.

Days and nights went by . . . Ashan didn't keep track of how many. Most of the time, Tor slept. When he was awake, the black centers of his eyes almost covered the dark brown. He babbled meaningless sounds. Ashan had once seen someone like this—a Shahala child with a cracked head who died after several days.

But Tor didn't die. When she changed the moss, Ashan wondered why. The fire-red, oozing hole in his chest looked worse every day. She wished she had spiderwebs to pack on it, but it takes a long time to gather enough, and she was afraid of leaving him. The sickness was inside him too. Stinking yellow-brown water came out both ends. Ashan didn't mind cleaning him, thankful for every moment he lived. She gave him a tonic of senna leaves and thornflower pods. She chanted over him. But most of her healing things—rattles to call spirits, throwing bones, powders for the fire—were in Anutash. She wondered if spirits heard her, and prayed that they did.

Ashan was so focused on her sick mate that she didn't feel hunger. But she must eat for the baby. Trusting spirits to watch over Tor, she left him alone in the tiny hut. Onion shoots, sweetfeathers, and fern heads were growing up along the riverbank; it was too early for anything else. She found a squirrel hole and stole its seed cache. Having no grinding stone, she chewed it, spat it out, and fed Tor.

Either spirits heard Ashan, or Tor was just a very strong man. The hole in his chest closed and scabbed. His skin turned from gray to brown. The yellow-waters stopped, and food stayed in him.

There were times when his mind was clear.

"How long has it been?" he asked one day.

"I don't know, but spring is near."

She took him outside to see the bright, hopeful green.

Ashan caught frogs and a turtle, but they needed better food. She made a sling; the stones it flung went wild. For a woman to use a spear seemed ridiculous; she didn't have one anyway. In the Misty Time, people had thrown rocks to kill their food. She tried it, and found that she was good! The day she knocked a flying squirrel out of a tree, she cried with pride all the way back to the hut. With onions and tender, curled fernheads, it made a fine stew in her new turtle-shell bowl.

Next she got a vulture, and the rabbit it was shredding. It wasn't bad; she didn't tell Tor they were eating carrion.

Ashan had become two different people who somehow lived in the same body. In the light of day as she hunted alone for food, terrible thoughts of the tribe stalked her. Who knew what would become of her people with no Moonkeeper? What would become of the world? There had always been a Moonkeeper, ever since Coyote made the First Woman.

Ashan ached to be with her people.

But was she willing to die? Sacrifice her baby? The swelling of motherhood could not be hidden forever. The Shahala would kill such evil. If Raga was still alive, she'd tell them to. Ashan herself would agree . . . if she was still Moonkeeper, and the child-carrying woman someone else.

Anyway, it was a waste of time to think of going home—she'd never get there without Tor, and why would the kidnapper take her back? Even if he agreed, it would be long before he could travel.

At times she thought of trying it on her own . . . thought of leaving him . . . to die.

But when the darktime came, when they held each other under a blanket of woven grass, Ashan knew she could never leave him, any more than she could leave herself, or the child not yet born.

Spring warmed the days. Tor progressed from lying in the tiny hut to sitting outside against a tree trunk, but he still didn't have enough breath for walking. Though she knew he was in pain, his words were all about happiness. And the baby . . . he talked on and on about his son, how he'd teach him to hunt and fight . . . or the daughter pretty as her mother, wise, wonderful and powerful, someday chief of a great new tribe.

Oh how Ashan loved him! Thank the spirits for saving him!

Nothing in life had made her happier than being here in the wildplace with Tor and the little soulmate growing inside. Pride and hope for a bright new life swelled in her.

Except when Shahala thoughts tortured her.

CHAPTER
23

One day Ashan realized the snow was gone; she hadn't even noticed it melting. Though she worked like a hive of bees—one animal of many parts—she could never find quite enough food, and Tor remained weak. Tempted to give it all to him, she made herself eat for the baby.

By the way belly overhung feet—she had to bend over to see her toes now—Ashan thought the child would come in about two moons.

Tor loved to hold his hand on her tight-stretched skin when the baby moved.

"It's a boy!" he'd boast. "No girl was ever this strong!"

Ashan just smiled . . . what he knew about women would fit on the nose of a flea.

The almost-mother used the evenings to prepare for the coming change. With bone needle and sinew thread, she joined the worked furs of soft little animals, and a blanket grew. She made tiny moccasins, cutting a small hole in the bottom of one. If the Ice Spirit came some night, the baby would say, "My moccasins are worn out—I can't go on a journey with you."

She started a cradleboard frame of thin, peeled maple branches, but Tor laughed when she showed him.

"Are you having a baby or a mouse?"

The cradleboard *was* too small, right for a little girl's doll. Feeling silly, she threw it in the fire and started again.

A little one's first bed should be lined with cougar fur—for softness, and for the cat's cunning and courage. But it was a joke to think of a woman killing such an animal. If she found nothing better, the cradleboard could be lined with a piece of her ramskin cape. At least there were thornflower bushes nearby for the hood that arched over the baby's head to protect it from bad spirits.

Too often, Ashan worried about bad spirits; about punishment for wrongful loving. In spite of her daily prayers for a healthy baby, knowing that mean or fearful thought can mark unborn skin, she worried anyway, and hoped the marks would be under the baby's hair.

Worry, worry, worry . . .

Often she awoke in sweat with a cry ready to jump from her lips at the terrible pictures she'd seen of her people dying without a chief. She tried to tell herself they were only dreams . . . ordinary dreams, not dreams of warning.

She thought all the time about being lost. She hated it! The Moonkeeper *always* knew where she was, by the sun or stars. Or by Pahto, the sacred mountain of her people, whose snow-shrouded peak could be seen from almost everywhere. But here in the wildplace, sun and stars told her nothing; scrub-pine mountains hid Pahto. Ashan did not know how to go back because she did not know where she had come from.

She worried about their miserable home—the small leaking hut out in the open by a river. What a terrible place for a new baby! It would be fine for a group of people who could protect each other, but a sick man and a child-carrying woman invited disaster. No animals or men had found them, yet. How long could such luck last?

Today Ashan felt like blaming Tor for everything, right down to the berry marks she pictured on their child's face—caused by its mother's worry, brought on by its father's rash deeds. But she remembered her own words to a woman whose mate had taken their son to the river, where he had fallen asleep and let the boy drown.

"There are times when I hate him!" Chuna had wept. "I think of killing him, who once I loved!"

The Young Moonkeeper had given ancient advice: "When

your mate does something that can't be fixed, don't waste strength on anger. Now you must come together. Shaptin will never need you more.''

Ashan shook her head. *Worry, worry, worry*, she thought. *It's all I ever do. My baby will be a mess of marks.*

She left her grump-faced mate and went to her power place by the river. Time there usually helped her feel better for a while.

A power place, called takoma, could only be found by a shaman's special wisdom. Raga said takomas were where high, invisible lines crossed . . . skytrails for spirits to use as men and women use earthtrails.

Ashan's power place didn't look special. A dip in the mossy riverbank cradled her back. Sometimes she trailed her feet in the water, but it wasn't warm enough today, so she tucked them under her skirt. Hidden by willows, she was close enough to the hut to keep one strand of her mind tied to Tor. All the rest she let loose to drift toward the sky.

This day, though everything looked the same, something was different. Ashan could not have said what, but it seemed *good*. Welcoming it as the soft moss welcomed her backside, she gazed into the sun-dappled, blue and green and black water. Its murmur was a soul caress. She closed her eyes, inhaling deeply the aromas of spring. As she had hoped, emptiness replaced worried thought. Silence and peace were sweet.

But it was only a little while before guilt intruded.

A Moonkeeper would do anything for her tribe—even die.

Ashan gave in to guilt's tears. She should have gone back to her people—at least tried! What was wrong with her?

The only thing stronger than a Moonkeeper's bond is a mother's.

Stunned, Ashan opened her eyes.

''A mother's bond,'' she whispered, then looked at the sky and said it again, fiercely.

''A mother's bond! For nothing and never will I betray it!''

Tingles ran under the skin of her face, and she knew . . . spirits were nodding with approval. It was time to accept what had happened to her . . . it made no difference that it was impossible. It was time to deal with reality.

Without dying, I've become someone else, Ashan realized. *Before, I was Moonkeeper, responsible for every Shahala life. Now, I am a mother, responsible for a single life not even named. This bond is stronger than the will to survive. It's the strongest thing on earth.*

For the first time, Ashan understood Shahala law forbidding the Moonkeeper to mate. The thing of real importance was that *the Moonkeeper not have children*. The conflict would tear her to pieces. The tribe would lose.

Ashan didn't know *why* the impossible had happened to her, but some powerful spirit, or a lot of them, had given her a baby—another soul—part of herself—to care for.

The old Ashan would do anything for her people. The new Ashan could do nothing to harm her almost-child.

The new Ashan still worried about her lost tribe, still grieved. But it was different now that she understood that it was not her fault, or Tor's.

It was the will of spirits. It had to be.

Ashan's new understanding of the mother-child bond gave her courage for a task she'd avoided: telling Tor about the death of his mother, Luka. The news saddened him, but didn't surprise him. He told Ashan of a dream he'd had in the man-eater's land, of his mother driven over a cliff by a stampeding herd of bison, of himself standing frozen, unable to help.

Tor had felt the breaking of the bond.

This was the sweetest day . . . warm, sunny, nature's laughter all around in bird song and flower scent. Ashan hummed, walking along the riverbank, farther downstream than she'd ever been. A new basket of cedarbark strips swung from her arm, looking more like a bird nest than a basket. She laughed at the old Ashan, the pampered girl who'd refused to learn basketmaking because it wasn't Moonkeeper's work . . . let others worry about small things like food, clothes and shelter . . . the Moonkeeper had *important* things to do, like sing to the wind and make bonfires for the moon. Not that these weren't important, but Ashan now realized the importance of the work of others—now that she had to do it all herself.

Well, her basket might be cause for laughter, but it did a good job of holding her morning's work—panku knobs dug

from the ground, several kinds of tender shoots, and a frog
. . . squashed because she'd used too large a rock, but meat
all the same.

Ashan came to a place where the river, still angry with too
much water, pushed out like a child-carrying woman's belly,
bending around an outcrop of tumbled shale on the other side.
The mossy bank was a good place to sit and rest; she could
see upstream and down. Her belly filled her lap. Blue sky,
fat buds, and fresh smells filled her soul. A prayer bubbled
out.

"Thank you, Amotkan, and all who love people! Thank
you for spring, for life old and new!"

Leaves rustled behind her. A small animal with red-gold
fur scampered to the river—some kind of squirrel with a
mouse's bare tail. It saw her, but showed no fear. She could
have thunked it with a rock, but why betray its trust? Today
was too nice a day to die.

"Hello . . ." What name to give it? ". . . Chumash, Naked-Tail Squirrel, a woman greets you . . . Ashan, Whispering Wind."

Watching her, Chumash nibbled purple flowers waving on
thin stems. Ashan tried one; it was sweet in the middle. She
picked some for Tor. She'd never seen this plant, but it
wouldn't surprise her to find medicine in it . . . for always,
animals taught people what was good to eat. It was the spirits'
way.

The strange-looking creature scampered off downstream,
stopping to eat more flowers, not knowing its luck that Ashan
allowed it to live.

All at once, she knew why: Watching Chumash, she saw
a miracle—Tor's horsetail rope, caught on a rock, trailing in
the water like a long-dead snake! Tor would be thrilled that
she'd found it! Like every hunter, he'd started it as a boy,
making it ever longer with the tails of horses he took. He had
felt worse about losing his rope than anything else!

Who-o-o-osh!

Feathers sliced air as a red-tail hawk swooped from the
sky. The naked-tail squirrel never made a sound as the hawk's
talons struck. The hawk screamed in triumph and rose with
its prey.

Open-mouthed, Ashan watched its flight . . . across the

river, in front of the outcrop, up . . . up to a small hole in a rock face above the tumbled shale.

Below the hole . . . a cave!

Shelter for the baby!

Ashan was so excited, she almost forgot Tor's horsetail rope. Pulling it from the water, she ran all the way back, not even stopping to coil it.

How big the cave was, she didn't know, but the mouth seemed tall enough for people to enter. She didn't know what the cave looked like inside, or how they'd cross the river . . . but she just knew it was their home.

Tor sat outside their crude little hut, yanking petals from a pinecone, flipping them into the dirt. His scowl told his mood, one she hated. He resented his woman for hunting, no matter that they'd starve if she didn't.

"Look, Tor! I found your rope!" She held it out.

Wonder swept his face, chasing away the winter-bear look. He took the rope and caressed it as if it was the softest female flesh.

"Oh Ashan . . . you don't know what this means to me! You couldn't have found anything to make me happier than this old friend!"

"I think I did, Tor!" A grin stretched her face; she could hardly keep from laughing.

"What?"

"I found our new home!"

"You did?"

"It's a cave, Sweetmate! It's high over the river. There's a slide of sharp, noisy rocks below. No one could sneak up on us!"

Tor's face lit up. He hated living in this dangerous place as much as she did.

"It's a very special place . . . a takoma," she said, though she hadn't stayed long enough to be sure. "I believe it is an omen . . . some kind of turning."

"I'm so proud of you, Ashan."

How sweet were his words and the look on his face. She prayed that the cave was as good as she was sure it must be.

Moving would be hard. Still weak and not breathing right, Tor would be little help. But Ashan didn't doubt that she'd find the way—her baby would be born in a decent place.

The biggest problem would be crossing the river. The water was deep and dangerous; boulders were far apart; the horsetail rope was too short. She prayed they wouldn't have to wait until summer drained the river of fury.

Ashan sat on the riverbank, looking up at the cave with a seeking mind. The answer was a long time coming.

The horsetail rope, she finally realized. *Make it longer*.

Tor had been making new tools. With a sharp blackstone axe, Ashan cut three young maples. Each was as thick as her wrist, and as long as one or two men. She stripped them of branches, and tied their ends together with her pledge bands. Now she had a three-part pole more than long enough to span the river. She tied the pole to the horsetail rope, and the rope to a good tree. They were the best knots of her life . . . she made sure of it as she let the thing out into the water. The current carried it down, and because of the bend in the river, across to the far side.

Ashan was pleased with herself for solving the problem, until she thought about trusting their lives to horsehair and sticks bouncing on furious water. But it was the best she could do, unless she wanted to wait for summer.

She took off her clothes and piled them on the bank to keep them dry, except moccasins—she'd need them to climb the rocks on the other side.

The icy water shocked her when she stepped in, but she ignored the cold and moved hand over hand along the rope, and then the poles; farther and farther until there was no bottom and the current took her feet; hand over hand on the slippery bark, fighting panicky memory with prayer, until her toes touched bottom on the other side.

"Yes!" she yelled, crawling out onto loose, sharp shale. Heart pounding, panting, she waited for the sun to dry her.

Bison dung! She'd forgotten about attaching the pole on this side. All she had were moccasins. She took them apart and used the thongs to tie the jointed pole to a rock, which she buried under more rocks. Now it would all stay in place for future crossings.

The loose shale was hard to climb with bare feet, and noisy. As she'd expected, chunks of rock clattered down.

Ashan pulled herself onto a shelf outside the cave's dark

mouth. She grinned . . . what a perfect spot for mother and baby to sit in morning sun! The mouth was lower than she'd thought. Very safe! Tor would be pleased! No one could come charging in while they slept.

She stooped to go inside. Bats spewed out! Lots of bats . . . flapping and chittering . . . after her hair to wrap up their babies, if a person believed the talk of old women. She threw her arms over her head and crouched, shuddering, until they were gone. No one liked bats—the face of a winged mouse was evil itself—but this was no real problem. The ugly things could be made to leave, or, better yet, be caught and eaten.

"Oh!" she said, standing up inside the cave. "Ohhh . . ."

In soft afternoon light, the cave looked as round as an oak fungus, as if Amotkan, making the world, had poured melted rock over a great bubble. Smaller than Ancestor Cave, it was just right for three. The rock above was higher than a man's reach, the bowl-shaped floor big enough for ten people to sleep without touching. And the floor was covered with ankle-deep dung. Bats had lived here long, which meant no one else had. If Ashan and her family were the first people to live here, that was even better!

On the way back to their tiny hut, she thought about where she and Tor would sleep, where the fire should go, and the birthing log, and all that she would do to make it a cheerful home.

Ashan went to the river the next day, tied her skirt and cape on her head, and crossed the water with the rope and pole. She gathered an armload of sticks and climbed to the cave, wearing dry clothes and re-laced moccasins, remembering yesterday's climb naked as a new-hatched bird.

A fire inside convinced the bats to leave, and gave her light to work. Happiness bubbled out in song as she scraped up dung that smelled so sharp it put fire in the nose and water in the eyes. She filled her ramhide cape time and again, carried it out and dumped the black muck over the broken shale, then swept out the last with a dug-up thornbush.

She couldn't believe she was cleaning bat dung . . . was covered with it! It was the most disgusting thing, worse than chewing skins! Yet Ashan had never felt better about anything she'd done in her life.

When at last the cave was clean enough for a baby, daylight was almost gone. Tor would worry if she didn't come back, but she wanted to be here by herself this night.

Ashan looked at her ramhide cape. The first skin she'd ever worked, so soft and pretty, was a stinking rag. She laughed until tears streaked grimy skin, then wadded the cape under her head and settled on the floor of her new home. The air smelled, but not that bad, more of smoke than dung. By morning, it would smell of woman.

Bats darted in.

As far as anyone knew, a bat's only enemy was sickness.

"Get out!" she yelled, waving the thornbush. "Or I'll tell the spirit of bat death where you are!"

That scared them. She knew they'd come back while she slept, probably be hanging upside down all over the roof when she awoke. But they were only animals, who would tire of the fight.

Ashan would win the cave for her family.

The Home Cave, she thought. *That's what we'll call it.*

Lying on her back, looking in the almost-dark for bats, Ashan saw that she was *not* the first person in this place. Someone had made a picture on the highest part of the roof— a black spot with a light hand shape in the middle. It made Ashan shiver. Who knew what that person might have left behind?

She thought about the Shahala ritual for ridding a home of evil spirits. Mother, father and almost-baby . . . all the family must be there. And of course, a shaman, who would wave a bundle of smoking juniper needles, chanting for all bad spirits to leave. When they were gone, each person in the family would burn a braid of sweetgrass, the favorite smoke of spirits who love people, to welcome them—and only them—to the new home.

Where did I see that sweetgrass growing? she wondered as she drifted into sleep.

She dreamed that the Home Cave was a takoma . . . one of greatest power. Many lines crossed overhead. In her dream, they were visible as strands of color that swept across the sky like smiles.

It took Ashan one day to move Tor and their things, and another to remove all signs of their hut by the river.

The new cave, and the knowledge that his family was safe, seemed to be what Tor needed for a cure. His black moods disappeared as strength came back. He took over hunting and gathering, acting as if it meant nothing, but glowing like a firebug when he brought his mate each day's bounty.

Nights were sweet beyond Ashan's dreams—she who had thought herself destined to sleep alone. She loved to feel Tor's warm, sleek skin curved around her back, his hand cupping her full breast or resting on her growing belly . . . a healthy Tor, as she knew from his breathing and scent.

Ashan had never been happier as she waited for the greatest gift of all.

CHAPTER
24

In the village of Anutash, on the second day of the moon called Spring Ends, the Shahala prepared for their long trek to the mountains of summer hunting.

How many more times will I see Ancestor Cave? Raga wondered. She knew the answer: *As many times as I must.* Spirits told Raga she had one more thing to do in this life: Only when she gave the Shahala a new Moonkeeper would Raven Tongue, the tired Old Moonkeeper, be allowed the peace of dying.

What a task it's become! she thought. *Spirits, give me patience!*

Tenka, whose name meant Rising Star, had seemed right in many ways. But the longer Raga worked with her, the stronger became her doubts. Daughter of Arth and dead Luka, sister of dead Beo and the Evil One, Tenka was an odd child, seldom smiling, keeping to herself. Her face was more long than round, and too solemn. Her eyes were too big, and the grief-painted smudges around them had never gone away. Her black hair was thick as a bush, and would not stay in braids. She was small for her nine summers—almost as small as Ashan had been. Raga wondered what had happened to the days of large women like herself—women who *looked* like chiefs.

Other girls played with dolls made of leather and grass, but Tenka had a herd of little stick animals, and a tribe of small stone people, carried in a waist pouch that she'd painted herself, to be played with when she thought she was alone. Raga had watched unseen as the child whispered to her stone people, walked them along finger-wide trails, dug little canyons to trap the stick animals, or stacked rocks to drive them over. Though she would never hunt, the girl had been born with a boy's understanding of hunting.

Tenka had no trouble sitting quietly to listen for spirit voices. She seemed so comfortable that Raga thought she might have tried speaking with spirits on her own. She learned easily about the moon and stars, and weather, and medicine. She didn't have to be taught how to paint. She loved to do it, and what she painted looked right—even better than Ashan's work—much better than Raga's.

But all of that meant nothing if Tenka didn't get over her fear of people.

This day, across from Raga in the Moonkeepers' hut, Tenka slumped on crossed legs, head down, crying without sound. The Old Moonkeeper had yelled at the Chosen One. She hadn't meant to—that was the worst thing to do with this mouse, who was more fragile than Ashan had ever been.

Poor little thing, she's only nine.

Raga, who felt like the world's oldest person, had an urge to comfort the child, who was simply overwhelmed by the demands being made on her. But sympathy would not work here. She'd learned that with Ashan.

"Look at me."

Tenka looked up . . . pitiful, small face almost lost in that mass of unshiny hair. She rubbed her eyes and nose with her fists, streaking her dirty face.

"I'm sorry," she blubbered.

"That's the point, Little Star. The Moonkeeper is *never* sorry."

"I know," she whined. "I'm sor— I mean—"

Spirits! What am I going to do with this one? Raga thought.

Well, it's a happier question than the one I cried inside, night after day—

—What am I going to do without the other?

Raga sighed, and thought back to the black time. For a

while after Ashan had disappeared, the Old Moonkeeper had believed she could not live. Lying in her bed, refusing all that people tried to do, she had meant to die by starving—too bad that her death would doom the people, and the world. When she thought of that hopeless time, even now, pain gouged her heart. She felt so sorry for the shattered creature who had been Raga two summers ago . . . not the same as feeling sorry for herself now . . . she was, thank Amotkan, not that poor woman anymore.

Tisu's baby had saved what was left of Raga—she who refused to be born without the Moonkeeper's help. Her father had named her Kiersa, Early Spring. Sometimes her mother laughingly called her daughter Grasshopper Legs, remembering the way she'd been born.

That a newborn could save a whole tribe proved the importance of every one of the people. Did it mean something else as well? For a time, Raga had watched for signs that Kiersa was the Chosen One, meant to take Ashan's place . . . perhaps the mark on her neck was a new moon and not a leaf, or blade, or fish.

Whatever else it might have meant, the birth of the marked child marked Raga's turning from death to life. Strength came back as she cared for the people and herself. Sometimes she felt . . . almost good. She had purpose again: To keep herself and her people alive until she could give them another Moonkeeper. But, oh . . . the loss of Ashan was a blade that shredded her guts many times each day. Even now, what Raga really wanted was the peace of death. But not at any cost.

"Tenka, have you finished blubbering?"

The girl nodded, biting her lip.

"Then tell me again what happened."

This time Tenka told it without blubbering.

Davi was a big boy of ten summers, a bully who'd taunted Tenka since Raga had named her the Chosen One. Davi was not the only one who doubted it . . . many did who were older and should have been wiser. It was hard to blame them. There'd been no magic sign, as with Ashan. Raga just saw little things that seemed to point to it, and one day she had gathered the people and told them.

Arth was only too happy to have his daughter go live with

the Moonkeeper. He had a new life now. After Luka's death, he had taken two women whose men had been lost in the massacre, and their five little ones. This was not the old way—one mate and her little ones were plenty for any man to care for—but in the Time of Sorrows, all the surviving men had done this. It was one reason why, two summers later, the Shahala community—though less in number—was still very much alive.

Today, when Tenka had gone to the bushes to make water, Davi had followed.

"He hid," Tenka said to Raga. "And *watched*! Then he jumped out at me. 'You're nothing special!' he yelled. 'Nothing but a *girl*!' Then he ran behind me and flipped up my skirt with a stick!"

The girl's humiliation singed Raga. "You should have set his insides to boil, not all the way to mush, but—"

"I don't know how!"

"Of course you do. You're the Chosen One."

"I don't know how to do any of those things. The people are my elders, and my friends. How can I hurt them?"

"You must, for their own good. People who do not fear you will not follow you."

"Then make me who I'm not!" Tenka's voice was bitter. "Teach me how to hurt who I love!"

"I can teach you knowledge," Raga said, "but not power. Power is given by spirits, and it's already in you. You must discover for yourself how to use it."

The little girl stared as if she had no idea. Raga wondered if Tenka was going to be the second great mistake of this life.

"I can tell you how it is for me when I must put the fear of spirits into someone . . . though that doesn't mean it will be the same for you. Each of Shakana's Daughters does the same things, but in her own way."

"Please," Tenka said with wide-open eyes.

"Well . . ." Raga frowned, took a deep breath, and rubbed her forehead to work up thought. She had never before had to explain the power—Ashan had figured it out for herself.

Raga opened her mind, cleared her throat, and her voice was deeper when she spoke . . . the power was in it.

"Anger helps. It makes me angry when someone does wrong. It should make you angry too. Moonkeepers and mothers have done a good job teaching every Shahala the proper way to live. They should know better.''

Now her words were flowing. ''So first I get angry. I clench my fists and grind my teeth. This makes me larger to look at. Then I work on the anger—twist it, punch it, puff it up—and it turns into power. I push it up through my body, gathering it into two balls behind my eyes. Now I glare at the sinner with less pity than a rattlesnake, thinking of what horrible thing should happen to him—and most often, it is a him. I mean, Tenka, really think hard, *hard enough to make it happen.* If I wish to freeze him, I think of ice, see him stiff and blue. If I wish to boil him, I think fire, see him writhe, smell his flesh cook. Now the power is ready. I know it, and he knows it. If I must, I will let it go—no, hurl it. But first I ask myself: Do I need to kill him? Or will hurting be enough? Usually, just the *threat* of hurting is enough.''

''And that's how you boil someone to mush?''

''Yes. Though I've never had to.''

''What?''

''People remember stories of what Moonkeepers before us have done.''

Tenka's look showed disbelief.

''That's what I want you to understand, Little Star. Fear is the Moonkeeper's weapon. The people believe I can do whatever I say, just as I believe it. We are all smart enough not to challenge. But if someone does challenge, you must find your power and use it to put him down.''

''I'll try.''

''Good girl. That's all I can ask. Would you like me to take care of Davi for you? Just this once?''

''Would you?''

''With pleasure. Shall I boil him? Freeze him? Turn him into a lizard?''

''I think it will be enough to beat him hard with a stick,'' the future Moonkeeper said.

CHAPTER
25

The baby grabbed her insides and twisted. Ashan sat up, instantly awake, sucking breath through clenched teeth.

Thank Amotkan! she thought. *This is the day!*

She shook her sleeping mate.

"Tor . . . time for you to go."

Rubbing his eyes, Tor looked at her with concern. "I've decided to stay. Women are not supposed to do this alone."

How well she knew. If she let it, sadness and fear would make her cry. She should be in Anutash, in the familiar safety of the women's hut, with mothers, sisters and grandmothers to comfort and encourage. And a Moonkeeper, in case something went wrong.

Her insides clenched again. Tears struggled up. She ground her teeth against them. Crying was a waste of strength, and she needed every bit for what was coming.

"Tor, this much woman power is poison to a man! You know this! Now go!"

"Ashan . . ." he whined.

She knew he'd given up.

"I have everything I need," she said bravely, thinking, *except the help of my sisters.* "You will stay away three days."

There were tears in his eyes, but he left.

The pains were far apart and not so bad. In between, Ashan
swept, cleaned what was already clean, and arranged the
baby's things all over again. She smelled burning and went
out to see what it was. Upstream on the far side of the river,
smoke rose above the treetops. Tor must have built a fire to
keep busy.

Ashan sat on the shelf outside the cave and watched white
smoke feathers drift across blue sky, imagining sitting here
on a sunny morning with her baby. She smiled at the pinches
inside—they weren't much more than the cramps of the time
of bleeding! Did women exaggerate the birth struggle to get
sympathy?

A huge hand gripped her insides; sharp nails dug in; strong
fingers tightened and squeezed. Gasping, helpless in its grip,
she realized that if anything, women *hide* the truth. Finally
the hand let go. When it seized her again, she knew it was
time to go back inside.

Tor, wanting to help in some way, had made a birthing
place like the one she had told him about in the women's hut
at Anutash. Near the back of the cave, a padded piece of
riverwood was held at knee level by rocks. The ground under
the log was covered with the worn but clean rag that had once
been her proud ramhide cape.

"Strong and comfortable," Tor had said, as if any part of
this could be *comfortable*.

In the way of women since the Misty Time, Ashan squatted
over the ramskin with knees spread, chest and arms on the
log for support.

Warmth flooded her thighs, and she looked down in surprise. She knew the water sack would break, but the feeling
was so . . . uncontrolled! Like everything else about giving
birth. She cleaned herself, and put a dry goatskin down.

The pains became closer—longer—harder. Ashan endured
waves of hurt worse than anything she'd ever known, biting
on a piece of leather, remembering what she'd heard in the
women's hut.

"Pant like a cougar in the sun!"

"Help your baby by pushing!"

"Go with the pain! Don't fight it!"

A baby must finish itself by tearing out a piece of its

mother's soul to add to its own. Of course such a thing would hurt. The greater the pain, the stronger the bonding.

But how could she *not* fight pain that grew and *grew* and became the whole world, trapped inside her and fighting to get out? She was made of pain; pain was her name; fingernails, eyelashes—it was everything, and out of control! Her body had turned against itself, and was trying to murder her! Oh, how she wanted to scream! But if she did, spirits might think she didn't want the baby. So she twisted shrieks into groans as a Shahala woman should, telling herself such pain was a sign of her baby's strength, courage and determination to live.

"You're doing fine, little mother!" someone would have said, if anyone was here.

"You're doing fine, little baby!" Ashan said.

In the pauses—and thank Amotkan there *were* pauses— she slumped on the log, and her mind drifted. But the pauses shortened, the pangs came closer, and then came on top of each other. There was no more mind-drifting, though she wished for it. Slimy with sweat, she panted like a cougar, grunted like a bear, and remembered to help her baby by pushing. Bearing down with all her strength, she pushed and *pushed* until she thought her eyes must pop and her skin ooze blood.

The head emerged, then shoulders. She reached between her legs to catch the slippery baby.

A boy! Ashan wiped his face. He let out a lusty cry.

"Tor!" she gasped. "See what I've done!"

A twisting of her stomach . . . oh so much smaller! . . . reminded her that the work wasn't finished yet. The empty sack that had been the baby's home must be born. She wrapped the howling boy in a lynx skin, put him beside her, and leaned over the log. A few more pushes brought the sack.

And an end—*thank Amotkan!*—to pain.

The baby had stopped howling. The mother tied the cord in two places with boiled leather thongs, and cut between with the white stone blade used only for this. A gift from Alhaia the Moon to Shakana the First Woman, it belonged to the tribe; but it had been in her medicine pouch when Tor kidnapped her, because someone had been about to give birth, and Ashan the Young Moonkeeper had wanted to be ready. No longer than a woman's thumb, very sharp, the blade had special power to cut the physical bond between mother and child, and at the same time nourish the spirit bond. Ashan was glad she had it for her baby, and sorry for others who'd be born without it.

She finished by making a knot in the cord tight against the baby's belly, then cut off what was left. She'd bury these things down by the riverbank . . . so this place would always know her son . . . so he would always have a home. He was the first Shahala child, she realized, whose birth remains would not be buried near Ancestor Cave or Anutash . . .

The time of work was finished, the time to enjoy begun. Ashan unwrapped her baby and washed him with water warmed in a turtle bowl. She marveled at his perfection . . . fingers and toes with tiny nails, little power staff . . .

Oh Amotkan, she thought, *mine is the prettiest baby ever!*

He had unmarked skin, not red like most newborns, but the rich gold-brown of polished agate; big dark eyes; well-shaped head covered with wet hair that would dry black and thick; a pink mouth like a thornflower bud.

Love welled up as Ashan gazed at her son . . . love achingly sweet, powerfully fierce, warm as swallowed sunshine. Kissing, tasting, smelling him, she understood ancient truth: Mother and child had known each other since time before time; time beyond time would strengthen their bond.

Ashan would kill for the tiny miracle. Or die for him. She swore it before all the spirits she knew.

Tor passed the time by the river, feeding a bonfire. It wasn't cold, but it gave him something to do besides worry. Like almost-fathers do, he worried anyway. First babies can take a long time. Ashan was so small; not strong at all, though she didn't agree. With no one to help her, and—

A high, sweet cry pierced Tor's heart.

"My firstborn!" he shouted.

The beautiful howling went on. Wonder swelled Tor like a strutting grouse. Grinning, shaking his head, he gazed at the river. Late sunshine dancing on dark water turned it into a living, laughing thing. *Sunshine and river, givers of life.*

Sun River, he thought. *A good name, be it son or daughter.*

Tor stood with face and arms raised to the sky and shouted as men have done since the beginning of time.

"Spirits of all who love people! Kai El, Sun River, is born! Give this child a better life than mine!"

Were Ashan and the baby healthy? Was he father of a son or daughter? Tor was eager to see them, but he waited as Ashan had said he must. On the third morning, he stood outside the cave.

"Woman, I wish to see my child!"

"Do you know this child's name?" Ashan asked, as curious about that as Tor was about its sex.

"Kai El, Sun River."

Ohhh . . . she liked it! Though it was different. People were named for one thing, with another word to say what kind—like "Whispering" says what kind of "Wind." Tor had named their son for *two* things—sun and river. A new way of naming seemed right for the first child born into this new world.

"Come in and see your *son*," she said.

He yipped like a dog and ran into the cave.

"A son! I knew it!"

Tor's face was full of wonder as he held the cradleboard. *As though*, Ashan thought, *he's seeing the face of a spirit*.

"Isn't he the most beautiful boy?" she said. "Not a mark? The darkest eyes, and all that hair? And the sweetest face! Tor, he looks just like you!"

"Don't insult me, woman!" Tor teased. "Your child has the face of a mud doll!"

They laughed a long time over that.

CHAPTER
26

On a hot day in Summer Ends, the Old Moonkeeper sent Tenka to a hillside near Ancestor Cave, the Shahala summer home. It was time to gather yew bark, medicine for more than one sickness. Enjoying the aloneness, the girl hummed for the spirit of each tree as she peeled a single, long strip of bark. Taking too much would kill the tree, and that would be stupid. Not only did trees deserve life, but if they died, the medicine would be lost, and people not yet born would die of sickness that could have been cured.

A herd of boys came charging down the trail, shrieking like man-eaters. Terror took Tenka's breath. *What will they do to me this time?* The Chosen One should have faced them, but she dropped her basket and ran.

Looking back, she saw Davi leap like a cougar. He caught her foot and they slammed to the dirt. His two friends and his little brother circled her, making ugly, scornful sounds. Tenka held her skirt down with both hands, but he wasn't after that. With a jerk, he broke the ties of her waist pouch, and held it in the air.

The painted horseskin pouch was Tenka's favorite thing— just about the *only* thing she had from the Time Before.

"Give it back!" she screamed.

Laughing, Davi shook it. Stone people and stick animals

196

spilled out, some in his hand and the rest on the ground. He stamped on the little elk made out of a cedar twig, and ground it into the dirt.

Tenka's skin burned; her ears thumped. A horrible sound tore out of her throat. She lunged, but Davi jumped back, and she hit the dirt. He flung her things as far as he could.

"Nyah, nyah! Stupid girl!"

Something came over Tenka . . . something hot and heavy with power. Her eyes blazed, and she knew the boys saw the flames. She stood with slow dignity and brushed herself off, never taking her eyes from theirs. They were frozen, their faces blank as if they couldn't think.

Which one? she wondered.

The one who believes, said a new voice in her mind. *Davi's younger brother, Bur.*

The Chosen One focused her stare on the condemned one. Everything left her sight . . . all but his round, black eyes, shiny-wet with fear. Tenka grew larger with hate. Bur seemed to shrink.

"You are cold!" she roared. "A fish who stayed in the river after the geese flew away for winter! You're alive inside the ice, but you're cold! Freezing!"

Bur fell to the ground, bare arms wrapped around himself, squealing like a speared deer.

"Ice is silent!" Tenka commanded. Bur stopped squealing and lay there shivering violently. His color paled to the blue-white of fish belly.

He is freezing! He really is!

The boy looked at her, pleading. "M-m-m-m," he said through chattering teeth. He couldn't get the rest of it out, but she knew he was trying to say "Moonkeeper."

"Stop!" Davi shouted. He held out her pouch. "Take it!"

"Not enough!" She kept her eyes on Bur, and pictured frost crusting over him.

"Find her stuff!" Davi yelled. "Every single one!"

The other boys dashed away.

"Don't kill him!" Davi begged. Tears streaked his white face.

Something snapped. *A Moonkeeper doesn't have to kill!* Tenka thought of a blanket of sun-warmed fur and spread it over the frozen child.

"You're all right," she said.

Healthy color washed Bur's pale skin. He sat up.

Tenka fixed her eyes on Davi. "On the ground!" she commanded. "Beg my forgiveness! And don't ever challenge a Moonkeeper again!"

Later, she who had found and used a shaman's power wept alone, with relief and sorrow. Bur, who'd believed he was dying, would tell everyone about it, even if Davi and the others didn't. The Chosen One should be able to control her people now. Raga would be proud, but Tenka felt no pride. It was a terrible thing to do. She hated it. Bur was just a boy following his big brother. He didn't deserve Davi's punishment. Maybe *no one* deserved such punishment. She hoped she would never have to do it again, hoped they would just believe in her now.

Tenka cried for a long time. *Why does it have to be* me?

Raga was a stew of feelings when she heard about the confrontation in the yew grove. Mostly, she was glad with relief. Tenka had found Moonkeeper power within herself, and used it. People would treat her differently from now on.

Now Raga understood the strange heaviness of the air that day. It was more than the wanderings of a worn-out mind, and more than just something in the air.

A real thing had happened that day, momentous: a passage of power from the lost Ashan to the timid Tenka, who had never been able to see herself as Moonkeeper, much less use the power within her.

That had happened, and more.

CHAPTER
27

The People of the Misty Time knew that life was a rugged trail stretching over four hills, marking the seasons of baby, child, adult, and grayhair. This newborn would travel, as everyone does, alone with the might of nature, with only the company of living creatures whose friendliness must be sought if he was to be safe on his journey.

When Kai El was ten days old, his parents took him to the creek below the Home Cave to present him to Creation—an ancient ritual taught by Spilyea, the Coyote.

It was a bright, warm day in high spring—sweet of air, the kind of day that, after winter's long visit, caused a person to flare her nostrils and breathe deep. Fine weather for the ceremony was a good, if minor, omen.

The sun shone and the water sparkled. *As if*, Ashan thought, *to honor the name Sun River, so cleverly thought up by Tor*.

Tor held his son. Wrapped tight in the cradleboard with only his head free, Kai El was alert, and quiet, as a Shahala baby must early learn to be.

Ashan had presented many babies to Creation—as a shaman. To do this for her *own* baby would be strange. But she knew that changes in tradition—adjustments in the ways—must be made for the reality of this new world they had been cast into . . . where mother and Moonkeeper were the same woman.

Ashan raised her arms. In a shaman's ringing voice, softened by a mother's love, she sang the ancient words.

"Sun, moon, stars, all who move in the sky! Into our world has come a new life! Make his path smooth so he may reach the crest of the first hill!

"Winds, clouds, rain, mist, all who move in the air! Into our world has come a new life! Make his path smooth so he may reach the crest of the second hill!

"Mountains, valleys, rivers, trees, all of the earth! Into our world has come a new life! Make his path smooth so he may reach the crest of the third hill!

"Birds who fly in the air! Animals who live in the forest! Bugs who creep in the grass! Into our world has come a new life! Make his path smooth so he may reach the crest of the fourth hill!

"All of sky, all of air, all of earth, hear me! Into our world has come a new life! Make his path smooth. Then shall this Shahala boy, my son, travel *beyond* the four hills!"

The tingle coursing through the Moonkeeper said spirits welcomed the new life, though much about his birth was strange—Kai El was the first Shahala born without a tribe, the fruit of a Moonkeeper mated to a man.

If Raga knew! Ashan thought, then wondered why she would think of Raga at a time like this. But . . . *if Raga and the people knew, it would be as if the sky had fallen down. Thank Amotkan they never would.*

CHAPTER
28

Twice, the seasons came and went, in plenty and peace. Life in the tabu mountains was good for the family of Tor, lacking only the company of others. The power of love between man and woman, and parent and child, went far toward replacing the love of a tribe.

Ashan awoke on a morning in late spring. She fit her mate's back like bark fits a tree. His sleek skin and full muscles awoke desire, but the need to make water was stronger. Ashan tied on a skirt, and went out to her private place at the far end of the ledge. She squatted there behind some bushes, admiring the work she'd been doing to make this place into a place of woman-power to hide her, and the daughters she hoped to have, in the time of bleeding. It would take lifetimes to collect enough antlers to make something like the women's hut in Anutash, or the women's corner in Ancestor Cave, but she had made a good start.

Sun peeped over the distant mountaintop. Ashan was glad the Home Cave faced Where Day Begins; there was extra power in morning sunshine. She sat on her special rock by the cave mouth—a good rock, just the right height for comfort, flat on top, with a colorful scattering of lichen. Below sparkled the torrent she had named Keecha, Crazy Creek, with its sweet-tasting water and bounty of fish and whipping eels. Trees rolled away like a spring-green blanket.

Ashan felt one with nature when she sat on her special rock. It was a fine place to think, or talk with spirits, or loose her mind to wander. She remembered the day Tor had found "the perfect sitting rock for his woman." Strong as he was, he'd barely wrestled the heavy thing up here. "My love is heavy as this rock," he'd told her. "It will never crumble."

Ashan smiled: Tor had kept his promise.

Her thoughts drifted as morning painted orange on the cloudless sky, and filled the air with scents and sounds of day—the first day of the moon called Spring Ends, as her shadow stick had shown.

It was hard to believe, but *two summers* had passed since Kai El's birth. They had been the best seasons of Ashan's life—in spite of the raw wound, named Shahala, that festered inside her, oozing pain and sorrow and fear.

The only thing that kept the secret wound from destroying her was that she believed she'd been given no choice. For reasons a person could not understand, spirits meant for her to be apart from her tribe. Going back would have done them more harm than good—not even speaking of what it would have done to her family. The Shahala would have *had* to kill their child-carrying Moonkeeper to satisfy spirits. But they *loved* her. That kind of conflict destroys.

Ashan thought her son was proof of a spirit plan. Spirits had given Kai El to her—there was no other way a little one could be born. She had sworn to protect him, as they'd known she would. They must also have known it would be impossible for her to protect *both* her tribe and her child.

She could only try to believe that spirits must have some other way to protect the people. Maybe Raga would live forever, or at least long enough to teach another Moonkeeper. If only Ashan could know for sure that her people were all right, she thought she could get beyond mourning. The trouble was this: The last time Ashan had seen Raga, the Old Moonkeeper had seemed near death. How could she still be alive after two turnings of the seasons?

In case Ashan was the only Moonkeeper left in the world, she had kept Shahala ways as best she could. Rituals made for a large tribe had to be changed for a little family. The first time Ashan held Kamiulka, the Autumn Feast, she tried to re-create what she'd always known—a grand three-day celebration of summer's bounty. She had sung to the moon, and tried to get Tor to dance the mating dance—but he had said Kai El was enough for now. Looking back, it was silly—the two of them and a baby trying to act like a whole tribe. Last autumn, she had adjusted the rituals to make them fit who they really were: just three souls hoping spirits still cared.

We must be doing something right, she thought. *So much about life is good.* She smiled, and her sitting rock felt good under her . . . something a person wouldn't even notice unless she knew a rock quite well.

Yes, much about life was good. Her family was healthy. Ashan couldn't imagine a better provider than Tor, the once-Shahala warrior. The lovers made love often, a perfect blend of sweetness and passion that grew in pleasure as their bodies grew in knowing.

And Kai El . . . she didn't have words for the joy he brought. No wonder Raga was such a grump-gut. How could any woman be happy without her own child? It seemed that her child was what life was all about. Ashan loved Kai El with the fierceness of a she-bear. Mother and father, called Amah and Adah, couldn't be angry even when he was bad—Kai El learned early how to get what he wanted with sweet or pouting looks. But the sweet-tempered baby didn't use these wiles very often.

As soon as Kai El could walk, Tor had made him a little spear. Father took son on short hunts. One day they brought home a flat stone, the blue of a robin's egg, the size of a lynx paw. Tor worked on it by the fire at night, while his mate worked on grinding or sewing. With the bone awl she used for piercing beads, he scratched Kai El's sign into the blue stone—a circle for sun, over three waving lines, for river. He used fine sand to polish it, pierced a hole, and strung it on a soft leather thong.

Fathers usually waited longer to make their little ones' neckstones—many died young, and a man's careful work was buried with his child. A Shahala father would never show this much attention to a son so young, but here in the wild-place without a tribe, they had to make up new ways.

As Ashan soaked up morning sunshine outside the Home

Cave, her old life seemed very far behind. Her family's waking-up sounds said more: *Lost to you, forever, Ashan . . . that's what your old life is.*

The afternoon was hot for the moon of Spring Ends. Tor spent it on the riverbank below the Home Cave. His mate sat beside him, flipping the water with her toes. What was making her nervous? He wondered if his face showed his secret thoughts.

"Two turnings of the seasons since he came!" Ashan said. She shook her head. "It's hard to believe so much time has gone by. But there he is."

Kai El stood in a shallow pool, slapping his hands on the water—a bit of pure fun to watch. In his second summer, the boy was all any father could want . . . happy, healthy, taller than Tor's knee, with sturdy arms and legs, and a bear cub's fat. He reminded Tor of Beo—smooth, heavy hair that reached his shoulders; long-lashed black eyes that sparkled with cleverness, danced with laughter, and glowed with love. Round cheeks, a little mushroom of a nose, and lips that wanted kissing. Soft, dark-gold skin. A voice that gurgled like water.

And smart: on Kai El's second birthday, his mother had said, "You are Amah's big boy now. Only babies suck." Kai El didn't ask for her breast again. It had been almost as easy to get him to make his messes outside.

Tor thought Shahala fathers—who liked to spend most of their time with other men—missed a lot of their children's gifts.

Ashan's voice broke into his thoughts.

"Let's sleep down here. It will be warm enough tonight. It's time I began teaching Kai El about the darktime sky."

"I don't want the boy sleeping outside. You know that."

"Oh, Tor . . . he's old enough, and so fat the Ice Spirit couldn't carry him off if it wanted him. Go up and get our sleeping things . . . please, please, please?"

How he hated that whine! "All right, woman!"

Tor began climbing the shale outcrop, as treacherous as the day they'd first come. He could have made a trail, but that would make it too easy for an enemy to reach the cave.

Ashan called after him. "Bring down some dried elk, and those yellow roots, and three huckleberry leathers. Then I won't have to cook."

Tor grumbled under his breath. "Yellow roots again! Raw!

Women are supposed to cook! And men have more important things to do than fetch! The woman wouldn't talk to her mate like that if we were with a tribe!''

But without a tribe, the old rules meant nothing.

Without a tribe . . .

Tor's whole face was a frown as he climbed. A familiar ache flooded the hollow in his chest. He loved Ashan and Kai El, loved them as much as spirits are said to love people. But they did not, and never could, make him complete. He longed for the company of men. Hunting with friends, reliving brave deeds around the fire, joking and telling stories only men like to hear . . . he missed these things that are so much of a man's world. Tor had been more with men than women in his life, and had to say he liked them better. They did not whine.

How sad to be doomed to a life without tribesmen! But at least Tor had memories. His son would never even know the joy of hunting with a band of men, would have no friends, no mate, no little ones. Doomed to loneliness, they were . . . unless Tor chose to believe in the dreams.

The dreams . . . Tor was having them again, and he was glad. Dark sight had come back like an old friend, after being gone so long he'd begun to doubt he had ever flown with eagles in the night. At first occasional and vague, now the dreams were frequent and clear. Sharp images and powerful feelings bled into the day. As it had always been in dreams, Tor saw himself and his family as part of a new tribe living on the shore of a great river in happiness and plenty . . . a peaceful community.

War was about to break out inside the man.

One side said he had all he'd ever wanted: his mate, his son, and freedom from stupid laws.

Another side knew he needed to belong to something more than a family. *Men are meant to live in a community*, thought the man who felt like a hiveless bee.

Yet another voice tried to be heard. *The future of people depends on you. You* must *find new land, and learn what men will need to know to survive in the changing world.*

Tor had heard this last voice before. What did it mean? How could the future of people depend on one man? Especially a man who didn't have any people?

"Bison dung!" he said, confused, angry. A piece of shale clattered down, kicked loose by his uncaring feet.

"Be careful!" Ashan yelled. "You could hurt us!"

At the cave, Tor tied their sleeping skins into a bundle. He took the stone lid from the storage pit. As he picked through pieces of dried meat, he saw that there was enough to feed ten people for two seasons . . . these mountains didn't suffer from lack of prey. Though it was against the law he'd grown up with, he'd been taking more than he should . . . hunting was better than sitting around poking a stick at a fire they didn't need.

Tor hadn't realized how much food there was.

Enough for ten people for two seasons. Well, maybe not. But enough for a woman and a child until winter . . .

Tor's confused thoughts took the shape of a plan; the heavy stone on his heart changed to owl down.

He would leave . . . he *had* to leave . . . just for a while. When he found Mother River, he would come back. Then Ashan would agree to move, would be so glad to see him that she'd agree to anything! And if she would not? He had forced her before; she'd accepted it in time.

The hollow in his chest filled with confidence as he checked the food again. Yes, more than enough to feed his family until winter. It couldn't possibly take that long to find his dream river.

Selfish Tor . . . very selfish! accused a voice inside.

Maybe. But no more selfish than Ashan, who insisted they stay here, as if the wants and needs of her mate meant nothing.

And what if the future of people does *somehow depend on me?* It seemed an arrogant thought, but . . . *what if it was true?*

Later, in the welcome cool of evening, Ashan sat with Tor at the riverbank, chewing the huckleberry leather he'd brought down. Kai El crawled in the grass, telling an ant about a leaf. Like any little one, he loved to talk, to anything, or to nothing.

Tor hasn't said a word, Ashan thought. *Not as if he's angry, as he so often is these days, but as if he's somewhere else.*

"What's the matter?" she asked. "You seem mountains away."

"Hmm?"

"I said, you seem mountains away."

He shrugged, and went back to that place in his mind where he spent too much time far away and out of her reach. It made her jealous, and that made her angry . . . at herself. Such feelings were stupid. Jealousy was what a person suffered when a mate desired another. There couldn't be another woman in Tor's life . . . not out here. *Maybe in his dreams!* she thought with spite.

His dreams . . .

Ashan stared at the swirling water. She had tried to ignore the signs, but she knew what was wrong with her mate: Dark sight had come back to him. He wouldn't admit it, but he was talking again about new tribes and great rivers, and where else did such ideas come from? It was *wrong* for a man to dream, and only a matter of time until spirits punished him. And who else got punished? Everyone! Tor seemed to have a way of splattering his sins all over the people around him. And there seemed to be nothing she could do about it, though she had tried.

Once she found some sleeping vines. A lot would kill, but a little would keep a person's sleep empty. She made a tea with lots of honey to hide the bitter taste.

"Please drink it," she begged one night.

Tor knocked the wooden cup from her hand.

"Why should I! Men don't dream!"

When he said that they should pack up and go search for this Chiawana, as he called his dream river, Ashan's anger flared.

"You are stupid as dirt if you think I'm taking my baby to wander in the wildplace, looking for something that is only in your mind! If we can't be with our tribe, we will live here. At least we have what we need to survive."

Ashan didn't understand Tor. He had everything he'd ever claimed to want. Why couldn't he just be happy?

Like you? whispered a voice inside. *Maybe, like you, he's too confused to be happy.*

Ashan sighed. She hid the wrong in her life under a mask of smiles put on with her skirt every morning. Her mate and son believed it. Sometimes she believed it herself. She couldn't deny the good feelings that being a mate and mother brought—Tor and Kai El completed her as a woman.

But Ashan was *more* than a woman. Once she had been Moonkeeper, chosen by spirits to lead a people. And she had failed—no matter how she looked at it. It still caused her grief when she thought of the proud Shahala starved or enslaved.

If only she *knew* what had become of them . . . but she never would. Tor would never take her home; he claimed he didn't even know the way. To take Kai El and try it on her own would be fatally stupid. And if she *did* make it, what would she find? Her people vanished? Dead? Or alive with murderous intent for their betrayer and her forbidden child?

Two summers! And still she struggled with this! Would Shahala grief last all her life?

Late that night, Tor took his undetected leave. Not, he told himself, as a rash young warrior acting on impulse, but as a man with nineteen summers of wisdom. In the dark of night, he could direct himself and control his feelings, and leaving seemed absolutely the right—in fact the *only*—thing to do.

But now the sun was rising. The light of day made things seem less absolute. Would leaving his family turn out to be the biggest mistake of his life?

She'll be waking soon, he thought. *What have I done?*

A sunray stung his eyes.

Left unprotected your mate and your son . . . the unthinkable, the impossible, the unforgiveable . . . that is what you've done. So many things could happen to them . . .

Worry overwhelmed Tor. He sat down. It was the first rest since he started his quest in the dark.

A sensible voice spoke in his mind. *Go back now and explain it away.*

But Tor, another voice said, *what about your dreams that have the mark of destiny—*

The sensible voice laughed. *Leaders have destiny. For others, destiny is to be a tribesman, a father, a mate. Is that not destiny enough for any man?*

But this sense of destiny, he said to himself, *it's the real reason I left them.*

Tor supposed that no man was entirely happy with his life, even a life as good as his own. But it was not dissatisfaction with life that had made him leave. That was just the excuse that had empowered him.

Tor had left because of his new sense of purpose about finding a people and a river home, of being part of some bright future. Whether in darkness or daylight, *that* still seemed real, and important.

But families should never be separated for more than a few days. Tor would have loved to have them with him as he set out on his quest. He missed them already. Ashan, with her shaman's knowledge, could probably have led them straight to the new future . . . if only she had believed him. Tor had done everything to persuade her, but it was impossible.

What if something happened to his mate and little one? How could he live with that?

I am selfish as a he-bear, without even courage to say good-bye.

You could not. She would never have allowed you to go.

Allowed? I am the man of the family. I do the allowing.

That was the way of the old world. In the new, men must have faith. The spirits would not ask of a man unless they meant to give what help he needed.

And so Tor set off walking again.

For a long time Ashan lay in half sleep, listening to morning songs of birds and river, eyes closed, mind full of pleasant thoughts. How good it had been to sleep outside; she was glad she'd talked Tor into it. She always felt *fresh* when she awoke outside . . . spirit-kissed. She drank in smells of sky and water and things growing, thinking how huts and caves were so stale—

Tor's scent was missing! Ashan's eyes flew open.

"He's gone!" she cried.

Kai El jumped up. "What's wrong? Where's Adah?" His little voice wound up to a shriek. "Adah!"

What made me say that? Ashan thought.

"A-a-a-dah!"

A child should never wake up screaming. If they were with a tribe, someone would slap him.

"Stop it!" she said. "Adah's hunting, that's all!"

"Noisy . . . baby . . . sorry," he gulped, chin trembling, bottom lip sticking out. Big eyes were liquid dark.

Ashan scooped him up. "It's all right, sweetbaby. It's Amah's fault, not yours."

She rocked him, wiping his tears with the back of her hand, crooning a cradle song.

"Adah hunts for baby; baby doesn't cry. He brings you presents when he comes; baby doesn't cry . . ."

But Ashan knew that Tor was not hunting. The skin he'd slept in last night was gone. A man doesn't take his sleeping skin on a morning hunt, and he would have told her if he planned a longer one.

He had left them!

From the moment she missed his scent, Ashan knew it—felt it in her heart like a blade. How could she have missed the signs? Weren't Moonkeepers supposed to be smarter than ordinary people?

Black terror filled her. She gripped Kai El too tightly, as if he were a twig at the edge of a cliff. Her voice quaked instead of crooning. She was losing control . . .

She put the boy down. "Stop sniffling," she said, as much to herself as to her son. "We have to go up now."

She slung the carrier over her back and knelt so Kai El could get in. When they got to the cave, she gave him an acorn cake, remembering to put the thornbush fence up so he wouldn't wander out . . . he should know better by now, but . . .

She stamped around the Home Cave scattering things. Tor's heavy spear was gone, and his three-stone sling, and extra clothes, and his horseskin sack . . . A man wouldn't take *all* his weapons on a morning hunt.

Her mind screamed. *You stinking dung-beetle! You cowardly son of a snake! You rotting hunk of carrion! HOW COULD YOU!*

But she kept the screams inside. Kai El had already shown that he couldn't handle her panic. Ashan had to think of her little one, especially now that she was his only parent.

Oh, my baby, she thought, *what will we do?*

The rage went out of her. She stumbled to the raised shelf where she slept with her mate, and lay there weeping. Kai El was soon in her arms, crying along with her, with no real idea why.

CHAPTER
29

"The world is changing," Tor said, giving voice to thoughts that spirits were putting in his mind. The loud words matched his powerful stride like chant matches drumbeat. "The future of people depends on new land that I am to find. The new land will teach me what we need to survive. I will find men and teach them what I learn." Over and over, "The world is changing. The future depends on me . . ."

With Colder at his back, Tor was on his way, talking to himself as if there were two men on this spirit-willed quest. He had started talking to himself when his life had changed two summers ago, and he had had to learn to hunt alone. At first, he had tried to stop—he had been taught that it was a sign of craziness—but now he accepted that a man must talk to someone. Talk can silence thought.

"I feel good!" he said often and loud, taking deep breaths of the different air, pounding on his chest. "Never better!"

He said it to fight the guilt pursuing him like his shadow. *What if, what if, what if . . .*" Finish the thought with any of the terrible things that could happen to Ashan and Kai El with no man to protect them. It was almost enough to turn him back, so he fought each *what if* as it sunk its teeth into his will.

Though this was only the moon Spring Ends, a strange heat
stayed in the air as he traveled through mountains toward
Warmer, where dreams had always shown Mother River to
be. He asked for a new dream to prove the rightness of his
decision, but none came . . . no dreams, no omens . . .
nothing. He fought his growing doubts, telling himself over
and over that he was *sure* he'd made the right decision, *sure*
he was fulfilling destiny, that he was somehow involved in
changing the future of men.

Late on the third day, Tor crested a mountain and saw that
it was the last. Lowering foothills stretched away, until the
land flattened to a vast yellow plain.

"Good work!" he shouted. "These foothills were the last
thing in my way!"

But beyond the hills, the yellow plain seemed endless.
Where was Mother River? Well, he was not about to give up
. . . she was out there. That night, on a treeless mountaintop
in a tabu land, under a cold sky bright with stars, he prayed
for a river dream. Takeena didn't hear, or care.

The sun became hotter as Tor made his way through the
foothills. It took most of two days to get to the plain. There
was no water on this side of the mountains. By the time he
reached the flatland, his water pouch was half empty. Tor
knew it wasn't wise to head into dryland with so little water.
He considered his choices. He could go back for more, but
what good would that do? He only had one pouch. By the
time he got back here, it would be half empty again.

Spirits wouldn't send him on this important quest just to
kill him. To keep going seemed the only thing to do. He had
to believe he would find Mother River before he ran out of
water. His heart told him Chiawana couldn't be much farther—even though his eyes saw no sign that this was true.

Several days later, Tor knew he'd made a mistake—one
that might kill him. The mountains were far behind him now,
the flatland hot and dry. The stony ground grew nothing but
scattered yellow and gray plants no taller than his shin. The
sun here shone bigger and brighter than it ever did on Shahala
land.

Hot sky; no shade; finally, no more water. His tongue
became thick in his dry mouth; his lips cracked at the corners.
The difference between day and night blurred; sometimes he

slept in the light and walked in the dark. Sometimes, confused, he went in the wrong direction. He kept going, more and more exhausted, longer than he thought any other man would last. Another would admit he was dying, but not Tor. *Remember?* said his drifting mind. *Spirits are on your side. You are the new "Chosen One," chosen to . . .* what was it? Too hard to think. Well, he'd been through this in the land of man-eaters, and just in time spirits had sent rain.

Once he came back from that place in his mind where nothing seemed to matter because nothing seemed real, and he saw that, somehow, he'd lost everything he'd been carrying. Everything! Skins, weapons, food, even his empty water pouch! The shock of what he'd done was too much. He collapsed in the burning sand.

"It is over," he said weakly.

Tor lay under the hot sky, wondering how long it would take to die, thinking about what it meant to die in a land that didn't know him, the victim of his own forbidden dreams. He thought of Ashan and Kai El, the innocents he'd condemned to the same cruel fate. He wept, pouring out what water he had left in tears to nourish the unforgiving land.

A stallion whistled.

In this forsaken place? What a joke! Another trick for his mind to play while his body died of thirst!

Tor heard the sound again, lifted his head to the barren hills, and saw the impossible. He rubbed his eyes, but rubbing didn't change anything. In the clear sky—so bright he had to squint—tendrils of mist were forming out of nothing, drifting and swirling into a cloud floating just above the ground. But not a *real* cloud, no. A spirit cloud, he could tell by the colors . . . pink, green, yellow, every soft shade except cloud-gray. The beautiful, impossible cloud reached for his mind and stroked. He forgot heat and thirst and death.

The cloud melted. A white stallion stood in its place.

Tor's mind was no longer his own to control. Staring at the snowy beauty, he thought he was back in Anutash, still living with his people, three autumns ago at the feast, something about the white horse captured by the First Warriors . . . he remembered whispering in its ear: *You are the one who will be freed. Someday our trails will meet. We will know each other.*

In a voice filled with awe, Tor asked, "Are you my spirit brother?"

The creature snorted. With a toss of his proud head that set his long mane dancing, he began walking. Tor found strength to follow. From time to time, the stallion turned and looked at Tor; when he lagged, the stallion slowed the pace.

Ahead, Tor saw green. *Shade*, he thought. But it turned out to be more than that. Horse and man reached a line of tall bushes, strung like a green necklace along a fold in the land. The cool shade would be a kinder place to die.

Tor flopped down exhausted, but his spirit brother took no rest. The beautiful creature pawed the ground under the largest bush, then looked at Tor, and did it again.

Tor remembered—finally—a thing he'd been taught as a boy: *Water had been found in dryland by digging under a certain kind of bush.* Since he came from a land where there was always plenty of water, Tor had never tried it.

"I understand!" he yelled. His yell was a dry squeak.

The stallion snorted, then he vanished like a shadow before a storm.

Tor dug frantically. It was true! When the hole was as deep as his elbow, he brought up damp fingers and licked them. It wasn't enough. He scraped out a place big enough for his head and shoulders, shoved himself into it, and sucked . . . not minding grit in his mouth, caring only for the water it gave up.

After a long, long time, it was enough. He relaxed in the shade of the bush whose water he had stolen, leaning against a cluster of trunks.

"I hope there's enough for both of us, friend, but if not . . . the life of a man is more important than the life of a bush."

Tor chuckled, pleased that his voice sounded almost human again. He thought he should make a plan, but . . . spirits! was he tired! Later would be soon enough to worry. He could stay right here for a long time, sucking the life of his friend the bush. He slept, and woke, and wondered what had saved him. A real horse? A spirit horse? Or just his own mind at work keeping him alive? He didn't know, and it didn't matter. What mattered was that he would not die of thirst. Not this day.

Life gives a man enough to worry about with the rising of every sun, he thought. *Why burden himself with tomorrow's worries too?*

In a sweet dream under the lifesaving green bush, Tor was almost ready to make love to Ashan, when he heard women laughing. *Doesn't belong*, he thought, opening his eyes.

Oh, Takeena! Three women were coming right at him! He backed into the bush and pulled branches around him. He watched through the leaves as they picked pods from low gray plants and put them in pouches tied around their waists. They wore woven hats shaped like anthills, *and nothing else*—no skirt, cape or moccasin. Two were young, about Ashan's age, and one of these was pretty. The third was old and wrinkled. With black hair and dusky skin, they could have been three Shahala gatherers. Except for their nakedness. And except for their speech, made of the strangest sounds Tor had ever heard people make.

The Shahala warrior Tor was not afraid of women, especially naked women with no weapons. But he stayed hidden. Their men might be near. Besides, they had nothing he wanted—not even water pouches.

An unpleasant smell pinched his nose as they came close. Sometimes men smelled this way, but women? He had never known a woman who didn't wash her smell away every day.

They sat in the shade, making sounds of relief, close enough to hear Tor's heart thud in his chest. Suddenly, the pretty one pointed at the new-dug hole. They walked up to it. So close Tor could have reached out and grabbed a bare foot, they knelt, staring at the hole and the dirt piled beside it, throwing wide-eyed looks at each other, clacking like baby owls.

With frightened faces, the women hurried away toward Where Day Begins. Tor stalked them like prey, not sure why. Over hills and down hollows, they kept a fast pace and didn't stop. He saw that the sun would soon go down. If they kept going in the dark, he would follow them. It was strange, but just being near people—*any people*—felt good.

The women disappeared over the top of yet another hill. When Tor got there, he dropped to his belly.

A village!

Tor looked down on a few mud-covered huts, squatting at the edge of a vast expanse of cracked, white land. The three women chattered like bluejays as they joined others. Everyone talked at once. Tor could hear well enough, but he couldn't understand a word. He counted nine men, twice as many women, and three little ones. All were naked or nearly so, except for their odd woven hats . . . which, when he thought about it, were not so odd. They were wide enough to shade the body, and out here where the sun was so close you could almost touch it . . . what a good idea to carry your own shade.

At least there were no mounted skulls . . . not exactly proof that they didn't eat men, but a good sign. Another good sign: The creature sizzling over the fire had four legs, not two—

A *coyote!* Revulsion choked Tor. Coyotes were sacred. Spilyea, the first, had made people. What kind of people would eat the sons of their maker? He wondered if they ate eagles too.

Well, he supposed it was better than eating other people.

The sun went down. The strangers shared their meat—men first, then women and little ones—in flickering firelight. Tor hated to admit it, but the smell drifting up, and the sight of their smacking enjoyment, brought water to his mouth, cramps to his gut, and a pounding ache to his head. He hadn't eaten for days. He needed some of their food—even if it was coyote—and the water they must have somewhere.

And then, he thought, *forget great rivers and new tribes, and voices that whisper of destiny! Forget everything! I am going home!*

More than anything, Tor wanted his mate and his son. The great invisible hole in his chest wheezed as he thought of the Home Cave, tucked in the tabu mountains of Snake Men . . . not precious Shahala land, but not so bad . . . far better than anything he'd seen since he'd left. It was a wonder anyone could survive in this cruel, waterless place. *Why did I leave my home? Does a man have to lose a thing to understand its worth?*

When the strangers had been in their huts for a while, Tor crept down by the light of the thin moon. He found a stinking pile where the savages threw bones. Hunger battled gagging as he picked through the mess looking for meat.

Crack!

Tor's head exploded in white-hot pain. He flew into the bone pile. Merciful blackness took him.

Knowing crept back. Pain pounded. He couldn't move. Terror gripped him when he opened his eyes.

Naked people stood over him, angry-faced, jabbering in meaningless clicks and clacks. Tor struggled, but he was wrapped like a wasp in a spiderweb—on the ground, on his back, helpless. A child poked his foot with a stick. An old man held a torch close to his face so everyone could have a look.

Then they left him. Hot panic changed to cold dread. Why was he still alive? He had seen no slaves. He must be food.

No man escapes his destiny, thought the man who should have died long ago with his Shahala brothers.

CHAPTER
30

The next day, the savage men went out early with their weapons, leaving behind a guard who carried a stone club and squatted close enough to bash Tor—as if a wasp in a spiderweb of twisted grass ropes needed guarding! His head was the only thing he could move as he lay face up, arms to his sides, on open ground among squatty mud-covered huts. His knowing drifted as the sun crossed the hot, bright sky. Hunger, thirst and pain tortured him, but self-hate was the worst. *How did I let this happen?*

The women who wore no clothes spent the day taking one of the huts apart. After chipping the mud away, they used the wood—precious in this treeless place—to make something in the center of the village, placing each piece carefully and tying it to others with grass rope.

The day that had lasted twice as long as any other ended. Tor was still alive to thank the spirits for dark, cool relief, and for turning pain into numbness. That night his captors buzzed with happy chatter. They didn't give him food or water. Were they waiting to see how long it took him to die?

The next day the women covered the frame they'd made with brushwood brought from the dryland. They dragged Tor to the welcome shade of the three-sided shelter. The guard walked along, shaking his club and rattling strange words in a fierce voice. But a softness about him said he was less fierce than he acted. Tor was sure he could take the man with a boy's face, but when the bindings were loosened, he was too weak to struggle. All he could think of was his blood flowing again, and how good the shade felt. The guard retied him in a way that felt better, with wrists bound together by a short rope, and ankles the same. From these bindings, long ropes went to the guard's waist, reminding Tor of the way stallions were led to Shahala feasts.

In the days to come, Tor was a well-treated, badly-confused prisoner. Why would people feed him when they barely had enough for themselves? With only a few hunters, why leave one behind as a guard? Why not do the easy thing and kill him?

The guard bound to Tor was fifteen or sixteen summers, and short, as most of these people were, with wide shoulders and chest, and arms so heavily muscled the veins stood up. He had dark gold skin, and a face that was pleasant to look at. His black hair, thick with grease, hung to his shoulders, except for the top, which was chopped short to poke straight up. A golden eagle feather trailed down the back. Like the other men, this eagle feather was the *only* thing he wore. Tor thought it strange that they left the parts that made them men hanging loose and unprotected like animals did.

Even though the guard could say nothing Tor understood, there was a keen spark in his black eyes that hinted of good thinking-power. He was quick to smile for reasons Tor couldn't see. He reminded Tor of a young bison bull, wanting to be fierce but wanting to play.

Some days the two men sat in the three-sided shelter. Other days, the guard walked Tor a short way from the village to a place where tall rocks jutted out of the ground. The guard made lines on a large, smooth stone by pecking over and over with a sharp pebble. Pictures already on it, all alike, made Tor think of suns the size of a man's hand. There were other pictures on other rocks, some faded and old, of animals, birds and . . . *fish*.

Where have these drylanders seen fish? Do they know where Mother River is? And what are these picture rocks for?

There was no way for Tor to ask.

Except for one, the women weren't pretty in Tor's eyes.

Most would have looked better with their bodies hidden under
something, especially older ones with breasts longer than
their hair. Some of them stared at Tor with looks that meant
desire in his language. He supposed in theirs it meant something else, but it made him uncomfortable. He'd never known
women who didn't cover their bodies, especially the place
where they hid their secret power. It wasn't safe for a man to
look there, but he found himself doing it anyway.

Each day a different woman brought some kind of
squashed, uncooked mess on a round, woven mat. It wasn't
easy, but Tor made himself eat. He didn't know, and didn't
want to know, what kind of food it was, telling himself that
at least it was dead, was not human, and whatever it was,
these people lived on it.

They brought water in baskets made of thin, coiled roots,
covered in tightly woven grass. Careful designs of colored
grass decorated them. They did not leak a drop. Tor, who
had never seen such baskets, admired them. The Shahala
carried water in animal bladders, and what baskets Shahala
women made were crude things for carrying plantfood. These
people didn't get many animals, and what they got had bladders too small to hold much. So they used what they had,
which was grass, to weave everything from hats to cooking
pots.

He didn't know where their water came from, but they
wasted none. They let him drink, but not wash. By the way
they smelled, it seemed they didn't wash either. Soon Tor
smelled as bad as the rest, and then he quit noticing it.

He was always a little hungry, though he had the same
foodshare as everyone.

Tor and his captors used hand signs for things like eating,
drinking, and leaving the shelter to make water. He came to
understand some of their spoken words. Water was "kahwit." His guard was "Wyecat." The pretty woman, one of
the three who had found him, was "Tsilka." The old man
who came to ask questions in the clackety language was
"Timshin." The tribe was called "Tlikit," meaning, Tor
thought, People of The Lake.

What lake? he wondered.

The Tlikit treated him kindly, but if they wanted him for

a tribesman, why not free him? Stupid question. These people hadn't learned as much as the Shahala, but they must know he'd run. *And would he!* Faster than an antelope runs from a cougar, back to his mate and child and home in the mountains, and the happiness he'd thrown away!

One night, Timshin, who seemed to be chief, brought a girl with shy eyes so young she didn't have breasts. The old man put his hands on her hips and rocked his loins, then pointed to Tor, smiling and nodding. With gnarled hands in front of the girl, he signed a child-carrying belly, then put his arms together and rocked as if he held a baby.

Oh Takeena! Tor thought, horrified. Shaking his head, waving his arms, he said, "No! Go away!"

Timshin brought a different woman the next night, and another after that. Then he brought Tsilka, the pretty one, and Tor thought, just for a moment, *Why not? Who would know?*

"Take her away!" he said, banishing the thought.

Tor was awake next to snoring Wyecat when Tsilka came back. He tried to pretend sleep, but he couldn't ignore her fingers walking across his chest like moths.

"Go away," Tor said. "I have a mate." He made the Tlikit sign for woman.

Tsilka took his hands, tied together at the wrists, and put them on her breasts. Her soft flesh ignited fire in his loins. She ran the tip of her tongue over her lips. The look in her dancing black eyes was the hungry look no man can resist, that begged "let me please you" in all languages.

Hot pleasure hardened him.

You snake! hissed the voice inside.

He took his hands away from the magic of Tsilka's flesh.

"Only one mate," he said in a quavering voice. "Only one—"

Laughing like a delighted child, eyes sparkling, she pushed him to his back and straddled his hips. She tapped his chest, chattering like a happy bird. Tor didn't understand the words, but he knew she meant, "I want you."

His eyes tasted black hair flowing over proud shoulders, ripe breasts, strong thighs, and the dark secret that had no name. Heavy hair brushed his face. Lips wandered over him leaving kisses. Gently, insistently, she rocked against him . . . and it felt so good. His breath caught in his throat. A moan slipped out.

Tor closed his eyes, and sent his mind away.

It's Ashan doing this . . . Ashan whose nipples trace my chest, who takes me in her hands and guides me home.

Ashan . . .

Tsilka's unwashed odor made a lie of his fantasy, but it didn't stop his hot explosion.

After that, Tor told himself that the Tlikit tribe was desperate for children they could not have, probably because they all shared blood. Even this primitive band knew the law against mating with those who shared blood. Tor, a father himself, couldn't blame them for what they were doing to him, not really. All people wanted little ones. Once he understood, there seemed no reason to deny Tsilka. But he refused others; he didn't think he *could* with them. Tsilka was the only one who pleased his eyes.

And who knew? Perhaps the Moon Spirit would send a child to temporary mates . . . though Tor didn't think it would be wise.

The seductive she-cat slept with him every night.

"I mean," he would say in a one-sided conversation, "spirits know I'd be with my *real* mate if I could!" As if this made up for what Ashan and Kai El would suffer if he didn't get back to them. Summer was half gone. They wouldn't survive winter alone. He thought about escape, but, bound and guarded, there didn't seem much chance of it.

Tsilka wanted to learn Tor's language, and so did a boy named Chimnik. Tor found himself having a new kind of fun. He drew lines in the dirt and made up signs to explain words. It felt good to work his mind so hard. At night on his way to sleep, with Tsilka warm beside him and Wyecat snoring a short distance away, Tor thought about what he would teach them next.

This way, the Tlikit learned a few things about their captive, while he learned much about them.

In the time of Timshin's grandfather, the Tlikit had been a people of great number. The cracked white earth had been a lake full of food. Then an important law had been broken. Tor wasn't sure about this part, but he thought a chief mated with his own sister. An enraged god, Wahawkin, Water Giver, had appeared as a wind and sucked the lake into the sky. Without the water, the Tlikit had suffered, dwindled, and would someday disappear, like the huge beasts of older times.

What a story! Stories were for teaching, and this one certainly taught the tabu against mating with blood relatives. But, the part about a god sucking up a lake . . . Tor would have laughed, but Tsilka looked so serious.

"Will Wahawkin bring the water back?" he asked with signs and words.

Tsilka shrugged. The Tlikit didn't know, but they prayed to Wahawkin to forgive them. No one had ever made love to one of his own blood again. Now all the people of mating age shared blood. Before long, the youngest would be old, and when the last died, only the land would remember the once-great Tlikit tribe.

Lightning struck Tor's brain. Confusion burned away. In one tiny but huge moment, he knew the meaning of "new tribe," and "great river," and "destiny." He was breathless with understanding.

The Tlikit were dying for lack of new blood. Tor was dying for lack of a tribe. All longed for a land of bountiful water.

I am the new blood. They are my new tribe. We will find the new land and the river of my dreams . . . together.

Tor thought about this instead of sleeping. *I must get free! Spirit-willed destiny demands it! But how?*

Tor knew that in some ways, he was smarter than any Tlikit. He could use their primitive fear against them . . . their fear of this water-giving god, Wahawkin.

For the rest of the night, Tor thought about how to *become* this Wahawkin in the eyes of his captors.

Early the next morning, Tor woke Tsilka and sent her for the chief, who was also her father. While she was gone, Wyecat snored on. Tor could feel the rope vibrating, but from Wyecat's snores or Tor's excitement?

This will work! he thought. *I know it!*

He practiced a stern, powerful look—chin to chest, brow lowered over slits of eyes, nostrils flared. His voice wouldn't be the voice of their captive, but of their god.

Timshin came on Tsilka's arm. He rattled something at his

snoring son that made Wyecat jump to his feet. The old man
looked at Tor, held his hands up and shrugged, meaning,
"What do you want?"

Tor spoke from deep in his chest. "I am Wahawkin!"

Three mouths dropped open. Tsilka fell to her knees. Timshin and Wyecat stood staring.

Tor spoke in words and signs.

"I am Wahawkin the god, not Tor the man. I forgive you
because you learned from the old ones' mistake. Now free
me, and I will return your water."

The old chief muttered, shaking his head, frowning so deep
his bottom lip pushed up to his nose and his plunging brows
almost covered the slits of his eyes.

Tor pounded his chest and bellowed.

"You miserable specks of dust! Free me!"

Tsilka fell flat on her belly. The two men jumped back,
jabbering too fast to be understood.

Tor roared. "Listen! The lake is dead! You will follow me
to a river of many fish! I will make the Tlikit great again!"

They were paralyzed with shock.

"Tsilka!" Tor said to the woman who thought pleasing a
man was everything. "Get up and free your god!"

Tsilka stood, keeping her head lowered. She glanced at her
father. He nodded, and she attacked the knots with her teeth.

For the first time in almost two moons, Tor was free!

He knew he should run the moment he could to his family
and his *real* life. But there was still time before winter to find
Mother River. And there was something about being a god
. . . something sweet and powerful that filled his chest and
head, and made his nostrils flare.

All that day, people with bright, hope-filled faces came to
chatter at their returned god. The boy Chimnik wouldn't leave
his side. Tsilka acted proud, as if Wahawkin were her own
special gift to her people. Timshin, like any chief would, said
he had known all along that the one they called Wixpoo,
Father of Many, was really the loved and feared god, the
Water Giver, the mighty Wahawkin.

Full of his god-self, Tor wondered if his head was swelling
up. But who cared? Being a god was better than being the
youngest Shahala First Warrior. Being a god was better than
anything . . . better even than being a mate and father.

Of course it was . . . it was his destiny.

The Tlikit people asked over and over, "What do you want of us?"

Their desire to please touched Tor's heart.

"Just be my tribesmen," he answered, but their faces said they would never be able to think of him as a brother.

So he said, "Follow me," and this they understood.

All would have gladly gone with him right at this moment, though they had lived by the dry lake forever. But it didn't make sense to take the whole tribe, when Tor didn't know himself where Mother River was. He'd have to find it first.

Tor spoke to the chief. "I will take Wyecat and Tsilka to be Timshin's eyes. If Chiawana makes them happy, I will send them back to lead you there. It will be the new Tlikit home before winter."

"Where will Wahawkin be?" the old chief asked.

"I told you long ago: I have a mate and a son. I must be with them by winter, or they will die."

"How can gods die?"

"They're not gods, but people like you. In the spring, we will all be together . . . together at Chiawana, our Mother River."

Tor, Wyecat and Tsilka set off the next day into the drylands toward Warmer, with the cheers of the Tlikit in their ears, and all the food and water the tribe could spare.

It wasn't much, but Tor was happy. The destiny he was born for was coming together at last.

CHAPTER
31

The Tlikit woman ran behind her brother and the man-god. Her thoughts swarmed over each other like a tribe of ants when their underground home is kicked open. Everything had happened too fast to understand!

Tsilka was a woman who knew—or *thought* she knew—about the world and her place in it: She would get what men—father, uncles, even a younger brother—wanted her to have. Tlikit men took pride in showing fairness. She trusted them to know what her share of food and water should be. As to her share of *life*—there wasn't much anyone could do about that: Tsilka was the last of her people, among the youngest ones who could not mate because of some ancient law.

"Unless," whoever told the story always said, "something comes to save us."

People couldn't be happy without hope, so they chose to believe that something would save them. The gods wanted punishment, they said, not extermination. The proof? Wahawkin only made life hard by taking away Tlikit water. He could have burned them up with lightning, or drowned them in a flood—a god could do whatever he wanted with his great strength.

Like a man, the Tlikit woman thought. *I guess that's why gods are "he," and the world belongs to "them." Men and gods . . . gods and men. How do I tell the difference?*

Tsilka gazed at the two running in front of her. Her brother was certainly a man. The other, who had seemed to be a man, now claimed to be a god. They didn't look much different, except that Tor-Wahawkin was taller, had uncut hair, and covered his good-to-look-at body with shapeless skins.

The ant swarm in Tsilka's head ran wild. *Is Wahawkin himself the thing that comes to save us? Is he a god just because he says so? Just because my father and brother believe it?*

Tsilka was tempted to believe. If he was only a man, it would be hard to explain the miracles his coming had brought. He had changed how everything was supposed to be. His new blood would make healthy children; the Tlikit would not disappear like giant beasts of old. And lucky Tsilka, who should have had neither mate nor children, had something like a mate, and a new chance for children.

But why didn't he tell us sooner who he really is? And why not just bring our lake back? Why look for water in drylands where no one has ever gone?

Shivering in the heat, Tsilka used her mind-foot to squash the wild ant-thoughts, and focused on her real feet running on unfamiliar grass. As shadows grew long behind her, she wondered if the man-god would stop to eat or sleep.

Morning birds squawked. In the Home Cave under the sleeping skin, Ashan ignored the sounds, too miserable to get up.

Two moons four suns, and still your scent lingers. I miss you, Tor. Please come back.

Tor is dead. I have to accept it.

Then what? Dear Amotkan, what will I do?

A scraping noise said Kai El was up, and trying to push the rock lid from the storage pit. Ashan poked her head from the skins.

"No!" she snapped. "I told you, that's for winter!"

"Want meat!"

"You're having berries and moss."

"Hate moss! Want meat!" Kai El stamped his foot, working up a tantrum. The child who missed his father threw bigger fits and more of them as the days passed.

"Please be a good boy. Moss makes the meat last longer."

Black moss is starvation food . . . not even food, but

something to fill hungry stomachs, to keep little ones from crying. Ashan's people ate it only in times of famine, mixing the tasteless strings with other food to make it seem like more.

If Tor didn't get to them soon, famine would come to the Home Cave sure as winter. It was her fault as much as his. She'd been so sure he wouldn't fail them, so sure he'd be coming back "any day now," she'd only gathered berries and roots—her usual woman's work. But she hadn't replaced the meat, and now it was getting low. When the snows came, she wouldn't be able to hunt. Ashan wasn't good at hunting anyway—no woman was. And what was a mother supposed to do with her son while she hunted? Leave him tied up in the cave?

But lots of black moss hung from the branches of tall pines. Yesterday, in the way of her people, Ashan had sent Kai El up the trees. Children were better climbers than heavy parents. Her heart beat a drum of fear, but she needn't have worried about the son of Tor. Kai El climbed like a bear cub, having a great time, paying no attention to scrapes and scratches. They brought home arms full. Ashan planned to do it again today.

Now Kai El "hated moss." Well, that's why Alhaia the moon gave babies mothers, instead of sending them into the world alone. There were times when mothers had to make them obey, whether they understand or not.

She put dry huckleberries in his turtle-shell bowl, and added water from the deer bladder that hung by the cave door. She tore up moss and mashed it into the berries with her stone grinder. Gritting her teeth, grinding too hard, she almost put a hole in Kai El's bowl.

"Little ones eat what their mothers give them!" She thrust it at him, slopping some on his chest.

Kai El ate. They went to gather moss. When morning clouds left, the sun was so warm Ashan could almost forget it was the moon Summer Ends. Kai El's mood brightened. He climbed trees like a squirrel, feeling big and proud.

Something moved in the nearby brush.

"Adah!" Kai El shouted.

A deer stepped out, stared at them for a moment, then dashed away, tail waving above white rump.

"If I had a spear, I'd kill you, Yamish!" Ashan yelled. "If I knew how to use a spear!"

Kai El was crying.

"What's wrong?"

"You know."

"I do. Adah will come home soon."

How can I still be telling him that? she wondered.

Tired and sweaty, Ashan trudged home at the end of the long day. Kai El rode in the carrier on her back, light and quiet as a shadow, knowing better than to bother his grumpy mother. Her mood was as black as the moss they'd gathered—as black as the Owl Cave where long ago in her other life she had almost died. She felt like hitting someone, but Tor, who deserved it, was long gone.

"Almost home," Kai El said. "Hungry!"

Thinking about what to have for a meal, Ashan started up the tumbled shale that led to the Home Cave. A stench hit her.

"Oh, no!" she cried. "A skunk!"

Rage erupted like a Misty Time volcano. "I hate you, Tor! Hate you forever!"

In a frenzy, she scrabbled the rest of the way up, sending rocks clattering to the river. Bouncing in the carrier on her back, Kai El cried in terror. Ashan barely heard him. As she stood on the ledge outside the cave, she could almost see stink billowing out.

"*Hate you!*" she screeched, forgetting the howling child on her back.

Ashan attacked her sitting rock—Tor's symbol of love that would never crumble. Grunting, she shoved it to the edge. It thundered down, broke in pieces and tumbled into the river. She wished it was Tor!

Kai El's howls finally reached her. She knelt and he climbed out of the carrier.

"Be Amah's big boy and see if Skeena is still in there."

Kai El stopped crying. "Big boy!" he said, and ducked into the cave.

Ashan crumpled on the ledge where her rock had been. A skunk in the cave was a small thing, compared to everything else, but it broke the dam holding back the lake of her despair, releasing a flood of tears.

Kai El came back. "Nothing in there but stink, Amah."

With her head in her arms, Ashan nodded, but she couldn't stop the gulping sobs.

"Only babies cry," her little boy said.

Ashan bit her lip and took a deep breath. "Right." She wiped tears with the back of her hand. "Let's get our things. We'll sleep out here tonight."

The cave was a mess. Firecoals were scattered. A mudspot stained the floor from a punctured water pouch. Kai El's pile of playthings, mostly rocks of different sizes, was knocked over. Pawprints of black fireash told of a skunk chased in by a fox, then back out again. The skunk must have sprayed the whole time. Ashan's eyes burned. How long would that stink last?

"Why my home?" she moaned.

They ate out on the ledge. The dried food from the storage pit tasted like skunk, which bothered Ashan but not Kai El—no more than it bothered him that the sleeping skin reeked. The boy of two summers loved to be outside, whatever the reason.

Ashan settled on the skin with arms behind her head. Kai El snuggled on the side of her heart.

"Amah smell better than skunk."

"Thank you. Go to sleep."

"Tell story."

Ashan just wanted sleep's escape from misery, but none of this was her son's fault. Telling stories was part of mother's work, a way for little ones to learn about life. Anyway, it was good for them both—she could forget her problems for a while.

"All right. Then you sleep. What story?"

"Star Boy."

Gazing at the dark sky, Ashan cleared her mind. With childscent sweet in her nostrils, she began.

"Long ago a boy wanted to hunt, but he was too young, so no one would give him a spear. One day when the hunters were gone, he disobeyed his mother and went by himself. The boy saw a horse and ran after it, ignoring signs that something was wrong."

"What wrong?" Kai El asked, though he knew . . . this was his favorite story.

"Well, the horse was huge—big as a deer—and blue as summer sky."

Kai El giggled.

"Even though he had no spear, the foolish boy ran after the strange horse, and caught its tail. It ran like the wind. Flying out behind, the boy held on. He didn't feel it lift off the ground, not until they were very high. Then it was too late to let go. The horse flew to its home in the darktime sky, and left the boy up there to be a star."

She pointed to the stargroup called Flying Horse. "Do you see him? The last star at the end of the tail?"

"I see him."

"When Star Boy looked down, he saw terrible sadness. His father, brothers, sisters, aunts, uncles, all the people of the tribe were weeping, but his mother cried the loudest. Do you know what he felt, Kai El?"

"Happy to be a star?"

"No. He was sorry that he hadn't listened. And lonely . . . Star Boy was so very, very lonely."

Wind shivered up from the river. Ashan pulled the skins over them.

"Love you, Kai El."

"Love you, Amah."

Ashan had trouble getting to sleep, not unusual in this summer without Tor.

CHAPTER
32

After leaving the Tlikit village, Tor, Wyecat and Tsilka traveled in a direction between Warmer and Where Day Ends. Tor disliked all he saw: hot sun, scorched land, flat-topped hills squatting one after another across an endless plain. Warm wind blew in their faces from Where Day Ends. Nothing lived here but low yellow grass and small herds of antelope and horses. There were no caves or trees; they slept wherever they were when night came.

On the fifth day as evening drained the sky, Wyecat stopped, closed his eyes and sniffed the air. Nodding with decision, he rattled in Tlikit and pointed toward Colder.

Tor shook his head. "Wrong way, brother."

"Brother say water," Tsilka said.

It sounded like "but-uh say wat-ah." The "r" sound was hard for her. Still, it was fun for Tor to see how fast Tsilka was learning Shahala—faster than any Outsider he'd ever known.

I'm coming to trust them, he thought, *whom I once saw as nothing but savages.*

The Tlikit ate sacred animals, went around naked, never washed, kept a man as a slave. Their idea of gods was childlike. They had no shaman to speak with spirits, work medicine, or even know what moon it was. They didn't wonder, as Tor did, what was on the other side of these mountains or that valley; the Tlikit never went so far that they couldn't get home by dark—about two looks in any direction.

But as they traveled, Tor's respect grew. Wyecat and Tsilka found water where there was none and food in things that shouldn't be eaten. Wyecat lured a rabbit from its hole with greens he picked when they dug for water under spear-leaf bushes; Tor had never thought of using food to lure an animal. They would have gotten lost out here because everything looked the same, but Wyecat had wisdom for that too. Whenever they stopped to rest, he left three stacks of rocks in a line large to small to point the way back.

And now the Tlikit warrior did it again. Excited as a child playing Find Me, Wyecat led them toward Colder, to a place where rock emerged from grassland to trap a puddle of rainwater.

Tor clapped him on the back. "Good work, man!" He dropped his bundle and knelt, drinking from his hands.

Tsilka shed her bundle and watched the two drinking. She wondered why this water had been found by her brother, not by Tor-Wahawkin, the Water Giver. True . . . Wyecat was the best man of the tribe for finding water, but still . . . the other claimed to be a god . . . a water-giving god at that.

After the men finished, she took a drink.

"Men rest," she said. "Woman make eat."

Tsilka walked into the dusk, thinking.

While she was gone, Tor talked to Wyecat—without hope of an answer, but just for something to do.

"How do you find water? By smell?"

Wyecat tilted his head, questions in his eyes. Tor wished the man would at least *try* to learn Shahala. Tribesmen should be able to talk to each other without a woman's help.

Tor dipped his fingers in the water and held them to his nose. He pointed at Wyecat, and made a loud sniffing sound.

"Smell water?"

Wyecat shook his head. He touched the water, put wet fingertips to the center of his forehead, and closed his eyes very tight.

Tor had no idea what he meant.

Tsilka came back with food on a flat rock, which she put in front of the men. She sat by herself, though she must be just as hungry. It was one of many strange Tlikit ways—women and girls sat watching until men and boys finished eating. Men saved enough for them, but it bothered Tor . . . the Shahala knew that, except for a Moonkeeper, no person was more important than another.

"Eat with us," Tor said, calling her with his hand.

She shook her head and looked at her lap.

"Phhtt! Women."

As Tor dipped into the food, he couldn't help noticing what it was—fuzzy leaves and yellow flower petals, mashed with small white worms. Washed down with swallows of the bitter water, it wasn't as bad as he expected.

When the men finished their share, they lay back with arms crossed behind heads. Wyecat belched, his way of thanking his sister for the meal. She ate what was left, and buried the food rock so no creature would know they'd been here. She sat beside Tor, twirling strands of his hair in her fingers.

"Your brother," Tor said, pointing to Wyecat, who seemed already asleep. "He finds water by smelling?"

Tsilka thought, then shook her head. "See behind eye."

"Like a dream?"

"What mean 'dream'?"

"Dark sight. Sleep pictures. In my tribe, only the shaman was supposed to dream, but I—"

Why bother? Tsilka didn't even know what a shaman was. How could she understand dreaming?

Tor was silent for a while, then he asked, "Has your brother seen Mother River behind his eyes?"

She shook her head. "Not see Mother River. Wyecat fear, but Tsilka trust Wahawkin."

As she gazed at him, starlight shone in her eyes. Her lips opened. She licked them, then gently bit the tip of her tongue. Tor's breathing was uneven as she snuggled down beside him.

Wyecat slept, or pretended to.

Tsilka's loving was as different from Ashan's as Tlikit words from Shahala. Ashan's fierce passion, her overwhelming need and love . . . well, why did everything have to be so serious? Tsilka made love seem like child's play, different each time. This night she kept him on his back, a cougar threatening to scratch him if he moved. Her torture was sweet to endure.

The arrogant Tor was wrong: Tsilka knew all about dreaming. Though the Tlikit called it something else, they knew that dream lives were being lived right beside the waking one. What happened in some dreams was as real as what happened in the daylight world, except that dream people were harder to control.

That night in the windy dryland, Tsilka dreamed that Tor was not the feared god Wahawkin, but a *man* . . . Tsilka's mate. They lived in their own hut in the Tlikit village. Tsilka was happy, they all were, because of the rain. It splashed, puddled and ran into the low spot where the lake used to be, filling it to shimmery vastness. Most of the raindrops were only water, but some turned into fish or clams. Two turned into babies. Love filled her as they swam to her.

"Your mate is a god," people said, bowing to Tsilka and her babies. "No, no. He's just a man," she was going to say, but they wouldn't believe her.

Maybe she was wrong, and he *was* a god. *Oooo!* she thought. *What kind of fabulous creatures will our babies grow up to be?*

"You, Tsilka?" sneered a dream person with no face.

Why not me? I've been a good woman. Good enough to catch the god Wahawkin. Good enough to be mother of a new god-people.

Flocks of gray geese and white swans began their flight toward Warmer. Long lines shaped like spread fingers darkened the sky. Like flying dogs, they barked in the language every Shahala knew: "Winter's coming. Go home."

Tor dragged along in some low valley, grumbling in his mind. *Any fool would know this windy land goes on forever . . . there's no river . . . it's just another lie . . . time to give up . . . say goodbye to these people, and the dream . . . get back to my* real *family and* real *life, before it's too late . . .*

"Look!" Tsilka shouted.

On a nearby hilltop stood a white horse with wind-whipped mane and tail. It whistled high and long, then galloped out of sight.

Wyecat chased after it.

Crazy! Tor thought. A man could never run a horse down. Four legs outlasted two every time.

Tsilka tore off after her brother. Tor could do nothing but follow. He ran up the slope, his long legs closing the space between them. Topping the hill a moment after his friends, Tor swayed.

The world dropped off!

The river of Tor's dreams shimmered at the bottom of a great canyon. He saw that since time before time, Chiawana had torn through the land from Where Day Begins to Where Day Ends, gouging a wide gash in yellow hills, deep into the rugged black rock of their roots. Far across the water, wider than ten rivers, the world stepped out and strode away on barren hills and plains.

As Tor stared in slack-mouthed awe, an eagle screamed in the wind-streaked silence, plunged to the water and speared a fish with its talons.

Tor saw that the river *moved* with silver . . . silver stitching blue with threads so close they sometimes touched, dipping up and down to make the water shiver. Chiawana was a living creature choked with salmon. Not so many that a man could walk on their backs, but enough to feed the largest tribe forever.

The fish called salmon was Amotkan's gift to the Shahala. The Creator made four kinds, each to travel up rivers in its own season. The one with firm meat, called bright fish, came in spring; the blue fish and brother fish in summer; the silver chief, Chinook, in spring, and again in autumn. Salmon were the bravest animals, fighting rapids, waterfalls, eagles and men to return to their birth streams, lay eggs and die, sacrificing their bodies to nourish their young. The salmon gave its courage to the person who ate the rich, red flesh.

Joy tripped over awe as Tor gazed down on the bountiful place. *Better than my dreams! Takeena, I will never doubt you again!*

No one lived down there—Tor knew it in his heart. Spirits

meant for the man who found it to decide who *would* live there. Part of him was sad—the Shahala, his birth people, should have been the ones. But he felt warm and good about his *new* people. The Tlikit treated him like a chief—no, more than that, a god. Tor knew he was no god, but he liked to hear it, especially since the Shahala had cut his name from their language.

Tor dropped to his knees, motioning for his friends to do the same. Arms stretched, head back, he sang thanks to spirits who love people. When he finished, he saw that the other two were bowing to *him*, not to the river.

Tor led Wyecat and Tsilka into the canyon through a deep cut made by a dried-up stream that had once rushed to join the Mother. By magic or spirit guidance, that same day, he found the new home for his new tribe. It seemed perfect in every way.

Curving away from the river, a wall of rock as black as moonless night loomed against the sky. Giant slabs heaped on slabs gave shelter from the constant wind that pushed against the current as if trying to hold it back. Once the river must have flowed into this bend to carve several long, shallow openings. A wide bank of pebbles spread in front of these caves and poked out into the water. The bank was strewn with weathered wood thrown up by the river—enough for a bonfire every night, forever!

They stayed in one of the long caves. Chiawana's bounty dazzled them. They took and took with no thought of what they would do with it all. Tor had fished before, but never like this. Wyecat and Tsilka—who had never except in legend known water greater than a spring, who had heard of fish, but never seen them—thought it was a miracle. They acted silly, laughing like children without a care, eating until they were stuffed, sleeping at the first hint of darkness like winter bears.

Tor made two Shahala fishing spears of light, straight pieces of wood, carving a back-pointing barb into the fire-hardened tips. From early morning until they could no longer stand, Tor and Wyecat rooted themselves in the Great River, toes clinging to slippery rock, spears poised over their heads. Waves slapped their thighs. Chiawana murmured in their

ears. The warm breeze smelled of sunshine and fish. They
laughed when they slipped underwater, unfooted by the swift
current or a silver chief.

The trick of fishing was to get the whole body working:
the eyes to pick out one fish and lock on, balance to keep
from falling, the brain to take aim, the arm to thrust . . . all
in a motion, all at the same time. The spear slipped through
water and pierced fat silver. With a powerful yank, out came
a fish longer and thicker than Tor's arm, hooked by the barb
at the end of the spear. With a smooth turn of the upper body
and a flip of the spear, the fish flew onto the bank.

Over and over came the shout, "Chinook!" and a speared
fish flashed in the sunshine and landed behind them. It could
have been either man who yelled in triumph. To Tor's joy,
Wyecat had decided to learn Shahala, which Tsilka called
"god speak." His first word? "Chinook."

On the gravel bank behind them, Tsilka waited with a wood
club. *Thunk!* and the salmon stopped flopping. She slit bellies,
threw guts in the river, and carried the slippery, heavy fish
two at a time to a pile in front of the cave. It was all she could
do to keep up. Tsilka's work, like any woman's, went on
long after the men had finished.

The Shahala had always lived near rivers . . . only *now*
did Tor realize how lucky they were. In the Misty Time,
Spilyea the Coyote had taught his people how to catch and
store fish. Maybe once, when their lake had been alive, the
Tlikit had known, but no longer. Tor had to teach them
everything. Making spears was easy, and showing Wyecat
how to fish was fun. A Shahala warrior never fixed food for
keeping—that was women's work—but Tor knew enough to
show Tsilka what to do.

There's so much my new people need to learn, he thought.
*Someday, Ashan will be their Moonkeeper, but for now, I
should teach them more than what to do. I should also teach
them how to think.*

He started on the first day by telling Shahala ways about
salmon. As the three rested by the mouth of their cave, setting
sun turned the water into blood, and the hills beyond into
distant flame. Rich-smelling fish rose in a heap between them
and the murmuring river. All the men of Tor's old tribe could

not have taken in three days from a puny Shahala river what he and Wyecat had taken from Chiawana on this one day. Tor was proud of what they'd done, though he knew spirits deserved the praise.

"Amotkan's gift is great," Tor said, spreading his arms toward the mountain of fish. "People thank Amotkan for making Chinook, and Chinook for giving up life."

"Uh-mot-kan?" Wyecat asked.

Tor swelled with pride. It was so good that his new tribesman finally wanted to learn!

"Amotkan is our Creator, a god even greater than Wahawkin."

Wyecat looked confused.

Tsilka spoke to her brother in Tlikit, as she did whenever Tor said more than two words.

"Mmmm." Wyecat nodded, stretching his arms to mean large. "Amotkan same Sahalie."

"Bigger than Sahalie," Tor said, wondering who *that* was. "Amotkan is the greatest god of all."

"Mmmm." Wyecat nodded as if he understood.

"Watch what I do," Tor said to Tsilka. "The fish must be cut up in a sacred way."

He took a gutted fish from the pile and placed it on a flat rock with its head pointing the way it had been swimming, slit, empty belly to them, back to the river.

"From respect, you must keep the blade sharp." He scraped his stone blade across his arm to show that it shaved hairs.

"Now watch . . . you cut the fish this way, the same every time."

He sliced the head off cleanly, then the fins and tail.

"You throw these parts in the river as you did with the guts, so Chinook's spirit will find its way."

"As you work, say, 'The people thank you, Chinook.' "

Tsilka nodded. "People thank Chinook."

Wyecat raised his fist. "Chinook!"

Tor grinned. "Right. Now, the skin you save for later."

With a scraper, he carefully peeled the thin, shiny skin away, leaving it in two pieces with no holes. Then he cut along the backbone, making two slabs of pink meat. He threaded the slabs onto thin willow sticks, and thrust them into the ground so they stood up by a small fire, whose smoke would flavor the meat, whose heat would dry it.

It was good that Tsilka was used to hard work. She would have to make many fires and keep them going, turning the meat often so it would dry evenly. When the slabs were thin and leathery, she would grind them into fine meal. Packed in the roasted skins, this could be stored for a long time, even buried.

Tor cut up four salmon before Tsilka was ready to take over.

He sat by Wyecat, cleaning his slimy hands with sand. "Men are glad this is women's work."

Wyecat nodded. "Women work!"

They smiled as if they knew something women didn't.

"Wait till we show your father!"

"Timshin laugh!"

And wait till I show Ashan! Tor thought. *She'll have to believe in me now!*

Weather was kinder than it should have been in the moon Autumn Begins. The warm air was rich with the smell of roasting fish. As hard as Tsilka worked, she couldn't keep up. Tor and Wyecat stopped fishing every day. They sat around watching her work, laughing and teasing her about moving too slowly. Once in a while, they helped—not with fish-cutting, but with fire-tending.

The two men, warriors of such different tribes, were becoming as close as brothers born of the same woman.

Now that they spent less time fishing, they had begun work on a rock picture Wyecat wanted to leave here. He had chosen a high stone—smooth, flat, broad as a man's chest—that looked down on the new river home. Wyecat was picky about the work, letting his friend know how lucky he was to be allowed to help. Tor kept his pecking carefully inside the lines charcoaled on the dark rock.

Carving made a rhythmic *tick-ticking*. Pecking away gave a man time to think.

Pictures on rock . . . Tor shook his head. He didn't understand why the Tlikit people made pictures on all kinds of things. These rock pictures took great time and effort, and seemed meant to last forever, but what were they for? Tlikit men carved designs in the wood of their spears and the frames of their huts. Women wove designs of colored grass into baskets and hats they made. It took a lot of extra time. Why did they do it? Could these designs be what kept Tlikit baskets from leaking?

Tor laughed to himself. *The carvings on the hut frames . . . they certainly don't stop leaking!*

The Shahala people—who in many ways seemed more *serious* to Tor than these dryland primitives—didn't have time for all this carving and painting, though it was true that his tribe sometimes painted for *sacred* reasons. Each Shahala person had a mark that, when drawn, would be like speaking the person's name to spirits. It was known that some signs, like those for men and women, had powers. In Tor's tribe, the Moonkeeper did most of the painting that was needed. *Well*, he thought, *except for Tenka. My sister paints for no reason on leather and wood, but she's strange in other ways, too.*

Lovely Tsilka climbed the rocks bringing the men their high sun meal. While they ate the salmon she had baked in a pit—a Shahala way that Tor could hardly believe they'd never thought of—Tor tried to find out more about this strange way her people had of wasting time.

"The Tlikit make pictures on everything? Why?"

Brother and sister looked at each other with questioning faces, shrugged, and looked back at Tor.

Finally Tsilka pointed to her eye and said, "Pretty."

Wyecat made motions with his hands, and said, "Good feel."

Tor shook his head. He didn't really understand.

Wyecat's design—a circle over lines that curved like smiles—was another thing that gave Tor cause for wonder. He'd seen it before, of course. Ashan had drawn the same thing and called it their son's namesign.

He asked them what it meant.

Tsilka pointed to the circle. "Moon. Lake," she said as she traced the curved lines below. "Sign mean people."

"Oh," Tor said.

The sign of the Tlikit people was also the sign of Tor's son. The very same lines that meant "moon" and "lake" to them, meant "sun" and "river"—"Kai El"—to him. How could this be? *How?* He wondered if in the Misty Time, Shahala and Tlikit might have lived together as one tribe. Was this shared design an omen that this coming together of peoples was planned? That all that had happened was the will of spirits?

Thinking about this gave Tor an idea for a name for the new home by Mother River. Naming was Moonkeeper's work, but where was Ashan?

"Our new home is Teahra," he said. "Shahala for Together."

Soon they had more fish meal than three people could carry. Did they stop? No. They dug holes and buried more. The tribe would eat like gods this winter in Teahra by the bountiful river. The three stayed too long. Tor couldn't think of leaving his life's dream coming true. Not yet.

But the flight of geese and swans came to an end. Day by day, the wind that blew on the river grew colder. Finally the voice inside Tor screamed loud enough to be heard.

Winter's not coming, fool—it's here! Every creature is safe in its home by now—except Tor, Wyecat and Tsilka.

Except Ashan and Kai El.

CHAPTER
33

"I t's time to go back," Tor said, as he and Tsilka cuddled after lovemaking.

"No!"

"We must bring your father and the others. You know that."

"Wyecat go. Tsilka and mate stay."

Tor pushed her away. "How many times have I told you? I'm your friend, maybe even your god, but I am not your mate! I will never be your mate! I *have* a mate!"

"No tell again!" she snapped.

He saw denial in her flashing eyes, clenched jaw and tense body. Heat rose from her as if something seethed under her skin . . . anger, frustration, or . . . what?

Tor shouted, not caring if Wyecat woke up and heard.

"I will say it again! And you listen! I never lied. I told you about my mate and my son. I will not leave them alone in winter. But I promise I'll come back with them in spring."

"Then Wahawkin have two mates?"

Tor thumped his forehead with his palm. "No! Where I come from, men only have one! Are you stupid? Can't you understand?"

"What if Tsilka make Wahawkin baby?"

Tor shook his head. As if spirits would send a child to such wrongful lovers. "A Tlikit baby would be lucky to have Shahala blood."

"Would you be father?"

"I would. But you *still* wouldn't be my mate."

"Tsilka want Wahawkin for mate!"

"Then stop being a rattlesnake!"

She snatched up one of the sleeping skins and crawled away.

"Trickster! Hate! Kill!"

Tsilka would get over it—women did. Tor was sorry, but he could never betray Ashan, his soulmate from time before time—Tsilka would just have to understand that. His father's words had never meant more: Women really are the most confusing creatures Amotkan put in the world.

Tor fell asleep to the sound of Tsilka's sobs. Did he dream of the Tlikit woman who'd done all she could to make him love her? No. He dreamed of making love with Ashan.

Tsilka was a different woman after that night. At first Tor thought it was nothing to worry about, only a woman's shifting mood, but it turned out to be much more. Her love changed to hate, completely, the new as strong as the old had seemed. Tor saw pain trying to hide behind her bitter scowl. The graceful looseness of her body became stiff. Somehow, the same woman was no longer pretty. She did her work, but refused to meet Tor's eyes, and would only talk if forced. She slept by herself, which made Tor feel bad, even angry, as he lay in the dark wanting what every man wants, needing what she would not give. *What snakes women can be!*

But, he told himself, *maybe this is good. Maybe she finally accepts the truth*. He had never lied, had only wanted to help her people in their quest for new blood. He didn't see how he could have treated her better. Why couldn't she just be happy for the time they'd had?

A few days later at Tor's command they left Teahra for the Tlikit village. Wyecat's rock markers pointed the way. Each shouldered a large bag woven by Tsilka, heavy with fish meal. The sun was hot for this late in the season, and Tor was glad for the shade of the wide Tlikit hat he'd gotten used to wearing.

It was a strange, silent trip—three nights sleeping and four days walking. Tsilka stayed far behind the men. Sometimes they lost sight of her. Wyecat's face said he knew something was wrong with his sister. Tor wished he could explain that she was acting like a rattlesnake—like a woman! But it was still hard to talk without her help.

Tsilka made him mad, but in his heart Tor knew her behavior was his fault, so he felt sorry for her too. But during most of the trip, he thought of Ashan and Kai El. How soon he'd be with them! Out of respect for his Tlikit friends, he kept his joy to himself.

The wanderers topped the last hill as night chased day from the sky. The Tlikit village lay before them. Wyecat threw off his pack and ran down yelling. Tor walked. Tsilka dragged.

The Tlikit people rushed up, shouting and weeping. They had long ago lost hope of seeing the three explorers again. As they hugged and pinched to be sure the three were real, the crying turned to laughter. A bonfire celebrated the return of Wahawkin and the Lost Ones, as they had come to be called. By its light, the people feasted on fish meal stirred in baskets with hot water. They chattered, laughed, slapped each other's backs, and ate until they were too full to talk. Finally it was quiet, except for fish-smelling belches and the crackling of the fire.

A grim smile carved Tsilka's face. It didn't fool Tor, but he was having too much fun to be bothered by a woman's bad mood. Tor was the Tlikit god Wahawkin, as full of himself as he was of fish, all swelled up with what his mother would have called "too much air in the head."

Wyecat stood. Tor settled back to watch a thing he truly enjoyed—be it Shahala man or Tlikit—a brother acting out brave deeds. By now, Tor understood enough of their language to follow Wyecat's story. Besides, Tor had *lived* the story.

Wyecat told his people about their new home. "Chiawana," he said, doing well with the Shahala word for Mother River. His hands showed that it was larger than their dead lake. He told how Wahawkin had called a horse, Kusi, who knew the way; how Wahawkin had called a fish, Chinook, so *many* that no one would hunger again. "Great god Wahawkin told us truth!" Wyecat said—or something like that.

Wyecat finished with a sweeping bow in front of Tor. The people gazed on their god with awe, waiting for him to speak.

"Tell my words," Tor said to Tsilka.

She gave him a hateful look, then dropped her eyes and nodded. Tor stood and faced the tribe, hoping the she-snake would say his true words.

"Wahawkin promised water, and gave it," Tor said. "Now Wahawkin must go to his other family."

Tsilka rattled something too fast for Tor to understand. It must have been right, because people shook their heads and made grumbles that meant no.

Tor went on. "Wyecat knows the way to Mother River. He will lead you. In spring I will come back, and be with you forever." For a nice touch, he added, "Wahawkin promises his favored people."

It seemed they understood, and accepted.

Timshin offered Wahawkin his own hut, the largest, and any of the women. But Tor wanted to sleep in the shelter where he'd been a captive, where he'd come to know and care for Tsilka and Wyecat. And he wanted Tsilka, one last time.

Making love to the silent, unresisting woman wasn't very enjoyable, but it drained him, and that was good—he needed sleep for the long walk home. Tor drifted off, hoping to dream of Ashan.

White fire jolted his sleeping brain. *Get away!* screamed instinct. He lunged, but something had him, ripping his flesh. As he threw his weight against it, pain became agony.

He shrieked. *"My leg!"*

Gasping, Tor grabbed the thing piercing his lower leg. His fishing spear! He'd been speared like a fish with his own weapon! Under his leg, the barbed end was jammed in the ground. Tsilka was lashing the butt of the spear to the frame of the shelter. If he struggled, he'd tear himself apart.

"There!"

"You're dead!" he screamed. *"Dead!"*

"Hah! Go on, kill me!"

Tor groaned.

"Can't hurt! No god! Only man! Tsilka's mate now!"

"Never!"

"You are! Need me! Can't walk! Other mate die, you glad Tsilka!"

As Tor screamed and screamed, part of his mind noticed that Tsilka had never spoken better Shahala.

Tor's screams brought people with torchlit, horrified faces. Timshin grabbed his daughter's shoulders and shook, shouting in her face.

She wrenched away. "He can't hurt us!" she said in Tlikit. "I used magic! His own spear!" With a look of triumph and hate, she kicked Tor in the side, and spat in his face.

"Come on, great god! Turn me into a lizard!"

Oh! How Tor wished he could do just that!

"See? The god is a trickster! He showed us water, but we won't find it now! Wahawkin scattered Wyecat's markers on the way back!"

So that's what she'd been doing when she was out of sight! Tor heard growls and grumbles. Someone kicked him; his leg tore. He couldn't help screaming.

Tsilka shouted. "Wahawkin wants to leave and never return? Hah! I say we *make* the trickster show us the way!"

CHAPTER
34

Fast as lightning, slow as cold honey, the summer without Tor slipped away. Days blurred together, while each night lasted forever. In the shortening daylight, Ashan buried her despair in work. She and Kai El gathered food, medicine and firewood. She saw to Moonkeeper tasks: greeting spirits every morning, keeping track of passing time, and making rituals, at least the important ones. Spirits might laugh at her puny efforts, but that didn't stop her from keeping the ways—she might be the only Moonkeeper in the world.

In the sleepless nights, her thoughts were dark as an unlit cave. *What had happened to Tor? What will happen to us? What should I do?*

Stay or go . . . Time after time, Ashan made up her mind, then changed it.

Yearning to belong made her want to go home—to her *real* home, Anutash. To have people again, to care for and lead, as she was born to do; friends for Kai El; loneliness just a memory.

How can we live without a tribe? We can't . . .

But how can we live without Tor? Now that she knew his love, could she bear life without it? Every moment he was gone reminded her how miserable a life without her mate would be.

Even if she could decide between tribe and soulmate, there

were terrible dangers to think about. Death seemed to be the result of either choice.

To go meant to travel with no man to protect them from animals or slave hunters, in a direction she wasn't sure of. If they were lucky, and the spirits guided them to Anutash, what would the Shahala do to the Moonkeeper who'd been gone nearly three turnings of the seasons? What would they do to Kai El, son of Tor, the Evil One? What if there *were* no Shahala?

But staying in the Home Cave meant the slow death of starving. The meat was almost gone, and people could not live on plants. Ashan shuddered, thinking of what it would be like to watch her child waste and die. Or be shredded by a bear, like her mother. This was not a foolish concern: A bear had tried to take their cave last winter. Ashan wanted Tor to kill it, but he had driven it off because they hadn't needed meat. If it came back now . . . she couldn't possibly kill a bear.

Of course, if *he* came home, all their problems would be over. But what made her think he would? Tor was probably a long time dead.

Dead, Ashan told herself over and over. *Tor is dead*. She needed to believe it to get on with life. But she was terrified to believe it. She'd mourned him once, and it had almost killed her.

Very confused, Ashan cried at night instead of sleeping. Each morning she had less strength, less desire, more numbness of mind and body. Why didn't she pray to the spirits for guidance? Because she was afraid of either answer.

One day the answer came anyway, not by spirit voice, but by a voice of nature that speaks to shamans: the swans and geese. It was not that they were winging overhead toward Warmer and their winter home, but that they had *stopped*. Now that she no longer heard their barking, she understood what they'd been saying.

"Home," Ashan said to herself. "Go home."

Confusion left her. With cold heart and clear head, she waited another day, but the answer stayed the same. That night she sorted through their belongings by the smoky light of the fish-oil lamp, packing her antelope carrier with things they would need for the journey.

"What doing?" Kai El kept asking.

"We're going on a long trek to our new home."

He didn't understand. As far as he knew, there was only one home, and it was this cave.

"Kai El stay," he said. "Wait for Adah."

"No. Little ones go with their mothers."

"Want Adah!"

Ashan was losing patience. "Kai El, you will love our new home. There are lots of people, and many little ones like you."

He shook his head. "Hate little ones! Wait for Adah!"

She had a sudden urge to slap him. Instead she yelled. "Adah's not coming! Not ever!"

Kai El crumpled in sobs. Ashan didn't go to him. She should have, but with all this to do, there wasn't time to make a child of two summers understand what she herself did not.

Kai El's tears put him to sleep, but Ashan didn't sleep at all that night. Not that there was so much to pack; fear with too many names kept her awake. The answer of the geese and swans may have taken confusion away, but it did nothing for fear.

As first light chased shadows to the back of the cave, Ashan pulled the horsehair rope tight around the skin-wrapped bundle. She sighed, looking at their home for the last time. It was too small, and soon the walls would drip their winter tears, but Ashan knew she'd never love another place like she loved the Home Cave.

Her eyes strayed from the pool of sunlight spreading on the floor to the medicine plants drying on the smoke-black walls, to the handprints over the door. She remembered the day they had made them—first Tor, then Ashan. "Up!" Kai El had said. Tor had lifted him, and the boy had spread his little fingers against the wall. Ashan had taken another mouthful of mud, and spat it around her hand. "No bigger than a lynx paw!" her mate had said, laughing. The sound of Tor's laughter rang again in her mind; her tongue remembered the slick taste of white clay. Sadness squeezed her heart; she shook her head and pushed the memory away.

Ashan checked once more the rocks that hid the storage pit. They looked as if they'd always been there. No one would think of moving them. But if *he* ever came back, he would have what she couldn't take—dried roots and berries, seeds, a riverwood bowl full of honey. *But no meat.*

Tears stung her eyes as sunlight touched the corner where Tor had held her through so many nights. She smoothed the pile of skins that had been their sleeping place. Her fingers traced the stone above where Tor had scratched their signs— Eagle From The Light, Whispering Wind, and, safe between them, Sun River. *No matter who shelters here*, she thought, *our signs will always say this was our home.*

Ashan shouldered the heavy pack, and awoke her son. They scrambled down the shale for the last time. Silent tears rolled down her face as they walked rugged ridges and forested canyons, keeping direction by the sun between Colder and Where Day Ends. Kai El walked for a while, then wanted to ride. She lugged two packs—the boy on her chest, and all their things in the antelope skin against her chest—and felt she was getting stronger with every step.

Tempted to rest at high sun, she only stopped long enough to eat. After berrycakes and sips from the waterpouch, they were on the way again. Frown-faced Kai El squirmed in the carrier. He didn't want to ride; he didn't want to walk. He wanted the Home Cave. He wanted Adah.

On the down side of a steep ridge, leaf trees replaced the needle trees of higher ground. They were coming to a river . . . a big one, by the sound of it. Ashan didn't remember any river when Tor had brought her this way. *Where are we?* she worried.

The swift torrent blocked them. Ashan headed downstream. The thick trees along the riveredge made it get dark sooner than it should have. She was wondering where they'd sleep, when the river changed direction—back toward the Home Cave.

"Bat dung!" Ashan said. Tired, unable to think, she dropped on a sandy curve of beach. "We'll have to sleep here."

Kai El got out of the carrier, gave her a mean look, and plopped on the ground.

Then Ashan saw a better place to sleep: As it made its bend, the river split around a bush-scattered island. They'd be safer there, and tomorrow maybe they could cross to the other side.

"We're going to sleep out there." She pointed to the island. "Get in, and hold everything high."

"No-o-o," Kai El whined, but he got in the carrier.

Careful to keep her balance on the slippery bottom, Ashan crossed slowly. Nothing got wet but her legs.

"This is good, Kai El," she said when they were on the island. "Animals won't swim to get us."

Ashan longed for the comfort of a fire. There was wood to burn, and she had fire sticks, but the light might draw something bad. She laid out their skins in the dark that had come so quickly. Kai El crawled in and slept. Ashan curled around him, sure that she wouldn't sleep a moment. She was right.

Sharp wind blew down the river, finding every gap in the sleeping skin. Rivernoise mixed with other sounds, making them strange. Was that coyote, or wolf? Dove or owl? And that—a bear's roar? The river-twisted sounds were the voices of her fears. Terrible pictures chased themselves through her mind.

What chance do we have, she thought, *a woman and child alone? Will we be eaten by animals? Taken for slaves? Or just wander in these endless mountains until we die? It would have been better to face starvation and cave-stealing bears.*

If death is our fate, she decided, *we'll meet it in the place we love.*

Ashan had never been more relieved to see the gray of any dawn. She awoke Kai El.

"Amah was wrong. We're going home, to wait for . . . Adah."

"Good!"

Ashan saw Chinook. Yesterday in the deepest part of the river, a few silver chiefs had brushed her legs. Today there were many more—so many they should be easy to kill. Slabbed, she could handle two or three—if she didn't have to carry Kai El. Once home, she'd dry it, grind it, and sprinkle the fish meal on whatever they ate. Salmon was the best food for its size. Whatever she took home would keep them alive that much longer. She could carry more if she stayed here to dry them, but that would take too long; desire for home was fierce.

"See the fish, Kai El?"

"Big!" He had only seen trout—the river below the Home Cave was too small for salmon.

"Chinook, silver chief. We're going to take some home. Kai El is a big boy who walks by himself? All the way?"

He puffed up like a strutting grouse. "Help carry Chinook!"

"Good boy. Now you sit here until I come back—I mean, *don't even move.*"

Kai El sat down, and poked his chest. "Good boy stay!"

Ashan stepped in. The water was cold, but she put it out of her mind. Rivernoise made it easy to forget everything but the task. She thought she'd be able to reach in and grab a silver chief, but they slipped through her hands. Time after time, she lunged, went under, and came up spluttering—with no fish. It was frustrating! And cold—you can't really forget that you're freezing! But a Shahala woman gritted her teeth and kept going.

Ashan realized that fishing with her hands wasn't going to work. She cursed Tor. *What a dung-beetle! Why didn't he teach me to use a spear?*

Then she had another idea. Once, when Tor's life had depended on it, she had hunted with rocks. She'd never heard of fishing with a rock, but it couldn't be worse than this.

Ashan picked a rock from the riverbottom—not too heavy to hold, but heavy enough to kill. Slowly, she made her way downriver. Staring into the water, she chose a fish, swung, splashed. Missed! Over and over.

Bat dung! This isn't working either!

She came to a shady pool, chest-deep, wide enough to slow the current. The salmon swam in circles, resting as if they knew about the rough water ahead. *Smart*, she thought. *But women are smarter than fish . . .*

She would have to trap one to kill it. She broke off a leafy branch and stood in the middle of the pool, scooping through the water, trying to bring a fish close. The rock was ready in her other hand. She let rivernoise drown everything out, and focused . . .

Caught by her branch, a Chinook nudged her thigh. She swung, and—*thud!*—connected. She fell on the fish, and squeezed hard. It wriggled for just a heartbeat, then died.

"Yes!" she squealed. The fish was huge—heavier than her son!

Ashan looked upriver, but couldn't see the island where she'd left Kai El. She'd gone farther than she realized. She waded upriver, pulling the salmon by the slit behind its head—easier than carrying it—water made things light.

Thrilled with herself—they *could* survive without a man!— Ashan shouted as the island came into sight.

"Kai El! Amah killed a—"

She saw a wide, wet spot where her son should be. Across the river, wet dirt trailed away into the trees—a lot of wet dirt, as if there had been a struggle.

In that instant, Ashan knew: her son hadn't just wandered away—he'd been kidnapped!

"Kai El!" she cried.

CHAPTER
35

I n unthinking horror—*Amotkan, not my baby!*—Ashan dropped the salmon and bolted for the riveredge, as if the riverbottom were dry land. For a moment she ran on water, then her foot slipped. And caught. The other flew. Arms flailing, she went down. The leg twisted under her. Pain shredded her senses, but she grunted instead of shrieking, and with her hands—*hurry!*—moved the rock trapping her foot.

She shrieked as her foot came free, grabbed her leg, squeezed, and fell back gasping at the pain. The water choked around her, over her. The sky looked shimmery wet.

Must be strong—Kai El will die!

Ashan gritted her teeth, sat up in the water, and became a medicine woman looking at someone else's injury. It was the lower part of the leg on the side of the heart. The flesh wasn't torn. The leg was straight—not pushed out of line as injured legs sometimes were. But the pain! She could not ignore it! Little men inside were chipping her bone into spear points! With this much pain, it had to be broken. She should get something for a splint to keep it straight, but there wasn't time, or anything here in the hateful river that could be used.

Ashan dragged herself through the water. The pain was horrible! *Make a friend of pain—that's what you must do.*

She babbled to it, asked it to help, to drive her until she found her son.

Going nowhere! answered her new friend, Pain.

As she pulled herself through the rushing water, she sent a thought through the door in her forehead.

Kai El! Amah's coming!

Their minds met. His fear paralyzed her! She had to block him out, not even *think* of how terrified he must be. Ashan allowed herself only one thought: *Get him!*

The riveredge was still wet where several people had climbed out. Ashan hauled herself up the slippery bank, tried to stand, and collapsed, choking back a scream. The pain would not even allow standing, certainly not walking or running. Her leg's message was, *No! I'm hurt, and you're not going to make it worse!*

"All right!" she said. "I'll crawl!"

Her fastest crawl would be too slow. When the footprints dried, how would she know where they'd taken him?

They . . . She wondered. *Who?*

No time for thinking. Ashan focused will on body. Arms and good leg scrabbled along the careless wet track. The bad leg trailed, screaming protest.

Over and over she told herself, *I am master of pain, pain will help me find him*—and found she could crawl faster than she thought.

Ashan dragged herself along a much-used trail, easy to follow even when the tracks dried. After a while, she knew she was following five men—four of them fat, or carrying something heavy. There were no little footprints, but that didn't mean Kai El wasn't with them. His faint scent said one of them carried him.

She'd never catch striding men by crawling. She tried to stand—*doesn't hurt . . . doesn't hurt . . . get . . . my baby!*—but the useless leg wouldn't hold her—it just *wouldn't!* She saw a long branch on the ground, almost as thick as her wrist. One end split like spread fingers. *A crutch to do what this useless leg will not*, she thought. With the split under her arm, she pushed herself up. The crutch reached the ground. She swung it out and took a hopping, jolting step with her good leg.

Amotkan! It hurts! But she could fight that. *Swing, hop, ignore the pain; swing, hop—it's working—keep going.* She was thirsty; she could fight that too. The hardest thing was weakness of will that came in waves. Some cowardly part of her wanted to lie down and rest, just for a moment. But if she lost even a moment, she'd never find them. She fought waves of weakness with thoughts of Kai El. What would they do to him? What would she do without him? What would she do when she found them?

Somehow, she vowed, *I will get him back!*

Mountainous clouds moved in from Where Day Ends, becoming thicker and darker as the worst day of Ashan's life dragged on. She crutched along the trail, keeping cries of pain inside. She slumped to the ground and crawled for a while when weakness demanded that she stop. When weakness became too strong to resist, she called to her friend Pain by jabbing the ground with her broken leg. When even Pain threatened to fail her, she made visions of Kai El in her mind, full of unspeakable torture . . . and knew nothing but her own death would stop her.

The thickening clouds threatened storm. Ashan was glad for the cool. When afternoon gloom turned to black—*how did night come so fast?*—she was heading toward the top of a ridge. In the dark, she had to crawl again, just to keep on the trail. Pain that would paralyze others drove her onward, but how long could she fight mind-numbing weariness? She who would stop for nothing prayed the baby-thieves would stop for the night.

In the dark, smells were stronger. Kai El's—of life, not death—gave her hope. She tried to ignore the stain of terror on it—the cruelest thing was that her baby should know such fear. Other scents said she was tracking hunters with fresh elk meat. She'd never smelled scent like theirs. They must be Snake Men. By their long, careless strides, she knew they must be on their way home.

She had a bitter thought of Tor, who had decided that none but his family lived in these mountains. Slave-taking Snake Men? Just another story, he said, to keep people from leaving the tribe.

A story has stolen our son, you fool!

The little men inside her leg chipping bones into spear points changed to pounding muscles with hot grinding stones. Pain did not stop to rest, nor did Ashan.

New scent bristled her hair. Panic froze her. *Cougar! More than one!*

Cats don't hunt people! yelled the voice inside. *Right*, she thought, and remembered the elk meat carried by the baby-thieves. Cats *had* been known to steal prey—it was easier than killing. For different reasons, she and cats were tracking the same victims!

Ashan prayed to the Cougar Spirit. "Puma, hear this mother who loves her son as a cat loves her kittens: Please, please, please help me get him back!"

Follow the cats, answered a mind-voice.

Stalking cougar moved with stealth, saving speed for the attack. Ashan heard no sound, but knew they were close—their thick scent covered all others. She smelled three—unusual, but not impossible; cats hunted alone, except for a short time when mothers taught their young.

The wind rose, beating the limbs of trees, tearing at Ashan's hair and wiping scent from the trail. Lightning flashed in the distance. The ridgetop was stark against the bright-for-a-moment sky. Thunder told of a bad storm on its way. Dry leaves rattled along, trying to escape the coming fury.

Ashan topped the ridge. The wind was fierce on the other side. Lightning showed a gradual downhill slope that turned into flatland with few trees.

A distant glow told of a used-up campfire. *Amotkan! There they are!*

She crawled down the slope, not knowing what she would do—just knowing that she must see her little one. The wind shifted; a mix of smells hit her: Kai El, Snake Men, smoke, cats, fear. She kept the fireglow in sight as she neared the camp. Lightning flashes showed what she faced: one man on guard by haunches of meat, others sleeping—

Kai El! She saw him! On the ground, tied to a board with only his face showing. *Now* Ashan must decide what to do.

Puma decided for her. Screaming cougars leapt from the darkness on the other side of the camp. A big one took down the man on guard. Two young ones went for the haunches of elk. The other men fled in noisy terror.

Ashan dashed into the chaos, grabbed the board with her shrieking son, and clambered away. Somehow—swinging a crutch, dragging a board with a child big as a coyote—she managed something like running, stumbling and getting up over and over again, feeling no pain.

Kai El howled. Wind and thunder deafened her. All around beat the fury of nature gone crazy. Balls of sky-ice pelted her. Rain poured. Little rivers streamed off her. Lightning streaked down. A tree near them exploded in flame. Ashan screamed . . . fell . . . the ground opened like a mouth to swallow her and the wailing baby. Down they fell . . . down into a hole . . .

Ashan knew no more.

CHAPTER
36

An ancient man rolled over with a groan as sunlight crept to the back of his cave. His bones ached every morning, but this morning it was worse; he might not make the effort to get up. Loneliness pierced him, sharper than usual. *A man can't get used to loneliness*, he thought. *Not ever.*

To help fill the emptiness of time, Ehr often started mornings thinking of the long ago. He closed his eyes. The sound of the waterfall outside his cave carried his mind to another time. He saw Ulak and Tren, his father and mother, and Moxmox, his older brother. Though he hadn't seen his family for most of a lifetime, clear pictures of them came.

His mother used to say that Ehr, named Shywash then, was a smart boy. His mind sparked with ideas of everything from trying new food to why there are stars. Some ideas were foolish; a few were very good. When he was as tall as his mother's shoulder, the shaman of his tribe became angry with him. As a child he couldn't understand why; later he realized the mean old woman had thought the clever boy a threat. Shywash was too young to have his ideas respected; it didn't matter if they were good or not.

Once Moxmox got sick from eating bad meat. The shaman came with her rattles and bones. Mumbling and yelling, she reached inside the young man's body—right through the skin of his belly. The hole closed when she pulled out her hand, leaving no mark. The ugly hag showed them "the sickness," a bloody hunk the size of a rabbit's liver in the palm of her hand.

Maybe because he was short, Shywash saw what no one else did. The shaman didn't really reach inside his brother's body—she just pushed on him, pretending. The bloody thing that was supposed to be the sickness had come from inside her robe.

Shywash made the biggest mistake ever—he told the truth. The shaman called it "wrong speaking," and cut off his tongue so he'd never do it again.

He became a man of mating age who looked like any other, but no woman wanted the one who couldn't talk—now called "Ehr" because that was a sound he could make. Even Moxmox wished they didn't share blood. Ehr only stayed for the mother who loved him in spite of all. When she died, the young mute left his tribe.

Ah well, the old mute thought. *It hasn't been so bad.*

Hrumph! thought another part of his mind. *At first it was worse than bad.*

Ehr had wandered, hungry, forgotten by people and spirits; lonely and wondering why he missed the ones who didn't want him. One day, curious about a creek that ran into the river he'd been following, he walked up a narrow canyon and found a waterfall. A large cave hid behind it . . . the finest cave . . . a home to live in forever. And he had been here ever since.

Once in a while, Ehr saw hunters by the big river below, but none ever came up the creek. Even if someone did, he doubted that they'd find his home. The rock behind the falling water looked solid.

Though he had shelter, food was a problem. Hunting alone was difficult; it took men working together to bring down prey. The best Ehr could hope for was a sick animal or a young one strayed from its mother. One day the hungry man sat on a ridge near his cave. Down at the river, animals came and went, crossing the same paths. If only they would *stay* there and wait for him . . .

Sudden as a rattlesnake, the best idea of Ehr's life struck: *dig a hole for them to fall into!*

He had picked a spot on a well-beaten path. With a sharp stick, he loosened the red-brown clay, then dug it out with his hands and piled it on a skin. He dragged the heaped skin and spread the dirt away from the hole, again and again. The animals stopped coming while he worked, and it worried him. Would they smell manscent and stay away forever? But Ehr didn't let worry get in the way of ideas. He was glad it was the dry season—rain would have turned the growing pit into a muddy mess. Day after day he worked, wearing the points from many digging sticks. As the hole deepened, he used a branched tree trunk to climb in and out. When it was deeper than a man with a child standing on his shoulders, and wider than a man laying down, Ehr decided it was done. To hide the pit, he covered it with leafy branches, an idea that came from thinking of how the waterfall hid his cave. After a time, the animals came back. Deer and elk fell in, and once a bear. Trapped, often with broken legs, they were easy to kill. With more meat than he could use, Ehr never hungered again.

As the seasons passed, he was comfortable, but lonely. He made friends of animals who came to drink from a little pool outside the cave. Sadly, there was always the day when an animal friend came no more. A new one would take its place, but the loss of each hurt . . . Ehr had outlasted so many. Most of them went somewhere else to live for the cold season, but a lynx and an old wolf stayed.

Get up, old man. Your friends need food, said one side of his mind in silent conversation with the other.

I won't be here forever. When I die, they'll have to make it on their own.

But you will care for them while you can. You made them this way.

Growling, Ehr got up. His old bones shivered in the damp air, but he didn't want the work of a fire. In the almost-dark, he put on loincloth, leggings, and moccasins. He ate sour red berries that he'd found yesterday. *Should have waited till they were purple*, he thought. Honey would have made it better, but his honey was almost gone. He loved honey, but at his age, bee stings seemed a lot to go through. So he made it last . . . as well as making food taste better, honey can soothe a man feeling sorry for himself.

Ehr put food for his animal friends in a waist-pouch. With a piece of stiff leather over his head, he walked through the falling water. It was bright outside. He hung the wet piece of leather on a branch, took a deep breath of washed air and looked around . . . wet rocks, more water than usual plunging over the fall. *Rain last night. It's about time. Good-bye dry season, hello cold.*

No more worry about fire, he thought, remembering dry summers and brushfires started by lightning, moving so fast they didn't burn trees, so hot, they killed most life. Ehr had managed to run to the cave to wait them out—all but once. That time, with the firewall between him and home, he had hidden in the pit by the river. His back had cooked as the fire rushed over him. He was sick for days afterward. Now he feared fire, and was always glad when the danger ended.

Ehr picked his way down the mossy rocks, squatted at the edge of the small, gravel-bottomed pool, and made throat noises.

Ayah, the lynx, stepped out of the brush, crossed the shallow pool and warily took a piece of meat from Ehr's hand. She splashed back across and sat on the other side, keeping green eyes on him as she chewed. Ehr had first known Ayah as a mewing kitten, bright with brown and yellow stripes, brought here with litter-mates by her mother. Ehr had also called the mother Ayah, No-Tail Cat, and she had been a very special friend, allowing him to stroke her fur, making purring sounds in her throat. This daughter of the first Ayah wouldn't let Ehr touch her, but he enjoyed her company. She was the only lynx who still came.

When Ayah left, a herd of striped chipmunks came. He tossed them shelled tree-nuts. One stood guard, stiff as a little stump, while the others stuffed their cheeks until that was the widest part of them.

Shiny, green-eyed blackbirds and their plain brown mates flew down for the grass seeds he threw on the ground, ruffling their wings and gurgling in their throats to keep a little space around them.

The chipmunks skittered away, and the birds flew off as Ehr smelled his oldest companion. A three-legged she-wolf limped out of the brush, tail and ears drooping. Ehr looked into the dull yellow eyes of his once-proud friend.

Tululkin, he thought, *do your bones hurt you too?*

The wolf growled and showed her teeth.

Ehr laughed. *So you are as old as I in your way. I think we get up for each other. The day you do not come, I will know it is time to die.* The thought of death didn't frighten the tired old man, as in his youth it had; these days, the thought could be a comfort.

No other animals came. Ehr gave Tululkin the meat in his pouch, and spread the rest of the seed on the ground for those who would come later.

The ancient man was thinking about a nap, and he didn't really need more food, but it was bad to let it spoil—rotten meat had almost killed his brother. So he went to check his traps, hoping they'd be empty. By long habit, the old she-wolf limped after him. Luck was with them: Nothing had ventured out in last night's storm.

Tululkin froze as they approached the pit by the big river—the first one dug so long ago, and still the best.

Ehr heard a thin sound over the rivernoise. He strained his ears . . . a child's cry?

Chief Above! No!

Ehr broke into a run. The wailing grew. He saw where something had crashed through the leaf cover. Then he was over the pit.

It was a child! Brown with mud, tied to a cradleboard, the helpless thing stopped wailing and stared up at him with terrified eyes. Next to it, half-covered with leaves—a woman!

Sickness rose. Ehr clamped his hands over his mouth. Dead, she was, with bloodless skin, lying on her back, a spike piercing her shoulder.

Why did I put in spikes!

Because that made it easier, you lazy dung! The food was dead when you got here!

But I never dreamed I'd trap people!

No, but that is what you've done—killed a woman and orphaned a child!

Ehr had never felt so bad. *Chief Above*, he begged, as he lowered the branched trunk and climbed in the pit, *trade my old life for their young ones! Give this baby a chance to live!*

He knelt in the mud. The woman wasn't dead, but close, breathing slowly in the kind of sleep you did not wake up from. Her skin was pale as salmon-belly; she had lost too much blood. Ehr pulled her limp body from the spike. The ragged hole in her shoulder began to bleed. He stripped off his legging, made a pad, and wrapped the wound.

The old man hauled the limp woman up the branched tree, and went back for the child. He felt sorry for the little thing, wrapped so tight it couldn't move, but it would be best to leave it tied so it couldn't fight him.

Tululkin could have packed the cradleboard—she'd helped him carry meat before. But Tululkin was gone. Ehr shook his head, strapped the cradleboard to his waist, and with a strength he thought long gone, picked the woman up in his arms. He loped, then walked. After a while he felt like crawling. When he reached home, his chest was throbbing with ragged-edged pain.

Leaving the child by the gravel-bottomed pool, Ehr carried the woman up the mossy rocks and got her inside—forgetting the piece of leather to shield them from the waterfall, soaking them both. He put her on his bed, took off her wet skirt and moccasins, and covered her with furs. *Still breathing. Maybe she will live.*

He brought the child in, this time remembering the leather. Untied, the boy tried to crawl away, but couldn't. The old man carried him to his mother, where he disappeared into the furs. Ehr heard muffled whimpering—a good sound. The little one needed his mother.

They must be cold, he thought. *Should make a fire . . .*

Tiredness overtook him. Though it wasn't even high sun, he collapsed on the sanded floor of his hidden cave.

CHAPTER
37

Ashan heard her son's laughter, muffled by a fur over her head. Pain wanted her attention, but it was far away and wrapped in fuzz. She smelled a trace of Kai El's scent, and smoke, and other smells strange to her. Unformed questions buzzed behind a door in her mind she did not want to open. It held back a flood of unbearable feelings.

Kai El laughed again—beautiful, peaceful sounds—wind and falling water—

Where are we?

Pain and fear are not allowed in the otherworld.

Ashan knew what had happened, and smiled. Mother and son were dead, and, thank the spirits, they were still together. Her baby wasn't lost after all. This made the horror of before seem unimportant.

My baby . . . Ashan's drowzy thinking cleared. She poked her head from the furs, and pain tore out of its fuzzy wraps. Her leg! Oh! She remembered that pain! A new one burned in her shoulder—bad, but nothing like the hot flame trapped in her leg. She shoved pain to the back of her mind. Biting hard on her bottom lip to keep from screaming, she sat up and looked around in the dim light.

She saw him, on the far side of the cave throwing stones in a small pool, splashing himself, laughing, looking anything but dead. Wherever they were, Kai El was happy. She propped herself on an elbow, trying to ignore knives of pain.

They were in a high, wide cave, bigger than Ancestor Cave where her whole tribe lived in summer. The sides disappeared in shadows. The smooth top couldn't be reached by four men standing on each other's shoulders. Blue sky showed through several small holes. Water dripped from one, splashing into the black pool where Kai El played, sounding like birdsong drifting past a distant waterfall.

Kai El threw his last stone in the water. "All gone!" he said, and walked into the shadows. "More?"

Ashan heard a grunt for a reply. In the shadow a man sat cross-legged on a rock. He handed Kai El something, and the boy ran back to the pool.

I should be terrified to find us with a man! she thought. *But I'm not.*

Sunlight from a roof hole showed that he was ancient. Lines and wrinkles carved his face. His hair was long, thin, and white. Deep black eyes sparkled over a wide, flat nose and smiling mouth. There was kindness and wisdom in his face. Most Shahala grandfathers were scrawny with memories of old famines. This grandfather was rounded and fleshy, as if he'd never known hunger.

Kai El pointed to a little mountain he'd made with the stones. "Look!" he said to the ancient man. He jumped up and stumbled over his creation, scattering the stones, hurting his pride more than his tough little body.

"Ahh-maahh!" he wailed.

Ashan told herself to go to her child, but her stiff, hurting self didn't want to obey.

The ancient stood. Using a walking stick, he limped to the crying boy, sat with a thump, and held out his arms. Kai El threw himself into them. Sobs weakened to sniffles as the old man rocked.

Ashan was alarmed at the sight of someone holding her son in such a personal way. She stood, swaying, and called in a puny voice.

"Kai El . . ."

"Amah!" he shouted. He ran and flung himself at her. She fell back on the furs, hugging him so tightly that she could have broken him. Her tears fell like last night's rain.

"My baby," she crooned, holding him, smelling him, tasting him, loving him more than life.

"Amah," he murmured.

Lost in the moment, Ashan forgot the stranger watching from the far side of the cave. She saw only Kai El, heard only his voice, felt only love and joy. He was alive! And fine—just fine! Her child stopped nuzzling, and fell asleep.

The sun was full on the old man now. She could see him clearly, sitting on his rock, watching.

Ashan should go to their rescuer and kneel at his feet. She couldn't quite remember where they had been before this, but she knew that it had been bad—so bad, that death had been the only escape.

She tried to stand, and fell back, dizzy with hunger.

"Do you have food?" Her voice was feeble.

He narrowed his eyes and tilted his head.

"Food," she said, holding a bowl made of air in one hand, scraping air-food into her mouth with the other.

Nodding, the old man said, "Ach." He disappeared in the shadows, and in a while, came back with food.

She took the wood slab—*How long since I've eaten? Two days? Three?*—gazing with hungry eyes and watering mouth at a mound of red berries drizzled with honey, and a mush of crushed grain. There were cress sprigs tucked around the edges, and in the center, *meat!*—a heap of dried strips, at least three different kinds.

She thanked the spirits and plunged in with both hands. Picked-too-early berries were sweet with honey. Hot mush warmed her belly, then her soul. Dried meat was best of all, with its taste of smoke and herbs. It started out small in her mouth, grew as she chewed, grew even more in her belly. Wonderful, wonderful meat! So long since she'd had any! Ashan felt a little guilt for not waking Kai El, but she couldn't eat it all if she wanted to. There'd be plenty left for him.

While she ate, the old man sat on a nearby rock with a wide smile on his face. And at the same time, tears.

When she couldn't eat another bite, she put the bowl down and licked her hands.

"Thank you!"

His look said he didn't understand her Shahala words. Why should he? Why didn't Amotkan give all tribes the same speech? Well, there were signs. She clasped her hands over her chest, then held them out, as though with a gift.

He smiled. For a while they sat and stared at each other. She wished she could tell him how much better she felt with a full belly.

A sound came from his throat, more grunt than word.

"Ehhhr."

Ashan shook her head. She didn't understand.

He poked his broad, wrinkled chest. "Ehr!"

"Ehr?" she repeated.

He nodded, grinning to show five yellow teeth. He pointed to Ashan and tapped his chest, then pointed to her again.

"Ah-shan," she said slowly.

"Ah-ahh," he said. He pointed to her son.

"Kai El."

"Aaa-eh."

Ashan waited for the old man to say more, but he didn't. He stared intently, as if he could look behind her eyes to see her thoughts.

He pulled one hand across his mouth, then made two short chops toward her.

"No talk?" she said, wondering how she knew what he meant. It just seemed to pop into her head.

He nodded.

Why doesn't he want to talk anymore? At least try?

Ehr made the sign again, then opened his mouth and pointed inside. Ashan didn't see anything. He came closer and opened wider. Five yellow, snaggled teeth, and . . .

No tongue! Nothing but a lump! Horror and pity washed over her. She shrank away.

"You *can't* talk!"

Something in his face made her realize he didn't want pity. What *did* he want?

Ehr was so kind, she could almost believe he was a spirit sent to save them. His eyes and smile put her at ease. She hadn't talked to a grown person in a long time; it didn't matter if he understood. She jabbered on and on about all that had happened since her mate had left—her decision to go back to her people; Kai El's kidnapping, and what she'd gone through to get him back; how they'd fallen into a great hole, doomed to death.

He listened, head cocked, smiling with sympathy . . . listened without understanding a thing. Her voice trailed; she looked away, frustrated.

Ehr took Ashan's hands in his and guided them through signs. It was almost as if he spoke inside her mind. She thought he meant: "Ehr speaks with hands. Ehr will teach Ashan."

If he could only understand *her*—there was so much she wanted to ask.

Ehr gently pushed her back to the skins, passing his hands over his closed eyes. Sleep. He was right—she wanted sleep more than anything. She pulled Kai El close and curled around him. As Ehr spread a fur over them, his crinkled, leaf-dry hand touched her forehead. *Everything's fine*, the touch said.

Ashan gave herself to healing sleep.

Ehr gazed at them, shaking his head. *Looks real*, the ancient thought. *Smells real*. He touched the sleeping woman's dirt-stiff hair. *Feels real, but*—No matter how he stared, he couldn't believe they were living, breathing bone and flesh, and not just another dream created by his lonely old mind.

Ehr pinched his arm. No, he was not dreaming. But he'd never known anything like this . . . happiness. There'd been times when he'd thought life wasn't worth living, but now he knew why he'd struggled. It was for these two. He reached to touch the woman, and stopped just over her cheek. It was enough to feel warmth rising from her skin.

Real, living people they are . . . not spirits come to take me to Chief Above. Real, and they belong to me.

No, old man. It belongs to you to care *for them, that's all. But in caring, you'll know what it means to be* needed, *and that will be the best thing in your life.*

The next day Kai El told Ashan about his ordeal, how he'd been scared the whole time, though the men had not hurt him. He held back tears until he told about one of them stealing his neckstone . . . made by Adah . . . the thing he'd valued most now that Adah was gone.

Once her son's tears started, Ashan thought they'd never stop.

CHAPTER
38

Tor, the once-proud Shahala warrior was—*again!*—a prisoner in the Tlikit village by the dried-up lake. He wallowed in self-hate worse than that which had crippled him in the man-eaters' land. It filled his mind, leaving no space for thoughts of escape. He beat himself with useless questions. How could he have let this happen? Why had he trusted savages who once had enslaved him? Any other fool learned from his mistakes, but not the biggest fool . . . Tor the Evil, the Hated, the Stupid . . . Tor let the same people—savages not even half as smart—capture him twice.

Winter came to the Tlikit village and ripped off the scab of self-hate to lay open raw grief. Tor's soul sank into it. Day after day rain dripped through the roof of the shelter where they kept him. In his mind, Tor saw snow falling in the mountains, sealing Ashan and Kai El in the cave that would be their grave. Sorrow was stones on his chest and knives in his heart; guilt was sickness in his gut. He *had* to escape, but there seemed to be no way.

Because of Tsilka's hatred, Tor's slavery was so much worse it made the first time seem like a nap in the sun. Sometimes the venomous snake slithered by just to spit on him. He wondered why she didn't have him killed; there were days when he wished she would.

Before, it seemed to Tor that brutal life had snuffed out the fire in Tlikit women. But it was flaring again in Tsilka. The growth of her power was frightening to see, the reason for her success clear. *She was the only human ever to have power over a god.* Tsilka never let her people forget that *she* was the spider who had spun the web strong enough to catch and keep him. Knowing better herself, she made sure they believed that Tor was Wahawkin and Wahawkin was a god, telling them over and over that he was an *evil* god, a trickster the other gods wanted punished. She said they gave this privilege to the Tlikit. Many were happy to spit, throw things, and call him names. A few didn't, among them Wyecat and Chimnik.

But no one would help the evil god who'd betrayed them. Tsilka was full of hate. Timshin and the rest were afraid. Wyecat, again his guard, seemed disappointed in the trickster he'd once called friend, and more determined than ever that he not escape. This time, in addition to bound ankles and wrists, a rope around Tor's neck tightened if he moved his hands. The only good thing was that his leg healed clean where Tsilka had speared him.

Wyecat was the closest thing Tor had to a friend, and seemed to be his only hope of freedom. One day as they sat out a thunderstorm in the leaky shelter, Tor tried again.

"Wyecat, please . . . you're my special friend. This rope around my neck hurts bad."

Wyecat pretended not to hear. Like all the Tlikit except the snake Tsilka, and the boy Chimnik, Wyecat refused to speak to Tor or even meet his eyes.

A friend's plea didn't work. Maybe fear would.

"You know I am the Water Giver. I took away your lake . . . what do you think I'll do with Mother River?"

Fear's sharp smell said Wyecat understood, but he didn't answer. Wyecat was more afraid of his own people than he was of a captured god.

Tor would need someone else's help.

Chimnik . . .

Tor guessed the boy was nine or ten summers. The Tlikit didn't keep track of age; it didn't matter to them. Chimnik's black agate eyes reminded Tor of Beo's, though he seldom showed them—they darted around as if he expected to be hit.

For reasons Tor didn't understand, the boy was treated badly by the people of his tribe. He cowered when a hand was raised, but that seldom stopped the blows. Chimnik limped, so slightly that it could be missed, dragging one foot before he picked it up. He was quiet in all he did, hoping no one would notice him. Like Tor's timid sister Tenka, only worse.

Tor felt sorry for the boy. He talked to him in Shahala, which the Tlikit believed was the speech of gods. Chimnik listened. Though he didn't say much, Tor knew he understood. He was a smart boy, like Beo.

Wind rattled the Tlikit village. With a water carrier slung over his shoulder, and drips running down his leg, Chimnik shuffled to a shelter where the god Wahawkin was kept. The warrior Wyecat, who was supposed to be the guard, lay on his back snoring to rival the thunder booms of arguing sky-gods.

What a lazy, Chimnik thought, as he filled their water basket—one of his many chores. *Guarding Wahawkin lets him sleep in the middle of the day while everyone else works.*

The sky-gods sent rain pelting. Chimnik lingered in the shelter, hoping Wahawkin would talk. It was fun to understand what the speech of gods meant. Now Chimnik could say things *two* ways—like what people drank. He could call it kahwit or water. If it fell from the sky, it could be uvia or rain. Chimnik thought it gave him power no one else but Tsilka had, though he saw no use for god-speech. Maybe fun was use enough.

Why isn't everyone like him? the boy wondered. *Nice . . .*

"Why do they hit you?" Wahawkin asked.

Chimnik felt the pull of the god's eyes on the side of his face, but he didn't look.

"Chimnik lazy."

"No, you're not. You work harder than any boy. And still they hit you. Even your mother. It's not fair."

A new word. "What mean fair?"

The god had to think. "Fair is how spirits want life to be . . . you know, balanced . . . same . . ."

Wahawkin tried to show something with his bound hands: one hand going up, the other down, then bouncing together. Chimnik didn't understand.

"I'll show you. Get that stick and lay it across this rock so it stays."

Chimnik did.

"That is balance, brother."

Chimnik saw what he meant. "Fair mean stay on rock?"

The god laughed his deep-chested laugh. "There's more to it than that. Pick up those two little rocks, and give me one. Now watch what happens to the balance . . ."

Wahawkin put the little rock on one end of the stick, and the stick tipped and fell.

"You do it with your rock," the god said.

The same thing happened. *As any fool would know*, Chimnik thought.

Wahawkin said, "Now we will do it together."

They placed their rocks on the balanced stick at the same time, and the thing they had made stayed . . . whatever it was.

"That is balance," the god said. "Everything in this world depends on it. Fair is the same . . . everyone working together, each one hard as the next, everyone getting the same."

"Tlikit not fair," Chimnik said.

"I know," the god Wahawkin answered.

Halfway through winter, because of the wonderful stories told by Tsilka and Wyecat, the People of the Lake made an unheard-of decision: they would move to Teahra by the great river. The matter was so important that Timshin, the chief, made sure it was the will of every Tlikit man. It was. But they argued over what to do about their ancient village. How should they know? They had never moved since time began.

Timshin wanted to leave the mud-covered huts standing. One evening, sitting with his people by the fire, he posed a question to the only ones who had seen the Great River.

"My son . . . my daughter . . . how do you know you can find this place again? How do you know it's not a magic river that vanished as soon as you turned away? I say we leave our village as it is. If we don't find this river of yours, we can come back to our home by this dried-up lake where our people have lived forever."

A magic river! Tsilka thought with scorn. The chief's daughter, who planned to show her people the way, was sure she could find the Great River. But if it took longer than expected, she would need something to keep the tribe with her. Having no home to come back to was the answer.

Though Tsilka no longer believed in gods, the others did, and that was good for her purposes.

"Father," she answered. "Destroying the village will confuse the gods, making it impossible for them to find the tribe. That is best. Gods are tricksters. All they ever do is hurt us."

Finally, she convinced them to leave no sign that there had ever been a village here. A plan for moving was made. They would carry weapons, bowls, skins and mats. What couldn't be carried would be burned, and the ashes scattered.

After several days of hard work by all, Tsilka stood in the middle of what used to be her village, looking at bare earth where huts had stood for all time.

It is done, she thought, filling her chest with familiar air. *We are ready. Tonight my people sleep under sky. Tomorrow we set off for the future.*

It was getting dark. No fire would be made on the cleaned ground. Around her, people were settling into their skins under brightening stars. She watched them, musing.

Tsilka now had power with her tribe that no woman had ever had before. The Tlikit could not believe that a woman had brought down a god. At first, they were terrified. How long before the wounded, imprisoned god decided to destroy them? When Wahawkin the Water Giver did nothing, they became afraid of Tsilka herself. If she could do this to a god who displeased her, what could she do to a mere man or woman? She must have magic power, they said.

Tsilka knew she had no magic power, as well as she knew Tor was no god. But their ignorance served her. Someday it might be important that the tribe believe both these things—magic and gods can be fearsome weapons—so she let them.

Of all her people, Tsilka was the only one to see Tor for the ordinary man he really was.

Why, she wondered, *shouldn't the smartest be the one to lead?* Not in this tribe. Whether or not he was capable, the chief had always been a man. In time, Wyecat—who was not even the smartest *man*—would take over from their father. *Why?* wondered the woman who was coming to see herself as the best one to lead. After all, Tor's tribe was led by a woman.

As she talked to people about the wonders of the new home they were going to—something her father the chief knew nothing about—their respect grew, and their awe. Tsilka had been thinking of how she could take power from Timshin, but there was no hurry. He was old. He wouldn't last forever. It would be easier to take power from her brother than her father.

This desire for power was new to Tsilka. Confusing, too, but not as confusing as her feelings about Tor.

Tor . . .

Tsilka went to the place where Wyecat and Tor had settled for the night. The moon came up. She stared down at the one who pretended to be sleeping under the skin she had been good enough to give him.

I hate you! she thought. *And love you! Sometimes I want to kill you, sometimes I would die to be in your arms!*

As Tsilka looked down on her moonlit lover, she didn't know what she would do about him. But she knew this: she could never let him go, even if he had to be a prisoner for the rest of his life.

A tear slid down her cheek. *It was much easier*, she thought, *when I believed him a god.*

Next morning, a layer of frost covered everything.

People grumbled about sleeping with no shelter. Tsilka rallied them with a story of the Great River.

"There is no winter in Teahra," she said.

It seemed to make them feel better. But the tribe was quiet as they set out for they knew not where, following a woman, carrying all they could—the heaviest burden being carried by their slave.

On the first night out, Tsilka took Tor's sleeping skin for herself, even though she already had one. From then on, the slave slept on bare ground.

For one moon, the ragged band wandered in bitter cold. Lost, rain-soaked, wind-blown and weary, hope turned to distrust to sullen anger. Tor could have shown the way, but why?

Finally, they found and crested the long last hill.

Mother River sparkled welcome.

Home! To sleep under shelter and be dry! To sit all day

instead of roaming! They cheered and danced. Happy but for Chimnik, who wasn't allowed to join in the celebrations.

And Tor. Tortured by guilt, loss, and slavery, he could never be happy again.

And now, as if he didn't have enough to bear, Tor found a coward lurking in his body. He could not make himself use Chimnik, though the friend-making had worked, and he thought the unloved child would die for him.

A mind-voice lashed him. *What's happening to you, Tor? A warrior does anything to get what he wants.*

But the boy will die . . .

The savages would know who had freed their highly-valued slave. They already disliked Chimnik. Tor believed it wouldn't bother them to kill him.

So? Tor tried to think. *He wouldn't be the first.*

That was the problem: too many innocents doomed in this life by Tor's selfish acts. Each one became a weight of sick pain to carry forever. Tor was so heavy with guilt now, he sometimes wondered how he could crawl.

When his thoughts were clear and cold, he knew it was too late to save Ashan and Kai El anyway.

His head tried to tell him they were dead, but his heart wouldn't let his soul believe it. How could he just give up? Not even *try* to save their lives, or at least care for their bodies? He began to think again of asking Chimnik's help. Was it so wrong to trade one life for three?

"The riveredge isn't safe for people to walk," Tsilka said to the kicking child. "Make it so."

I hate her! Chimnik thought. He'd been working all day, picking up rocks that were big enough to stumble over, carrying them to the slapping water and throwing them in. He was nowhere near finished, though he *should* have been. The rattlesnake, as Wahawkin called her, wouldn't let Chimnik do it *his* way—throw some in a pile, throw the pile on another, and finally all would be down by the river.

"Take the rocks all the way every time. I don't want to see them again," Tsilka had said, first in Tlikit, then in the speech of gods, just to show she could.

Chimnik grumbled as he carried out his endless task.

"Doing it her way will take days! Women think backwards! That's why they shouldn't be chiefs—something my people have forgotten!"

The extra work made the boy angry. His life was worse in the new home by the Great River than it had ever been in the ancient village by the dried-up lake.

Though there was food and water enough, life here was worse for them all. Tsilka was wrong about this being a never-winter place—it was very cold; icy wind howled most of the time. But it was more than the weather. Something about the tribe had changed. The mood of the people was different now; they were without laughter. The Tlikit now argued: the women at the men, the men at the women, both at the children. They were more cruel than ever to the slave-god Wahawkin. They found more reasons to abuse Chimnik, and the abuse was uglier.

He was only ten summers, but he wanted to know *why*. The Tlikit taught their young that things happened for a reason—knowing reasons made it easier to bear life's burdens.

It made it a bit easier, the boy supposed, to know the reason for his life-long abuse: his mother told him that a tribe must have someone to give its bad moods to, to keep them from spreading everywhere. The kicking child was never *really* injured. It was an honor, she said, to be picked. Chimnik thought *that* was a handful of dung.

Before, he mused with a sigh of longing, *when we lived in our village by the dried-up lake . . .*

Tlikit warriors were always the first to eat. Though stronger, they were good enough to give proper share to the women, who did the same for the children. Even a slave was fairly fed.

That was our balance, Chimnik thought, remembering Wahawkin's lesson, *though we had no word for it. Everyone knew what to expect. Each would do right by the others, according to their place in the tribe. It depended on knowing who you were. It depended on respect for one another.*

But suddenly, the warriors were not so careful to make sure the women had the food they needed. At times they were hungry—in this place of plenty—and the women were angry. They had done nothing to make the men throw away their promise.

People so angry found much use for a kicking child.

Why? Chimnik wondered. *What is different now?*

The answer was the chief's daughter. Tsilka was making people sour. They knew they shouldn't have to listen to a woman, but they were afraid of her. No one called her chief, but everyone knew. She had stolen a place in the tribe that wasn't meant for a woman.

Worst of all, she did not treat people with respect.

The Tlikit chief—a man, of course—never had to tell people what to do. To be chief meant mostly the resolving of arguments—something men were naturally better at than women.

But Tsilka wanted to control—everything and everyone. And though the people followed her, they hated it.

That, the kicking child decided, *is what's wrong here . . . this place is fine, but the woman has destroyed the balance of the people.*

His arms hurt from carrying.

"I hate her! I hate them all!" he said in the speech of gods—if anyone heard, they wouldn't understand. Chimnik glanced at the slave. "Everyone rests but my friend and me!"

Wahawkin's neck-rope was staked to the ground. He sat rubbing the inner side of a fresh doghide with spit and stone. It disgusted Chimnik to see god or man—whichever he was— doing women's work.

"They don't even make me do that!" he muttered.

Chimnik watched his mother walk up to Wahawkin. Frowning as she usually did now, she held out a flat rock the size of two hands.

"Grind me a bowl," Euda said to the slave in Tlikit—the only speech she knew. "Careless Chimnik broke mine."

With a sly glance at Chimnik, Wahawkin looked at her stupidly, as if he didn't understand.

Euda smacked him on the ear. "Grind me a bowl, you cursed creature!"

Her sister Yak jumped up. "The slave is mine today! I need this doghide worked!"

"Well, when do I get him?"

"How should I know? Ask Tsilka."

Euda threw the bowl-rock down and went to find Tsilka. For no reason, she slapped her son as she strode by, making him drop a rock on his foot. Chimnik howled, but she didn't slow down.

CHAPTER
39

A touch awoke the prisoner.

Dark blanketed Teahra, the new Tlikit village by the Great River. Tor couldn't see, but his nose knew Chimnik. The boy put something in his hand. It sliced him as he closed his fingers.

A stone chip flaked off in blade-making! Tor sucked in his breath.

"They'll kill you!"

"Wahawkin be free."

"But you—"

"God more important than kicking child."

He would die for you, Tor. For once you will do the right thing.

"We will be free together, my friend," Tor said, without thinking of how that might change his life.

Tor felt the warmth of Chimnik's unseen grin. The boy took the stone chip and began gnawing the ropes. Put on wet to dry tight and tough, the twisted strings of sinew resisted cutting. The lazy guard Wyecat proved once more that he could sleep through anything.

Gray hazed the sky when Tor and Chimnik slunk away.

"For the *last* time!" Tor vowed, as they distanced themselves from the evil people, from the cruel river and the dream of destiny ruined by . . . he didn't really know. Spirit joke? A man's selfishness?

They ran across yellow plains toward the mountains—toward Ashan and Kai El and the Home Cave—sweating in the chill of the cloud-covered day. Chimnik's limp disappeared, and he kept up with no trouble. It rained in the afternoon, then stopped, leaving them wet and cold, but no longer thirsty. Tor thought it didn't matter that they had no food—he wasn't hungry. They reached the foothills. Old snow dusted the ground, deepening to crunch underfoot as they made their way higher into the mountains.

It was wonderful to run with a brother—even one so young—better than Tor remembered. A fire of excitement burned inside; he couldn't wait to hold Ashan and Kai El!

Storms of doubt—*what if? WHAT IF*—tried to put out the fire, but he fought doubt by not allowing bad thoughts.

Tor would have kept going all night, but he had the boy to consider. When the sky purpled, he stopped and slumped against the trunk of a low-branched juniper.

"Pffft! This old man is wearier than he thought."

Chimnik grinned. "Old man rest. Boy make fire."

He gathered wood, smiling with his whole face, and soon a fire was warm between them. Light sparkled in Chimnik's agate-black Beo-eyes as he gazed into Tor's. It pleased Tor: This child didn't look at anyone unless ordered.

"You're a good boy, Chimnik. I've never known better."

The boy dropped his eyes. "Boy not Chimnik."

"No? Who are you?"

"Elia."

In Tlikit speech, "chimnik" meant "spoiled food." In Shahala, "elia" was another word for "friend."

Tor nodded, smiling broadly. "Elia . . . yes. That is what you truly are, and from now on will always be."

As they sat in comfortable silence, Tor realized that he'd never had a better friend. A friend deserved truth, not lies.

"I'm not who you think, Elia. I am Tor, a man—not the god Wahawkin."

Elia smiled. "I know. I and Tsilka."

"You never told me? Why you little dung-bee—"

Tor stopped; he would never again call anyone a humiliat-

ing name, now that he himself knew the sting. He grabbed
the boy and they tussled in the way of brothers.

Chimnik's laughter—Elia's—*what a good sound!* Tor
thought, realizing he'd never heard this child laugh.

They sat by the dwindling fire. Hearing a loud growl
from the boy's gut, Tor wished there was something to feed
him.

"Tor?"

"What?"

"Why you bring Elia?"

Tor had asked himself the question. He wasn't really sure.

"You were as much a slave as I. You deserved freedom,
too."

"Where we go?"

Tor smiled to think of it. "To my home over the mountains.
It's a good cave, the Home Cave. You will live with my
family."

"Family?"

Tor had told the boy many times. Talking about them made
him feel good, and the boy never tired of it.

"Ashan, Whispering Wind, my mate. She's beautiful, with
a smell like flowers, and sweet, and kind. She will be like
your mother, only *much* nicer. Kai El, Sun River, my little
boy, will be like a brother to you."

"Family maybe not want me."

"They will. They are Shahala. Nothing like Tlikit. Shahala
people love each other enough to die."

"I am Shahala?"

Tor thought about it. Such a thing was not his to decide,
but what would it hurt—the only Shahala people Elia would
ever know were Tor and his family. It seemed that, by risking
his life to save his friend, the boy had earned the right to be
called anything he wanted.

"Elia . . . Friend," Tor said with respectful dignity.
"Now and forever, you are Shahala."

Elia glowed.

They slept on the ground beneath the drooping branches of
the juniper tree, close together because of the cold, wishing
they had sleeping skins.

Tor dreamt that he was a winged man. He didn't fly as
usual, but stood on a high place, spreading cloud-sized wings

over the world, casting a shadow of light over dark ground, as though he were bringing in the day.

Elia surprised Tor in the morning: he, too, had had a dream . . . of eaglets in a high nest, flapping untried wings.

Before setting out, they chewed bitter juniper berries, and talked about what it might mean.

Tor believed eagle dreams were sacred dreams, sent by Takeena with messages for people.

"Ten summers am I," Elia said. "Time boy become man by killing first eagle."

The thought made Tor cringe. Eagles were sacred animals, never to be killed.

"Eagles help Shahala boys become men," Tor said, "but not by dying. They help by allowing themselves to be caught, so a boy may take a tail feather. Then he is known as a man."

"Maybe dream tell boy watch for eagle."

"Maybe," Tor said. For both to dream of eagles on the same night . . . it must be an omen. "Becoming a man is no easy thing, Elia. In our tribe, when the right time comes, a boy chooses a man to help. It's very special . . . the feather hunt makes them spirit brothers. I will help if you want."

For Tor and Elia, that very day, it would be so.

A smell caught Tor's nose as they loped through a thin forest of grandfather trees. He dropped to a crouch. Elia dropped beside him.

"Do you smell that?"

Elia shook his head.

"Close your eyes. Still your mind. Take a deep breath. Eagle scent . . . seek it on the air."

Elia closed his eyes, lifted his head and flared his nostrils. His breath went slowly in and out. His head moved as he caught different drifts of air. Then his nostrils quivered. With his nose high, he sniffed short breaths, like a fox sniffs a trail. His eyes popped open.

"I smell it! Let's get it!"

Tor hesitated. It could take days to catch an eagle. He wanted to be home with Ashan and Kai El at the nearest moment. How could he let anything interfere?

But . . . Elia had received his dream of manhood, and had chosen Tor to share his rite of passage. A man could not refuse such a high honor.

They were lucky—they quickly found the nest, a great tangle of wood in the high top of a dead tree. The eagle wasn't there. Tor hoped it had not moved away for winter, as eagles sometimes do.

"Feather in nest," Elia said. "I climb tree and take."

"No. You must pull it from the living bird. It takes great cunning and courage."

Tor explained that, though the man might guide him, the boy must make his own plan.

"How you did?"

"First, I caught a ground rat, by sneaking up and throwing a rabbit skin over it. I didn't kill it. You know that loud, squeaky noise they make?"

Elia nodded.

"I used the noise to call the eagle. But first, I dug a hole deep enough to hide me. My father's brother, Kaiman, who died before he was old . . ." Tor sighed to remember the good man. "My spirit brother Kaiman put leaves over me, then staked out the ground rat with a thin rope on its leg. An eagle heard its cries. Kaiman whispered to me from his hiding place: 'Get ready.' "

Tor remembered how his every muscle had been coiled tight as a good rope, how his heart beat so loud, the eagle should have been warned. When he heard the rush of air that meant attack, he sprang from the ground at just the right moment. He caught it by a foot and jerked a feather from its tail, howled as talons raked his arm, and let go. The outsmarted bird flew off screaming. But Tor had his feather. The spirit of the eagle was in him. The boy had become a man.

Elia was impressed with the story, but made a plan of his own. Tor listened, and thought it would work.

He covered the boy's naked body with sharply fragrant pitch, scraping it from the tree trunks below woodpecker holes, then stuck clumps of moss to his sticky skin. When the boy looked and smelled like something that grew in a forest, he climbed the dead grandfather tree. He found a spot right beneath the huge nest and clung there, as invisible as a moss-covered boy could be.

Tor hid himself in brush, and watched and waited. He thought about the sacred event taking place in the tree overhead. He prayed to Takeena the Eagle Spirit. He thought about Ashan and Kai El.

It came home in the dusk—a very large black eagle with white head and tail—Tor's favorite kind. It did not see or smell the boy under its nest. As it landed, Elia's hand flashed out. The eagle screamed and flew away, leaving one of its precious white tail feathers behind.

"I did it!" Elia shouted. He was down in a moment, running with the feather in his hand, so excited Tor couldn't believe it.

The man placed his hands on the boy's moss-covered shoulders.

"Elia, this day you are a man, brother of the sacred eagle, who gives feathers to no other."

Tor drew a beaming Elia up and hugged him, not caring that pitchy moss stuck to him.

"We are spirit brothers now, closer than brothers of flesh."

Powerful warmth flowed between them. Tor was glad he'd taken time for this.

Beo would have chosen his big brother to go on his feather hunt, and Tor would have been proud to do it. But Beo had not lived that long.

The next evening, the spirit brothers crossed Keecha Creek, and scrambled up the shale outcrop.

Tor burst into the Home Cave. Bats swished out. *Bats? Amotkan! They're gone! Not just out gathering! GONE!*

"Ayiiiii!" he screamed. "NO! No, no . . ."

Tor collapsed, pounding the floor with his fists, gasping and choking. He barely felt Elia's arm around him. The small hands patted and stroked as if they could wipe away pain. If the boy said anything, Tor didn't hear. His own screams filled his ears. Blood pounded in his head. Tears spewed. Shredded guts tried to retch up his throat. The inside of him was dying.

Sleep took Tor just before death got there.

The next morning, he awoke exhausted and empty, lying on his back on the cold stone floor. Sorrow lay on his chest like a great burial stone. Breathing took all his strength, leaving none for moving.

Ashan . . . Kai El . . . without you I cannot live. My mate . . . my son . . . dead, dead, dead . . .

Tears overflowed the sides of his eyes, ran down and puddled in his ears. Struggling for calm against sobs wrenching
up from his gut, he made fists so hard that his fingernails dug
flesh. He clamped his jaw. The muscles in his neck stood
out. All the strength of his body and soul he focused on a
single thought: *NO! THEY ARE NOT DEAD!*

Tor *had* to believe it. He *did* believe. It was the only way
to go on.

He jumped up, shouting, "They're alive! They are!"

Elia cowered. Tor had forgotten about him.

"They're alive, boy! We'll find them!"

"Find our family!" the child answered with a grown-up's
voice.

"Maybe I brought you for more than one reason," Tor
said.

Tor searched the cave and found the food Ashan had left.
It gave him hope. Taking the food, Tor and Elia left the Home
Cave that day. Snow hid the tracks that knew which way
Ashan had gone, so they just started walking, lost as the ones
they sought. Like a crutch for a broken bone, Elia kept Tor's
broken soul from collapsing under the weight of desire to lie
down and die. The boy listened when the man babbled about
bears eating his loved ones, or finding their bodies, or maybe
walking right by them buried in the snow.

Elia knew better. "We find our family—alive!"

Later, Tor would wonder how a boy of ten summers kept
a crazed man going. And Tor *was* crazy. By light or dark,
asleep or awake, he stumbled through a strange world that
wasn't really real, except for a searing agony that was *too*
real.

CHAPTER
40

Where had winter gone?

Willows were greening when Tor and Elia found Ashan's pack on an island in a river. Tor fell to his knees and buried his face in the faded leather. The scent cleared his mind, bringing a picture of his mate and son, smiling, healthy . . .

His voice was ragged. "You were right, boy! They *are* alive!"

Neither mentioned the weather stains on the pack that told of several moons on the island, or asked why she would abandon such a thing. It was reason to hope, and they needed it.

They gathered strength by spending the night on the island.

"Ashan and Kai El slept here."

"I know," Elia said. "I feel them too."

In the morning, they left the island and followed a trail. The weight of Ashan's pack on Tor's shoulder seemed to lighten the weight on his mind. For the first time in many moons, he could hold thoughts long enough to think about them.

He realized that he and the boy had *not* been wandering aimlessly. They'd been heading toward the Shahala winter village as if led by an unseen power. The faded pack proved

that Ashan had also been going to Anutash, taking Kai El
where she thought he belonged.

Some part of Tor must have known it all along. *Where else
would she go?*

As they had all his life, Tor's *what-if's* put up a battle that
threatened his plans. *What if his family had never made it to
Anutash? Or what if they had? What had the people done to
the runaway Moonkeeper? And her son, forbidden by ancient
law to exist? What might the Shahala do to The Evil One, as
they called Tor, and this Outsider boy who named himself
Friend?* Though he liked to think of them as being more
advanced, Tor's people, like any other, had their ugly side.

Tor knew he must go to Anutash, but he was afraid—not as
a coward, but of what he would find. If his family wasn't
there, he'd have to admit they were dead. He thought he
could survive anything but that.

Somehow Tor kept himself believing that he'd find his
family safe with their people. But it was summer—the tribe
would be at Ancestor Cave, far away on a slope of the sacred
mountain, Takoma. Tor told himself there was no reason to
get to Anutash before the Shahala moved down, so he spent
the summer wandering in places he'd never been, teaching
Elia warrior skills . . . and putting off the day of knowing
for certain his family's fate.

Spirit brothers since the feather hunt, Tor and Elia grew
even closer from sharing: an antelope hunt that went perfectly,
and gave them meat and sleeping skins; a near-dying experi-
ence when a bison herd turned to run them down and at the
last moment, a boulder had appeared, and they'd crouched
behind it as the herd thundered past.

There was plenty to talk about by their night fires: experiences shared in their new life together; unshared experiences
from their old lives; Tlikit ways compared with Shahala—
and usually found lacking. Tor described wonderful scenes
of the future: He and Elia would rescue Ashan and Kai El
. . . they would love Elia too . . . the family of four would
live a happy life in the Home Cave . . .

Elia, who meant never to speak Tlikit again, understood
and spoke Shahala almost as well as one born to it. The boy

seemed like a gift from spirits to the man who'd lost his brother.

On a late summer day, the spirit brothers found tracks of a small goat, and a pile of still-warm, shiny goat-berries—as people jokingly called goat dung. The larger tracks of the mother should have been there, but were not. The young goat was lost. They followed the tracks and found it, standing in an open place, browsing on yellow grass.

"I kill," Elia whispered.

A few days ago, Elia had finished making the heavy Shahala spear every warrior needed. There'd been no chance for him to blood it.

Tor nodded. "Come from downwind, low and quiet."

The man watched the boy creep through the grass, until the boy became invisible. The little animal grazed unaware. Elia stood and hurled his spear. A streak fast as lightning, in less than a heartbeat, it pierced the neck behind and just below the head.

The goat squealed once and went down, without having seen the coming of death.

"Good work!" Tor shouted.

Elia pulled his blooded spear, hefted the carcass to his shoulders and brought it proudly to Tor.

"We'll spend a few days here," Tor said, pointing to a rise of boulders that would hide them.

When they found a good place, Tor had Elia dig a hole in the dirt, slice the animal's throat, and let the blood drain into it. They shared the heart and liver, still warm with the creature's spirit. The guts were put in the hole with the blood, and buried. Tor enjoyed this work that men did together. It was a time for old warriors to teach new ones.

"This goat was really too small. Shahala warriors don't usually kill the young, except in bad times."

"You call this bad times? What a woman!"

Tor laughed. He loved Elia's jokes.

When the goat was skinned, Tor said, "As I've told you before, it's best to cut the meat into thin strips to dry, but it takes too long. Warriors on the move do what they need to do, even if it's sometimes wasteful."

They cut large hunks and spread them on rocks. In a day or

so, there'd be air-skin on the meat. For a while, the middle would be good to eat. When it stank to the treetops, just before the fumes made their eyes water, they'd bury it and kill again.

"Let's go wash in that creek we crossed," Tor said when they had finished. They could have cleaned themselves with dirt, but cold water on hot sticky bodies would feel better.

"Make noise trap?" the boy asked.

Smart, Tor thought.

The scent of a kill traveled far to tempt thieving animals or men. They hadn't seen anyone since they'd left Teahra, but it was practice for the boy. Tor nodded. Elia set up a pile of small rocks by a piece of meat, so a thief would cause a clatter.

"You learn as fast as any Shahala boy."

Elia glowed like an oil lamp.

They walked to the creek and squatted in shallow water. As they washed, Tor heard a faint clatter.

"Bat dung! Stay here. I'll see what it is."

He hurried back to the camp. There, with his back to Tor, a lone man stuffed meat in a pack.

After all our work! Anger ripped through him, but stealing food was nothing to kill for. Tor charged with his spear raised.

"Stop!"

The thief spun around and dropped the meat-laden pack, hands out to show he had no weapon.

Tor jabbed his spear. "Go!"

As the stranger backed away, a round blue stone swung across his chest.

Tor shrieked. His Shahala spear flew—pierced the thief's gut—pushed him back. Tor threw himself on the gurgling screaming man and ripped the thong from his throat.

"My son's neckstone!" he screamed. "Where is he?"

The dead man didn't answer.

Elia came. "Why?" he asked. "You call my people savages, but we're not so fast to kill."

Tor was too crazed to explain. He couldn't stand to spend another moment with the proof of his stupidity a bloody mess before him. Leaving the goat meat and the thief unburied, he fled, not knowing or caring if Elia kept up. He couldn't stop raving as he staggered along.

"They *are* dead! And I killed a man who knew where to find their bodies!"

The next day they came upon a camp with no shelter but thick, dark green forest. A few trembling women held each other, staring like owls at the intruders. Little ones hid behind their mothers.

Do we look so fierce? Tor wondered.

"Do they understand Shahala?" Elia asked.

"We'll see."

With words and signs, Tor questioned them about a woman and a small boy. Elia asked the same in Tlikit. The terrorized women didn't understand either language. Tor showed them the neckstone, and saw recognition they tried to hide.

"They know of your son," Elia said in a sad voice. "Will we kill them?"

"No," Tor groaned. "Too many dead."

They left the women of the forest camp unharmed.

"Too many dead," Tor moaned as he stumbled in blind despair. "Oh, Amotkan . . . my family . . ."

"We find them, Tor! You see!"

Elia's words didn't help this time. Tor had given up hope—finally, completely, forever.

His loved ones had been dead all along.

Dead dead dead . . . It was all Tor could think as he sat that night in the crisp air of almost-autumn. He barely noticed Elia gather wood and make a fire.

Might as well lie down and die, said a voice inside, *the sooner to join them in the otherworld. . .*

No, said another voice. *That was the young Tor, and you have learned . . .*

Learned that I cannot live without them . . . want to die of my pain, as my own mother chose to do.

Don't you know, Tor? There is no graver insult to the spirits, to your destiny. Learn from your mother's mistake, don't repeat it.

Of course, Tor knew. He always had. But life seemed more important, now that he was older.

"Ashan," he said aloud. "I pledge to your spirit that I will search until I find how and where you died. Then I will wander until the spirits decide it's time for me to die . . . alone, my love, until I join you in the other world."

As he made his promise to his soulmate, somehow Tor

knew that he would never again have to decide this matter of ending his own life.

"You won't be alone. Elia wander too."

Tor was startled. He'd forgotten the boy.

What about the boy?

Tor knew better than anyone how important it was to be with people. *He* had no choice, but how could he condemn another to wander tribeless?

He couldn't. He would take Elia to the Shahala.

"We're near the winter village of my people," Tor said, "but it won't be like we thought. Ashan and Kai El won't be there." The ragged choke was gone from his voice; there was no feeling at all in the droning sound.

"Dead . . . my family's dead." He deliberately said *my* family, not *our* family, already breaking away from the best friend he'd ever known. "I am condemned to live without a family, to live without a tribe. But you, Elia . . . you don't deserve my fate. I will take you to Anutash, and leave you there."

"No!"

"My people are kind. They don't beat boys."

"Don't leave me!"

"I must. The Shahala hate me worse than the Tlikit hated Chimnik. Me they would kill. But they will want an Outsider boy like you."

Tears shone in Elia's eyes. "Please, Tor . . ."

For some reason, Tor thought of his dead brother, and his heart ached.

"I love you, friend. But I don't know what else to do."

Elia shook with silent sobs. Tor put his arms around the weeping child.

"It's best for you. You're Shahala now. You should be with your people."

The next day the spirit brothers awoke to a strange and frightening sight: a great smoky plume rising out of the sacred mountain, Pahto. Huge, it blocked the sun for a time. A high wind carried the dark cloud toward Colder, and the lands of the Shahala tribe.

Tor said, "I've never seen such a thing, or heard of it. Have you?"

Elia's eyes were wide with fright. "Never."

CHAPTER
41

It was known that spirits summered on Takoma's high peaks, which helped make it a fine place for people. That summer, while the Shahala tribe lived in their ancient and beloved Ancestor Cave on Takoma's flank, a terrifying, never-before thing happened . . .

. . . Pahto, the other sacred mountain, fell ill.

Though the days were warm, Pahto, She Who Makes the Waters of Life seemed to have cold weather sickness. She coughed many times over several days, spewing high smoky plumes that hid the sun as they drifted over the Summer Hunting Ground, dropping gray ash and small reddish stones—even though the sick mountain was far away—many days' walking toward Warmer.

One day Pahto shuddered as if with fever. The ground trembled, then shook violently for a few heartbeats that seemed much longer. People trying to run for the safety of Ancestor Cave were knocked down by the quaking earth.

A tree fell, crushing a Shahala little one and her mother.

Now people would not leave the cave to hunt and gather. Mountains lived forever, they believed, and did not get sick.

Only Raga and Tenka knew that such a thing *had* happened before in the distant past.

Much was known to Moonkeepers that was kept from oth-

ers. This time, a secret had been kept for the tribe's protection:
If people couldn't trust a sacred mountain, how could anything be trusted? Fear was a powerful force: In one or two
people, the Moonkeeper could manage it, but mass fear was
another thing that sometimes could not be controlled. And so,
ordinary people weren't told certain things unless it became
necessary.

Now it had . . . When the earth quaked, Raga knew it was
time to tell the tribe what she had learned from Tsagag, the
Moonkeeper before her, about the sacred mountains: Takoma,
son of the sun, and Pahto, daughter of the moon.

"Long ago," Raga said, "in the time of the Third Moonkeeper, a sacred mountain got sick—"

The young man Davi interrupted. His mother and baby
sister—full of life only yesterday—were now wrapped in
leather, awaiting The Soul's Growing.

"How can a mountain get sick?" he asked. "Pahto got
mean, not sick!"

"We are not told everything. It just happened: Once, Takoma Who Shelters Spirits got sick."

The People could not believe this. When they were outside,
Takoma's white peaks loomed over them. Ancestor Cave was
a hole between the mountain's roots.

Raga continued. "Such a thing had never happened before.
The Third Moonkeeper took some people and fled to the
Valley of Grandmothers, but most were afraid to leave Ances-
tor Cave. They thought it would protect them.

"They were the ones who died when the side of the mountain blasted away. The mouth of Ancestor Cave was buried
under deep ash, sealing the people inside. But the people in
the valley survived. Many seasons later warriors returned to
the mountain. It was hard to recognize their ancient summer
home under thick gray ash. They dug out the mouth of Ancestor Cave, and found the bones of their relatives huddled in
the farthest corner. Eventually, what was left of the tribe
came back to spend summers. As people were born and died,
the tragedy was forgotten—by all but Moonkeepers, who
knew that if a thing happened once, it might happen again."

"And so we will die?" someone asked.

"No. I will go to Pahto and heal her, as I heal you when
you get sick."

"You can do this?"

"Of course. I am the Shahala Moonkeeper." Raga took a deep breath and finished the story.

"When Takoma blew up the first time, one of the Shahala who lived was the Third Moonkeeper. A mountain spirit told her that a shaman's prayer could stop such a thing from happening again. The mountains were healthy for the rest of her life. Before the Third Moonkeeper died, she taught the prayer to her successor, who taught it to hers. Much later, a sacred mountain got sick again, and that Moonkeeper cured it by climbing the shaking slopes and praying there for three days and nights without food, water or sleep, until the mountain quieted."

And so the sacred mountains had stayed healthy. Until now.

Raga made a plan. She and Tenka would walk to Pahto—a long way for an old woman—Raga would have to make courage take the place of strength. It was good she had Tenka—such an old woman might die on the way, but a girl would keep on. The people must go to the valley and wait, for the mountain had become a dangerous place.

Raga could hardly believe it, but some said they would not go. They were afraid to do anything so different as living somewhere in the wrong season. The Shahala were *supposed* to live here in the summer. How else would they get the deer? The yew bark? And the berries?

"What difference do berries make to the dead?" Raga shouted, but she could see that some would not change their minds.

Raga and Tenka did not have to make their terrible trek. The people did not have to go to the valley until it was the right time. Pahto got well on her own.

CHAPTER
42

"**A**nutash. Valley of Grandmothers," Tor said with love.

Embracing the sight, he breathed deeply of the moist air of home, sweeter than any he'd tasted since he'd left on the tragic mammoth quest . . . long ago, in that *other* life.

At dusk, he and Elia crept to a hiding place near the village burial ground, close enough to see but not to hear his people.

His people: a pale reflection of a once-great tribe. *Amotkan! How few there are at a time of day when everyone should be here!*

"You said there'd be more," Elia whispered.

Tor was too shocked to answer. He started to count, and closed his eyes to make himself stop—it would kill him to know how many were dead, and who. He knew about his mother and grandmother, and the warriors lost to man-eaters. But the grayhairs . . . where were they? And there should be more little ones . . .

Still, the tribe had survived. There was yet a creature in the world named Shahala. The People of the Wind, if less than proud and mighty, were alive.

But Tor saw that they had done a terrible thing for survival: They had trampled on ancient law forbidding more than one mate.

Had they forgotten the story of Qumish and Ashrat, snow-topped mountains who'd been Misty Time women? Both had wanted the same man, Tucanon, who had thought it was a fine idea. And so it had seemed, until jealousy had started. Who gets his body tonight? Are these children mine or yours? Their fighting had annoyed Amotkan, who had sent Coyote to talk with them. In a trickster mood, Coyote had eaten their children, turned the women to mountains, and Tucanon to a river between them. Now the greedy ones looked at each other, but could never touch, reminding men that having two mates was not good.

Leave! Leave now! Tor's mind yelled, but sick fascination held him, burning pictures of sin on his mind.

There was his father Arth, squatting by the skin-covered hut where Tor had grown up, sharpening a blade on a leather strap. At the nearby stump where his mother used to work, *three* women were grinding grain: an Outsider Tor did not know; Mirda, once mated to Yon, killed in the massacre; and Tashi, Ashan's time sister born the same summer. By the way they sat as a family, Tor saw that Arth had taken the older ones for mates, and Tashi for daughter. Little ones ran in and out of the hut in a game of silent chase, as Tor had done with Beo and Tenka—as if it were *their* hut. *And so it is*, he reminded himself. *They are Mirda's children, and so the children of Arth.*

Tor sighed. *Tashi* . . . He had once looked at her full breasts and wide hips, and imagined making love. A crazy idea grabbed him. *Run down there! Be part of a family and a tribe! Arth wouldn't let anyone hurt the only son he has, would he?*

Tashi stood up—oh, Amotkan—swelled with unborn baby. She leaned over Arth to whisper. The old, *ancient* man stroked her belly with wonder, as almost-fathers do.

You're disgusting! Tor wanted to scream. *She's young enough to be your daughter!*

He ripped his eyes away.

He saw Raga slouched against the Moonkeeper's hut—older, smaller, more tired than fierce—with the time ball of the Shahala people in her lap. Beside the shriveled vulture, Tor's sister Tenka twined grass string to lengthen the sacred object that told the story of the tribe.

It meant that Tenka was the Chosen One. Raga wouldn't let anyone else touch the time ball.

Tor shook his head. *My little sister? The Moonkeeper? Are they in trouble!*

Solemn-faced Tenka looked older than he had expected, but she was still a child. Tor loved his sister, but she was a strange one, sometimes living inside herself for days, needing no one else in the world. How could someone lead who could just *go away* like that?

What choice did they have, Tor, after you stole Ashan?

Tor saw one thing that was right in the winter home of his ancestors. By the hut of Lar's old ones, two friends played with a girl Kai El's age: Lar, Tor's spirit brother; and Mani, Ashan's spirit sister. How Tor had loved them, and still did. Seeing them together with a child was good. Much was wrong in the world, but not every single thing.

Elia whispered, "What we do?"

It took a moment for the question to sink in. "I have no idea," Tor started to say. But when he saw trust in the boy's eyes where there had been fear, he found he had a plan after all.

"In the old days, a warrior would guard the village at night and rest the next day while others hunted. There are so few, I doubt they bother anymore."

"No guard?"

Tor shook his head. "We'll hide up here until the village sleeps. Then we will say good-bye."

Elia gulped, stiffened his lips and nodded. The brave Tlikit child was a valuable gift for the people Tor had harmed.

"You will take the meat and skins we have. Your people, the Shahala, need them more than I. Sit by the firecoals until morning, and when they come, pretend you don't know Shahala words. They'll think you're just a lost boy. Soon you can pretend to learn, and they'll think you're very smart."

Loneliness iced Tor like a winter pond. "Do not tell them about me," he said. "Not ever."

The village slept unguarded. The moon never lit the still, cloud-draped night. When the time came, Tor spoke in the dark.

"Go now. I will not forget my spirit brother."

"I will not forget my spirit brother," Elia answered in perfect Shahala.

CHAPTER
43

Winter had been approaching when "the children"—as Ehr thought of them—had come to the cave hidden behind the waterfall. A moon had passed since then, and now winter was here. For the first time, Ehr was not prepared for the long, cold season. He had food and firewood, but that was only part of it. The traps must be made harmless so he wouldn't have to go out in the snow and check them. It was a lot of work for an old man, and he put it off. For a while, the woman needed constant care, and after that, he just wanted to be with them.

One morning Ehr awoke shivering. Snowflakes floated through a hole in the roof. *This is the day to tend the traps*, he thought. *But first the children*.

They were sleeping where Ehr used to sleep—a cozy place away from drafts. Wrapped in a soft deerskin, Ehr started fire with his sparkstone. Smoke smelled good as it left by the smokehole in the roof. The air warmed. He heated grain mush that had soaked all night, tasted it, and thought, *needs honey*. Since the children had come, he'd been putting honey on everything, and now it was gone. If he had only himself to feed, he'd do without until spring. The bees needed their food for winter, and would punish a man who tried to steal it. Even so, this morning he thought of raiding the hive by the river.

Stings weren't that bad, not if gratitude was the reward. And the children were so grateful for everything he did.

He thanked Chief Above for sending them to cure the loneliness that hurt like flesh thrust in a fire. Ehr glanced at the shiny, scarred skin on the back of one hand. Except for his mother, he remembered people as cruel. These two were nothing like that. They were a miracle sent to gladden his last days. He knew he deserved it: He'd lived a good life. Another man with his fate would have become hateful, but not Ehr. His mother had taught him to *love*, and he had never forgotten.

As his inner voice had said, being needed was better than anything. The old man would die to save the woman and boy from harm. He wanted to believe they'd stay here after he was gone. It was wonderful to think of someone living in his beloved cave, feeding his animal friends, missing him.

Smiling, Ehr put the mush into bowls and took them to the children.

"Ah-ah," he said, but she didn't move. He touched her forehead.

She stretched, smiling. "Good morning, grandfather."

Because he couldn't talk, Ehr used his mind to know the thoughts of others. Ashan's mind was easy to reach. Ehr wasn't sure why, but he suspected she might be someone like the shaman of his old tribe, trained to send and gather thoughts—except that the shaman was an evil hag, and this girl gentle as a moth. Ehr and Ashan both took pleasure when mind-touching worked. Soon it would be as if they'd grown up with the same language—his version silent thoughts, hers spoken words he was coming to understand. Shahala, she called it.

He put the bowls down.

"Thank you, Ehr."

What a beautiful smile, he thought. He would like to sit and watch, but it made her uneasy. She'd say, "You go eat," so he saved her the trouble, and sat by the fire with his bowl.

A chill shivered him. *Yes, it's cold, but you're going out to tend those traps.*

All right. Now leave me to enjoy my food.

Ashan was licking her bowl when Ehr stood.

"Ehr oh," he grunted, pointing to the cave door.

She smiled. He'd tried to say the Shahala word ''go.'' Was he going out to hunt on this snowy morning? A thought came to her: *make traps harmless*. She knew the old man could send thoughts, but this time she didn't understand what he meant.

What good is a harmless trap? she wondered.

When Ehr had gone, Ashan hobbled with Kai El to the long tunnel where they left their body waste.

At first she'd been too weak to stand, so the old man had carried her. She didn't like it, couldn't help remembering Tor, and how he'd done the same thing when he'd kidnapped her—part of life she'd like to forget.

Well, it *was* one thing that made her try hard to walk again. First steps were shaky and hurt only a little less than giving birth, but she thanked Amotkan: being able to get around meant being able to do for herself and Kai El.

Today I should go out and set up a shadow stick, she thought. She'd have to guess how much time had passed, but a guess would be better than having no idea at all. It bothered her not to know *when* it was. Many things must be done at the right time. Knowing *when* was a shaman's job.

Lately, though, Ashan had begun to wonder if time was as important as she'd been taught. She had missed rituals in her weak time, and the world had not ended—though for a while, it seemed possible that it might.

Ashan hadn't seen the signs herself; she was still very weak, and spending most of her time in her bed. But Ehr's hand signs and frightened thoughts told her what was happening. Pahto, She Who Brought the Waters of Life, was sick. Pahto could not be seen from the land around the Hidden Cave, but Ashan knew the mountain lay in the direction of Where Day Ends, and that was where Ehr saw the strange cloud with a tail that touched the earth.

''Huge cloud,'' he had signed. ''When one goes away, another comes.''

Ashan had prayed for strength to go to Pahto and chant healing prayers. But she had no strength. Her legs were like things made of wet clay: they looked fine, until she put weight on them, and then they crumpled under her. Maybe Ehr could have carried her to the mountain, if she could have explained the importance to him.

After several days of Pahto's puffing, the ground shook horribly. Bits of the cave roof fell. Ashan awaited the end of everything.

Thankfully, she waited in vain. Somehow the mountain got well without her help. Maybe it had meant that Ashan was not a *real* shaman. Or that Raga still lived, and had strength enough to heal a mountain. Or that there were other shamans in the world.

Ashan had not known then, and did not know yet.

As she left the dark tunnel, she wondered if Ehr ever hauled the smelly stuff out. Now that she could get up, she'd take the oil lamp back there and do it herself. *But not yet*, she thought, as faintness took hold. She staggered to her bed and collapsed, napping on and off as she did every day.

Though Ashan was still so tired it hurt, she knew Ehr had done a fine job of healing. He used medicine that no man had ever been shown, and even knew some things she didn't . . . she, with the wisdom of every Moonkeeper since the Misty Time. He made tonics she'd never tasted, and used some kind of mold on her torn shoulder, where she would have used spiderwebs on such a wound. She couldn't believe how quickly she healed.

If only she could get over the painful tiredness. She vowed to drink more of Ehr's nasty tea. It tasted like bugs and dirt, and she poured it out when he wasn't looking, but he believed it was good for tiredness . . .

Ashan dozed, still aware of her son, who was playing with a new toy the grandfather had made—a wad of gray fur on a long string. Talking to it as if it were a real animal, he pulled it behind him, making trails on the cave's sandy floor. When Ashan got up to feed the fire, Kai El came running for a hug, then went back to playing with his "mouse." She sat poking coals into flame with a stick.

A wall picture caught her eye: three stallions, legs stretched, beards, manes, and tails flying. Only paint, but somehow they looked full of life and joy. Flat on her back, Ashan had gazed at them for days.

She hobbled to the picture-covered wall. As she touched the images with her fingers, they touched her with wonder. *Did Ehr make them? Why?*

Not that painting was so strange. There were times when

the Shahala Moonkeeper painted on people, to say things to spirits and others of the tribe, like, "This day I am a woman!" Or on certain sacred objects, like the pouch that held the Moonkeeper's robe. Ashan enjoyed the time spent gathering plants, rocks, and other things used to make paint. She was proud of her pictures: People could tell what they were supposed to be—not true of Raga's smearings.

But all Ashan's painting was nothing compared to what had been done on the walls of this cave. She didn't see what all the time was for. A Moonkeeper's painting had purpose, but what good did it do to paint on rock hidden inside a cave? Rock didn't need to say anything. And she thought it might be dangerous to make something that would last forever. It was believed that only spirits could make things to last forever. Wasn't Ehr afraid of offending spirits?

Did he even believe in spirits? Some tribes did not—Ashan wondered how they thrived.

She would have to talk to Ehr about this . . . talk, or whatever she should call this understanding of thoughts. Kai El had even figured it out, and had no trouble letting the old man know what he wanted without speaking.

Yes, she thought, going back to her bed. *The old man and I will have to . . . thought-speak about this.*

Mmmm . . . good word . . . Ashan drifted off.

In winter, once the traps had been made harmless, Ehr stayed in the Hidden Cave most of the time, leaving only to feed the few animals who still came to the pool below the waterfall. *Never happier!* he often thought. But sometimes it seemed unreal. *So long were you sad, old man, you thought it was happy*, said that voice inside that always tried to make him look bad.

Since Ehr's teeth had left him one by one, his food had to be ground and soaked, and today he needed to do grinding. But he'd been sitting all morning instead of working, watching the boy play with his new toy. Ehr had made four more balls of fur, smaller than the first one, and tied them together with horsetail string. Now Kai El had a family of mice to drag around the cave.

Tails, Ehr thought, *mice need tails.*

Anything but real *work, old man?*

Ehr got a basket of grass seeds and his grinding stones—the flat-bottomed one with its scooped-out middle, and the club-shaped smasher that fit his hand so well—and settled by the fire. He poured some seeds onto the bottom stone and began.

Ashan limped over and sat by him. She pointed to his wall of paintings.

"How do you make them?"

Signing for her to wait, Ehr walked into the shadows on his side of the cave and brought out a leather pouch. He spread it open before her.

"Ohhh," she said with a little gasp. The pouch held a small grinder and two flat stones the size of her hand, one for crushing paintstuff into powder, the other for mixing powdered colors with fat. There were small leather fold-ups for paint—some of it already turned into powder, some waiting to be crushed—stones, dried berries, green and black beetles.

She closed her eyes and drew in a deep breath as if paint had the most wonderful aroma in the world.

Do you like it? he thought.

"I used to have a paint pouch!" she said. "The smells bring wonderful memories!"

Did you paint your cave?

"The Moonkeeper painted on people's skin." Ashan sighed. "They were always so happy . . . pictures are for the wonderful days in people's lives. I could paint almost as well as you, not quite, but people could always tell . . ."

Ehr loved the sound of her voice, but she stopped.

Talk more, he thought.

"I don't understand, Ehr. Why do you paint where no one can see it? Why on rock? I know you've had no people, but . . ." Her voice trailed off.

Keep talking.

"What good are these paintings? And why put them inside a cave where they'll last forever? Aren't you afraid spirits will be angry because you're trying to outdo them?"

Hard questions, he thought.

"Do you even believe in spirits?"

Ehr knew painting and spirits were linked, but he hadn't

thought about it for a long time. He just painted in the way of his tribe, enjoying without thinking about why.

He looked into Ashan's curious brown eyes. *I will think and tell you later*, Ehr said in his mind. For the rest of the day, he ground seeds and thought about her questions. That night, he put tails on the mouse toy. Next morning after a meal of berry mush, Ehr spoke.

"Ah-ah," he said, and thought the rest: *We will paint, and I will tell you why.*

Ashan and Kai El watched quietly as Ehr drew lines with charred wood on a soft-lit wall that had no pictures. As he worked, the shape became a half-size woman with a fierce look on her face. Lightning streaked from her head. She held a snake like a living staff. A small bird of prey flew from her other hand.

When he finished drawing, Ehr taught Ashan how to paint on rock. He chose each color, showed her where it went, then sat and watched her work, slowly and carefully, rubbing paint inside the lines with her fingers. Sticky pine pitch added to the last layer—something she'd never heard of—made the pictures shiny, made them last and keep their colors. It smelled good, too.

Late that night while the others slept, Ashan lay watching the dying coals. A flame jumped up, swayed and died away, and then another . . . *The good scent lingers*, she thought.

It was dark, but she could see in her mind the picture she'd been painting: a shaman, what else could it be?

Why did Ehr make a picture of a shaman?

They had painted, but he hadn't told her why.

CHAPTER
44

I n the Shahala winter village of Anutash, thin gray light showed through the smokehole in the Moonkeeper's hut. *Another day, and still I live.* Raga's first thought, this and every morning, could make her happy, or angry, or too tired to move.

A dream-memory tickled. *Still I dream of you, Ashan . . . what was it, though?* The Old Moonkeeper was losing sharpness, whether she was trying to recall a dream or yesterday's meal. But dreams of Ashan were worth the effort; seeing her in dreams was better than not at all.

Raga picked through the webs in her mind, and found a dream middle with no beginning or end. The ancient woman focused on the fragment . . . the winter village, the people a blur around the ceremonial ground as the sun rose in a cloudless sky; Ashan, facing the people, giving off her own golden light, splendid in the Moonkeeper's ancient robe of furs and feathers, the horsetail headplace flowing down her back; Tenka standing beside her—a woman, not a child. Ashan took Kusi's tail from her head and pinned it into Tenka's wild black hair. The golden light leapt to Tenka, enclosing both. They clasped hands and thrust them high. The dream stopped there, with the strange picture of two women, each wearing half of the Moonkeeper's garb.

Where was I? Raga wondered, and realized she had seen it all as though lying on the ground.

CHAPTER
45

Ehr thought the young woman, Ashan, was the most curious of people, always asking questions, interested in everything he did. Like painting: It wasn't enough that he taught her *how*, she wanted to know *why*. He couldn't explain, not because he couldn't speak—there were other ways. Ehr didn't remember why his people made paintings.

Though he'd forgotten much, much was still in Ehr's mind: old ways learned from his people; new things he'd thought of himself; knowledge to make life easier, that old age was slowly taking away. It seemed sad, and wrong, that something so valuable be lost.

Ehr decided to teach Ashan what he knew. It was a way for him to outlast his body, almost a way of living forever.

Ashan smiled as she watched Ehr and Kai El play a game. It was easy to become fond of the old man whose arms were full of hugs, whose eyes were full of love, whose mind was full of the most interesting ideas. Ashan was amazed by what Ehr knew that her people had never thought of—like the traps for hunting and fishing. She understood that the traps were made harmless for winter because Ehr had enough food stored, and didn't want to go out and check them every day. Winter, he believed, should be an easy, restful time. In spring, he would make the traps ready again, and food would come and wait to be killed. A man alone, or a woman, could get everything needed this way. At least, that's what she understood from thoughts shared with Ehr.

Certain that she'd never see Tor or her people again, Ashan was as eager to learn as Ehr was to teach. The old man could teach her how to provide for her son without the help of mate or tribe.

Winter brought days of rain. In good weather, Ehr took them to see new things. There was another trap like the stake-bottom pit she and Kai El had fallen into. Ehr had made these pits harmless for winter by opening the tops so animals would see them. In spring he would hide them again with branches and leaves.

She learned to make a snare for small animals with thin, nearly invisible sinew, tied to a branch that would whip into the air when some creature took the meat that held it down. The sinew would catch the animal's neck or leg.

Ehr showed where a fish trap would go across a narrow place in the river. Pole tops stuck out of the rushing water. In spring, he would weave sticks between the poles, to slow the fish so they could be speared from the bank. Not all the fish, he thought-spoke, would, or *should*, be caught—many must lay eggs so there would be fish tomorrow.

Painfully remembering her one try at spearing fish, Ashan told Ehr that she didn't know how to hold, aim or throw a spear. He promised to teach her that and more: how to use a two-stone sling, how to make fire with a sparkstone instead of sticks.

Ashan learned from Ehr, and took pride in knowing, valuable man-skills that no Shahala woman had ever been taught, and new things that even Shahala men didn't know. She could not imagine a better place to live. The Hidden Cave had everything, except fresh air, which little ones needed to grow. So she took her son outside as often as weather allowed.

One late winter morning, they were invited to go out by sunshine splashing through roof holes. Ashan made hot mush of grass seed and soaked meat. She and Kai El finished eating before the almost-toothless grandfather.

"We'll wait for you in the sunshine," Ashan said.

Mother and son put on warm robes, covered their heads,

and ran out through the falling water, laughing as icy tingles attacked them.

Kai El went to wait for Ehr down by the gravel-bottomed pool.

Ashan said, "The rocks are slippery! Be careful!" knowing that he always was.

The young mother stood on a flat stone, filling her chest with crisp air, listening to a song of splashing behind her, thinking how pretty was the ice piled and swirled at the sides of the waterfall. Sun sparkled on ankle-deep snow. Ashan smiled, squinting in the brightness.

Ehr splashed through the waterfall behind her with his pouch of food for the animals. He gave Ashan a hug, and picked his way down the rocks to squat beside Kai El.

One of the strangest things the grandfather does, she thought. *I'll never understand it.* But her son loved this part of the day. At first he wanted to touch the animals, but Ehr had let him know that they wouldn't like it. Kai El obeyed. Ashan was proud: Her son was growing up.

Ehr allowed Kai El to feed the animal friends—except for the lynx and the wolf. The lynx wouldn't take meat from the boy's hand, and Ehr would not allow him to feed the wolf. Kai El needed to learn the danger of wolves, even an old, three-legged one.

Ashan watched, satisfied and peaceful, as Ehr handed Kai El the food pouch.

With throat noises that sounded just like the old man's, the boy called chipmunks.

Ashan laughed. Kai El knew the chipmunks were in ground holes sleeping the winter away. But his child's way of thinking told him that if he called them every day, they'd get up and tell spring to hurry.

The chipmunks were smart—they knew it was too early.

Scattering seed, Kai El called for birds with a sound he'd made up himself: "Chir, chirrr . . ."

Leaving Kai El by the edge of the pool, Ehr shambled to his favorite sitting rock.

"Ah-ah." He motioned her to come. His look said: "time for teaching." Like Raga, Ehr wanted to pass on all he knew, all he believed. Ashan understood Raga's reason—the tribe must have its new Moonkeeper. Why Ehr wanted to teach, she never understood, but she was thankful.

She climbed carefully down the slippery rocks and stood before him with a face that said, "ready to learn."

Ehr gazed into her eyes, opening the pathway between their minds. Ashan felt her other senses close down as a trance bound them.

Without breaking gaze, Ehr touched the rock, then his forehead. Holding up his hands, he looked to the sky. Then again . . . rock, man, sky. He went to a tree and did the same, then the water in the creek.

Ashan understood. "Yes," she said, "there's spirit in everything, and each is important . . . all connected . . . all one."

Ehr nodded with a toothless smile. Then he thrust his face and arms to the sky as if beholding something wonderful.

Chief Above. Creator.

Sensing his thought, she said, "The One my people call Amotkan."

Ehr nodded. *Chief Above made us all. Chief Above provides and we are thankful.*

Ashan smiled in agreement.

As the once-Moonkeeper of Amotkan's favored people, there was one thing she took pride in knowing all about: the spirit world. It pleased her that the old man shared her important beliefs. Ehr knew there was a Creator, as anyone would just by looking around. He called Amotkan Chief Above—a good name, she thought. Like the Shahala, Ehr recognized a spirit in each tree, rock and animal. But—and here was a wide canyon separating their ideas—Ehr believed these spirits had no real power over people.

Spirits, he said with his mind, *are friends who give of their own desire. There is no need to beg.*

The Moonkeeper inside Ashan warned, *This is dangerous!*

Things happen in the world, the old man thought, *because Chief Above created it so . . . not because a shaman says some words.*

"I don't agree," she said. "I am . . . I was . . . a shaman."

I know, Ehr thought. *But child, I am sure of it: the moon*

and sun need no help to shine; the seasons change by them-
selves; food comes to those in need because of the love of
Chief Above.

"Then what is a shaman for?"

Ehr made signs that said, "I don't know."

Ashan sighed. Ehr did not know many things that the
Shahala never questioned.

But about this matter of shamans, she had troubled thoughts
of her own. Like all her people, Ashan knew that a shaman
was necessary to keep the Balance—she was the link between
spirits and people. Spirits had no time to speak to everyone,
and people had no time to learn how to listen. So this work
was given to one person. And of course, that person would
be the chief of Amotkan's favored people, the Shahala.

Yes. It made sense. Because the world depended on a
Moonkeeper, after Tor had kidnapped her, Ashan had kept
every important ritual—except for the times when she could
not. And that troubled her: the right things kept happening in
the world, whether she was able to help, or not. How could
this be? Was Raga still alive? Were there other shamans
somewhere who kept rituals?

Or was Ehr right? Could the world get along quite well
without human help?

If people depend on spirits for everything, Ehr's thoughts
asked, *how can they develop the strengths within that Chief*
Above gave them to use?

"But . . . if we change anything . . . there is fear . . ."

I had to change. Fate gave me life without a shaman,
forcing me to go beyond fear and look in myself for answer.
So I took fate in my hands. I learned to catch food without a
pack of hunters. I learned that I did not need permission from
spirits. I learned to rely on myself. You can see that I have
survived.

"But if we only need ourselves—" Ashan swallowed,
wondering why this frightened her so. She took a deep breath.
"If we don't need spirits to help us—"

We do need spirits to help us, and it's just what they want
to do. We have faith that they will provide, so why should we
beg for what is already ours? It makes us smaller than we
are. There is no need to beg. What spirits want from us is
respect, and appreciation.

"What do you mean by respect?"

Respect the Balance, and we care for tomorrow. Use well what is given. And appreciate. Show thanks. I do this by painting, but there are many ways—one for each person born.

"Oh," Ashan said. To herself, she thought, *Fine, but I will still get up to raise the moon on Nights of Balance, and I will still have an Autumn Feast, and I . . .* Ashan shut her thoughts down. She did not want Ehr to hear.

Her other senses came back as the trance ended.

Later, after foaming her long hair with soap leaves, Ashan held her head under the waterfall to rinse it— *Brrr! Cold enough to wake a wintering bear!* Sitting on a sun-warmed rock on the cliffside, she shook her head, flipping the hair tips to get the water out. She ran her fingers through it to make it all go the same way, envying women like Mani, whose hair never looked like a bird's nest. As she sat, the sun dried it—much more pleasant than drying it inside the cave by the heat of a fire as she usually did in winter.

Ashan looked down on a pretty scene: the only people in her life, sitting together by the little pool. Wrinkled old arm around young, smooth back, they quietly watched brown and black birds peck in the gravel for seeds. The love between the old man and the boy was so strong that it gathered in a haze around them—something only a Moonkeeper could see. From the first, Kai El had been charmed by the grandfather. Ehr was the only person he'd ever seen besides his mother and father, and that was part of it. But mostly it was this: Ehr was the kindest person Ashan had ever known.

The birds flashed away as the lynx poked her gold-striped head from the leafless brush on the other side of the pool.

"Kai El feed Ayah?" her son asked the grandfather.

Ehr shook his head, signing, "Lynx fears boy."

"Kai El play with Ayah when sleep."

Oh no, Ashan thought. *Not again . . .*

Ehr raised his eyebrows in question.

"Me . . . her . . . sleep-friends," Kai El said.

Ehr nodded and handed a piece of meat to Kai El. "Go slow," he signed.

Ashan's hand flew to her mouth as Kai El stepped into the water—a lynx could shred his flesh!—but she stopped a

"No!" before it could get out. He was showing bravery, young as he was—not yet three summers. Mothers must encourage bravery in sons who would one day be warriors.

The lynx did not move. Kai El slowly crossed the pool, stopped at the edge and held out the meat. Boy and animal stared, as if they were the only two creatures in the world. The lynx stretched out a stealthy paw and put soft weight on it, never taking her eyes from Kai El. Another step, and another. She stopped, reached with her neck, opened her mouth. White teeth gleamed sharp. Ashan held her breath. The no-tail cat took the meat as gently as she would carry a kitten, then turned and disappeared, a gold-brown flash noisy in the winter brush.

Kai El splashed back, yelling, "Ehr! Amah! See?"

Ehr clapped his hands and hugged the wet, excited child.

"What a brave young man!" Ashan said. She thought, but didn't say, how proud Tor would be of his son.

Ashan worried: Kai El had said he played with a lynx in his sleep—another way of saying that he dreamed. All little ones dreamed at first, but soon it would have to stop. No one but a shaman could dream. It was too dangerous for anyone else, dangerous enough to die from. Yet . . .

The once-Moonkeeper and the wise old man had thought-spoken about it. Ehr dreamed. The ancient who was right about so much was astonished at Ashan's belief that dreaming was deadly to anyone but a shaman. To Ehr, dreaming was a game to play at night, and he enjoyed it. It was the only time he could be with people. Dreams had given him important ideas. He couldn't imagine how a person could stop.

Had a lifetime of dreaming harmed him? He didn't think so, but Ashan wondered if that was why he'd been banished to live alone.

And what about Tor? she thought. Dreaming had not been good for him. It was where he got all his bad ideas. But he hadn't died from it, as Raga had told everyone he would.

Or had he?

Now she didn't know what to think about dreaming. But she didn't try to stop Kai El.

CHAPTER
46

Called enough times by a little boy, chipmunks came out of their holes and brought spring. Geese and swans barked their way toward Colder. Green things sprouted. As always in spring, the heart of the once-Moonkeeper yearned to migrate—a useless desire. In this life, there was no need to move. Everything was here, except the ones Ashan bled inside for. Having long ago accepted that mate and tribe were lost to her forever, she pictured the rest of her life here in the cave hidden behind the waterfall. She'd have Ehr until he died; Kai El, until he grew up and wanted a life of his own. Then she would live out her days a comfortable hermit. There were worse lives.

In the warmth of that summer, when Kai El turned three, and all the world was in high growth, Ehr's strength failed. The only thing he did was feed his animal friends. It saddened Ashan to see the grandfather weaken, but she was glad to take care of him as he once had cared for her.

On top of her woman's tasks, Ashan now hunted. Shahala warriors let women believe that hunting was the hardest possible work, but with Ehr's traps, it was so easy that the work part was dragging the food home. She could have used Kai El's help, but thought it best for him to stay with Ehr. They so enjoyed each other . . . how much more time could there be?

She tried not to think of Ehr dying. Her feelings for him, strong and full of thankfulness, were sweetly different from anything she'd ever known. Ashan would have loved her father Kahn this way if the spirits had allowed more time.

Autumn blew summer away.

On a chilly morning, Ashan awoke with a throbbing head and itching eyes. Her nose bubbled as if she'd been crying.

Bison dung! Now I have it!

The day before, Kai El had complained of cold-weather sickness, a mean, but brief, illness that traveled from person to person. By tomorrow it would probably attack the grandfather, and this scared her.

The ancient man was failing—she could see it day by day. Bruises with no cause blotched thin-enough-to-see-through skin. He claimed it was too hard to eat with no teeth, and his flesh was shrinking. Sometimes his loud, ragged breathing seemed almost too much work. A small sickness could kill a person in his condition. But there was nothing anyone could do about it—not a medicine woman, not even a spirit. Unlike mountains and rivers, people only had so much life in them. When it was used up, they died.

Aching all over, Ashan heated grain mush with sharp-tasting sage leaves, good medicine for cold-weather sickness.

"We're staying in our beds today," she said, giving Ehr and Kai El their bowls. The boy whined, but his tired, watery eyes said that he didn't really care.

The old man ate for a change.

Ashan put crushed sage and kinnikinnick into neck pouches for each of them. Breathing the healing smells, she dozed with Kai El curled up beside her.

Later Ehr got up to feed his animal friends. Frail as he'd become, he never missed a day. Kai El stirred, and wanted to go with him, but Ashan said no, and in a moment her sick child was sleeping again.

Rising to her elbow, she said, "Be careful, grandfather." The words scratched her throat.

Ehr smiled, nodded, and was gone.

Ashan sank back, pulled the sleeping skin up to her chin, closed her eyes, and sighed.

Tor . . .

As time went by, Ashan thought of Tor as often as ever, but less with tears, more with smiles. For the second time in her young life, she was coming to accept that her mate was dead. It helped when she thought about their good times together. This morning, she remembered another time she and Kai El had had cold-weather sickness. Tor, who never got sick with anything, had taken wonderful care of them. He'd made hot tonics, and got them to eat more than they wanted by covering their food with honey. To make them laugh, he had danced wearing one of Ashan's skirts.

In her mind, she smelled the Home Cave, and heard Tor's silly chant. The memory made her smile. She breathed a good sigh.

And then she thought, *my lost people . . .* and the thought was like a hand closing on her throat.

Nothing helped when Ashan thought of them . . . not focusing on good memories . . . not even time. The best she could do was chase Shahala thoughts away.

Shahala-grief was different from Tor-grief. It hurt more, and it would never lessen. Tor was dead, and that made a difference. It was possible to put the dead behind you. But Ashan didn't think the Shahala were dead. They were suffering. She knew, because she'd been taught to feel their pain.

Sometimes her yearning to be with her people was so strong it tore her apart. But she *could not* be with them . . . what would they do to Kai El? Nor could she think of leaving Ehr, whose life now depended on her.

Anyway, it *was* senseless to believe that a Moonkeeper was responsible for the fate of the world.

Yes, the best thing was for Ashan not to think of her people. If only she knew how to stop.

Ehr ducked through the waterfall with a skin over his head. The short dash left him breathing hard. *How,* he sighed as he hung the dripping skin on a branch, *can a man this tired still live?*

He looked down and smiled. Sitting on her haunches by

the pool, the three-legged wolf heard him and looked up. Animals didn't smile or frown like people, but their faces told Ehr what they were thinking. Tululkin's eyes reproached him.

Sorry I'm late, he answered in his mind.

You're old, the wolf thought. *I understand*.

Ehr started down the rocks.

A cougar sprang from the brush behind Tululkin, slashing with outstretched claws, slamming the stunned wolf to the ground. Yelping, the wolf thrashed free and floundered into the water. The cougar bounded and caught her. Overcome by size, strength and youth, Tululkin went down.

"Unnhh!" Ehr screamed, waving his arms, bolting down the slippery rocks with a young man's recklessness.

"Unnnnhhh!"

The water was alive, roiling cat-yellow and wolf-gray, tumbling legs and heads, barks and growls of hate and pain. Tululkin yowled, then gurgled as the cougar gripped her neck and shook her body.

Ehr hurled a rock into the cougar's flank. The cat whirled around, dropped the wolf, and screamed—ears flat against its head, golden eyes filled with hate, blood dripping from its teeth. Was it crazed? Was it going to attack him? The cougar screamed again, then crashed away through the brush.

From the edge of the pool, Ehr stared at his crumpled friend, unmoving in the bloody water, unseeing eyes wide open.

The old man splashed toward her—

—Fire seared his armpit, streaked past his elbow to his wrist. A monstrous hand gripped him, crushing his chest. *Chief Above! The pain!* He tried to scream, but his throat was blocked; he couldn't even gasp. Swaying, he clutched his exploding chest. The invisible hand squeezed until agony was bigger than the world.

Ehr fell in the water beside Tululkin. He reached out, touched her paw, and pain evaporated like sun-warmed fog. His sight blurred, fuzzed to yellow, then white. Light in his brain grew brilliant.

So, Tululkin, it is the day to die, he thought, as his fingers lost the feel of her fur.

The wolf's glazed eyes flashed a spark of life.

Yes, old friend, but we have done well, Ehr heard before he brilliance consumed everything.

'Owww.''

Squirming beside his snoring mother, wishing he were outside with the grandfather, the little boy frowned, bottom ip sticking out as far as it would go. Aches chewed him. He coughed, and goo bubbled in his throat. Snorting, he swallowed the bad taste, thinking how mean cold-weather sickness was and how he hated it. Amah's skin—warm, good-smelling, soft as a flower—was the only nice thing in the world. Kai El snuggled up tight and tried to go to sleep, that place of games and friends and never being sick.

What was that noise outside? Fighting animals? Like the ime a short-eared dog and a badger fell into the big pit by the river? And were down there trying to kill each other when the warriors Ehr and Kai El came to kill both?

Oh no! the boy thought. *Ehr is outside! Alone!*

Kai El squirmed away from his sleeping mother. He was acing a moccasin when Ehr cried out. There was fear in the cry! Ehr needed him! Forgetting the other moccasin, the boy ran through the waterfall.

Wiping the drips from his eyes, he saw Ehr and Tululkin in the pool below, still as boulders.

"Ehr!"

Kai El slid down the slippery rocks and splashed into the pool. Anyone could see the torn-apart wolf was dead, but Ehr had no hurts on him. Why was he sleeping in the water?

"Wake up!" Kai El shook the grandfather. His head flopped. Something was bad wrong with his friend. Fear made Kai El shake. He felt like a baby as he scrambled back up the rocks, crying.

"Amah! Help!"

Water swirled around their ankles.

"Wake him!" Kai El begged. "Hurry!"

Ashan could see that Ehr was not sleeping.

"Sweetbaby, the grandfather's dead."

"But he has no hurts!"

Her son knew nothing about the death of people.

"The grandfather was old," she said, "and very tired Sometimes people die from that."

Bottom lip sticking out, eyes brimming, Kai El whined "Amah fix . . . Kai El love grandfather."

"I'm sorry, little one, death cannot be fixed. But I promis you will see the grandfather again. When your time comes t die, Ehr will be there to help you."

"No-o-o! Want him now!"

Kai El threw himself at her legs, sobbing. She scoope him into her arms and sat on the ground.

"I'm sorry, baby, so sorry."

She crooned and rocked, stroking his hair. She stared a the bodies in the pool, wondering why she wasn't crying too so much did she love the kind old grandfather. Had all he tears been used up for Tor and her people?

Kai El cried himself to sleep. She put him down withou waking him. Feeling like a dead person herself, she went t the cave for soap leaves, fat, sweet spices, and leather.

Kai El was still sleeping when she returned. It was on good thing about being young, she remembered: Childre could sleep away pain.

Ashan pulled Ehr from the water, stretched his body on th ground, and looked back at the mangled wolf. They had die together. How and why, she would never know, but it seeme important. To Ehr, Tululkin had been more than just an ani mal. She was his friend when he had no other. Ashan knev she was doing the right thing when she dragged the beast out

Souls should go to the otherworld clean. Ashan washe Ehr's body with wet soap leaves, dried him with soft bark and rubbed fat and spices into his skin—all very slowly, ther was no reason to hurry.

When the wolf stopped bleeding, Ashan washed and drie the Shahala. She considered the pouches of fat and spice. The Shahala did not give animals the honor of sacred burial. Bu this was an animal of exceptional worth, perhaps the onl one ever to befriend a man. And so she treated it the same She would always remember how strange it was to rub fa into fur, and how spice smelled different on a dead anima than on a dead person.

Ashan spread out an elkskin and placed the bodies on it

azing at them, a sad frown on her face, but still without
ars, she was strangely calm, almost as if she weren't really
ere but had left behind a clay-woman to do the things that
d to be done.

She awoke Kai El, and they dragged the bodies to the place
ar the Hidden Cave that the grandfather had loved more
an any other—the high bluff where he'd been sitting when
first imagined making a trap. In spring the bluff was lush
th grass and flowers, and you could see far on a blue-sky
y.

Ashan believed he would want to be buried here, though
ey'd never thought-spoken about it. Ehr had tried, but
shan had refused, as if thinking about his dying would make
happen. Of course, it had happened anyway, and now she
ished they'd talked about it. She didn't know how his people
red for their dead. Shahala ways would have to do.

Kai El watched with dull eyes as Ashan wrapped Ehr's
iffening body in long strips of leather as wide as her hand,
ginning at his feet and working her way up.

It's not as if I thought he'd live forever, she told herself.
ut couldn't he have died in comfort . . . in his sleep?

Ashan looked on Ehr's face once more, then wrapped it.
ears trickled out. *I will miss this one*, she thought, *and even
ore will my son.*

"Not cover eyes," Kai El whimpered. "Ehr not see."

"He doesn't need to see," she answered. "The ones al-
ady there will guide him."

Kai El looked confused, and so sad.

"There's much I will tell you while we sit with our friend."

Ashan laid the wolf close to the tan person-shape, smooth-
g its gray fur instead of wrapping it in leather. Since animals
ore no clothing, she didn't think Tululkin would want to be
rapped.

Kai El wanted to stay with the bodies, so Ashan went by
erself to the Hidden Cave for sleeping skins, food and wa-
r—enough for herself and Kai El for three days, and more
r Ehr to take on his journey to the otherworld. He'd also
ant his favorite things. She picked out some paints, a spear,
d his "thinking rock," a small stone clear as water that
hr had liked to rub in his fingers while he sat lost in far-
way thought.

Now began the time of keeping company with the de
and the time for a mother to teach her child about dying.

"Ehr was old. Ready to go to the people who love hi
the ones already in the otherworld. He will be happy to j
them. We're glad for him."

"But I want him here."

"I know, so do I, but we must think of Ehr. You an
will stay with him for—" she held out her fingers, "o
two, three days, so his loved ones can find him."

She wondered . . . his loved ones had hated him enou
to banish him. What made her think they would welcome h
now? Ah, well . . . that was not in her hands.

"We'll get lots of wood, and make a great fire to burn
body and free his soul—"

"No! Fire hurt him!"

"Nothing can hurt the dead. You will see his soul fly aw
in the smoke, and hear him laughing. When the fire is dor
we'll bury what is left, and find a pretty rock to put over hi
We will always love and remember Ehr, and when we wa
to feel close to him, we can come sit up here. Do you unde
stand?"

"No . . ."

Do I? she wondered.

CHAPTER
47

Because of Ehr's gift of knowledge, winter in the Hidden Cave was easy for those he had left behind. Ashan was grateful. She had long been wise in a shaman's way, but the teaching of the grandfather had made her strong in other, more important ways. If Ashan could not be with her people, at least she could now provide for her child.

She often thought of Ehr. People were selfish: Knowing the dead were better off, still the living missed them, and wished them alive.

It did surprise her that she wasn't lonely . . . though she and Kai El might as well be the only people in the world.

A precious bond grew stronger between them. Every mother loved her child, but this was better and more than other mothers felt. If Ashan had known this feeling was possible, she would have told Raga to find another Moon-keeper. She would never have been willing to give this up.

The only two people in the world needed nothing but each other for happiness. Or so Ashan desperately believed.

"Let's paint," Kai El said on a rainy morning.

By her shadow stick, Ashan knew Ehr had been dead for almost two moons. Winter would soon be over; in spring, there would be little time for such things.

"What would you like to paint?"

"Finish cougar."

Ehr's last—the picture he'd been making when his strength had failed. The black ash lines of a leaping cougar were drawn on the wall, but he hadn't filled in the fur.

Cougar color was made from a soft stone. Among Ehr's things, Ashan found pieces of the yellow-gold rock.

"Do you want to make the paint?" she asked Kai El, who was jumping around behind her.

He nodded. "Ehr teach me."

She handed him the grinding stones. Sitting cross-legged by the fire as the grandfather used to do, he put a yellow-gold rock on the bottom stone, tapped it into smaller pieces with the grinder, and began mashing. When the soft rock turned to powder, Ashan put a lump of hard goose fat on the stone to be ground into it. When the paint was slick and smooth, she scraped it onto a piece of leather. Kai El ground more rocks into paint, not leaving the smallest lump.

Ashan thought he must be getting tired. "I'll grind for a while," she said.

He shook his head. "I want to. Ehr watch me."

Sitting up straight, looking proud of himself, humming low like the grandfather, stopping only to go out in the rain and feed the animal friends, Kai El spent the rest of the day making enough paint to finish the picture.

In the morning, he could barely wait until they ate their meal so that he could start.

Ehr had drawn the cougar around a slight bulge in smooth rock that spoke of a body shape. Its legs were stretched leaping. Two graceful lines were the balancing tail. The cougar's belly was at the height of Ashan's chest, the head and tail-tip as high as she could reach.

She gazed at it, looking for the best place to start.

"I paint," said her son.

"No. It's too high."

Kai El had never painted, and she didn't want him to ruin Ehr's last picture . . . how the finished pictures looked had been important to the old man.

"Ehr want me to. Amah hold up."

Oh, what would it hurt? If he messed it up, she could fix it later. She swung him to her hip.

"Higher," he said. "Start at tail."

It made her laugh to see that her little boy had a plan of his own. She would have started at the head.

"Sit on my shoulders," she said, hoisting him. When his weight was comfortable, she held up the leather with the paint and he dipped his fingers.

"Now," she said. "Rub paint in between the lines, very hard, and—"

"I know," he said. "Watch Ehr."

He did know, and did it well enough to delight his mother. With paint-sticky fingers in her hair, paying no more attention to her than he would to a sitting rock, with greater care than she herself would have used, he rubbed paint into paint until no more would stay on the wall.

He's in a trance, Ashan realized, *one with paint and picture, all else forgotten.* Trance was a mind-place where a shaman spoke with spirits. Ashan had never seen it in a child so young. It wasn't natural, but had to be taught. Or so she had believed.

Kai El hummed like Ehr, and once in a while mumbled, not to Ashan, but to the picture . . . or . . . ?

"Tail. Then body, then head. Last most dangerous eye."

From tail to eye—this was the way Ehr had painted an animal, though Ashan never understood why; it seemed backward to her. She wondered how Kai El knew. He must have been watching when she thought he was playing.

"Mean, bad cougar, stuck on wall, can't hurt me now." He chanted the words like a song.

"What do you mean?" she asked.

Startled by her voice, Kai El almost fell from her shoulders.

"Ehr tell," he said. "You not listen?"

"What do you mean *listen*? The grandfather couldn't talk."

Kai El laughed. "Silly Amah!" He rubbed his belly. "Make food. I tell what Ehr tell."

Good idea. She was hungry too, and achy from holding him. While she patted soaked grain into cakes and sizzled them on a hot rock, Kai El—with much halting and starting, and signing with his hands—said the longest thing he ever had said.

"Picture . . . trap. For *spirit*. Paint food animal . . . it come. Paint bad animal, it not hurt anymore. Paint hold spirit inside rock, so make worst part last. Eye. See?"

Ashan was proud. Never had her son spoken so well. But she was not sure she saw anything. Was that really why Ehr had painted? To capture a creature's spirit? Ashan thought it had more to do with thanking. She had to admit she'd never understood the why behind the old man's work. How could a child know?

Or had Kai El thought the story up all by himself? She was beginning to see signs of Tor in him—her son had the same clever way of making things up so others believed it.

Ashan always looked forward to the coming of young animals in Summer Begins, but she'd never seen them as close as when they came to drink at the pool below the Hidden Cave. Watching them brought smiles, and warmth in the heart. She was beginning to understand why Ehr had gone to all the work of feeding them, and why Kai El continued.

Baby squirrels and chipmunks were like their parents, but smaller, brighter of color, and softer-looking. They chased each other like the children of people. Their flips and slides, chirps and growls kept a person laughing.

It was funny to watch young blackbirds mob the parents frantically trying to feed them, dragging one wing as if it were broken, peeping as if they were starving, refusing to pick up a single seed for themselves. Being a human parent was easy compared to that.

The lynx kittens were best of all. Ayah brought three golden fuzzballs to show off. Ashan thought the lynx might disappear when the old man died, but the cat became as friendly with Kai El as she had once been with Ehr. Ayah still didn't want to be touched, but the kittens tolerated it. While they chewed on a piece of meat, snarling at each other, Kai El lightly stroked their backs. They'd take it for a while, then snap at him, except for one—a girl-cat who growled, but didn't scratch or bite.

"This one likes me," Kai El said.

The family of no-tail cats stopped coming. After a few days, Kai El wanted to search.

"Ayah was Ehr's special friend," he said. "I love her."

"I think she may be dead, Kai El."

"Then we find kittens. Too young to be alone. Like me."

Who could resist when Kai El put on his "pitiful baby" face? Ashan remembered a boy named Beo who'd had the same talent.

They searched for the lynx family, but found no sign.

One day Ashan watched from Ehr's sitting rock as her son squatted by the pool trying to get a gray jay to eat from his hand. Two skinny, matted lynx kittens straggled through the brush on the other side of the pool. Kai El threw meat. They grabbed it and disappeared.

The kittens returned. The girl-cat Kai El had befriended before soon came to him again. The other would only eat with a good distance between himself and people. The boy named his new lynx-friend Ayah, which he said meant "pretty cat," though Ashan thought it meant "no-tail cat." The other, he named Ghar, "scared cat." Sometimes he tried to entice Ayah into the cave, thinking it would be fun to sleep with a furry live thing. Of course, a lynx—even a kitten— was smarter than that.

Among the Shahala, the teaching of children was shared by many, but here in the wildplace, the boy had only his mother to show him how to survive on his own. Shahala little ones stayed with the tribe's old women while their mothers gathered; Kai El spent every moment with Ashan.

On stormy days, they stayed inside the Hidden Cave. Kai El liked to feed the fire, poke it with a stick, mumble to it. Like often-remembered Ehr used to do. Ashan didn't tell her son that people usually don't talk to fire. What difference did it make? He might never see another person. It seemed natural to him to watch it, even while he did other things, and he began to know what it wanted. Before long, Ashan didn't even have to think about fire.

"Only four summers!" she said, shaking her head. "If Adah could see you now!"

As Kai El's speech grew up, talking with him became richer. He was so smart, she often learned from *him*.

She told him about his father.

"He loved us, but it was time for him to die."

"Why? Was he old?"

"No. But his mother wanted him. She and his brother were in the otherworld, and lonely for him."

"Could they come and take me?"

"No. I wouldn't let them."

"What is a brother?"

That was a hard question, but she did her best to explain.

Ashan told about the tribe they came from. Kai El didn't understand, but someday he would. It seemed important for him to know who and what he was, or used to be, or, by a miracle, might be again someday: a proud Shahala warrior.

As Tor would have done if he were alive, Ashan taught their son a warrior's ways. Together they crept unseen, disguised in animal skins or leaves. Together they set the traps, killed the catch, and hauled it home. And then the boy helped make it into food, work the skins, carve tools of bone and antler, and learned all the other chores of a woman. The mother realized her son might never have a mate to do this for him. He might never know a shaman either, so she taught him Moonkeeper things . . . medicine, spirit speaking, rituals, and keeping track of time.

Once, from up on the ridgetop where Ehr was buried, they saw a band of men walking on the river trail. The men stopped at the place where their small creek ran into the river, but they did not go up the canyon. Even if they had, Ashan didn't think they would have seen the cave hidden behind the waterfall.

CHAPTER
48

Tor was soul-sick after he left Elia at the Shahala village.
Grief—the mother of sorrow, guilt, and pain—followed his aimless footsteps through mountains and grasslands, as he searched for but never found a sign of Ashan—grief that ground him under its heel, but in greater cruelty, refused to stamp out his life. The lonely wanderer barely noticed seasons passing: a winter . . . a spring . . . a summer . . . an autumn . . . another winter . . . gone by, and little remembered.

Tor was as miserable as a man could be, until spring touched the land, and he had a dream that awoke hope. It was a flying dream, like he used to have, the kind that carried spirit messages.

He dreamt he was an eagle soaring over a river valley. The bird-man circled lower and saw a creek on its way to the river. He flew up the creek to a waterfall. There stood a woman with her hands on the shoulders of a boy. Beckoning with a silent smile, she held out her arm, making a fist for him to land on. He scooped air in his wings to slow himself, extended his talons, and—wait! He would hurt her tender flesh!

A dream couldn't hurt anyone . . . Tor wasn't real . . . Ashan didn't see him. She sighed and dropped her arm.

When Tor had the same dream the next night, hope began to beat fresh wings.

They're alive . . . somewhere . . .

CHAPTER
49

M other and son headed home on a spring afternoon. "Empty traps!" Kai El said. "Good day!"

Ashan laughed. "Full traps" was a good day to her, but she knew what her son of almost five summers meant. Turning a large animal into food was a lot of work; getting it home without losing it to a predator was dangerous.

They approached the Hidden Cave from the ridge that was behind and above it. There was never anyone up here on the ridgetop, though hunters were sometimes seen down by the river that crossed Pusha, the valley they had named for the grandfather Ehr.

Expecting no one, still Ashan was watchful.

Her breath stopped. She slipped to the ground.

A man! Right on top of our cave! I should have made sure the fire was out!

Kai El flattened behind her. "What is it?"

She whispered, "A man over the smokehole, looking down into the cave."

"Will he go away?"

She shook her head. "He'll bring others. He must die."

"But—" Kai El stopped. Little ones did not argue at times like this.

"I know life is sacred, Kai El, but ours come first."

"What if . . ."

She knew what her son was afraid to ask.

"You're old enough to live by yourself. If something happens to me, the spirits will help you."

Ashan almost lost courage at the thought of her boy being left alone in the world. They should flee and never come back, find a new home . . . no . . . there was no home like the Hidden Cave. She didn't think they could survive without it.

"Hold this till I need it." She handed Kai El her spear.

His whispered answer faded as Ashan focused her senses on the enemy who must die because of her carelessness. Wrapped in dark fur, he crouched over the smokehole, peering down into their home between puffs of smoke.

Ashan stepped into the open, praying he wouldn't turn around, and took her sling and its three fist-size stones from her pack. She put two at her feet—hoping she wouldn't need them—and snugged the best one into the soft leather pouch of the sling. Eyeing the enemy as an eagle eyes a rabbit, she narrowed her sight until all was dark but a tunnel of light between her and the back of his head.

She asked Shala the Wind Spirit to take death swift and straight.

The pouch whirled at the end of its thong, round and round her head, gathering force and speed. Her wrist snapped. The rock flew.

Crack! The intruder crumpled without a cry.

Kai El put the spear in her outstretched hand.

Ashan had never faced a man with her spear. Or destroyed human life. It wasn't easy, but she forced herself to cross the invisible tunnel that connected them. The enemy lay unmoving, face-down over the smokehole, a heap of dark fur with human hair and moccasined feet.

On the ground next to his head, Ashan saw something round and blue: Kai El's lost neckstone!

The thief who stole her baby! Up flashed her spear!

A scent stopped her. Ashan fell to her knees and turned the man over.

Tor! Knocked senseless, but alive!

"It's you!" she cried. "Kai El! It's Adah!"

She lifted his head to her lap. "Oh, my love . . ."

The handsomest face in the world seemed more asleep than senseless—eyes closed, flesh slack, breathing slow and even—a little blood in his hair, but none in his mouth, nose or ears.

Kai El came running, and slammed into his father's body, throwing wild punches.

"Dead like Ehr!" he howled. "Hate you bad!"

She pulled him off. "He's not dead! See him breathe?"

The boy quieted. Ashan turned him loose. He knelt by his father and lay his head on his chest.

"Amah fix," her little boy begged through tears.

Time stopped. Sight blurred. Shock, love and rage tangled and fought within her. Rage killed the others, and hardened into a hatred strong enough to destroy life.

Ashan kicked the unconscious man with the sobbing child on top of him.

"You chunk of vomit! You made me a liar! I told your son the only thing that could keep you from us was death!"

Tor's eyelids fluttered, but he didn't wake.

Shoving her son away, Ashan trussed her mate with his own horsehair rope, making a cocoon of the bearskin he wore, tight enough to turn skin pale—just as he'd done to her.

She barely heard Kai El howling; his puny blows to her legs were less than bug bites. Hate consumed her like fire destroys yellow grass. With strength borne of fury, shrieking every ugly word she could think of, she dragged Tor by his hair, thumping and grinding, over the grassy ground above the cave, then down the rocky side, with no mercy.

"Fly maggot in the bottom of a bat cave!"

She would torture him! Kill him!

Tor's senses flooded back. *It's a lie that death is painless! Death is a woman shrieking filthy names! Tsilka! The rattlesnake has me again—*

"You stink ant!"

Filthy *Shahala* names. *Ashan?*

"Beloved!" he cried. "You're killing me!"

"Not yet, I'm not, you pile of steaming dung!"

Crazed with rage, savoring his howls of pain, Ashan hauled her trussed-up mate to the Hidden Cave, making sure the waterfall soaked him as she pulled him through. She tied her prey to the treetrunk that Ehr had brought inside for hanging meat. She wheezed like an animal and her chest was about to explode, but she had one more thing to do before she collapsed.

"I want answers, Tor!" she shouted in his face. "Why?"

"I love you—"

"I don't need love like that!"

Kai El headed for his father with outstretched arms.

"My son," Tor said with a crooked smile.

"Go to your rock!" she yelled at the boy. "Don't move until I say!"

"Ahh-maah—"

"He's our enemy!"

Kai El did what he was told.

Ashan jerked hard on the last knot. She strode back and forth in front of Tor. Questions asked and never answered spewed out.

"Why did you leave us? Where have you been? What kind of man are you? First you kidnap me, then you leave me to die! And your son! Your mate, I can see—I must have angered you—but your own son? How could you, Tor?"

Ashan started to cry. She couldn't help it—she felt so bad for what he'd put them through.

"We mourned you, Tor! We suffered!"

"I mourned you, too, Ashan. I know how it feels to think the one you love is dead."

Her voice turned shrieky. "I don't love you! I hate you! I wish you were dead! I wish I were dead! I can't go through this again!"

Ashan stumbled to her sleeping place, pulled a skin over her head, and sobbed. *How can this be happening—again? How many times will I grieve for this man, only to have him turn up alive?*

She'd used up her strength dragging the worthless beast into the cave. Her mind was beyond thinking. She was too exhausted to fight the sleep that wanted to carry her away.

If he's gone when I wake up, so what? What do we need him for anyway?

* * *

I've seen mad women, but nothing like this! Tor thought as Ashan stamped back and forth hurtling questions like rocks.

When she emptied herself and stumbled away, he saw that this cave was large enough for a whole tribe. He heard the sobbing of his mate, muffled by furs, and outside, the splash of the waterfall that had nearly drowned him . . . but no sounds of other people.

Tor's bearskin cape had saved his flesh from shredding, but she had trussed him too tight. Parts of him were numb; other parts hurt so bad he wished they were numb. He had to get loose before pieces of him died and fell off.

And then there was his head, going *whoom, whoom!* What had she hit him with? The trunk of a tree?

Ashan's crying became sleep-breathing.

Tor whispered to the boy who sat on a rock, hands clamped between his knees, pale with fright.

"Untie me, son."

"Shhh! You'll wake her!"

"Come on. It's all right."

The boy shook his head.

"Kai El, I'm your father."

"She would kill me."

"Your mother wouldn't kill you, son. You know that."

"Maybe not. But she *will* kill you."

Tor wondered. Could she? Who knew how much his soulmate had changed?

As if Kai El saw his thoughts, he said, "She will."

"You can't let that happen. You must help me."

The boy glanced at the heap of skins that was his mother. A troubled sigh said he wanted to help, but fear was too strong.

"Please, son, don't let me die."

Kai El clenched like a fist, then his little shoulders drooped. He came to his father. Small fingers attacked the knots. Tor ignored bursts of pain as parts were freed and feeling rushed back.

"I'm sorry," Kai El whispered. "I tried to stop her."

"I can't believe how big you are!"

"I've seen animals crazed like that, but not my mother!"

"And how well you speak!"

When Tor was free, Kai El disappeared in his embrace. Sweet explosions of light filled his head. *Amotkan! The child thought dead—in my arms and wriggling with life!*

"Will you take me away, Adah?"

"I'm not leaving."

"She'll kill you!"

"I'll take the chance. We need to talk. Is it safe outside?" Kai El nodded.

With a piece of leather over their heads, they ducked through the waterfall. Tor squinted; the sun had gone down, but it was bright after the dimness of the cave. He turned and looked at the waterfall. The way it hid Ashan's new home impressed him.

Tor followed his son to a mossy rock wide enough for two, near enough the waterfall so its voice would cover theirs, far enough so they wouldn't get splashed.

"Who else lives here?" Tor asked.

"Lynx. Chipmunks—"

"I mean people."

"Oh. There was Ehr."

"Ehr?"

"The grandfather. He died."

"You and Amah live here alone?" It was hard to believe!

"You left! What else could we do?" Kai El stared hard at his father. "Why, Adah? Why did you leave?"

Tor swallowed. "How smart you must be to take care of your mother!"

"Why did you leave us?"

"You talk like one fully grown!"

The boy wouldn't be distracted. "Why—did—you—leave—us?"

Tor took a deep breath. "Well . . . I had a dream . . ."

Did his son even know what the word meant? Ashan believed dreaming brought disaster. Why would she allow Kai El to do it? But the boy was listening—demanding—so Tor went on.

"In my dreams, there was a river, so wide you could barely see one side from the other. And fish so many you could walk on their backs. There we were, living a fat, happy life. You, me, Amah . . . and a tribe of people."

The only faces Tor saw in dreams were Ashan's and Kai El's. Once he had thought the Shahala were the people of his river dreams. When he understood that he could never be with them again, he knew the faceless ones were Tlikit. The dream was not so sweet after that.

"This river, boy . . . I dreamed it was the best home in the world. I had to go and look for it. I was going to come back for you and your mother."

"Did you find it?"

"Yes. It's even better than in my dreams."

"Then why didn't you come back for us?"

Tor hesitated. How could he explain? "I couldn't come back, until now. I'll tell you the reason some other time."

For a while there was only the sound of the waterfall.

"I dream too," Kai El said.

Tor was surprised. "Didn't your mother teach you the danger?"

"She tried. It bothers her, so I stopped talking about it."

Love filled Tor—for this boy, for himself, for men and the way they thought, no matter what age.

"My son," he sighed. "It's so good to be with you again. We'll tell each other our dreams."

They smiled warmly at each other.

"Soon, Kai El, I'll teach you to be a warrior."

"They already did . . . Amah and Ehr."

"Oh."

Darkness came. Tor's flesh numbed, this time from cold. They went into the cave. The boy brought a goatskin for his shivering father to wear.

The furpile with Ashan under it had not moved.

"Do you have wood?" Tor asked.

Kai El nodded. "I'll make fire."

"You know how? At your age?"

The child laughed. "Didn't you?"

"Of course," the father lied.

Pride swelled Tor. Growing up without a tribe must have required much of the boy. What a job Ashan had done! Of course, look what she had to work with: Tor's son, with the blood of Shahala warriors farther back in time than anyone remembered.

The man who had missed so much watched in wonder as

his child made fire with practiced ease, and then food. Kai
El couldn't keep his eyes open long enough to eat. He went
to a pile of furs near his mother. Tor followed and knelt
beside him.

"I love you, Kai El."

"Will you be here tomorrow?"

"I'll be here forever."

Kai El looked doubtful. "Not unless you tie her."

"Don't worry. Go to sleep. Spirits keep you from harm."

"I love you, Adah. I'm glad you came back."

"So am I, son. So am I."

Tor tucked furs around his child. *The most ordinary thing,
unless you thought you'd never do it again.*

As Tor sat by the fire, his insides felt like one big smile.
The most peaceful sounds filled his ears, sounds he'd thought
he'd never hear again: Ashan and Kai El breathing in sleep.
Life sounds . . . theirs and mine . . . He poked the fire and
gazed into the flames. *I'm with my family! What a place!
Prayers answered! Happiness forever!*

Except for one thing: Ashan wants me dead.

Tor went to where she slept under enough furs to keep five
people warm. He saw no part of her, but she was in there;
ever so slightly, the furs rose and fell. He sat there shaking
his head. *Women!* How could anyone sleep at a time like this?

She won't sleep forever. What are you going to do?

Tie her. Even Kai El said so.

The thought cast a heavy cloud over Tor's joy. It had
worked before; eventually, she had come around. But at
first—what a miserable time!

That seemed so long ago—almost like another life. Tor
had been a rash young warrior, always thinking up crazy
plans to get what he wanted. All he ever got was disaster. It
had changed him. He was no longer the same *boy* who in
the heat of passion, without thought of consequences, had
kidnapped his lover. Since then, he'd been a mate and a
father. He'd been treated like a god, and a slave. He had
lived through loss, to become a man who understood responsi-
bility in new ways.

No. He couldn't tie her. Maybe it was time for honesty.

Tor honestly wanted to make love. At this moment, it was
the only truth he knew. He slipped under the furs, molded to

the missing part of himself, and was whole. He didn't care if he died for it.

What a dream . . .

Warm and sleepy under a sky like an upside-down lake, Ashan lay naked on meadowgrass soft as fur. Her mate stood over her with eyes full of love and desire. His loinskin fell. Memories of ecstasy coursed through her. Breathing hurried. She gasped as he lay on her . . . strong and sleek, the weight and scent of a man . . . *so good.* Her center caught fire as she moved with him and against him. Their bodies melted together, seeking to be one. He opened her lips with his tongue. She had forgotten his sweet taste . . .

This is no dream, Ashan. This is your soulmate, your Tor.

Amotkan! I knew how good this would be. Just like I knew I was giving up when I went to sleep.

There was one thing Ashan had to know.

"Are you on your way somewhere, or are you staying?"

"I'll stay forever if you let me."

"Mmmm . . . good."

The two were one again.

CHAPTER
50

Ashan was a smile riding the sky on a cloud, as sleep gave way to waking. She heard man-breathing, but no child noise, so she opened an eye. The light from the smoke-hole said morning. Kai El would be outside. Smiling, she snuggled to her lover's body, soaking up the best kind of warmth. All she could think was how *good* she felt, inside, outside, body and soul.

Tor awoke and touched her cheek. "It's true . . ."

She nodded, smiling.

He rose to his elbows and looked around.

"Where's Kai El?"

"Outside."

"By himself?" He sounded worried.

Ashan smiled. "Your son is older than you think. He'll be down at the pool getting a fish for our morning meal."

Tor's face showed his disbelief.

"Come on. See for yourself."

It feels so good to smile! she thought.

Tor's mate tossed him a piece of stiff leather.

"Hold it over your head. Stay on that ledge. Watch your feet. Fast is best."

"Do you ever get used to running through water?"

She shrugged. "It keeps things out of our home. Remind me to tell you about the skunk that almost ruined the Home Cave."

Tor wasn't sure he wanted to hear that story.

Ashan came through the waterfall dry. Tor got soaked. He shook himself and held a hand over his eyes against bright sunlight.

Below, his son stood at the edge of a shallow pool, slender spear poised, gazing into the water.

"Hello!" Tor shouted.

Kai El waved, and touched a finger to his lips—the sign for silence. Turning back to the pool, he raised his spear and stared into the water—just like a Shahala warrior, except for size.

Tor shook his head. *What a boy!* he thought.

Ashan looked the same as when he had left, a beauty to take his breath away, but Kai El surprised him. Tor had left a fat stumbler who babbled. Now he had come back to a short warrior who talked. He had known the boy would grow—he just hadn't realized how long he'd been away.

He followed Ashan to the rock where Kai El had taken him the night before. They sat touching. Everything was sharp and bright. His chest swelled with sweet air, his heart with love. Ashan nudged him, so he put his arm around her. Loving the feeling, her scent, the sight of his boy down there, Tor drank deep, like parched earth welcoming rain.

Kai El hurled his spear. A rainbow-colored fish exploded from the water and thrashed in the sun, as if to shake off death, but there was no shaking off the spear in its gut.

The boy threw himself at the water, arms out, belly first—splash! He came up sputtering and empty-handed, lunged, and missed again.

Tor burst out laughing. He'd never seen anything funnier: a fierce, determined warrior no taller than his thigh, chasing a fish through waist-deep water, without a chance of catching it. Ashan shook with laughter beside him. He thought they both might fall backward off the sitting rock.

Tor caught his breath. "If he tied a rope to the spear, that wouldn't happen."

"I never thought of that."

"I don't suppose you would!" Tor couldn't keep from

laughing. "It's a good thing you had that old man! If you'd had to count on the boy, you'd have starved!"

He felt Ashan stiffen. "You couldn't be more wrong. Kai El could feed us all. He could live alone. That has been my purpose since you left."

"Ashan, he's a wonderful boy, but he's only four summers."

Kai El yelled. "Got him!" He wrestled the huge trout out of the water, threw it on the ground, hit it with a rock, and flopped down beside it.

"Look at that!" Tor said. "It's huge!"

Ashan's voice was prideful. "They're his animal friends. He feeds them so they get fat. When he wants a special meal, he catches one."

Animal friends? What a strange idea. Scratching his head, Tor couldn't think of anything to say. Could Ashan be right about the boy?

"You really believe Kai El could survive alone?"

Smiling, she held out her hand. "Come back in the cave and I'll show you."

Tor thought Ashan seemed taller as she took him around the cave showing him her caches. She had enough food for several seasons: deer, elk, antelope, marmot—everything but horse—leathermeat, chipped meat, marrow, fat, berries, grains, nuts. Tor could not believe how much food there was.

"As you can see," his mate said proudly, "there's plenty for us *and* Kai El's animal friends. Ehr was very clever about catching food. He taught us everything he knew."

Tor thought there was too much food; there would be waste.

"Where do you get all this?"

"From traps."

"Traps?"

"You know . . . things to keep animals until you're ready."

His lips curled. "Like man-eaters keep live food?"

"Not at all. You'll see."

Without knowing exactly what she meant, Tor didn't think he liked the idea. But, seeing her pride, he decided to wait to tell her what he thought about keeping animals until they're needed.

"What would you like to eat?" she asked. "You can have anything."

"Those salmonberries looked good."

Watching her work, Tor smiled. No one made food like his mate, once she taught herself—not even his mother. Thinking of salmonberries, his mouth watered. Named for the pink-orange color that was like salmon meat, fresh ones were sweet and popping with juice. They only grew in lush places. He hadn't seen any since he left the homeland of his ancestors. Ashan didn't stop with salmonberries, bringing a food bowl with several kinds of fruit mashed with honey. It was delicious! He hadn't tasted honey in so long. The Tlikit didn't even know about honey. Tor finished and licked his fingers.

"What a place, Ashan!"

"I know. It has everything. And now it has *you*."

She took his hand, ran her tongue on his sticky skin, then pushed him back.

"You're sweet," she said. "I'm hungry."

The root of Tor stirred. "The boy . . ." he said weakly.

"He'll be busy with that fish for a while."

"We can't do it right here . . . in the open . . ."

Ashan smiled as she led him to her sleeping place. They made love hidden under furs.

In the afternoon, Kai El cooked the trout over a fire and proudly served his parents. They made much of the rich, oily taste of the firm orange flesh. Tor thought it was good to hear Shahala people admire food with words. Tlikit people only knew to belch.

Ashan spoke as if she were giving her mate a gift: "You don't have to do a thing. There's so much food stored, we can take a long time enjoying ourselves just being together."

"Hmmm," Tor said, wondering if having nothing to do could be such a good thing.

They made love that night, after she had rubbed his back—something he'd tried to get Tsilka to do.

How did I ever leave this woman? Tor wondered. *Nothing,* he vowed, *will ever separate us again!*

The next day, they went to see "Ehr's traps." Tor thought it odd that they still said "Ehr this" and "Ehr that" all the

time. It showed how important the man they called grandfather had been in their lives.

They found the traps empty. Kai El said he was glad, an
Tor agreed—they certainly didn't need any meat. The trap
were all different—and clever, Tor had to admit, as Asha
explained how they worked. She did something to each on
to "make it harmless": covered it, took it apart, or whateve
had to be done so that nothing would get caught.

"Harmless traps don't have to be checked," she told him
"We usually do it in autumn, so we don't have to go out i
the cold. But I don't want any work for us now. I just war
to spend time enjoying you."

Tor was confused by what he saw. He didn't know animal
could be lured to traps. Weren't they smarter than that?

There was no balance in this trapping, no pitting of strengt
and cunning that was a warrior's pride. What about ancier
laws? Selecting which animal to take? What about respect
He couldn't deny that traps were useful for a woman wh
didn't know how to hunt. His family would probably be dea
without them. But for a man? Were men meant to live s
easily? Every creature had to work hard for food. Plant-eater
had to graze all day. Predators missed far more often tha
they hit. It kept things in balance. It was fair.

"I don't like this trapping, Ashan. Now that I'm back
we'll get rid of these things, and I will hunt."

"Hunt if you like, but I'm not getting rid of Ehr's traps."
Her voice had new strength to match her new wisdom.

CHAPTER
51

Two moons passed, slow as flowing honey.

Alone in the Hidden Cave on an early summer day, Ashan sat cross-legged in a patch of light let in by the smoke-hole, punching sewing holes in the elkhide bottoms of moccasins that were a secret present for Tor. The pleasant work would have made her hum, but didn't.

Except for a gnawing void inside, Ashan might have been completely happy. But when she was alone, she found herself thinking of her beloved, lost Shahala. It made her sad, guilty, and in a way, empty.

Inside Ashan, a hollow was growing where purpose used to be. All her life, purpose had been thrust upon her. When she was young, it was learning to lead. Tor kidnapped her, and it changed to surviving and getting back home. Then Kai El was born, and Ashan understood why the Moonkeeper was denied a family: as children do, Kai El became purpose more important than any other could ever be.

But what purpose did Ashan have now? Tor had taken over protecting, providing for, and teaching Kai El. Of course, the child still needed his mother, but not enough to fulfill *her* need.

Ashan sighed. *The happiness on my face does not reach the hole in my heart.*

But then she thought: *Enough whining*. She was skilled blocking unhappy thoughts. She did it by thinking happ ones.

Life is good. Plenty of food. And love . . . sometimes think that's the best of all.

Sleeping with a man was so much better than sleepin alone. In the dark, the lovers took what their bodies wante and gave back what they needed to give. And the strange thing was that each night's love seemed better than the las

Talking was good, too. She and Tor had never talked th much before. At first there was so much to tell that their voice got tangled. Ashan told everything the way it happened. To seemed to, but she suspected that he left things out.

She remembered last night's conversation . . . sitting clos to her found mate, gazing into the embering fire . . .

"I worry about our people," she had said, wistful voice

"I know, my love. I'm sorry."

"It's getting worse now that we're back together . . . guess because you've cured my other worries."

Tor patted her, but comfort didn't come.

"If only I knew how they are," she said, "I could mak myself stop worrying."

"That would be good."

"If I could see them one more time—"

"You know they would kill us."

Ashan sighed, and gave herself to watching the ember But she couldn't let it drop.

"Maybe we could go there, just to look—"

"It's too far. I don't know the way."

"My mate, the Shahala warrior, doesn't know the way? Ashan laughed. "If you don't know the way, how do yo know it's too far?"

Tor gave no answer.

"I think I know the way," she said, her voice wistf again. "Someday I might try it on my own. I did once, yo know."

"And a big mess you made."

"At least I tried . . ."

Ashan had realized that she sounded like a little girl wit no one to help find her lost doll. It wasn't good for Tor, o anyone, to see her like that. She had cleared her throat, and said, "So . . . you were right about your Great River, and even the tribe you said you'd find."

"I have always been right, my love."

She hadn't laughed, though *that* was funny.

"If this tribe was so great, why did you pretend to be a god?"

Tor hesitated, then cleared his throat. "It was fun."

"Terrifying people? What a strange idea of fun."

"Isn't that what a Moonkeeper does?"

She huffed. "Not unless she has to. And it is not fun."

"Oh, I see," he said with a hint of sarcasm.

"So . . . if these Tee-likit were the best people you ever knew, and this river the best place, why didn't you stay there?"

"Tlikit, Ashan. You say the first part all at once."

"Tlikit," she said perfectly. "Why didn't you stay with them?"

He hesitated. She had the feeling there were things he was afraid to say.

"I needed you and Kai El to make my life complete. But Chiawana, and the place I named Teahra . . . it really is wonderful. And the Tlikit are nice. They make pictures on rocks like your friend Ehr. Someday we'll go there, and you'll see—you'll want to live there."

"No, Tor. You're the one who will see. If I were going to live with any people, they would be our own Shahala. Since you say that's impossible, we will live by ourselves."

Tor had made a disgusting noise.

"You'll be happier when you accept it."

"I can't accept life without a tribe! It isn't natural!"

That had been the end of last night's conversation.

Now Ashan noticed that sunlight no longer lit the work in her lap. She picked up her sewing things and moved into brightness again.

"It's lonely in here," she grumped out loud. "I'd rather be out with my boys."

She told herself it was good to see the growing bond between father and son. Mother and son had to grow apart so that the boy could grow to be a man.

"Ouch!" The bone needle popped through the elkhide into her finger. She licked the drop of blood and went back to work, wiggling the needle instead of forcing it.

It might be nice to have another baby, she thought. *I miss the time when my boy and I were the only creatures in the world.*

Ashan heard them coming, and hid her work; she wasn't ready for Tor to see his moccasins yet.

Kai El's gift of wilted flowers made her smile.

"It's strange," Tor said. "Were there horses in this valley when you came?"

"Not many after the first winter."

"This seems like a place they would love."

"Ehr said there used to be great herds. Like Anutash."

"I've seen hardly any since I've been here. I wonder why?"

Ashan shrugged. It wasn't something she worried about. When they'd lived with the tribe, horse had been the main winter food, prepared in every way possible. By the time spring finally brought other animals, Ashan would rather have eaten treebark than horsemeat.

"I would enjoy a fat horse steak," she admitted. "But we don't really need horses, now that we have Ehr's traps."

Tor was glad for this good autumn day: Rain had kept them inside too long, and the cave had a musty smell.

"Kai El and I are going walking," he told Ashan.

"There's grinding to do. Then we can all go walking."

He frowned.

"Well, go by yourself if you don't want to help."

Tor went by himself. He walked along the river, kicking rocks into the water, muttering. "You'd think she was chief of this family—"

He heard the squeal of a hurt animal. Deer?

No! Horse!

He ran to a nearby trap, the deep pit Ashan called her best. She had covered it with logs to make it harmless, but a tan and black horse had fallen through. It squealed pitifully as it struggled to stand on broken forelegs. At the sight of a man its dark eyes rolled, flashing terror's shining white.

Tor slid into the pit, jerked the head back, and ended its agony with his blade.

Oh Amotkan . . . the first horse he'd seen in how long. And a mare . . . he had killed a mare . . . forbidden by Shahala law. Sadness filled him as he knelt in the mud, stroking a soft ear flecked with blood and foam.

"Forgive me," he said to her spirit. "I did not mean for you to die."

But you knew traps were wrong, said a voice in his mind. *You knew animals should be hunted by warriors with courage, not lured to a stinking hole in the ground.*

Tor should destroy the shameful pit—start right now—dig a trench to the river and flood it, so it could never kill another innocent.

Why didn't he?

Maturity got in the way. To destroy another man's work demanded careful thought. And there was Ashan to consider. Destroying what meant so much to his mate would have been the rash act of the young Tor. A different man now, he knew it was unfair, and unwise, to use his greater strength against her.

This new life called for words, not muscles; persuasion by reasoning, not bag-you-up-and-haul-you-away.

So he pulled the dead horse out of the pit, slung it over his shoulders, and walked home. Ashan was thrilled with the catch, and fire-blackened slices for a meal.

Tor waited until their son slept to speak about what was on his mind.

"Ashan, I'm a warrior, and you've always respected my knowledge of hunting."

"I have."

"Then believe me: Catching food this way is wrong. Shahala law tells everything men need to know, yet doesn't speak of trapping. I'm afraid it will upset the Balance. You know better than anyone . . . the world will end if the Balance fails. That's why Amotkan gave us laws about selecting, and told us to respect animals, and not cause unnecessary pain." He paused, then said firmly, "These traps should be destroyed."

"But Tor, they work so well. How can a man who dreams of fathering a new world destroy new ways, simply because it goes against what's been done in the past? Life is different for us now. We have to make law fit reality. It's a truth I learned from Ehr."

"There are more important things in the world than you and I and some old man. Ashan, the Balance—"

"The Balance does not depend on how animals die. I know these things."

"But if you're wrong—"

Tears shone in Ashan's eyes. "I'll never be happy if Ehr's lifetime of work is destroyed. He trusted me to care for his things." The tears spilled out. "And you don't know, Tor, how terrible it is to have no meat for your little one. I'll never feel safe without the traps."

Here was the bad part about Tor's reasonable new way: half the time, it didn't work.

He sighed. "For you, I won't destroy them. But neither will I use them."

CHAPTER
52

Land Dancer, Amotkan's favorite, was disappearing.

As he hunted that autumn with his son, Tor saw only a few small bands of the beautiful creatures. He remembered with longing the herds of his youth, a sight Kai El had never seen. He told the boy how horses once roamed Shahala winter valleys, so many that their meat fed a large tribe. Horses were an important part of Shahala life, and Kai El was a Shahala warrior. Even if his son never saw another, Tor wanted him to know their ways—the best any men had, he was sure, now that he had seen the ways of others.

More than once that autumn, they found rotting horses. What was happening to Kusi's kind? It must be sickness, or poison, because scavengers left the bodies untouched.

Not wanting to frighten Ashan, they mentioned none of his . . . until the day they found the last stallion.

On a windy afternoon, father and son hunted far from the Hidden Cave. From the top of a ridge, Tor looked under his hand into the distance, and saw a narrow canyon.

"Let's go," he said. "Sometimes animals hide in places like that, not realizing they can't get away."

The horses they found there were too weak to even try. Four mares stood together, missing patches of fur like spring bison, heads hanging, breathing hard. The pitiful creatures did not move as the hunters approached.

A white stallion lay on the ground, with barely enough strength to hold up its head.

"It's you!" Tor said, gazing into sorrowful eyes. "You who saved my life!"

He heard in his mind its plea for death. His stone blade answered. The sun went down in colors of fire as the last stallion turned cold in his arms.

The *last*? Why would he think so?

Because the mares should have fled when their stallion died, to find another and join his band. But when Kai El chased them off, they circled back.

Everything came together in Tor's mind . . . disappearing herds, decaying corpses, mares with nowhere to go. As sure as he'd ever known anything, Tor suddenly knew that Kusi's kind was dying out . . . like Manu's.

How could such a thing happen? Did Amotkan weary of them? Or punish them for the sins of people?

"Why me!" Tor yelled. "Why must *I* kill the last of kinds?"

"Don't know," Kai El whispered. Tor had forgotten him. Sometimes the boy seemed invisible.

When they got home, Tor blurted: "Ashan, I killed the last stallion!"

"There's no such thing as the *last* stallion. Just because there aren't many here—"

"Listen! Kusi's kind is gone from the world, just like Manu's! I know! I brought death to them both!"

Her eyes widened. "You killed a mammoth?"

"I don't know why," he said bitterly, "but it's my destiny to kill the last of kinds. First the Earth Shaker, now the Land Dancer. Once they're gone, they can never come back." Tor put his head in his hands and moaned. "We cannot begin to know the tragedy of that."

Ashan knew a kind could die out. She didn't doubt it when Raga said Manu was the last mammoth. It seemed no tragedy—people didn't need mammoths—Ashan had never ever seen one.

But the last horse? No. Too hard to believe. Too scary

Horses were as many as snowflakes, as faithful as winter. The wearing of Kusi's own tail by the Shahala Moonkeeper at the Autumn Feast made sure they would come forever.

If horses died out, as Tor believed they had, what would it mean to the Shahala? Horsemeat, lots of it, was critical for the tribe's survival. Could her people find some other way to live?

That night, Ashan found a forgotten bit of dried horsemeat and boiled it with mild, thumb-size roots. Her family praised the faint taste of horse in the stew. Was everyone wondering if it was the last?

Her mate was asleep when she crawled in beside him— carefully—once in a while, it was nice to go to sleep without lovemaking. Soaking up his warmth, she thought of the stew. Would she ever taste horse again, or see the great, many-colored herds?

"Strength to you, Kusi, and your kind," she murmured.

Ashan dreamed: she was a wind, blowing over her childhood home, looking for horses. But there were no herds on the yellow grassland, none on the hillsides or at the watering places—not one horse in all of Shahala land.

And then—whoosh—she was in Anutash, in the Moonkeeper's hut. People with dread-filled faces crowded around a withered crone lying on her back, a bag of bones with eyes closed, skin white against a black bear robe—Raga. Ashan saw the old woman's life force floating above her, faintly glowing, held by the thinnest of strands. Raga's glow flickered. The people began to wail: the death of the last Moonkeeper meant the end of the Balance, of the tribe, of everything.

"Your Moonkeeper is here!" Ashan cried.

They didn't hear, any more than they had seen. She reached out, but her hands went through their bodies, as if she, or they, or all of them were made of air.

In the morning, she remembered having a bad dream— nothing more. But a nameless fear stayed with her.

"Tor . . . what if Raga died, and the Autumn Feast came . . . and here I am in the wildplace, so there was no Shahala Moonkeeper to wear Kusi's tail?"

He gave her a narrow look.

"Well, think about it," she said. "Without a Moonkeeper,

the Balance would shift. Maybe horses would be the first to go—they were the first created."

Tor shook his head. "Do you really believe that the fate of the world rides on the breath of one woman?"

"Well . . . yes."

"I would laugh, but there's nothing funny about the death of horses."

"No," she said from her heart. "Nothing could be sadder."

After a time, Tor said, "Oh, I don't know. What about a family with no tribe?"

Here we go again, Ashan thought.

"Without a tribe . . ." He sighed as if it were the most tragic thing ever. "The man hunts alone. The woman has no one to chatter with, so she turns sour. The child plays with animals instead of other children. Ashan, it's not right for you to deny us a tribe."

"Tor, there won't be any tribes if there are no horses."

"Wrong. The Tlikit tribe doesn't need horses. Chiawana's fish will keep them from hunger."

"I'm glad for them. But I already told you: if I was going to live with any tribe, it would be my own."

CHAPTER
53

In the Misty Time, people knew the moon and sun as friends.

Enemy of the night, but destined to dwell there, Alhaia the moon continually struggled with the Spirit of Dark. She fattened and shrunk, lived, then died, always to return. Like the butterfly, Alhaia showed people life beyond death.

Kai the sun ruled the day, warming the world, and lighting it so Amotkan's creatures could see. He was stronger than his sister: though his path through the sky changed with the seasons, he kept his shape, even when he hid in clouds—round and whole, a never-changing circle of brilliance.

People could trust the moon and the sun—as much as they could trust anything—as long as the Balance was kept.

But on this autumn day, the Balance must have come undone, for on the battlefield of the sky, the sun was dying. So too—plunged into never-ending night—would the world die, and Amotkan's every creature.

Tor sat on sun-warmed grass near the Hidden Cave, with arms around his knees, tipped-back head, eyes following a small cloud as it scudded across the midmorning sky.

His eyes flicked past the sun, and . . . there was a spot on it!

Impossible!

He rubbed his eyes, and squinted—but the sore on Kai's flesh was still there—a hole into night where the edge of the sun should be.

Tor jerked his eyes away—staring too long could blind a man—looked back for a moment, then away. Each time he looked, the black spot had grown. It was eating the sun.

His soul needed a shaman. Without a clear thought in his mind, he ran home yelling.

The panic in Tor's voice frightened Ashan. She hurried outside, and found him—mumbling, white faced, staring at the sky. She'd never seen her mate like this.

Ashan looked up, and gasped. Last night's unremembered dream crashed into her mind with all its terrifying details: horses gone, Raga dying, people wailing, Ashan powerless.

"Oh, Amotkan!" she cried. "The sun is dying!"

Moonkeepers knew much that others were not told—too much knowledge made people worry. One secret was that the sun had died four times before. Four times a Shahala Moonkeeper brought it back to life, but Ashan had no idea how. There hadn't been time to learn—if Raga even knew—in Ashan's lifetime, the sun had been well.

Sick to her stomach, dizzy, Ashan tore her eyes from the blinding ball and the black shadow chewing its top away. She grabbed Tor's shoulders.

"It's the end, Tor! I dreamed it! Raga's dead! There's no Moonkeeper to help the sun!"

"You're a Moonkeeper—"

"Not by myself! I need a tribe to finish the magic!"

Ashan slipped to the ground, sobbing.

Tor had never told his mate that he'd seen the Shahala tribe, nor had he intended to. It could only fan the flame of her deadly dream of returning.

But now . . . Tor couldn't think . . . how could this even happen? A rounded shadow like a mouth slowly devouring the giver of life? Light fading from the world in the middle of the day?

He blurted: "Ashan, the Shahala have a Moonkeeper, even if Raga dies! Surely she will know what to do!"

"They have no Moonkeeper, Tor. I was the Chosen One."

"Tenka took your place."

"Your dreamy little sister . . . Raga has better sense than that."

"Raga had no choice."

Ashan looked up, suspicion in her eyes. "Where do you get these ideas?"

Tor took a deep breath, swallowed.

"I saw them."

Her mouth dropped. Her eyes grew. She spoke very slowly.

"You? Saw? Them?"

"Yes, I did. And Tenka was the Ch—"

"You never told me?"

"I—I—"

"I ought to kill you, Tor."

I really should! Ashan thought. *Later*. She took deep breaths to calm herself, put Tor out of her mind, and focused on remembering all she knew about the sun. In the gathering silence, Ashan thought she heard the ground cry and the sky moan.

"Hurry!" they pled. "The Spirit of Light is losing!"

In the Shahala village of Anutash, it was an ordinary morning . . . until someone saw the missing edge of the sun. A fearful hush fell. The wind stopped. Animals stilled. People held their breath in wonder. In Anutash, and everywhere, all things waited in the gathering dim, shocked to silence, watching the impossible happen in the sky.

Even Raga, weak as she was, had been brought on a litter to the ceremonial ground. Raga no longer had much voice. But she had the Chosen One.

Squatting beside the Old Moonkeeper, Tenka was eaten by fear like the sun was being eaten by that . . . whatever-it-was.

Raga whispered like a dry, crumpled leaf.

"Stand and sing, Rising Star."

"Spirit mother, I don't know the words!"

"Reach in your heart to find them."

I'm only eleven summers! Tenka thought. *How could I know a song to give life to the sun?*

Her heart fluttered like it was full of bugs, her muscles felt runny like melted fat, but Tenka understood that she—almost-Moonkeeper of the Shahala people—was the only person in the world who could even hope to do anything.

Standing with her arms to the sky, she made up some words: "Kai! Be strong! We need you!" and sang them in a pleading voice.

Kai was more than half gone. It was twilight, becoming night, and still he shrank. Panic squeezed like a hand around the Chosen One's throat. *Help me . . .*

Words sprang from Tenka's heart. Her voice rang out.

"Earth was born of the timeless struggle . . ."

". . . between Dark and Light."

Far away, outside the Hidden Cave, Ashan had also found a shaman's resounding voice, and the words of an ancient song:

"In the Misty Time, Amotkan gave power to the Spirit of Light. But Dark never sleeps. Forever must Shakana's daughters keep the Balance."

A Moonkeeper did not show fear, so Ashan shouted as loud as she could.

"Spirit of Dark! Go back to the night where you belong!"

Ignoring her, the shadow advanced.

"Spirit of Dark, you're tired! Very, very tired!"

Help me, Kai! she thought. But the ball in the sky was nothing but a thinning crescent with no power over the dark engulfing the world.

What am I forgetting? she asked.

To threaten . . .

"Spirit of Dark! Give up this fight, or we'll kill your favored creatures! The bat! The owl! The night mouse!"

. . . almost . . . gone . . .

"All you love will be destroyed!"

But it was too late. The sun vanished. Dark robed the world. In the lonely, midmorning night, a shiver ran through Ashan, as if Kai twitched as he died. But it was a shiver of strength from the not-quite-bested sun. He began to struggle, fatten, chase the shadow back.

"Thank Amotkan!" Ashan gasped. "It worked!"

"I—I did it!" Tenka yelped, clapping her hands.

Raga went weak with relief. *But it shouldn't have worked,*

the old woman thought. *Why would spirits listen to one who is not yet a Moonkeeper?*

We have been saved for some special purpose.

It fit with Raga's other ideas: about the mountain who coughed ashes; the death of horses; her own dreams of a better future that she wouldn't live to see, a future more of fish than meat.

In a bruised whisper, the Old Moonkeeper told the Chosen One what to say to the awestruck tribe. When Tenka spoke, her voice was stronger than it had ever been—almost a Moonkeeper's voice.

"My people! We have been saved for some great purpose! We must prepare ourselves for a new future!"

Tsilka, unrecognized chief of an unhappy tribe, had never known such terror. When the world began to darken in the middle of morning—not from clouds, but from a dirty spot on the sun—with the rest of the Tlikit, she had run for shelter.

The noise in the long, low cave was awful. People babbled and sobbed. The fear of so many in such a small place took on a hot life of its own, spreading like wildfire, stealing the breathing air.

Tsilka huddled back as far as she could get, clutching her little daughters as if she thought someone would tear them away. She couldn't keep from looking out the cave mouth, where the light of day faded and faded.

Never-Ending Night was coming, as threatened by an ancient story. Because of the wrongdoing of people.

Hiding her face in her daughters' hair, Tsilka rocked back and forth, moaning, "Oh, my babies . . . only two summers . . ."

How she loved them . . . two instead of one . . . twice the love inside the body of one woman. And twice the pain to think of what would become of them in the Never-Ending Night. Against her terror, Tsilka forced herself to think pleasant thoughts of Tsurya and Tsagaia. So lovely that people smiled to see them, they looked alike as seeds of grass. But their natures were different as the graceful water skimmer from the big tan cat, whose names they bore. No Tlikit woman had ever made two babies at the same time. They were miracles, these daughters of the god Wahawkin . . .

Someone poked her shoulder—her father—and the old chief was angry.

"The very sky speaks against you! It is you who caused the Never-Ending Night! You captured a god! You changed the old ways! You ruined the balance of our tribe!"

The truth twisted like a knife in Tsilka's heart.

Timshin said, "You brought this on us. You are the only one who can stop it."

"Look out there, Father. Nothing can stop that."

"You have to try. Give me the babies."

The babies . . . She swallowed. *For them* . . .

Weak as overcooked mush, Tsilka crawled outside to a place she thought was special. The sounds of wind and river seemed muted in the darkening morning. The scariest thing was loneliness: She could still see familiar things in the fading light, but in the Never-Ending Night . . . how lonely it would be to never see.

On her knees, Tsilka raised her face and her trembling arms. She opened her mouth, but for the first time in her life, she could not make a sound. So she thought words, thought them very hard, tried to push them out her forehead.

Sky gods! Spare us! I'm sorry for the wrong I've done!

"What wrong?"

It might have been the sound of wind, but Tsilka thought it was the voice of Sahalie, god over all.

Keeping a god, she answered in her mind. *Stealing power from men. Changing the ways.*

The voice said: "Be your brother's helper, not his enemy."

"I will change," Tsilka promised.

The god over all gave her, and the world, one more chance.

CHAPTER
54

Ashan opened her eyes, and thanked Amotkan: The sun was whole again, shining morning on the world.

Anger soon intruded on relief. Tor *had* seen their people! What other lies had he told?

No point in asking now, she thought. Tor still gaped at the sky, face blank and stupid, like a man who has seen the end of the world . . . almost. He didn't notice when Ashan left.

Tired, she asked spirits to help as she walked to the most sacred place she knew: The ridgetop where Ehr was buried. There she sat on a special rock.

"The sun died," she said to the sky. "What does it mean?" No answer.

"Someone has to tell me!"

Ashan thought she heard laughter, but it was the wind whipping up. Clouds thickened, hiding the sun. Fear teased her, but she knew it was just an ordinary, autumn thing— clear sky, then cloudy, then clear again, many times in one day.

The mottled sky dripped. She turned her face to the wet that smelled and felt so clean.

On the clouds, a vision appeared . . .

. . . Ashan's beloved Shahala tribe, strung out one by one,

traveling with all they possessed across the dry plains of the tabu land. Her people looked weary, starved, frightened.

An impossible, sheer-sided gorge slashed the plain before them. Its ends could not be seen—if indeed it ended.

On the distant side, Ashan saw Tor leading another tribe to welcome the Shahala.

But that gorge . . . there was no way across.

The wind spoke: *You are the bridge for people to walk.*

Ashan envisioned herself growing, strong and tall as many trees. She lay herself across the chasm. The Shahala walked into new life.

The sweetness, the rightness, the beauty of the vision made whatever anger she had for her mate as nothing.

Rain in Tor's face brought his senses back. He desperately wanted to talk about the sun, and what Ashan had done to save it. But she was gone.

He went through the waterfall, into the Hidden Cave. Kai El was napping—had he slept through the whole thing? Tor was tempted to wake him, just to have someone to talk to. He knelt by the boy, and tried to think, but it was too hard. So he gave up the effort and lay his head down, face so close he could smell Kai El's sweet breath.

A strange thing happened: Tor's mind drifted to a place that was almost sleep, but not quite. There he had an awake-dream, so clear, so real, he believed that . . .

. . . Outside the Hidden Cave, the sun was shining in the kind of sky you could see into forever. Tor was watching Kai El feed birds down by the pool.

Ashan said, "I'm going to bring you something good."

"Berries and honey?" Tor asked, but she had already passed through the waterfall.

She never came back.

They searched the cave. She was gone, which was impossible, unless she turned into air and escaped through the smoke-hole. They dashed outside, up to the ridgetop, and looked into the distance.

"Ashan!" the man called.

"Amah!" the boy called.

With a hand over straining eyes, Tor scanned the Valley of Pusha. Nothing. He shook his fist.

"Takeena! Help me find her!"

Tor saw a distant movement, something coming from Colder—and there—something else from Warmer—two herds of—

"What is it?" Kai El asked.

As they approached, the herds turned into masses of people, who turned into individuals.

"Two tribes. Coming together. To us."

The tribes met, mingled, and came up the ridge, silent as mist in motion. Shahala people bumped into Tlikit people, into Tor and Kai El, and the touch was warm and filling. Then the people backed away, except for two with fearful faces.

Raga and Timshin held out pleading arms.

"We lost Ashan," Raga said, "and ran out of food!"

"We ran out of new blood!" Timshin said.

Elia-who-used-to-be-Chimnik stepped up and grasped the hands of the two old ones.

"Help us, Tor," his young friend said. "We must find the lost Moonkeeper."

Taking Kai El's small hand and Timshin's old dry one, Tor linked them all as one.

"Together we will find her, and survive. Without her—"

Tor awoke and sat straight up, shivering, sweating.

His mate sat on her rock, snuggling their son.

"I understand!" he blurted. "Everything!"

"So do I."

"No, listen!" He had to get this out. "Remember when I had my first dreams of the Great River, and I saw a new tribe, like a stew of Shahala and Outsiders, and life came along and made me think *that* part of the dream was impossible, so I put the Shahala behind me, and focused on the new people I found?"

Ashan frowned. "What are you talking about?"

Sometimes she made him feel like a little boy learning his words. But she *must* be made to understand this . . . this revealing.

He slowed himself. "Like I told you, I named the new home Teahra? Together? Because I really think . . . no, wait . . ."

He breathed deep to fight frustration. "Over and over I

dreamed of a bountiful river. It was the river I found in the
tabu land, and it is bountiful, beyond imagining. You were
always in those dreams, Ashan, there at the river, mother of
our children, leader of our people. You were happy, and so
was I.''

Tor was beginning to make sense.

"The people I saw in those dreams, the new tribe—there
was always mystery about them, because I never saw their
faces. I never really knew who they were. Until today . . . I
saw their faces for the first time . . . in a dream.''

Now Tor had her full, smiling attention.

"The new tribe," he said, "the ones who will live with us
by the Great River, they are a joining of old and new . . . the
Shahala of my boyhood, still in my heart, and the Tlikit of
my manhood, whom I have come to love . . . all of us living
in peace and plenty at Teahra by the Great River.''

He took her hands. "Ashan . . . you have knowledge of
the old ways, and faith in the new. You are the one to bring
the tribes together.''

There was peace on her face. He thought a faint light came
from her as she spoke.

"I know, Tor. I too had a vision. The old way is closing:
without horses, the Shahala will starve. But a new way is
opening: your Great River has enough food for two tribes.''

Her light brightened. "I am the bridge for my people to
walk. Everything points to it—all I've been through—all I've
learned. I will teach them to live in the new time and place.''

Tor was breathless with awe. "It was always you, wasn't
it? The one with power and wisdom . . . the one with
destiny . . .''

Ashan squeezed his hands.

"You are no less important, Tor. You are the bridge to the
Outsiders.''

They held each other as the meaning of their lives sank in.

Ashan thought it would be easier to accept destiny than to
make it happen. The truth was, considering everything, it
seemed impossible to bring Shahala and Tlikit together to live
as one.

"How?" she asked.

"We'll go back to our people. They'll be at Anutash now. You're the Moonkeeper. You'll persuade them—"

"All three of us?"

"Of course."

"Tor, how many times have you said the Shahala would kill you and Kai El? And probably me. I—I'm afraid I believe it."

Tor said nothing.

Ashan's heart broke with understanding; rushing off to Anutash with Kai El would be too dangerous. She'd have go alone, trust Tor with him for a while. But, oh! It hurt to think about it. What if she never saw her baby again? She didn't have the courage to leave him for a single moment.

It's not a matter of courage, a spirit said. *Mother to more than this child: You have no choice.*

"Maybe I should go to Anutash alone," she said through tears. "In time, I think I can talk our people into . . . everything. You will take our son to the Great River, and ready the Tlikit people for our coming."

"You can't go by yourself, Ashan. You'll never find it."

"No. You'll have to show me. And then leave me there. We'll mark a trail so I can find the way back. When the willows green, I'll come here again, with all who will follow. By then, they'll know about the two of you. And then you can take us the rest of the way."

Tor shook his head. "All that would give us is time. The boy and I will have to face them someday."

"Time would be good—"

Tor looked into her soul. "No, Ashan. I vowed to you before every spirit I know that I would never leave you again. And I will not. We will go together."

Kai El did not understand why they had to leave the home of Ehr. He wanted to howl and shake his fists and hold his breath like a baby. But he was the son of Ashan and Tor—a young warrior, not a baby. So he bravely made plans, like his parents were doing. He would take Ehr's paints, his blade for carving wood, the mouse toy. Kai El was too old for such a toy, but it smelled of Ehr, reminding him of the grandfather's love.

Before he said good-bye to home for the last time, the boy

left lots of food for the animals. That Ehr's friends might starve worried him more than anything.

Several days later in the dark before dawn, Ashan and her family neared Anutash, the Shahala winter village. It was the third day of the Autumn Feast—*if*, she thought, *the people still have strength for that*. She had chosen a special day for coming home. Spirits would be gathered for the feast, and for a change, Ashan believed that she and spirits were on the same side.

They stopped on the hillside above the burial ground, where Tor had agreed to leave her. He and Kai El would stay in hiding for days or moons, until Ashan let them know it was safe.

For a while, the little family stood close together watching gray outline distant mountains.

"It's time," Ashan said, embracing Tor. If any tears were left, they stayed down.

Until she picked up her son. "Oh, Kai El . . ." Ashan squeezed him to her breast, buried her face in his hair. Tears squeezed from her eyes. *Amotkan, I was wrong! I can't do this!*

Kai El wriggled loose.

"Don't cry, Amah," said her baby who was growing up so fast. "You promised we'll be together again. I believe you."

Ashan needed that for courage. "You're right," she said. "We *will*. Now go, you two."

They disappeared into the brush.

"I love you more than life," she whispered.

CHAPTER
55

After her family had gone, Ashan gave herself to tears but for a little while. Sensing the presence of spirits, she raised her arms in supplication.

Destiny, they answered, *is about faith.*

Ashan arranged her wrap of many feathers, gift of a condor—huge, hard-to-catch bird of carrion—outwitted by Tor. The long, black-tipped white feathers draped the returning shaman from shoulder to knee—almost as imposing a garment as the ancient Moonkeeper's robe.

Morning was on the way, wearing not one cloud—morning of the third day of the Autumn Feast—a most sacred time. More alone than she had ever been, Ashan started down the hill. From the village, drums were calling spirits. She brought the rhythm inside her, and walked with it.

Anutash . . . she smelled home before she saw it. Familiar scents filled her soul . . . lost friends, the smoke of an oak-wood fire . . .

No one guarded the trail. The people were gathered around the ceremonial ground in the center of the village.

Ashan drew near, saying, "Let me pass."

Utterly shocked, they opened a way for her. In their midst, she saw a litter, and on it a withered bag of bones. *Raga* . . .

Sensing gasps of wonder and murmured prayers, feeling

sweet touches, Ashan passed by her people without seeing them. She knelt by her spirit mother, swept with old forgotten love.

Dawning recognition turned Raga's face to an upside-down rainbow of joy. The old voice was a bruised whisper.

"Are you a spirit, or are you real?"

"Real."

Fleshless arms encircled Ashan's neck, pulling her down for a wet kiss.

"Oh thank Amotkan," Raga murmured.

Someone tapped Ashan's shoulder.

"This was to have been my day," Tenka said, "but Amotkan has brought you back to life."

She offered the robe of furs and feathers worn by Moonkeepers since the Misty Time. Ashan reached for it.

"Wait," Raga said. "Sit me up so I may speak."

Two men took off their wraps and tucked them under the old woman's back.

"My people," Raga croaked. "The spirits have returned our beloved Ashan, and we are full of thanks. But it won't be like you think. Times are changing."

Raga's eyes closed. Her nostrils flared in slow, deep breaths. Ashan could see her exhaustion and pain, but the old shaman found strength for more words.

"This I have been shown: Ashan has come back from a different world—the *new* world where *we* must learn to live—a world of no horses, but much fish, and people of new blood."

Ashan wondered how Raga knew these things. She must have been having her dreams, too.

"A new home for all seasons. Ashan will lead you there."

Raga was gripped by coughing.

"Ahhh . . ." she said when she could speak again, "I am so very tired." The dry-leaf voice sounded like the oldest thing in creation, so weak now that Ashan was the only one who heard it.

"In the old days," Raga said, "one woman could do everything—keep the ways, lead the people, speak with spirits. In the changing world, it is too much for one."

"What do you mean, Spirit Mother?"

"Windpuff . . . of all the Moonkeeper's duties, listening

to spirits and obeying their wishes . . . that's the most important . . . even more than leading the tribe. And there must be loyalty . . . Tenka would never leave the people.''

"But I was stolen—''

"I know. But Tenka would have come back long ago.''

"Are you saying I'm not the Moonkeeper anymore?''

"No. The problem is this, my child: in Tenka, the people see a shaman who talks with spirits, but they don't see a leader, strong and wise. The girl can't even see herself that way. But you must be very strong, very wise, or you wouldn't be alive.''

Ashan began to understand.

"I must know this, my daughter . . . are you with us?''

"Now and forever.''

Raga sighed in deep relief. She gathered herself and spoke with power.

"Hear me!''

The Shahala crowded close.

"In the changing world, a tribe needs two Moonkeepers.''

Shocked sounds rose.

"Yes, two: a shaman, *and* a chief. I give you these, my daughters. Tenka will speak with spirits, do the rituals, and keep the ways. Ashan will lead you as chief.''

CHAPTER
56

A few stars could still be seen when a high, clear voice offered an ancient song four times to the four directions.

"Spirits of all who love people! Arise, and bring us this day!" Then, in a whisper, "Chief Above, guide me."

The prayers of the girl Tenka were accepted.

Wrapped in a robe of pale morning, the Spirit of Light, Ah Ah Nay, peered over a mountaintop, sniffed the Balance, and then—trailing daylight—slipped across a plain.

People perceived the coming of day as a single, smooth motion. But the Spirit of Light, moving in another version of time, could pause as desired, and did so today before the Shahala village where the greeter sang.

Anutash. Early as it was, the place was alive with activity, and conflicting emotions. Hope rose up in patches of mist, colored like spring, that only the Spirit of Light could perceive. Tension stained the air with brownish bubbles that burst and fell back, to mire people's souls, argue with their hope, and even their courage.

Not wishing to startle creatures already so tense, the Spirit of Light crept forward on silent paws to the near edge of the village, and stroked the skeleton of the women's hut. The women slowly circling it didn't notice. Having removed the covering skins from the ancient framework, they were trying to decide the best way to take the woven antlers apart.

Some thought it foolish to move the women's hut . . . the tribe could only carry so much on this journey into new life.

"It's been here since time began," they argued. "It should remain."

"Why not make a new hut?" others said. "Our bountiful new home will provide antlers enough to make it even larger, for the women of the other tribe who will be as sisters."

Another asked, "What if we have to come back here to live?"

With the confidence of the goose who flies at the head of the flock, Ashan said: "We will not come back. These antlers that sheltered our mothers and grandmothers are full of memories, and cannot be replaced. They will go with us to the new land."

No one wanted to argue with the Lost One who had returned to them—blessing, miracle, mystery—awesome in power and wisdom, as no Moonkeeper had ever been. Ashan gave her people hope. Hope gave them faith, and courage to challenge the unknown.

The Spirit of Light moved on to the cluster of family huts.

The man Tor smiled up at the awakening morning. The one who had shown astonishing bravery by returning with his young son to a tribe who thought they should die, was helping his father, Arth, prepare the family's things for the journey to a river that only Tor had seen.

Arth moved in a glow of peace; a sweet smell rose up from him. The man had lost too much to ever again be happy in the way of the young, but he felt better than he thought possible. His beloved son was home—with a miracle called Kai El.

Arth did not believe the story, told by the Lost Moonkeeper, repeated by Tor, that blamed the kidnapping on maneaters, and lauded Tor for her rescue. The Evil One was now seen by the Shahala as a hero. And why not? They who had been through so much needed heroes to give them something to believe in.

Knowing his son, Arth knew Tor himself was Ashan's kidnapper, but it was easy in a man's old age to forgive the rashness of youth.

Arth *did* believe that Tor had seen the new home. As he looked at his three mates, their six children, the boy Elia taken to raise because he reminded Arth of Beo, his miraculous new grandson, and his beloved Tor—how unimportant the past seemed to one thinking of what he had now, and what he expected of the future.

This, and all, was known to Ah Ah Nay, the Spirit of Light, who each day traveled over this place, Anutash, winter home since time began of the people Shahala.

The Spirit of Light moved on, touching the woman Mani as she laced the cradleboard that held her baby girl, renamed Yayla, for promise, when Ashan came home. Then Mani shaped acorn cakes, for Lar, her mate, and for Tahm, her boy of five summers . . . thinking how very brave her people were . . . to leave everything they knew . . . to pick up and follow a suddenly returned leader to what they hoped would be a wonderful new life . . . but which might not be . . .

Anything we do, Mani thought, *is exactly the same as everything we've ever done. We go to the summer place, then the winter place, gather berries on Pahto's flank, grass seeds from the plain, the same places at the same seasons. But now . . .*

. . . nothing would ever be the same again.

The Spirit of Light passed over others. Some noticed, some did not. They were heroes, all of them . . . not because they were unafraid . . . heroes are wise enough to be afraid, but brave enough to go on with what destiny requires despite their fear.

The Spirit of Light left the village, climbed the hill behind it, and stopped before the burial ground. There was an uneasy soul lingering here . . . the woman called Raga, dead in flesh, but not at peace . . . unable or unwilling to join her ancestors in the otherworld.

The dead woman's essence plucked nervously at the Spirit of Light. *The feet of the people are leaving the sacred ground! We in the earth are being abandoned! How will I protect them now?*

The Spirit answered: *Raven Tongue, what is in the earth is but a useless fragment. The rest of you must rise from your grave, and, if you wish, go with them.*

Having many more places to visit, the Spirit of Light

crossed over the Shahala burial ground, and away. Behind in the brightening day, the air vibrated as Raga's soul arose.

The next day, the Spirit of Light brought morning to the Shahala village of Anutash. Finding it abandoned, Ah Ah Nay moved on, to encounter Raga's airy soul. Drifting high together, they came upon eighty-three Shahala people strung along a never-traveled trail, each man, woman, and child loaded with all they could carry, and dragging more on travel poles . . . heading into Warmer, the tabu land. Ashan, splendid in her garb of condor feathers, led the courageous strand of humanity, with Tenka on one side, Tor and Kai El on the other.

The Spirit of Light, who had so often traversed Shahala ground, touched the people one by one, met their leader, and settled on her. Bathed in light, Ashan reflected it back . . . like a shiny rock when a sunbeam crosses a meadow, catches it, and makes it brighter.

Ashan looked up in wonder. "Raga?"

May we give them an omen? the Spirit of Raga asked.

The Spirit of Light swelled in response.

As the sun climbed the backs of distant mountains, with dawn only moments away, a rainbow colored the cloudless sky.

People gasped. "A miracle! A rainbow with no rain . . ."

The rainbow vanished. The sun burst free of the mountaintop. Dawn splashed the tribe. Talking all at once, the people of the Misty Time sounded like migrating swans.

The spirits moved on.

FALL IN LOVE...
WITH REBECCA BRANDEWYNE!